C000302952

Darcy (Dressed to Kill)
Copyright © Marie Mistry 2023

ISBN: 978-1-915066-30-5

www.mariemistry.com

Cover art and design by JODIELOCKS Designs.

Edited by Kaye Kemp Book Polishing.

Darcy

DRESSED TO
Kill

Marie Mistry

In memory of Chester Bennington.
And for those he saved.

Contents

AUTHOR'S NOTE

Darcy is a contemporary reverse harem novel containing explicit sexual situations, including scenes featuring multiple consenting partners over the age of 18. This series is written in British English and contains foul language, violence, discussions of past self harm, drug addiction and relapse, and multiple explosions. For a comprehensive list of trigger warnings, please check out my website.

Self-care is important, so if such subject matter upsets you, please don't read this book.

This book has been professionally edited, but we're all human. So, if you spot a typo, please contact Marie directly using the form on her website or any of her social media links.

Darcy
1

BOOM!

The windows of the penthouse apartment shatter above me as fire shoots out in a glorious explosion that paints the rainy night sky golden. Glancing up from my phone, I revel in the sight for an instant before returning to my screen and wiping away the rain splattering it. I love explosions, but I have work to do. Thankfully, I have a drone filming everything, so I can rewatch the footage later.

> **Tommy**
> babe you got a sec?

I dismiss the message with a sigh of impatience. Tommy has been getting more and more clingy lately, and I can't deal with him mid-mission. I have a few minutes at most to move the funds from my mark's accounts before his people catch wind of what's happening.

Swiping down, I check the upload status of my calling card... almost there. God, I wish this rain would just stop. I'm soaked through.

Sirens pierce the air—that was fast—and I grimace at the reminder of how little time I have.

Months went into planning this, but it always comes down to these final few minutes.

Tommy
I just wanted to let you know that I'm sorry, but this ain't working for me anymore.

What?

Dismissing his irritating messages again, I flip between apps. Bingo. The funds from that corrupt senator's little nest egg are now sitting pretty in one of my shell accounts. I'll give it a few days, then begin the process of wiring it to the dude's victims—minus my cut, of course.

Tommy
I want to break up. You're gorgeous, and the sex is great, but you're just not into me, and it's not fair to keep stringing me along like this.

I pause, but only because I'm waiting for the notification —there.

Upload complete. Every single device the senator owns is now wiped. His money and his data are mine, and all the cops will get off any of his tech is a new little screensaver that reads *Game Over.*

Satisfaction curls my lips into a tiny smile as I disconnect from the server and—

"Put your hands up!"

Oh, great. I remove my glasses with one hand and pull up the messaging app with Tommy's latest break up text. Mustering a sob, I turn to face the officer. His gun is shaking in front of me.

"He broke up with me!" I wail, inconspicuously dropping

my glasses into my handbag as I brandish my phone in the cop's face. "By *text*! Why would he do that?"

The poor, fat, balding man sweats as he tries to figure out if I'm a threat or just really as stupid as I appear. I can't blame him. No sane person would stand calmly below a building that's just exploded, in the pouring rain, ranting about a break up text. Eventually, he must figure that I'm just an airhead—thank you blonde stereotypes—because he lowers his weapon.

"Miss, you need to get to safety. There's been an incident—"

"I thought he loved me." I pinch my brows together, thrusting the phone at him again. "He said he did, and now look! I planned our life together. I even had a Pinterest board! And he just..." I manage a huge, hiccupping sob, allowing practised tears to fall freely. "Why do they always leave me?"

His expression hardens, and despite my poor vision, I can practically read the words "dumb, emotional bimbo" as they flit through his mind. No sympathy from this dude, sheesh.

"Miss. This isn't the time or place. I'm going to have to insist you get behind the safety cordon, immediately."

I wipe my hand across my eyes, sacrificing my mascara to the cause with an embarrassing sniffle. The cop just sighs and grabs my elbow, dragging me out of the dark side street and over to where his colleagues are already ushering civilians away. The moment I'm among the crowd, I stop my fake tears and start making my way around the block. Pulling a hat out of my bag, I tug it over my distinctive hair, flipping the collar of my trench coat up to hide the rest, before heading for the metro.

Just another face in the crowd. Nothing to see here...

Once I'm seated and the train is rattling along the tracks, I fish my large black-framed glasses out of my bag and send a quick text confirming the mission was a success back to Man. Then I take a deep breath and open Tommy's chat.

Five new messages. Ugh.

Despite my dramatics, I just don't have it in me to care about the multitude of excuses he's listed. They all come down to one simple truth...

I got bored.

Just like every other time, I thought I was in love, but in the end, it turned out I wasn't. God, I *wanted* to be. Tommy was decent. Stable job. No gambling or other addictions. Good family. Wanted kids. The whole picture. I did so much to keep myself in the box he expected: outspoken, but not too much, sexy, but not slutty, interested, but not nagging. It was so tiring, but I thought maybe it would be worth it...

My head falls back, and I let out a long sigh. The car I'm in is mostly empty, so there's no one to see the small, genuine tear when it finally escapes.

I'm not crying over Tommy. Not really. There are other guys out there, so I'm not sure why I'm upset. Perhaps it's just self pity.

Scraping the evidence away with one hand, I dig into my bag for my panda ear headphones with the other. I know Man will be annoyed that I'm letting my guard down, but I'm certain of my anonymity. The music will help drown out my background thoughts and allow me to focus on erasing any lingering security footage of myself from the incident.

It takes almost an hour until I'm satisfied I've left no trace of myself behind, and by that time I'm more than ready to hop off the metro and board my plane back to Colorado. Once in the air, nestled in a business class suite that I took the liberty of upgrading myself to, I let the sounds of Hazardous's latest album take away my ability to feel. The band's haunting vocals—at times screaming, other times whispering fervently against the mic—take the place of thoughts.

I must've fallen asleep, but I wake to the bing of the seat-belt light alerting me that it's time for landing.

I check my phone again. Ten new messages from Tommy.

Block. I don't even want to know what they say. If he's changed his mind... Well, he shouldn't, because he's right. All I want to do is stuff my face with pizza and ice cream, create a blanket pile, and hide for the next week until I feel like myself again.

I wish that ritual wasn't as familiar as it sounds, but Tommy is the latest in a string of "the ones" who didn't work out. My never-ending streak of breakups is honestly more upsetting than the end of the relationship itself.

We've been over for a month, maybe longer. No use pretending otherwise, and I have no interest in the whole "let's stay friends" lie. I don't need to be reminded of my failure to settle down on a regular basis.

Most of the other Belladonnas have paired up—or really, grouped up, given that they've all started their own harems— and I can't even keep a relationship going with one guy.

A new notification pops up, jerking me out of my maudlin thoughts, and a small smile quirks the corners of my lips.

[HzD]D0dgeVip3r
getting our asses kicked, where tf are u?

Dodger's message is an instant dose of dopamine straight to the brain. My thumbs move of their own accord, tapping out my reply.

D4rk4ngel
Omw home from business trip. Be back on in a few hours.

Chucking my phone back into my bag, I make my way through baggage claim and out of the airport. My driver, Pierce, is already there, waiting for me by the open door of the armoured Bentley, and I slide into the back seat with a sigh.

His baby-blue eyes meet mine in the rear-view mirror, and he offers me a gentle smile.

"Did you enjoy your time in Chicago, miss?"

I beam at him. "Yes, thank you."

He nods, face fixed into a pleasant mask. "Back to the house, miss? Or will we be stopping somewhere first?"

"Home, please," I answer, turning back to my phone.

[HzD]D0dgeVip3r
Proph3t rage quit. We need our healer.

D4rk4ngel
Is he going to beg this time?

Radio silence follows the message, and I snort. My clan has been regretting making me pick a healer class for three years. When too much blatant monetisation convinced the five of us to switch from playing Clans of Carnage to Runes of Chaos, they decided the fresh start was an opportunity for the group's only girl to play a more "suitable" character.

I've been making them pay for their misogyny ever since.

At one point, Slate actually begged me to switch classes and go back to being their tank, but I've invested too many points into the druid and healing skill trees to respec now.

Until we start a new game, they're stuck at my mercy, even proud, silent Prophet.

The car pulls down the empty country roads, sleek and silent. Man likes his privacy, so it's a good twenty minutes from the nearest town to the manor, and I gaze silently at the trees as we pass, mulling over Tommy's texts and trying not to feel disappointed.

When Pierce finally brings the car around the circular drive, I jolt out of my funk and shove open the door. The late afternoon sun is a welcome change from the chill of the AC, and I let it wash over me for a second before I head inside.

"Thanks, Pierce," I call over my shoulder, leaving him to put the car away. "You rock!"

He says nothing, but I catch the flicker of a smile at the corner of his mouth before I turn and jog up the front steps of the house.

The sun-bleached coral walls of the manor haven't changed since I was a girl. Man's immense home is adorned with white gables, imposing pillars, and arched windows. From the outside, it could be the house of any run-of-the-mill eccentric millionaire, but beyond those dark front doors lies the base of operations for one of the deadliest assassin agencies in the world: the Belladonnas.

I dump my bag on the gleaming tile floor of the Mediterranean style foyer, ignoring the imperial staircase in favour of heading to my second favourite room in the house—the kitchen. I half expect my sister, Karma, to be here baking up a storm, her long brown hair bound out of her face while she works, but she's been gone for weeks now.

Groaning at the thought of having to feed myself, I grab a pizza from the freezer, decorate it liberally with canned pineapple chunks, and chuck it in the oven.

Tabby and I are the only two Belladonnas here at the moment, and we rarely cook. I'm probably going to develop a nutrient deficiency without the others here to scold me for my bad diet.

I'll eat an apple later. Probably. If I remember.

Darcy
2

T he others' absence hangs heavy in the air as I skip
back through the house with my plate of pizza in
one hand and a tub of ice cream in the other.

I was the first Belladonna; a five-year-old runaway Man
picked up on a whim. Growing up, I was alone a lot. He was
dedicated to my training, but otherwise distant. For years, I
never questioned the echoing emptiness of the big house. That
changed with the arrival of the other girls.

I considered all of them my sisters from day one. It didn't
matter that only Naomi and Ivory are technically related.
Together, we brought plenty of noise and life to a house that
was otherwise cold and lifeless, and I miss that.

The living room was once Raven's favourite haunt, and
part of me still expects her to be there, watching endless
reruns of her favourite medical drama, and covering her eyes
to hide from the gory bits. If she wasn't there, it would be
because Harlow kicked everyone out to watch a football
game.

Now the room is unused.

Juggling the ice cream to my other hand—because it's *cold*
—I take the stairs two at a time and sigh in relief as I reach my

floor. As I fumble with my food and attempt to turn my door handle with my elbow, my eyes skip over to the others' rooms.

Harlow's is at the far end of the corridor, and normally her grungy metal music would be blasting out of there. Ordinarily, I wouldn't mind the loss too much, because my taste is definitely more metal*core* than heavy metal, but it was still background noise.

Tabby's room beside mine is empty because she basically lives in the garage—nothing new there. Royal is currently AWOL on her own little vendetta, and Raven's moved in with her sexy thieves. Across the hall, the green glow of Selena's Mountain Dew vending machine is still peeking out beneath her door, but she moved in with her three hot mafia dudes months ago. I half expect her to pop out, headphones on, just to rib me over being caught off guard by that cop on my last mission.

Huffing out a breath, I force myself to turn away.

Maybe later I should go down and bother Tabby. She and I are the only two left, after all.

It's all just so *quiet*.

Unlocking my door with no hands is tricky. I end up freezing my boob by holding the tub of ice cream under my arm while I turn the key, then I use my hip to open it, letting me into my own private sanctuary.

"Lights on," I command.

The neon purple glow of the honeycomb LED panels across the far wall snap to life, followed by the matching glow strip behind my desk and below my bed, and finally my floor-to-ceiling lava lamp.

Ugh, I shouldn't have done that. Now I can see all my dirty laundry scattered across the floor and my unmade bed.

"Computer on," I add, smiling as the near-silent fans inside my rig—affectionately known as Beastie—whir, and the glass side panel starts to glow beneath my desk.

Sticking my pizza on the desk, along with my ice cream, I quickly change out of my clothes and into a baggy sleep shirt that reads *This is my sexy lingerie.* I groan in relief as I chuck my bra as far away from me as humanly possible.

"Take that, you stupid tit prisons," I grumble, sliding into the throne that is my enormous gaming chair and slipping my headset on.

I flick through my messages, ignoring most of them as I wait for Runes of Chaos to boot up, munching happily on my pizza. The clan is already in the lobby, waiting for me.

"Miss me?" I ask, sliding into the voice chat.

"Hey, *cariño*," StoneRE1—aka Slate—croons, and I blush. "Have fun on your trip?"

"It was a blast," I reply. "Sorry, just let me scarf down this pizza and finish my ice cream, then I can come save your asses."

Prophet's scoff is barely audible, but Dodger covers for him.

"Pizza and ice cream again, Dark?"

He calls me by the first half of my username—they all do, except Slate with his silly nicknames—because they don't know my real name. The topic came up organically a couple of times, when we swapped numbers, and again later. But Man would never have allowed me to disclose anything that major about myself. Assassins are supposed to be ghosts. I didn't have the heart to give them a false identity, so I dodged the question. Eventually, they stopped pushing.

Strictly speaking, I know I should've respected their anonymity as they respected mine, but I'm a hacker. I wasn't going to spend years of my life playing with people without getting a little bit curious.

We've gamed together for a decade, but four years ago, I couldn't stand it anymore, and I went snooping.

I nearly shit my pants when I discovered their real identities. Dodger, Arlo, Slate, and Prophet are the four members of the record-breaking metal band, Hazardous, and I never once suspected a thing.

They don't know that I know, and I made a vow never to bring it up. We were friends before they were even a band. For years, I assumed they were a bunch of college dropouts living in their moms' basements, and I didn't care. Their fame changes nothing for me.

"No answer," Fr0gg0—Arlo—notes.

I sigh, hating that they're familiar with my break-up rituals. "Tommy broke up with me, by text, if you must know."

"What a piece of shit," Dodger commiserates, and perhaps it's my imagination, but he doesn't actually sound too sad about it.

"Complete loser," Slate agrees.

"Did he give a reason?" Arlo asks.

My next sigh is louder. "The same reason they always give, Frog. I got bored, and he knew it." I scoff. "At least it wasn't the good old you're-just-too-much excuse. Oh, but he let me know the sex was great—on his end, at least."

"Why do you keep dating these limp-dick losers who can't even get you off?" Slate asks. "You deserve better."

Prophet makes a throaty noise of agreement.

"You know why," I retort. "He was stable and sweet and—"

"Boring?" Arlo adds, helpfully. "You're worth so much more, Dark."

I stuff my face with more pizza to give me an excuse not to reply.

My phone chimes, the *ribbit* noise letting me know that it's Arlo before I even look.

[HzD]Fr0gg0
Soz if I upset u

I frown and quickly type back—cursing my greasy fingerprints on the screen.

> **D4rk4ngel**
> You didn't. It was over for at least a month, but I'm still disappointed in myself.

> **[HzD]Fr0gg0**
> Not ur fault he was a shithead

Isn't it?

After the first two break ups, yeah, it could've been them. But I've lost count of how many times I've been here. Surely, at this point, any smart person would see that the common denominator is me.

I can't even tell what I'm doing wrong.

I had one ex tell me my intelligence was "intimidating," so I dumbed myself down, only for the next to tell me I wasn't challenging him enough. I'm too enthusiastic for most, but too demure when I try to change. I talk too much, or too little. I give too much affection, or I'm too distant.

And whenever I manage to get it right... I get bored, and the whole thing falls apart, anyway.

I just can't win.

"How's the pepperoni and pineapple?" Dodger asks, shattering my grim reverie.

"Glorious," I reply, but my mouth is full of cheese, so the word is mangled.

A drop of the sauce drips free, and I grimace as it lands on my blanket. Ugh, the price I pay for stuffed crust goodness.

Arlo chuckles. "Only you could eat something that sounds so..."

"Fucking awful?" Slate finishes for him.

I can feel Dodger cringing. "It's definitely a questionable choice of topping."

"Unique." Arlo steps in to save his clan mates. "Just like Dark."

I fold my last slice in half and down it, cleaning my hands with an antiseptic wipe I stole from Harlow on her last visit. Pizza down, I crack my knuckles and grin.

"Enough judging my gourmet meal choices." I fire up the game and take control of my avatar as she drops in from the heavens in a burst of fire that cracks the ground. "You ready to beg, Prophet?"

The grunt of annoyance from his end makes me smile.

"Very mature," Dodger grumbles, as his halfling appears beside my fallen angel in the dark and creepy dungeon we've been tackling.

"At least I don't still have my *Call of Duty* clan tag in my username. What are you, twelve?"

"Hey, that's not fair," Slate argues. "You know they charge you to change it after the first time."

I smile secretly. It's not like the band can't afford it, but I suspect they secretly like having those three little letters telling the world that they're brothers by choice. I'll never admit it, but in my daydreams, I've wondered what their reactions would be if I changed my own username to match.

"Don't you think this begging game has gone on long enough now?" Arlo asks. "You've held this grudge for years..."

His druidic gnome pops up on screen, immediately followed by Slate's enormous stone golem and Prophet's orc. The latter is sagging, his green skin glowing red with the injuries he's sustained in my absence.

"Grudge? Whatever do you mean?" I grin. "I'm just an innocent little do-good healer." I pause. "I'm not asking much. It's a bargain, really, given the cost of healthcare in the real world..."

My phone chimes again, this time with the *ba dum tss* that I've assigned to Prophet. Everyone else goes quiet. By now, they all recognise the quirky ringtones I've assigned the four of them.

[HzD]Proph3t
Please.

My evil grin spreads, and I whisper against the mic huskily. "You know that's not enough."

In all honesty, I'm surprised he's given in. Usually he'd rather die, be sent back to the spawn point, and lose his entire inventory than submit to my demands. I guess he's looted something good from one of the bosses down here.

Slate lets out a breath. "This must be a record."

"Don't jinx it," Dodger warns. "This dungeon has been tearing us a new one, and I want out of here."

Ba dum tss.

[HzD]Proph3t
Pineapple belongs on pizza. Now *please*
heal my ass.

I cackle and—with the press of a button and a little mana sacrifice—Prophet's orc roars, standing straight, all his status ailments gone in one sweep.

"That wasn't so hard, was it?" I coo.

Prophet grumbles what sounds like a curse. "Don't push your luck."

"When are you going to give us better ringtones, *cariño*?" Slate asks, changing the subject before I can tease Prophet into regretting his actions. "Mine is just..." He makes a noise that can only be interpreted as a verbal shudder.

"Aww, but I thought you liked it," I smile. "It fits you so well."

"Stop teasing them," Dodger says, his avatar making a

rude gesture which smoothly returns my attention back to the game. "Come on. We've got a dungeon to finish."

"Yes, sir, Dodge, sir." I use the honorific just because I know it will drive him crazy, but there's no drawing a rise out of him.

Not yet, anyway.

Darcy
3

The message comes as we're winding down for the night—well, morning, really, given that it's well past midnight. The tone—a deafening tyre squeal—matches his car obsession.

[HzD]D0dgeVip3r
stay online

Two words that set my heart racing. I knew this was coming. I'll never admit it, but I've been silently hoping for it since that stupid break up text.

The second the clan has said our goodbyes, Dodger drags me into a separate, private, voice chat.

"Five seconds," he requests.

The sounds of rustling and doors closing fill my ears, along with a few masculine grunts, until it's silent once more. When we're alone like this, every note of his voice whispers over my skin like dark velvet, and I can't help my shiver.

"Was that little bratty display earlier a sign you're ready to play, baby girl?"

I bite my lip, knowing I should say no. Any sane person

would consider the night after a breakup to be too soon. But Dodger and I have been playing this game for so long that it's less like a rebound and more like coming home.

I must take too long to answer, because he hums under his breath.

"You rethinking our agreement?" he asks.

If I said I was, he'd wait. He's done it before, when I was too raw from a toxic relationship to do anything. But that was a long time ago.

"No," I whisper back.

"Good." One word, but he doesn't even try to conceal the lazy satisfaction behind it. "I wish I could say I'm sorry that the latest 'Mr. Right' didn't work out, but since it means you're finally mine again..." He trails off, and somewhere deep in my chest something aches.

Because, yes, I am his. Until the next one. Our first virtual hook up was an accident, and I quickly broke it off. After all, this isn't going to go anywhere. Whatever relationship we could have is doomed, and I'm looking for more than he—or any of his band—could give me. But we're like two asteroids, forever orbiting one another, and after I broke up with Michael—or was it Daniel?—we found ourselves back here again.

Still, sometimes I like to pretend...

"What makes you so sure you're not 'Mr. Right' yourself?" I tease.

I can feel his dark smile through the headphones.

"Because I'm all wrong for you," he reminds me. "That's why you like this so much."

I wish he wasn't right. The reason I'm already melting in my chair, softening, is precisely because he's nothing like the many guys I've tried to date. Try as I might to wrestle the deep part of my psyche into liking good guys, it just isn't working.

"Now, put those pretty fingers inside your panties and tell me how wet you are," he orders.

His words yank me out of my funk, and I grin. "Err, unfortunately, I can't do that, sir. You see, human beings don't possess hygroreceptors, and as such, we can't actually detect wetness—"

His dark chuckle cuts me off. "I missed your big brain and your smart mouth, baby girl. But I've got a long memory, and you've used this one before. We don't have hygroreceptors, but we *do* have the ability to detect changes in texture and temperature. So pull your fucking panties down, put those fingers in that gloriously soft cunt, and tell me if you're all hot, slick, and *wet* for me."

My mic is sensitive enough that I know he hears the tiny hitch in my breath as I squirm on the seat. My thighs rubbing together isn't helping the situation, and I bite my lip as I spread them. My hand bunches the hem of my sleep shirt, raising it enough to expose the neon-green pickle-covered panties I chose to wear, before delving beneath the elastic.

I'm wet, not that I needed my fingers to tell me that. My forefinger slips and slides directly over my clit, and I gasp as even the light touch sends a bolt of need through me.

"Still waiting for the verdict, baby girl," Dodger reminds me.

"Yes," I hiss. "I'm wet for you."

"Good. Pull your panties off and hook your legs over the arms of your chair."

I circle one finger around my clit, and don't bother hiding my rebellious moan.

All part of the game.

"Baby girl." A dark warning.

I reluctantly remove my hand, yanking down my panties and kicking them away before hooking my knees over the cool armrests of my gaming chair. The move spreads them obscenely wide—thanks gaming chairs designed for men—putting my pussy on full display.

"Done," I whisper.

"Now give those tits a squeeze for me, just the way you like."

My hand slides up my body, skating up my ribs as I try to ignore the slight soft pooch of my stomach and focus on the generous swells of my breasts. In my eagerness, I'm rougher than usual, and my breath hisses out.

"Tell me how it feels," he commands, and I hear the rip of a zipper in the background.

"It's not enough," I complain. "I want more."

"Always so greedy." He tuts. "You'll get more when I say you've earned it. Now play with those pretty tits, lift them up nice and high and lick your nipples through your shirt."

Ever since he found out that my flexibility and boobs allow me to do it, sucking on my own tits has become a regular part of our play.

The dry cotton of my sleep shirt dampens quickly, the warmth of my own mouth adding to the sensations bombarding me. The contrast of cold air on my pussy and warmth on my breasts sends a shiver up my spine, and it emerges as a shocked gasp.

Dodger's answering groan is quiet, but it's definitely there.

At times like this, I wish I had a webcam, but no one in my business trusts those things. Too easy to hack.

Besides... I kind of like the thrill of knowing it's just his voice and the darkness. If I close my eyes, I can pretend he's right here in the room with me.

"My shirt is damp," I murmur, knowing he'll like the visual. "And my pussy is soaked."

"You making a mess of your chair?" he asks, voice husky.

I don't need to look down to know that I am. I can feel my own body's slick dripping down my thighs.

"Yes, sir."

"Good. You'll think of me when you clean it up."

I shudder, hating the truth in his words. "Yes."

"Pinch your nipples. Both of them."

Obediently, I shift my hands and apply just enough pressure to make me moan.

"Harder."

I lick my lips as I debate it. "But I like it like this."

"You'll like it better when they sting as you let go," he promises. "Now harder, baby girl. Don't make me ask again."

My exhale becomes a full-fledged hiss as I do it, pinching through the fabric harder than I normally would.

"If I were there right now, I'd kiss that sting away," Dodger promises. "Then I'd suck those pretty buds right into my mouth and worship them properly." He pauses. "Let them go."

I whimper as the blood rushes back to my nipples, and my clit pulses in sympathy. The burn quickly fades, turning into a deep ache.

His low chuckle doesn't help.

"One of these days, I'm going to record that sound. I can't decide if I like the sound of you in torment more than the little screams you make when you come."

My hand inches lower before I can help myself.

"I know what you're up to," he growls. "But I'll let you get away with it, just this once. I've missed you, and you deserve a reward for letting me have my way with you."

Permission granted, I flick my finger over my clit once, then twice. Far from relieving the aching emptiness, it just makes it worse, and I groan in frustration.

"What's wrong, baby girl? Struggling to get there?"

He's playing with me. Well, two can play at this game. "I wish I had you inside me."

His breath hitches, and my fingers pick up speed. I can come like this. I'm getting closer and closer with every breath.

"I'm so empty without you. If you were here…"

He growls, and I swear the husky sound strokes along my sensitive skin like a physical touch.

"If I were there," he finishes for me. "I'd bury my face in that perfect pussy of yours and eat you until you screamed. Now dip a finger inside for me."

Damn, I'm so close. I don't want to stop stroking my clit, but my curiosity wins—barely. I want to know what he'll do next more than I want to come.

I slide my finger inside, just to the first knuckle, teasing myself.

"Deeper," he encourages. "Find that G-spot for me."

It isn't hard. Thanks to many years of long-distance relationships, I'm an accomplished masturbator, and I know my body well. The second the pad of my finger rubs over that pleasure point, I let out a moan, biting my lip.

"Good. Two fingers. Fuck yourself with them. I want to hear the sexy wet sounds your body makes as you finger yourself over the edge. I want to imagine it's me making those noises as I fuck you into my mattress."

My second finger slips in easily, and I moan as I finally get the stretch I've been waiting for.

"You'd feel so good inside me," I whisper.

A real cock is always so much better than my fingers, and I've seen the swagger that Dodger struts around the stage with. I've been with enough guys to know what BDE looks like.

He's touching himself now. The rhythmic sound of his hand stroking his shaft, combined with his laboured breathing, fills the silence.

"You're not fucking yourself like I told you to," Dodger warns, his voice husky and breathless. "I want to hear, baby girl."

My head falls back, and I do what he asks, drawing my fingers back, only to plunge them back inside over and over. The slurping, wet sounds fill the air, just like he wanted, and my breath starts to come in little pants as my orgasm draws closer.

"If I were there, I'd have a finger in your ass too," he says. "I bet you'd clench so fucking hard around me."

I lick my lips. "Was that an order, sir?"

He groans. "Nasty girl. You want to play?"

I slip one finger free and trace my own lubrication down to the crease of my ass. I'm already sopping wet, so slipping inside to the first knuckle is easy, but when I draw back and forge forward a little deeper, I cry out.

"You like playing with your little ass for me?" Dodger demands. "I'd fuck you there too, you know. And you'd let me, wouldn't you? You'd let me stretch you open and fuck your ass until I filled you up with my cum. Then I'd plug it, so you could walk around with me trapped inside you for the whole day."

"Yes, sir," I whimper.

"Touch your clit," he orders. "I want you to come, and I want to hear every glorious second."

My spare hand lowers to follow the command, strumming in that familiar rhythm. Dodger's laboured grunts reassure me he's striving for his own release, and in my mind, I picture him fisting his cock, arm muscles flexing as he strokes it.

I come, legs clenching hard over the armrests of my chair as I fall apart with such loud, reckless abandon that I wouldn't be surprised if even the soundproofed walls of my room aren't enough to muffle me.

"Fuck." Dodger groans, the sound reverberating through my ears as my body slumps, finally relaxed.

For a long minute, we say nothing, both of us finding

comfort in the sound of the other's harsh breaths slowly evening out.

"Draw yourself a bath," he whispers, the order softer, laced with regret. "I'd do it for you, but..."

But the distance is too great. *But* this is just about mutual stress relief, nothing more. *But*, despite our earlier words, I'm not *his* to do that stuff for.

Too many thoughts weigh down the pause, and a bitter taste fills my mouth as I curse myself once again for being so stupid.

Because Dodger isn't part of the plan. The plan is to find someone who's nice, stable, reliable, husband material. Not one single member of my clan—of Hazardous—fits those criteria. No matter how much I wish otherwise.

"Okay," I promise, even though I don't have the energy to move. "Goodnight."

"Sweet dreams."

I tap the side of my headset, disconnecting the call.

Leaving me alone with my thoughts.

Darcy
4

The knock comes too early. *Way* too early. I'm barely conscious as I rub sleep out of my eyes with one hand and feel around my nightstand for my glasses with the other. Once I can actually see, I glance at the alarm clock. It's eight in the morning. Ugh.

Stumbling my way across my darkened bedroom, I trip over my own dirty laundry as I make my way to the glowing outline of the door.

Opening it blinds me. My room is a sanctum of darkness, but beyond it, the summer sun cascades through the windows, illuminating everything, and I have to squint to make out who dared disturb my slumber.

Oh.

Man stands in front of me, one brow quirked in amusement. I swear he does this on purpose. He *knows* I hate mornings.

I meet his blue eyes and let my displeasure show on my face. Normally, there's some downtime after a mission before he expects us to get back into training. Not much, but a day or two to decompress.

Then he lifts one hand and crooks two fingers at me in a

familiar signal. Not waiting for me to respond, he turns and strides down the hallway, grey hair glinting in the light.

My gut sinks.

Now? So soon after the last mark?

Normally, he leaves us a little more time between targets, and I had hoped for a week of gaming with my clan before they start the next leg of their tour and schedules get messy. Plus, I was going to work on that app, and...

I retreat back to my room, determined to at least put on some pants before I follow him to his office. Once dressed—albeit haphazardly—I plod through the ridiculously bright house and into the basement.

The training room is empty, which only makes the old repurposed ballroom feel larger and more imposing. Above me, frescoes of angels look down judgementally, as my bare feet pad softly over the marquetry floor. Man's office is just on the left, beyond the cupboard, and the door is ajar, waiting for me.

My phone squeals in the pocket of my sweats, alerting me to a message from Dodger, but I flick it to silent.

A new mission always leaves a buzz in my veins, and I want to know where I'm going next, and which mark Man wants me to blow up.

The other Belladonnas take missions because they believe in our family's criminal brand of justice. Me? I just love explosions.

The door snicks closed behind me, leaving me enclosed in the mahogany panelled room. Sleek, shiny, and modern, the office is brightly lit with spotlights that make it hard to remember that we're underground. Aside from his desk and the handful of chairs around the room, the only decoration is a feature wall and two bookcases.

Man is already in his leather chair, with a single manilla folder waiting on the desk in front of him.

My mark.

"Who is it this time?" I ask, curious.

I don't expect him to answer me. We're not supposed to talk in here, but his silence always pressures me to fill it, and after all these years, he's given up trying to stop me. Anticipation thrums beneath my skin as I pad across the cold tiles towards him.

"Another senator?" I hum as I take the seat opposite. "Those guys just can't seem to catch a break... but I suppose they're all shady fuckers. Ooh, I haven't blown up a cult in a while..."

Man doesn't comment, merely places two fingers on the folder, twirls it to face me and slides it across the desk.

That's when I see the word scrawled along the tab and my gut drops to the floor.

'Hazardous'

"No." My voice is dead cold as I shove out of the seat I just took. "No fucking way. They're not—"

Man's hand, rough and calloused, grips my wrist when I would've stormed out of the office.

"Read."

Man rarely speaks, so that single word snaps my mouth shut. My butt lands in the chair before I realise what's happened. He releases me, then flips open the file.

There, on the first page, are three mugshots, all men I don't recognise. Not one of them is part of my clan.

"The Rosales brothers," I read, frowning as I skim the lines of information.

The trio runs a cartel, and a bloodthirsty one at that. They seem to have dabbled in every illegal substance under the sun. There's the usual—cocaine, meth, and heroin—but they've also started absorbing human smuggling rings and turning them into a trafficking business. Oh, and torture, extortion, and assassination.

It's all pretty standard for an international narcotics distribution setup, but none of it explains why my clan's band name is on their file.

I flick over the page, and my scowl deepens as I come face to face with the most candid shots of the band I've ever seen.

Dodger is first, his dark shaggy hair and stark tattoos making him stand out from the crowd that surrounds him. Even in plain clothes, he looks like the metal-head he is. Black gauges decorate both of his ears, and silver rings adorn hands that I'm used to seeing passionately cradling his mic on stage. I stare for a little while, wishing they'd gotten a bit closer, so I could see the rich hues of those sparkling brown eyes just a little better.

I force myself to move on, smirking as I realise they've caught Arlo outside, in daylight, without his staple sunglasses. The guitarist always wears long sleeves. Even in the height of summer, with dead brown grass all around him, his leather jacket stays on. I've always been curious to see if he has tats like Dodger and Slate, but his sun-kissed skin is kept under wraps at all times. His trademark black aviators are in one hand as he wipes the lenses on the hem of his shirt, but his brow piercings and general expression are hidden from view by his wavy, jaw-length blonde hair. He's the youngest of the group at thirty-three—just under a year older than me—but he looks younger.

Man shifts in his seat, and I quickly move on to the next photo.

Slate's been caught bare-foot on the beach. The bassist is ripped, and his loose tank top shows off every inch of his bronze skin. Unlike Dodger, whose tattoos are a colourful mix of dragons, skulls and flowers, Slate's are black and grey. Words scroll across his skin in a mix of Spanish and English, surrounding a huge crucifix tangled in rosary beads on his left collarbone. I know from magazines that he's got a chainsaw gun down his spine, but unfortunately, it's not in this shot. A gold cross earring dangles from one lobe, beginning a trail of studs that climb all the way up the outer shell of his ear. His box braids are tied into a small man bun at his crown, and he's levelling a black-eyed scowl at his photographer.

Last, but not least, Prophet has been caught shirtless in the gym. The drummer of Hazardous is the oldest of the bunch at thirty-five, but he's no slouch either. His dark skin is glowing with sweat under the cold fluorescent lights as he keeps pace with a treadmill. His headphones are massive, swallowing his ears and hiding most of his cropped tight black curls. The photo only shows one of his stunning, mismatched eyes—the baby blue one—and maybe that's for the best. If he'd been staring straight at me, I'd never be able to look away. The corners of his mouth are turned down, as usual, but it just draws attention to his full lips and well-trimmed goatee. Unlike the others, who all have piercings, Prophet has none. He's the least outwardly metal of all of them, and I've always wondered if that was a conscious choice. The only thing that outs him are his black leather wristbands.

The photos have caught them completely off guard, so different from the posed cut outs I've kept pinned inside my closet for years.

Man clears his throat, and I grimace. Shit. He's caught me gawping at their photos. Time to move on, and fast. I can stare at their pictures later; right now, I need to know why their band name is on this file.

According to Man's intel, the band is in deep with the cartel. Miguel—the youngest Rosales brother—owns their label, and Hazardous's contract with them is... indefinite?

That can't be right. Most contracts last a year, or five, at the very most. No artist is contracted to a label indefinitely. That would be madness. I make a note to look into that later but skim past to focus on the rest.

The band's tours are used as a cover for the cartel's distribution and money laundering operations. Narcotics are hidden in the vast amount of stage equipment that's dragged with them everywhere. Humans are trafficked as roadies or interns in small numbers every time they cross a border.

It's the perfect cover, but I can see the drawbacks. Namely, they had to find a band with enough potential to warrant all of the logistics of touring every year, and Hazardous is the biggest band signed with the label. Cartels—like most businesses—are all about scaling up their operations, and there are only so many multi-platinum bands out there.

This seems like a pet project of Miguel's, and the next page confirms it. He's younger than his brothers by almost twenty years, and this is his baby. He's made himself the band's tour manager—though it looks like he has an assistant who does most of the actual work for him.

The contract is for all three brothers. No other casualties; though I know Man won't mind the loss of a couple of cartel thugs. Take them all out in one hit. Make it look like it could have been an accident... All the standard stuff.

I flick over a page until I come face to face with my cover for the mission.

"Pyrotechnics expert?" I look up at Man. "Like... flamethrowers and fireworks? Yes! Oh, this is going to be so much fun!"

My face falls as I realise something else. "They're going to recognise me."

The band may never have seen any pictures of me, but we've been gaming together for years. They're going to recognise my voice, and if I'm working for them, at some point, the truth will come out.

Man raises a single brow, and I scowl at him. "I'll still do it, but it's bound to happen."

I don't want one of the others to take the mission. They're

all experts, but if my clan got hurt in the process, I'd hate myself.

If—when—the band recognises me, what does that mean for us? For our friendship? Are they going to believe it's a coincidence when I turn up as their new roadie?

Maybe I'm worrying for nothing, I think to myself much later, as I reread the file while sitting on the kitchen island, devouring my second pepperoni and pineapple pizza in as many days. After all, they're Hazardous; one of the biggest metal bands in the world. They're probably above talking to—or even acknowledging—their roadies.

In fact, I'm willing to bet they won't even notice me. I can tone down my makeup, wear my glasses, and keep my head down. Most days I slob around in hoodies, anyway. I'm hardly the type to catch their attention—though I could be if I tried.

Plus, I only know their online personas. In real life, they're probably stuck up or rude, or high on the drugs their cartel buddies are peddling.

I flick through to the back, admiring the faultless ID that's been provided. I could've made my own, but Man always sets us up for our missions. I like to think it's his way of taking care of us.

"Darcy D'Angelo," I murmur, stroking the plastic identity card.

It's a bit on the nose—I had no idea Man paid attention to my gamertag—but I'll take it. He's given me a load of false references from other smaller bands, along with detonation and munitions training at a military college.

On paper, I'm the perfect pyrotechnics expert. In real life... Well, it's been a while since I played around with anything as tame as iron wool and butane.

Something slips out from the back as I move the folder, and I frown at the slim piece of paper.

'Hazardous is pleased to invite you to join them for the road

crew kickoff party, celebrating the start of the third and final leg of the Broken Chains *tour, hosted by the Museum of Contemporary Art. Dress code is black tie.'*

I raise my eyebrows. If the dress code is black tie, does that mean the band will be wearing suits? I highly doubt it, but I really want to find out.

My clothes are currently in the laundry, so while I wait for Martha, the housekeeper, to save me from my own crusty laundry, I head to the garage to gather some more practical supplies.

I have my laptop, my phone, and spares of both—I learned the hard way how one impromptu swim can easily ruin even the best laid plans years ago—along with C-4, fuses and white phosphorous grenades. But I still need my gadgets. My last bot bit the dust after I sent it through the ventilation shaft with the explosives I used to kill the senator, and I'm not exactly sure what happened to the drone... It might still be buried in my case somewhere.

Walking into the garage is always a bit of a trip hazard. Tabby may have a place for everything, and her own system of organising things, but I can't figure it out for the life of me.

I hear her before I see her. Her domain echoes with the clatter of metal and the squeal of machinery as she leans over her workbench in a set of baggy coveralls.

Pierce is leaning over the hood of the car, but he's not even pretending to look at the engine. His eyes are glued to her ass as she focuses on whatever she's working on.

"How did the chocolates go?" I ask, sneaking up beside him.

He jerks, and I grin, delighting in being able to surprise the unflappable ex-cop.

"She had the box sent off to a lab to be examined for bugs," he mutters under his breath.

I can't help the giggle that escapes my throat. Pierce is so head-over-heels obsessed with Tabby it's adorable, but she's completely oblivious. On more than one occasion, she's had me hack into his accounts, looking for proof that he's a spy.

She's convinced he's here to arrest us all, even though he left the force ages ago.

"She'll figure it out eventually," I promise.

Tabby is one of the smartest women I know, but when it comes to dating, she's almost as hopeless as I am, just in a different way.

"Tabby-cat!" I have to shout over the noise of whatever she's doing.

She pauses, turning back to stare at us both with suspicious eyes. Oops, better step away before she decides I'm a co-conspirator in Pierce's evil plans.

"I'll leave you two," the driver murmurs, picking up his suit jacket from the chair and heading for the door.

The moment he's gone, Tabby is there, inspecting the car where he was working, looking for proof of sabotage or whatever she thinks he's up to now.

"Nothing," she mumbles to herself.

"Hello to you too," I reply. "I came to pick up some stuff."

She jolts, looking at me as if she's just remembered I'm here. "New drone?" she assumes, heading back to the workbench.

"And a bot as well. I have no idea what I'll need."

"Well, this one has a laser cutter." Tabby throws a collapsed hexapod robot at me, and I tuck it safely into the front pocket of my hoodie. "And I've added night vision and an infrared camera to this one." She tosses me a drone, the four arms folded down for easier transport.

I add that to my pocket as well. "Awesome." All the better to spy on my guys—I mean, marks—with.

Her eyes narrow. "You're usually more excited when you've been given a new mission."

I chew my lip but shake it off. "Boy troubles."

"Need me to dismember Tod?" she asks. "I can rewire his toaster so it electrocutes him every time he turns it on."

I grimace. "Tommy, and no. I'm good." I go to hug her, then think better of it and settle for a nod. "Thanks, Tabby-cat. See you when I get back?"

She nods, drifting back to her worktable—me and my boy drama already forgotten.

I don't take it personally as I weave my way back through the house. My absence has given Martha all the time she needs to get through my laundry, and my clothes are neatly folded in my closet by the time I return. I admire the piles before I mess them up by stuffing them into my case. Then I dig in the back of the closet for my favourite dress.

That invitation did say black tie, after all.

Darcy
5

My first thought as I step into the gallery is that they've gone all out for this event. My second is that I should've worn black if I wanted to blend in. And my third is that if one more dude checks out my boobs, I'm going to have to battle my dress to get to my gun.

All of that falls away as I cross the threshold and have to evaluate whether I've tripped and fallen into an alternate dimension.

One where a hyper-realistic version of my Runes of Chaos avatar has been recreated painstakingly in charcoal and spray paint on a canvas the size of a garage door, and hung from the ceiling facing the entryway. The artist has abandoned the cel-shaded character art of Runes of Chaos to create a bright, gritty, realistic portrait.

One of the lures of the game is the incredible customisation options, and my avatar has many of my features, including my soft blonde waves and the long oval face shape. But, because it was just a game, I may have gotten a bit fanciful with some stuff.

Namely, the glowing white eyes, cutesy black feathered wings, and mystical, full body vine tattoos. Of course, I was limited to the skimpy armour bestowed upon female characters by the devs. Because, as we all know, a loincloth and metal bra are the best protection against goblin hordes.

The artist hasn't even bothered to supply that much coverage. The sketch ends at the upper slopes of my avatar's breasts, leaving my collarbones and shoulders bare. My avatar's pouty lips are turned up in a smug, sensual smirk that makes her appear powerful.

It's gorgeous.

It's also very obviously a nude.

Without thinking, I slip my phone out of my clutch and snap a picture, loading it up into the group chat to demand answers.

> **D4rk4ngel**
> Confess! Which one of you did this?!?

But I'm interrupted before I can hit send. "I reckon you like the exhibit?"

His voice has the rasp of a heavy smoker, with a deep, rumbling Texan accent. I turn to see an older man waiting patiently behind me on the doorstep.

"Sorry." I move out of his way.

"Not to worry, girl. I was waiting for you to get here. Darcy D'Angelo, right?"

I nod, scanning his face for some clue as to his identity. He must be in his late fifties, and he has the face of someone who's worked hard and laughed harder. His foppish grey hair has been badly half-tamed in an attempt to clean up, and he has a voluminous moustache that covers his upper lip entirely.

"Sully," he introduces himself. "Production manager for the band."

And my new boss.

"Good to finally meet you in person." I extend my hand

before I realise I'm still holding my phone, and the other is still clutching my purse. Grimacing, I stuff my phone away and offer my palm again.

Mercifully, he ignores my blunder. Sully's hands are massive, and his calloused palm engulfs mine as he shakes it, grip light, as if he's afraid to break me.

"You don't look like someone who'd choose to spend their time playing with explosives," he says.

I might be offended, but he says it with an air of honest, open curiosity that stops any anger in its tracks. Maybe I should've worn my glasses rather than the contacts. People tend to take me more seriously with them on.

"Let me guess, I should be fifty pounds heavier, bald, and male?" I raise a critical brow.

He shrugs. "Yeah, that'd do. Maybe a bit less... colourful....."

"I left my hair dye, fishnets, and leather choker at home," I deadpan.

His face splits in a wide grin, and he fishes out a cigar case from his jacket pocket. He offers me one, shrugging again when I shake my head, and pops his own between his lips.

"You'll do, girl. Just make sure ya don't blow up the audience."

I nod sagely. "Or the band?"

Sully laughs. "Mad bastards would probably enjoy it." He lights his cigar, courteously blowing the smoke away from me before waving me forward. "Enjoy the gallery. The real party will kick off soon enough, and then it's all work tomorrow."

Sensing the dismissal for what it is, I head into the gallery proper, following the dramatic trail of canvases through the open space with the other guests. Most of my co-workers seem to know each other, and the horrible new-girl-at-school feeling settles over me as they continue their conversations, oblivious to my presence.

Understandable. Most of them have probably been through the European and South American legs of the tour together. I'm an outsider right now, but that'll change.

This party might be mostly for the crew, but there are still journalists everywhere, rubbing shoulders with one another as their eyes flick around the gallery, scanning for any sign of Hazardous. I don't pay them any attention, and in return, they barely spare me a cursory glance.

One of the band's older albums is playing softly in the speakers, but Prophet's heavy drum solo is muted by the loud hum of conversation. It's a shame. I'd rather be here alone with their music while I try to figure out which one of them is the mystery artist.

Is it the stoic drummer? I can't see him plastered in smudges of graphite and paint, pouring over a canvas. A few seconds later, I find the portrait that proves it's not him.

Prophet's avatar—a bulging orc barbarian with a giant axe—is on his knees with his palms raised in supplication to a floating black feather shining with dark radiance.

I chuckle-snort. Prophet has proved hundreds of times he'd rather lose all his in-game loot than beg me to heal him. Even on the few times he has backed down, he definitely never did it with such a look of awe on his face.

"I always thought this one was more moving than funny." A woman's unimpressed voice interrupts my reverie.

I turn, trying hard to tame my lingering smile as I come face to face with a curvy goddess with bold, slashing eyeliner, waist length pink ombre hair, and a pale lavender dress. She's one of the few other women who haven't gone for a black on black look, and the two of us stand out like sore thumbs.

"Very moving," I agree quickly. "Unbelievably so."

She scans me from head to toe, taking in my sleeveless blood red dress while lingering on the thigh slit and sweetheart neckline.

"You're not familiar, but you're not wearing a press pass."

"I'm new." I hold my hand out. "Darcy. And you are?"

"Emma." She pauses, waiting for... something. "I work in makeup and costumes."

"Oh, cool. That must be intense."

Her eyes, which have been narrowed the whole time, relax slightly, and she shrugs. "At least the boys don't need to change every three songs and be winched into corsets."

"I guess not."

I can only imagine what female artists go through. A part of me notes the easy familiarity with which she calls Hazardous *the boys*, and I bite my lip, making a mental note to look this woman up the second I get a free moment. Most of my research has been into the cartel, but I need to know more about the other roadies if I'm to survive here.

Who knows how long it will take for all of my marks to be in the same place at the same time? Making friends in the meantime will help me blend in, and I might be able to get information out of them about how the cartel is blackmailing the band.

Emma hums, waiting for me to say something else, but when I disappoint her, she sighs. "Well, I hope you enjoy the rest of the party."

She turns without waiting for me to reply, heading farther into the Gallery without speaking to anyone. I quickly shuffle away from the stunning piece of art and onto the next.

"Ladies, gentlemen, and everyone in between," Sully begins, his distinctive voice echoing through the gallery's speakers. "If you could make your way to the main floor, the band has a few words they'd like to say before you return to drinking yourselves stupid."

The good-natured chuckles that go up around me tell me a lot about how well liked Sully is by the crew. Even a few of the journalists smirk and raise their bottles in the air. Not wanting to stand out, I snag a bubbling champagne flute from a passing waiter, but I have no intention of drinking it.

Unfortunately, I'm a total lightweight, so drinking around my marks is a no-go. I don't do my best work when I'm a giggling mess.

Following the press of people through the hanging paintings, I finally manage to breathe when they open up into a clear centre space that's obviously intended for dancing. A bar has been set up to one side, but I ignore it in favour of finding a spot against the wall, with a clear view of the stage that Sully is standing on.

Behind him, in the shadows, I can make out four silhouettes. My eyes linger, but I'm too far away to make out the details of their faces, and my attention is quickly captured elsewhere.

As Sully steps down, a good-looking man, in his late twenties greets him and slaps him on the back. His shoulder-length hair is tied into a low ponytail, and his dark eyes shine with enthusiasm as he takes in the room. The older man stiffens at the touch, but it's so subtle that the rest of the room doesn't notice.

Miguel Rosales's perfectly white, easy smile makes it obvious that he's used to getting his own way, and the matching tailored suit he's wearing screams money and professionalism. I know it's all a lie—Man's information is very rarely wrong—but his easy demeanour is so at odds with the shark I know he is.

"Hey, everyone."

My eyes are yanked back to the stage, and my breath catches as I finally see the guys in person. Slate has stepped up to the mic, the rest of the band fanning around him, their matching white hoodies glowing under the brilliant spotlights. All four of them have the hoods up, casting their faces in shadow, and Arlo has tugged his trademark leather jacket over the top. They're gods, standing above us all, and not for the first time, I question Man's wisdom in sending me on this mission.

"So, we just want to say thank you for everything you've put into making the last two legs of the tour so unbelievably smooth."

Slate's presence is so magnetic that I find myself leaning away from the wall to be closer to him. I know, I've heard him before over my headset, but that was nothing compared to the reality of him. All of them seem to possess this incredible draw, even though they're standing up there in relaxed leather and oversized hoodies, while the rest of us are dolled up to the nines.

Applause follows his words, and he has to pause to let it die down before he continues.

"I know you've all been waiting to hear who'll be supporting us on stage for this last leg of the tour, and I'm pleased to finally announce, we're playing alongside Rottenheim Twins and Yesterday's Cascade!"

As he announces it, the two other bands leap onto the stage, grinning. I've heard of both, and I love a lot of Yesterday's Cascade's solo work, but my gut takes an uneasy turn at the sight of the twins.

Beautiful, leggy, with bright green hair for days, the Rottenheim Twins were relatively unheard of before they collaborated with Hazardous on one of their latest songs. The music video between the two women and the band was literal fire. At one point, the twins very nearly kissed both Slate and Arlo during the instrumental, which sent the rumour mills flying. Now they'll be in close proximity to the band for months...

Are they seeing each other? I thought they were a little young for the guys—barely out of college—but this is show business, after all... Stranger things have happened between the rich and famous.

Suddenly, the very real possibility that I might be interfering by making myself known to the clan wiggles into my brain. I always assumed that Dodger wasn't with anyone else, because he was so eager to take advantage when I was single. If they have girlfriends—which, given who they are, they probably do—then can I really just pop up in their lives?

What if I've been the other woman all along? Even if I wasn't, a lot of women don't like meeting their man's female friends, and I don't want to cause that kind of drama.

Looking at the grins on those beautiful girls' faces, my stomach sinks, and I take out my phone to delete my last message.

I'm here for the Rosales brothers. I'll take out my marks and free my clan from whatever blackmail they're dealing with. After that, I'll disappear.

"Both of them have agreed to give you all a little taste of what they're bringing to the tour," Slate finishes, grinning out into the crowd. "So give them all you've got."

The two bands leave the stage, leaving the twins to grab their guitars and step up to the mics.

They're good—not as good as Hazardous—but they certainly have a way with the crowd, and their enthusiasm is infectious.

I leave them, inching closer to where Miguel is slowly making his way out of the crowd and towards the doors. His phone is in his hand, and I grab mine. If he's connected to the free Wi-Fi, that's my in.

Public networks are a godsend. In a few swipes, I'm in the router's DNS settings, and matching them to my own. All I need to do now is wait for that phone of his to reach out to the router, and I can redirect him to a fake site under my control, prompt him to download a file with a rootkit inside and bam, I have control of his phone.

It's a bit of a blunt tool, and I'll probably catch dozens of other fish in the net, but I'll be able to discern his device from all the others when I start looking at his files and emails.

Once everything is set up, I'll be a parasite in his system. He won't be able to swipe right without me knowing about it.

"Ah, here she is!"

Sully's voice distracts me, and I curse under my breath before turning on my heel and freezing. Panic chases my heart-beat into my ears, until it merges with the harsh bass coming through the speakers.

The entire band is there with him. This close, I can see that someone has lined the inside of their hoodies with red fabric, and the spotlights above filter through, making their faces look like they're bathed in blood.

"So this is our pyro?"

Dodger's voice breaks through the fuzz in my brain, and my cheeks warm. Did he really just call me that? And did I really just blush? His narrowed, almond-shaped eyes seem to pierce right through me as he gives me a slow once over.

No. Bad, Darcy. We are not doing this. No blushing, no giggling, definitely no flirting.

Unfortunately, my normal fall-back of acting like an airhead isn't going to help me here. I don't want to get fired, and they *will* fire me if they think I can't be trusted to handle the most dangerous part of their show. As it is, their eyes are tracing sceptically over the form-fitting lines of my dress.

"Nice to meet you," I mumble instead, keeping my voice calculatedly quiet, so that the noise of the Rottenheim Twins drowns me out.

"This is David's replacement?" Prophet demands, looking pissed. Those mismatched eyes, one ghost-blue, the other warm russet brown, are narrowed as he turns to my new boss. "Sully..."

"Her qualifications are just as good as David's were, and Kenway says her background checks out." The older man's expression softens. "Look, we all miss him, kid, but after that shit he pulled, Darcy is who we've got."

Note to self: find out what Man did to get my predecessor fired.

Slate steps forward, elbowing Prophet to the back of the group and offering me an easy smile. "Don't mind the grump; he doesn't mean anything by it."

I scoff internally, and my expression sours slightly. It's illogical, given he has no idea who I am, but I was hoping for one of his flirty Spanish nicknames.

I glance at Arlo, the only member of the band who hasn't spoken, but his sunglasses make it impossible to tell what he's thinking. He sticks to the back of the group, watching us all with his lips softly parted.

If this was our group chat, he'd have reached in to check in with me. But it seems real-life Arlo keeps his cards close to his chest.

"Look forward to working with you." Dodger's tone is pleasant, but bland. A far cry from the husky voice of the man who coaxed me to orgasm with his words only a few days ago.

"Likewise," I mouth.

Sully offers me a small smile, then stretches an arm out, gesturing for the band to head towards the doors.

They're leaving their own party early? Really?

Multiple journalists try to approach them as they cross the gallery, but they're ignored. The boys move as one impenetrable unit, and every reporter is iced out.

I track them as they leave, watching as Miguel joins the back of their group, slinging an arm around Arlo's shoulders.

No one else sees the small plastic bag that makes its way into the guitarist's back pocket, and if they do, they don't care.

I'm too far away to tell for certain, but my heart clenches at the sight.

In the band's early days, Arlo's drug problem was legendary. Stills of him doing lines off girls' asses were plastered over gossip sites.

Has he fallen back on old habits? Was he ever clean?

A long sigh escapes me, and I reluctantly force my attention back to my phone. I have a job to do, and dwelling on how... anticlimactic our first meeting was isn't it.

I suppose this is why they say don't meet your idols.

Darcy
6

My first day at my new job is a late start, and, God, do I need to sleep in. After my mark and the band left, I stayed to maintain appearances, and I might've downed a few champagnes in self-pity. Hey, the band was picking up the roadies' tab, and the least they could do after disappointing me like that was help me get smashed.

Unfortunately, I'm not sure I can face any of my new coworkers now. Giggly, drunk Darcy danced with just about all of them.

To make matters worse, Miguel left and didn't return, taking his phone out of reach of the Wi-Fi before I could get my digital claws into him.

My only saving grace was that neither Sully nor the band returned all night. It doesn't mean I feel any less nervous as I show security my pass and step into the chaos that is backstage at a metal concert.

"Ah, Darcy, just in time." Sully claps me on the back before I even notice him approach, and drags me into the chaos. "The pyro cages are kept over there." He points at a far-off corner of the room, empty of anything except the wheeled cages. "There's a safety checklist they need you to fill out at every venue—health and safety, covering their asses as usual—that's lying around somewhere. Make sure you find it, or I'll get my ass handed to me."

He continues talking at a hundred miles a minute as he gives me the quickest tour of the cavernous backstage space, ending with the stage.

"The band will be arriving later, and then you can go through their safety check. I've got the choreography David—the guy before you—used, written down here." Sully hands me a folded piece of paper. "The band doesn't mind if you want to change things, but you need to make sure they know where not to stand, so be up here for rehearsals so you can do the safety checks with them. One of the dry ice machines is also temperamental..." A loud clang makes him tense, and he looks over his shoulder. "Be right back."

Abandoned and alone amongst people rushing around with their own problems, I unfold the paper and groan.

It's all iron wool, dry ice, and electronic cartridge-based explosives. Not even a hint of nitroglycerine or C-4. Sure, even dry ice can be explosive under the right conditions, but this is so... tame.

I leave the stage—which is bare and empty in the bright daylight—and head towards the cages full of my baby incendiary devices. Only to stop as I see the clipboard tied to the front of one.

There's so much paper trapped on it that the clip at the top looks like it might break.

"No."

Not paperwork. Not today. Not while I'm hungover.

I glare at the clipboard and crack my knuckles. "Ah, bureaucracy, we meet again."

I'm barely ten minutes into the world's most anal

checkbox exercise when my phone buzzes in my pocket, followed by a *ba dum tss* that alerts me to the fact it's Prophet.

Unable to help myself—because Prophet so rarely initiates any kind of conversation, and I'll do *anything* to escape the purgatory of paperwork—I draw my phone out and glance at the screen.

[HzD]Proph3t
We needed you last night.

Accusatory, grammatically perfect, and so very like him. I sigh, slipping the phone back into my pocket without replying, condemning him to the unread pile with the slew of other messages.

They all reached out last night, trying to cajole me into going online, but I'm irrationally angry at them still.

Yes, I know I'm overreacting, and I should be *happy* that my cover is safe and they didn't recognise me, but we've been gaming together for years. Years! And they didn't even—

I press the pen into the paper so hard that my next tick makes a savage rip through the box.

"Careful," a familiar voice warns. "Trying to find a pen around here is nearly impossible."

I look back and find Emma standing there, hand on one hip, as she eyes me with amusement. Unlike me, she's immaculately put together, makeup on point, and wearing a floaty teal romper that stands out amidst the sea of black shirts almost as much as my unicorn hoodie does.

"I blame the hangover," I mutter. "Plus, shouldn't this whole process be digitised? Who uses paper and ink nowadays?"

The wardrobe mistress snorts. "Oh, I'd love to hear you tell Sully that." Her smile fades, becoming one of fond exasperation. "Seriously, don't even try. I've been nagging him since I joined the tour, but that old goat will not learn new tricks."

"Noted," I reply.

"As for the hangover..." She moves closer, rummaging in her purse, and pulls out two luminous energy drinks. "I snagged these from the vending machine. Figured you'd need one after last night."

I grimace, accepting the bottle and flicking open the cap to down it. "Was I that bad?"

Emma smiles. "Well, your giggle fit was definitely an icebreaker."

If there is a god, please don't let Man find out about that...

"In my defence, it wasn't intentional," I mumble. "I kinda... got carried away."

My phone chimes again, this time with Arlo's *ribbit* followed quickly by Dodger's *squeeeal.*

"You gonna answer that?" Emma asks, frowning.

I sigh. "No. I'm mad at them."

The other woman quirks the corner of her lip sympathetically. "Is it those boys you were cursing out last night?"

I did that?

Shit. Disaster control, now.

Berating myself five different ways, I shrug as nonchalantly as possible. "How much did I drink, exactly?"

"Enough," Emma admits, her smile returning. "Don't worry. You didn't say anything too embarrassing, though you did keep ranting about how people are never as cool in real life as they are in games."

I let my head fall back and groan. "Just forget I ever said that, please? Besides, I'm here to work, and..."

The loudest, most obnoxious, girly giggle I've ever heard in my life interrupts us, and I trail off. Craning my neck, I struggle to work out where the sound is coming from. Jeez, I thought I pulled off a good airhead act, but that is either grade-A acting, or the woman in question has been cursed with the world's most unfortunate laugh.

Then her fake tits come into view, and I realise it's neither of those options. Just as quickly, I curse myself for being judgemental. Maybe she really loves metal... and the girl behind her... and the girl after—Jesus! How many are there?

Damn it, Darcy. Women policing other women's sexuality is a tool of the patriarchy. We've got to be better than this.

"Ugh..." Emma echoes my thoughts. "I know they make a shit ton from VIP ticket sales, but sometimes the VIPs are just..."

"I'm sure she has a wonderful personality," I grind out, watching not one—but four—metal-barbies assemble, complete with leather corsets, bright neon space buns, platform boots, and tiny rah-rah skirts. "Or... donates to charities that save drowning kittens or... something."

Emma bursts out laughing. "Oh, we're going to be best friends. You can counter my judgemental bitchiness with your strained positivity."

"I can barely counter my *own* bitchiness most days," I retort, grimacing as I take another sip of energy drink and try *not* to focus on the thong I can clearly see from all the way over here. More power to her if she can survive having her butt cleaved in two like that, I guess... "How am I supposed to counter yours as well?"

Emma cackles, and the two of us watch as the group of ten VIPs—six of whom look mercifully normal, for metal-heads, anyway—are ushered away by a brunette with blunt bangs who's wearing a suit and a strained expression.

"Gabrielle's got her hands full," Emma mutters, noticing the woman. "Poor thing. She's shy, but she's Miguel's assistant, and he always makes her do this shit."

She was in my file, and I'm relieved to put a face to the

name. Miguel's assistant is an intelligent nobody, put in place by his older brothers to keep this whole show running. She might be a good lead if I can't get to her boss.

"I didn't think a metal band would attract those kinds of fans..." I mumble.

Emma gives me the look. "The band has money, and wherever there's money, there are people who'll sell their dignity to get their hands on it." She tosses her pink hair back and sighs. "Thankfully, the band got out of that phase pretty quickly in their careers. Those ladies will be disappointed."

I am *not* relieved.

"The band doesn't like groupies?"

I couldn't judge the clan if they did. If hot men were throwing themselves at me on a nightly basis... Well, I'm not sure I'd be strong enough to resist.

"Sully said they used to." Emma shrugs. "But it was before I convinced Arlo to let me join. Dodger might fuck one every now and again, but it's rare. I think the boys got fed up with having the details of their sex lives leaked to the press." She pauses. "I do feel bad for the girls... the VIP experience can cost upwards of ten grand a ticket, and they're wasting it because they think their magic vajayjays are going to enchant the boys into making them Mrs. Hazardous." She waves a hand. "Anyway, the band will turn up for rehearsal soon, which means I've got to bounce. See you 'round, and try not to get into any more fights with that pen."

She disappears in a sashaying breeze, leaving only the pleasant scent of her perfume behind. My eyes fall back to the clipboard, and I moan. Damn it, what do I have to do to convince this paperwork to do itself?

Another *ribbit* echoes from my phone, this time followed by the creepy *mwahaha* I assigned to Slate. I get a few looks from other roadies for that one. A frog croak is cute enough, but Jigsaw's laugh is decidedly not.

I could turn it to silent, but I'm a masochist. Besides, the other Belladonnas have a habit of messaging me when I'm in the middle of something, even while I'm on missions. If one of my sisters needs me, I don't want to let them down.

Or at least... that's my excuse.

I bite my lip as I check my phone for the fifth time in two minutes. In a few moments, we need to be on stage; I shouldn't be agonising over this.

"Still nothing?" Prophet grunts, tapping his sticks against his legs. He likes to pretend he wouldn't be here if he had a choice, but I can read the adrenaline already buzzing through his body. He's just as addicted to the rush of this as we all are.

I sigh, picking at the ripped leather pants Em bullied me into. God, these things are tight. "Not a peep."

My hand has been glued to my phone all day. I kept sneaking glances at it all the way through rehearsals. I ignored most of the team meetings—including the safety talk with our hot new pyro—and spent most of my time in my head, wondering what Dark's up to.

If I get torched by a gerb on stage, it's entirely my own fault.

This is the longest Dark's ever gone without a reply, and the silence feels... terse. Like she's mad at us. Normally, she responds within seconds. I seriously wonder sometimes if the woman even sleeps. But she wasn't online yesterday, even though we left the kickoff party early to hang with her before the next leg of the tour steals all of our time.

Not that she had any way of knowing that, but still.

"She said she had another trip," Slate reminds us, accepting his guitar from Gavin as the crowd roars a final applause for Yesterday's Cascade. "I'm sure she'll read our messages when she's got time."

As usual, there's an impatient undercurrent to his voice when it comes to talking about Dark. Not because he doesn't care—no, he's just as besotted as I am—but because Slate doesn't do emotional "what ifs."

In Slate's mind, either Dark wants to speak to us, or she doesn't. She's either interested, or she isn't. He doesn't waste time worrying about the why, and he hates the games that a lot of the girls we dated in the past liked to play.

Dark's not like that. She never has been. She's funny and sweet, and...

Dodger clasps arms with Tidus as Yesterday's Cascade jog off the stage, but I can't pay attention to the pleasantries between the lead singers as I slip my phone out of my pocket and check the group chat again.

[HzD]Fr0gg0
Are you ignoring us?

Slate's phone buzzes, and he groans, but my ears prick up as I hear a distinctive *ribbit* chime come from our left.

I whirl in place, but before I can see where the noise has come from, Rick is pressing my guitar into my hands. In the crowds above us, the chants have begun.

I heard her ringtone. I swear—

Dodger frowns at me. "Get your head in the game, man."

A bright stage light cuts through the gap in the black curtain, momentarily blinding me.

"I heard—"

"On stage in five, four, three..." Sully counts us off on his fingers while his other hand holds his earpiece in place.

Then we're running, diving headfirst onto the blackened stage. My fingers find the neck of my Les Paul, and I wait for Prophet to start the beat. Two seconds later, the loud pounding beat echoes out over the crowd, and my hands move automatically, strumming the first lines without thought.

"Los Angeles!" Dodger roars into the mic as the flames whoosh out beside me. "How you doin'?"

The screams that answer him drown out all thoughts of Dark, and I slip into the only drug that's ever really mattered. Music.

Darcy
8

The band jogs off stage, grinning widely and covered in sweat. All four of them are completely ignorant of the blush that's stealing over my cheeks at the sight of them. I'm still trying to ignore them, but it's damn near impossible now that I've spent the last three hours listening to them blow the roof off this place.

From my spot backstage, I had a panty-melting view of Prophet's back flexing as he thrashed the drums like they personally offended him. I even caught glimpses of Arlo, Slate, and Dodger as they jumped around, lost in the grip of their music.

I thought watching Dodger cradle the mic as he sang into it on video was intense, but in real life, he made it look intimate as he alternated between soft vocals and harsh screams that gave me goosebumps. Even when he wasn't singing, his dancing...

I swear at one point, he made love to the fucking floor.

Sometimes I had to remind myself I was supposed to be working and drag my attention back to the gerbs—which I learned today is the technical term for all things on stage that go boom. More than once I almost missed my cue to shower them in titanium sparks or set off the butane flame throwers.

To be honest, the band is doing a better job of ignoring *me*. As a roadie, I'm invisible. Even when I mumbled the safety instructions at them during rehearsal—certain that they'd recognise my voice—they just looked right through me.

I shouldn't be surprised. I've been infiltrating organisations since I was a teenager—I'm good at it—but this time, my heart just isn't in it. I know I'm making mistakes, and I can't bring myself to care. I keep berating myself for not treating this like any other job, and then in the same instant, silently pray for them to figure out who I am so I can take this opportunity to spend time with the four men who are my best friends.

Unfortunately for that vain hope, it seems like even with my own self-sabotage, they're completely oblivious.

Hell, Arlo was just endlessly scrolling on his phone or gazing off into space.

Was he high the whole time? With his sunglasses on, I couldn't read his eyes to check for redness or blown pupils. His favourite accessory has gained a new meaning now, and I can't help but wonder how long he's been using.

At some point during the show, Dodger lost his shirt, and so did Slate. The two of them are eye candy, and it's making it hard for me to focus on my stupid paperwork—because yes, there's an after-show list of safety precautions *as well*. They don't even make eye contact with me as they hand off their instruments to the guitar and bass techs beside me, before they're ushered towards the post-show VIP meet-and-greet by Sully.

"Good show tonight, everyone!" the old Texan cries, as the band disappears down a corridor to the left. "Let's make it a quick pack down, so I can get some shuteye before my flight tomorrow."

A chorus of agreement follows, and he strokes his moustache with a smile before heading my way.

"You did good tonight, Darcy," he says. "I know the health and safety talk made you a bit nervous, but you powered through, and what a show!"

I can't help my smile. "It was fun," I admit. "I could do with less paperwork, but..."

He chuckles and pats me on the back. "You and me both, darlin'."

He's gone without another word, leaving me to pack away in silence.

It goes faster than I thought it would. After a long, tiring, and stressful day with very little progress on my mission—or even a peep out of my mark—all I want to do is go back to my hotel room and crash. The knowledge that our flight tomorrow is at an ungodly hour only makes me more determined to get some sleep where I can.

I've just finished my final box and am tugging on my oversized, pastel tie-dye hoodie in preparation to leave when someone bumps into me, almost sending me flying. As it is, the clipboard and a whole bunch of water bottles that they were carrying drop to the floor.

"Sorry! Sorry!" my unintentional assailant cries, putting a hand under my elbow to steady me.

"It's okay," I return, automatically dropping to my knees to help gather the lost stuff. I manage to grab two of the bottles before they roll away, but when I look up to give them back, I freeze.

Miguel's assistant looks a lot worse for wear than she did earlier. Her hair is wild, and there are huge bags under her bloodshot eyes.

"Thank you!" She blushes beneath her long bangs. "Sorry, I know we haven't met. You're Darcy, right? The new hire? I'm Gabrielle."

"Hi," I reply, handing her the water. "You look—" Stressed. Run off her feet. "Tired. Are you okay?"

She hums, grabbing her clipboard. "Mr. Rosales keeps me busy, but I'm used to it. Promise. I just have to get this water to the band, inspect the trucks before they depart, and call ahead to the next venue to confirm set-up times for tomorrow... Sorry, I know you don't want my to do list."

Damn, she still has to do all that? It's almost two in the morning already. Against my better judgement—she *is* my mark's assistant, after all—I find myself nodding in sympathy.

"Can I help?" I ask, without meaning to.

She looks up, sharply, her bright brown eyes wide with shock. "You mean it? Really?"

She looks so hopeful that I can't find it in me to take my offer back. "Yeah, I mean, I'm pretty much done for the night. I could do one of the smaller things—"

Gabrielle loads the water bottles into my arms without giving me a second to back out. "Ohmygoodness! Thank you so much!" she gushes. "The band are in the VIP suite still, just getting the last photos taken before they go back to their hotel. It's easy to find, I promise. If you could just sneak the bottles inside, that would be so great! I won't forget this. Thank you!"

My stomach sinks as I realise what I've just signed myself up for, but Gabrielle is already racing away, heading for the loading bay doors with single-minded determination.

I glance at the water bottles with annoyance.

"So much for keeping out of their way," I mutter to myself.

Putting the bottles down for the second I need to secure my last few boxes of gear, I take a deep breath, complete the last few pesky check boxes, and then, when there's absolutely nothing left for me to procrastinate with, I finally head down the corridor towards the dressing rooms and the VIP suite.

Gabrielle was right. It's not hard to find—which destroys my plan of getting lost on purpose. Even if I struggled, the huge bear of a man guarding the room would be a dead give-away. From behind the door, with its obnoxiously large sign, I can still hear those high-pitched giggles, and I grimace.

Watching the band flirt with groupies was not what I signed up for.

The security guy takes a look at me, my lanyard, and the bottles of water, then admits me. Taking a deep breath—and grimacing at the amount of perfume that hits me even from this side of the door—I shoulder my way inside.

Just put the bottles down and get out as fast as you can, I console myself. *Don't even look—*

Too late.

Damn it. I should've known I'd never have the strength to not look.

The band is lounging around on overstuffed couches as the VIPs chatter away excitedly. Dodger still hasn't managed to find a shirt, and this close, his tattoos are magnificent. I pick out a familiar pair of crossed short blades stretched out across his collarbones. The two knives are linked with chains and edged with flames, but the view is obscured by a set of long, feminine fingers tracing the ink.

I force my gaze up to his face.

Mistake.

His eyes might be empty, but he's giving the woman who's claimed his lap an easy, charming smile that says he doesn't mind her attention. Her hands are all over his chest as she kisses him, tracing the lines of his tattoos, lingering on the small hazard symbol tattooed over his heart.

As I watch, the groupie leans back, then drops her head and presses a soft kiss over the band's symbol, then darts her tongue out to lick the skin.

That should not hurt as much as it does.

We're not exclusive, I remind myself sternly. *We're just friends with phone sex benefits. I said I didn't want to see him at the same time as I was seeing other people, but he never said the same. He's allowed hook ups with other women.*

No matter how much I reason with myself, the irrational pang in my chest isn't getting any less painful, and I yank my gaze away to find a safer target.

Arlo is on the seat across from them, chattering animatedly with a teenager and his friend, both of whom are looking at him like he's hung the moon. Prophet is posing against the wall for another photo with more guests, and Slate... is nowhere to be seen.

Forcing myself to abandon the search for him—because I don't want to know what he's doing—I hastily chuck the bottles of water onto the nearest table and flee.

Of course, I don't make it. Slate is right there, standing in the doorway, unintentionally blocking my exit as he frowns down at his phone.

The next five seconds seem to happen in a horrifying kind of slow motion. His thumb comes down on the screen, and—two blinks later—my phone erupts with a creepy and unmistakable horror movie giggle.

Mwahahaha.

The sound—so out of place in this cosy smoozefest—stuns the room to silence. Slate's head snaps up, and I don't need to look back to know that the rest of the band is staring as well.

My cheeks heat, and my brain snaps into disaster mode.

Deny, deny, deny.

"Oh, shit! I thought I had it on silent." I bite my lip, keeping my eyes downcast. If I play dumb, perhaps they'll put it down to coincidence. "I just came to deliver the water for

Gabrielle." I wave awkwardly at the bottles on the table. "Anyway, have a nice night."

Before any of them can stop me, I duck around Slate and flee into the corridor, rushing down the long, straight hall as fast as my legs will carry me.

I'm not fast enough to out-run the sounds of my own traitorous phone.

Ribbit. Ba dum tss. Squeeeal. Mwahahaha.

"Oh my God! Shut up, shut up, shut up!" I growl at the device, snatching it out of my pocket as I turn the corner.

Unfortunately for me, my stupid hind-brain decides to look back before I'm completely out of sight.

Four immense bodies spill out into the hallway behind me, watching as I run away as fast as my short ass legs will carry me.

I keep running until I reach the hotel, too wound up to even think about calling an Uber. I take the stairs two at a time, cursing myself over and over for being so stupid.

This entire mission is shaping up to be a disaster. They know who I am, although I suppose they must believe their own anonymity is still intact. Even though some of their usernames are less than subtle, it's plausible that I might not put two and two together and connect Hazardous, the band, to my clan. I'm just a newbie who got nervous when her weird ringtones called attention to her.

But are they really going to believe my being here, out of the blue, and working for them, is a coincidence?

Ugh! The whole thing is making my head hurt.

To top it all off, Miguel wasn't here at all today, and I've yet to see either of his brothers.

I burst into my room, collapsing onto the scratchy sheets with a long, drawn-out groan. Then, because I have zero self control, I pull out the traitorous phone and scroll through the group chat.

[HzD]D0dgeVip3r
where are you at???

[HzD]StoneRE1
yo, @D4rk4ngel? What's keeping you?

[HzD]Fr0gg0
we've gotta beat this dungeon today. Won't
be online tomorrow.

Those are just the start of yesterday's messages, all of them
sent after they left the kickoff party. It's stupid, but my heart
beats a little faster. Did they leave that party early just to play
Runes with me?

I'm reading too much into this.

I scroll past their messages and reach the ones they've sent
today. After Prophet sent his message this morning, all of
them checked in, asking if I was okay, both in the group chat
and privately. Arlo alone sent half a dozen messages.

Taking another deep breath, I scroll past those and read
the last messages.

[HzD]StoneRE1
if you're pissed at us do us a favour and tell
us why before Fr0gg0 loses his mind

That was the message that outed me, and it explains the
glower on his face as I bumped into him. Then, beneath that,
are the four that sealed my fate.

[HzD]Proph3t
Hey.

[HzD]Fr0gg0
Dark?

[HzD]D0dgeVip3r
baby girl?

[HzD]StoneRE1
cariño?

I have to say something, I realise. Otherwise, they're going to corner me at work, and things will get awkward fast. A newcomer waltzing straight into the band's inner circle will put me directly in Miguel's path. I'm not like some of the other Belladonnas. I never take my marks on face-to-face. I could, in theory—I've been trained to shoot, to slit throats, and more—but that's not how I like to work.

I'm at my best when I'm invisible. It gives me space to observe and plan. I set up my marks' demises with calculated precision, and they never suspect a thing until my bombs detonate.

Pushing up from the mattress, I brush my hair out of my face and start disaster control.

D4rk4ngel
Sorry guys, I'm not ignoring you. First day at my new job and I really want this one to go well, kk?

There's a pause, and then their messages come flooding in at once.

[HzD]Proph3t
You never told us you were applying for a new job.

[HzD]D0dgeVip3r
I'm sure you rocked it

[HzD]StoneRE1
what job?

[HzD]Fr0gg0
congrats! *cheer emoji*

[HzD]D0dgeVip3r
are they paying you enough?

I let out a breath.

Okay, they bought the excuse. I don't feel great lying to them, but it's not like the truth would go down well.

Hey guys, by the way, I'm an assassin here to resolve the little blackmail issue you've been having by blowing up your tour manager and his two despicable big brothers. Fancy grabbing pizza while I start the long and arduous process of moving all of their money—minus my cut—to charities who need it?

Nope. They'd either think I was insane, or they'd call the cops. Best to stick to my cover unless there's no way out.

D4rk4ngel
thanks! It pays meh but my boss is nice.
Super tired now tho, gonna catch some zzz

I don't feel bad at all about calling them out on their shit pay rates. Hell, I doubt the band is involved in wage discussions for roadies, anyway. But it's only fair to let them know Sully has been nice to me.

[HzD]Fr0gg0
sweet dreams

[HzD]D0dgeVip3r
night

[HzD]StoneRE1
get some rest

[HzD]Proph3t
Night.

My smile breaks free before I can remind myself that real-life Arlo is not this sweet. Then I lose it entirely as I remember that I still have to shower because we're leaving for the next city at six-freaking-am tomorrow.

Who on earth decided that was a good idea? I bet it was Gabrielle. She acted nice, but I bet she's a peppy morning type person.

Slate

P rophet storms into the hotel suite like a man fleeing for his life. The asshole doesn't drink—none of us do —but tonight he heads straight for the bar, grabbing a bottle of whisky and downing it neat.

"Fuck." Dodger sums up the feeling that's been gripping all of us since we watched her—watched *Dark*—flee the VIP suite like her ass was on fire.

And what an ass it was...

The meet and greet collapsed after that. We didn't even have the energy to pretend for the fans anymore, and they could tell. The genuine ones were good enough about being sent on their way with a few autographs and a photo, but the girls...

God, they were impossible. I swear one of them was trying to surgically attach herself to Dodger.

I'm just glad Dark didn't see that. Shit, she probably saw enough.

Arlo collapses on the sofa, barely taking in the room. "She's real. She's here."

"She's our employee," Dodger growls, looking at his

phone—probably at her last message. "And she's not getting paid enough."

"She's not *our* employee," I correct, leaning against the wall. "The agency hired her."

Though, I'll admit, it grates to know that she has financial ties to Miguel and his brothers.

He's not listening. "How much do roadies even make? I thought Sully promised it was a living wage…"

I'm not getting through to him. That much is clear. He's hyper focused on the money—like always.

Dodger isn't a dollar chaser, not really, but money's his fixation. We all know what it's like to go without, but Dodger's the only one who's ever been truly homeless.

Arlo, of course, is harder to read. Now that we're alone, he's taken off the glasses, and is pinching the bridge of his nose like thinking is hurting him. A second later, he stops, fishing out his phone.

Is he messaging Dark?

Prophet slams the bottle down, and I grimace as I realise he's downed half already.

"Ease up, man," I caution. "This is a good thing,"

We've been friends a long time—longer than the others, though not by much—so he immediately glares at me.

"Don't even think about it."

I hold my hands up, trying to paste an innocent expression over my smile. I probably just look pained.

"What?"

"You *know* what." He scrubs both hands down his face.

I grin. "Don't pretend you've not thought about it. We've been friends with her for years; since way before we ended up here."

'Friends' is putting it lightly. I'm pretty sure all of us are half in love with her, but before now, it was never going anywhere. She's always been cagey about her real name, so none of us ever dared suggest we meet up in real life.

This is new. This is a chance for all those unspoken crushes to finally lead somewhere.

"And you want to drag her right into the middle of our shitshow," Dodger accuses. "You're plotting, Slate, and you're not even being subtle about it."

Arlo's head falls back, and he groans. "Please, guys, not tonight."

"No, if Slate's planning something, we should know," Dodger says, pausing his pacing. "Especially if it puts Dark—"

"Her name is Darcy," Arlo interrupts. "I got Gabrielle to send her records over."

Darcy. It suits her. Delicate, but with a hint of steel.

Prophet hisses under his breath.

Dodger groans. "Great. Now you've put her on their radar."

"Relax, I told her I wanted to look over all the new hires, and we've taken on over a dozen for this leg of the tour. Fortunately, Darcy's the only woman."

Dodger walks up behind him, resting his elbows on the couch as he inspects the file Arlo has got up in front of him.

"It's her," he grumbles. "Remember that time last year she let slip she was in Florida? That was apparently a training course."

"We're not letting this pass us by," I insist. "The band contract states—"

"Fuck the band contract," Dodger growls, stalking off. "We were what? Seventeen when we made that thing up?"

"Nineteen." Legal adults. "And you signed it."

By that point, I'd just finished busting my ass through online school to get my degree, and I used all of that knowledge to make sure it was ironclad.

"Worst mistake of our lives," Prophet grouches.

Beneath my skin, my temper roars, demanding I answer Dodger's and Prophet's anger with my own. I won't.

I learned control the hard way.

"She's the only woman who could possibly fit."

The terms are very clear. One woman for all of us, or none of us date seriously. I wrote them in myself, which is how I know it's all legally ironclad.

"We included that clause because we didn't want a Yoko coming along to break up the band," Arlo mumbles. "Now, thanks to the contract we signed with Miguel, we *can't* break up, even if we want to, so it's pointless."

"It doesn't matter, because we won't be putting her in danger like that," Dodger adds.

Prophet grunts in agreement.

"She would never be in danger," I reply. "Because, between the four of us, we'll make sure that Miguel never gets a whiff of who she is."

Because she *is* something to us. Now that Fate, or God, or maybe plain fucking luck, has landed her in our laps, I have no intention of walking away.

"She's our friend," Arlo replies. "You don't think this will wreck that?"

I roll my eyes. "She's been more than a friend for a long time, Lo. How long have we known her?"

He doesn't hesitate. "Ten years."

"And how many of those have you had a crush on her?"

"*Boys* have crushes," he retorts.

"So what do you call it?" I tease.

He pinches the bridge of his nose again. "An obsession," he mutters, guiltily. "It doesn't matter. I won't risk her. Miguel has enough people to threaten if we step out of line. I won't give him her."

Dodger nods. "Agreed."

I raise my brows at him. I honestly thought he'd be the

first one to jump on board with my plan, given the sounds I've heard coming from his room after the rest of us hang up.

Does he really think I'm that stupid?

Prophet lets out a long, slow sigh. Without looking at any of us, he stands and heads for one of the bedrooms, slamming the door behind him. I'm not surprised by his response. The label contract is the only thing keeping him in the band, and he's made sure the rest of us know it.

Dodger meets my eyes and shakes his head. "Drop this one," he warns. "I know what you're like, and I get what you're thinking, but no. Leave her alone."

He leaves as well, but not before giving Arlo's phone one last look.

That leaves the two of us.

Arlo yawns. "He's right, Slate. I know you love the band, and you think this will fix things... but not even she can fix this."

I shrug, refusing to answer him directly. Instead, I head for my own room, ignoring my suitcase as I head straight for the shower.

It doesn't matter what any of them say. As far as I'm concerned, Darcy being here is a gift from God. Maybe he's gotten bored of pissing on us and has finally decided to throw me a bone.

I've lost count of how many Sundays I've spent on my knees, begging for a way to stop the rifts between us getting any wider. For the last few years, gaming with her has been the only time I've been able to feel even a fleeting reminder of the genuine friendship we used to have.

This band is all I have—all any of us really have—and if Darcy is the way to save it, then I'll do whatever I have to to ensure she ends up between us.

And if Miguel lays a finger on her...

Well, I went to juvie for a reason. I'll happily serve more time if it takes the bastard out of the equation.

I turn the dial to cold, trying to freeze out those thoughts.

Killing Miguel will accomplish nothing. His brothers would just come down on all of us harder for it. My death, I could live with—but Prophet's nieces and nephews? Arlo's sister? No fucking way. The cartels don't make empty threats, and after they finished destroying everything we care about, we'd still be no closer to freedom.

Getting out from under their thumbs and persuading Darcy to give us a chance will take work, but it'll be easier if we're all working together. Only one problem with that: we're barely able to collaborate long enough to make music.

How the hell are we going to work together to show our dream girl she belongs with us?

Darcy
10

I stomp through airport security, cursing the asshole who booked our flight for six in the morning. The road crew doesn't get to travel on a fancy private jet, unlike the band, so we file into economy like the peasants we are.

I should've paid to upgrade my seat, but I didn't want to stand out. Ugh. Now I'm sandwiched between two lighting techs whose names I can't remember, one of whom is munching his way loudly through an entire pack of Doritos. They're friendly, but they quickly start talking over the top of me.

Next time, I decide, *I'm risking it and upgrading myself to first*. I should be sleeping right now, but I can't even nap, thanks to the uncomfortable sensation of being surrounded by men I don't know.

It's barely more than an hour in the air, but touchdown can't come fast enough.

"Enjoy the city, but don't forget, bright and early for set up tomorrow," Sully calls as we deplane into the bright San Jose sunlight. "The band's trying to hook us a nice bonus this tour, so we gotta make sure we earn it."

His words barely register through my sleepy fog. Ugh, why is it that even the *sun* is so peppy this morning?

My Uber is late, because *reasons*, and then we hit traffic almost as soon as we leave the airport. To make things worse, my driver is one of the awkward silent ones. I spend a lot of the journey to the hotel wondering if he's a serial killer, and then trying to figure out which one of us would make it out of the car alive if he was. I'm almost certain it would be me, but I don't have a chance to test my theory because we rock up at a moderately nice hotel.

As a result of all the morning stress, I'm almost brain dead as I scroll through my phone, waiting for the receptionist to find my booking.

"Miss D'Angelo?"

I look up in alarm at the sharp tone, only to realise from the exasperation on her face that she's clearly been trying to get my attention for a while. I offer her a bright, apologetic smile that probably doesn't meet my eyes.

"That's me, sorry."

"Your booking has been cancelled," she repeats, slowly, as if she's silently doubting my intelligence.

It... has?

"Then I'll need to re-book," I suggest, smiling hopefully at her.

"That won't be necessary."

A deep voice, smooth and rich, interrupts, and a hand appears at my elbow before I can protest. I don't need to see who it is; I've heard him often enough.

Slate moves me past the line and towards one of the posh brass elevator doors. It takes me half a glance to realise he's got my suitcase in his other hand, and another to realise he's staring straight ahead, not looking down at me.

And he would have to look down, because up close like this, it's never been more clear that he's giant. Now that I've given myself permission to notice him, the scent of his after-shave washes over me like a drugging haze. Rich, smoky, and undeniably Slate.

What on earth is he doing? I glance down at the point where his warm hand is still firmly holding my arm, then up to the mirrored wall of the elevator.

I take in his oversized hoodie, pulled up over his distinctive braids, and the dark—almost black—eyes gleaming with satisfaction from beneath.

"What—?" I barely get the word out before he grins at me.

"Hey, *cariño.* No running away this time, 'kay?"

My mouth drops open in shock, and it's not an act. I was expecting the guys to bring the subject up... I was not expecting to be kidnapped into an elevator and confronted before I've even had my coffee for the day. Then my cheeks begin to heat as I finally experience the full effect of being called one of his cute nicknames in person.

No. Bad Darcy, we're not falling for the sexy Spanish. We are strong, damnit.

"Wh—"

"I'm going to explain everything, but first we've got to get you settled in. Want some coffee?" He interrupts me again, and I roll my eyes before I can help it.

"Coffee... would be good..." I admit, still thrown by whatever game he's playing. "Am I... dreaming?"

He laughs, right in time for the elevator doors to spring open. "Only if it's a good dream."

It doesn't escape my notice that he only releases my arm when the elevator door has closed, sealing me into their suite.

This place is *fancy.* The open plan living space is massive, with two corner sofas bracketing a low coffee table already boasting two half-full coffee cups.

"Get comfy," Slate orders, already on his way to an open kitchenette on the far side of the room.

Now that he's out of the public eye, he shoves his hood down and his sleeves up, revealing muscled arms covered in tats. I know he said to get comfy, but my brain is still trying to figure out how I got here. I may as well have stumbled into an alternate world for all the sense this turn of events is making.

In all my imaginings about how today would go, this wasn't it. I visualised myself wandering around San Jose by myself, possibly finding Gabrielle and needling her for information to work out Miguel's schedule while I have the down time. I hadn't prepared myself for encountering any of the band. My worst-case scenario was them bringing up our connection during the safety talk tomorrow.

But Slate—ever bold and impatient—is now throwing all of my plans into jeopardy. At least I don't have to fake my shock and confusion.

"What on earth is going on?" I finally blurt.

Slate looks over and frowns. "I mean it. You can sit down."

I'm not sure I should. I have the distinct feeling that Slate is up to something. Bringing me here, with the rest of the band conspicuously absent? Red flag. He may be the bassist, but he's also the one member of the group who always has a plan. Even in-game, he always makes the decisions.

I shuffle over to one of the crushed velvet sofas and almost purr as I sink into it. Pure comfort. I wiggle until I'm sitting on my legs, my hoodie dragged over them for warmth, and watch as Slate tips plenty of sugar into my caffeine.

"I never told you how I like my coffee," I whisper, as he turns and presents it to me like a prize.

Milky and candy-sweet.

"You've brought up enough bad coffee dates that I figured it out by process of elimination," he retorts. "Too dark, too bitter... I never once heard you say too sweet."

To spare myself the indignity of gaping at him some more, I raise it straight to my lips and take an immediate gulp.

"Careful, it's—"

I silence him with a look. "Cold coffee is a crime."

Unless it's iced coffee...

His concern fades, replaced with a lazy grin. "God, you're exactly like I imagined." He coughs, then looks away. "I know this is probably a bit odd, but..." He holds his hand out, like he expects me to release my coffee to shake it. "StoneRE1, but you can call me Slate."

This is the part where I'm supposed to say something, or shake his hand, or something, but I just stare at him with wide eyes. After a few moments, it gets awkward, and he rushes to cover the silence with conversation.

"Anyway, this suite has more than enough rooms so, seeing as yours got cancelled, I figure you can spend the day with the band, and take one of the spare beds tonight," he continues a few seconds later, dropping his hand with a shrug and plopping down on the sofa beside me.

He's got this all figured out, I realise. Suddenly, the coincidences begin to make a lot more sense. I bet my room was cancelled as part of whatever he's up to.

"You're not serious," I finally stutter. "What...? Wait. You want me to stay with you? Here?" My voice is getting higher pitched with·each word, my careful plans being destroyed with every second that passes.

There's no way I'll be able to bump into Gabrielle if I'm being constantly distracted by the band.

"Here will do... for starters. You can stay in our hotels during the tour, and when it finishes, we can look into finding a place together..."

Oh, God. I recognise this tone. This is what he sounds like when he's on a mission to get something. Slate is as stubborn as an ass, and if he's decided he wants me to stay with them, I'm going to have a battle on my hands to change his mind.

"Slate." Prophet's voice is like a whip, making me jump so hard I almost spill my coffee.

The drummer has just emerged from the room opposite, shirtless and wearing only a pair of workout shorts, with his headphones wrapped around his neck. Both of those beautiful mismatched eyes are focused on his bandmate, fury blazing in them.

He doesn't even spare me so much as a glance.

"Prophet needs no introductions, given that his username is just his name in leetspeak," Slate continues, ignoring the raging bull across from us. "Dodger and Arlo will be awake in a bit, then we can go for breakfast."

"Breakfast?" I echo. "I... Slate, don't you think this is a little bit... fast?"

His easy grin never slips. "Don't you believe in soul mates, Darcy?"

What the actual fuck? I'm so stunned by the ludicrous question that I can't do more than blink at him.

Prophet grabs him by his collar and physically lifts the bassist from his spot, dragging him towards the open door he emerged from. "Slate. A *word*."

"Enjoy your coffee," Slate calls as he allows the drummer to bully him from the room.

A second after the door slams, the yelling begins. It's too muffled for me to make out any specifics, but it's easy to tell that Prophet is pissed.

Great, so Slate is trying to manipulate me, and Prophet doesn't even want to look at me.

"He could at least pretend he's happy to meet me," I grumble into my already half-empty coffee.

"He is." My head snaps up, and I crane my neck uncomfortably to find Arlo standing in a doorway behind me, arms folded over his chest. He's already dressed, and even wearing his damned sunglasses indoors. "It's just Slate has been..."

For a second, Prophet's voice booms loud enough for me to make out a few words. *"You impatient, two-faced, defiant—"*

"Slate can be a lot. Especially when he wants something," Arlo finishes, moving closer hesitantly, like he's afraid to scare me off. "If you haven't guessed, I'm—"

"Fr0gg0," I finish for him, offering him a smile. "I'm sorry I crashed in like this. Honestly, the receptionist just told me my room was cancelled, and suddenly Slate was dragging me up here."

The lead guitarist groans and presses the palm of his hand into his forehead. "Jesus, Slate."

"What's he done now—?" Dodger asks, emerging from a different door on my right, his hair wet and dishevelled and a towel hanging loosely on his hips. My cheeks heat as the horny part of my brain begins to utter a prayer to the gods of gravity, and a small disbelieving sound escapes my throat before I can stop it.

He freezes, staring at me with wide eyes, before cursing and retreating back into his room, slamming the door after him.

My stomach drops. Of all of them, Dodge and I have the most intimate relationship. I was hoping for a hug or a hello, heck, even a nod.

Not a slammed door.

"I need coffee for this," Arlo mumbles, heading towards their high-tech machine. "Trust Slate to get his own way."

"Does stuff like this happen a lot?" I ask.

He turns, holding his mug to his lips simply to breathe in the steam. "Bringing old friends into the middle of our hotel suite during a tour? No, that's a new one. Pissing the entire band off by doing things 'for our own good?' That's pretty normal."

I raise my own mug, only to frown when I realise it's empty.

"Another?" Arlo asks.

"Please," I mumble, holding the mug out to him. "He wasn't... serious, was he? About moving in with you guys?"

My mug falls from Arlo's hand, smashing against the tiled floor with a loud crack.

"He said that?"

I wonder if Arlo heard the smooth line about soul mates but decide not to mention it. "Have you guys got a broom?" I ask instead. "We should clean that up."

Arlo startles, already midway through grabbing a new mug from a cupboard. "Right... yeah. Erm..."

He wheels around, looking lost.

"You have no idea where the cleaning stuff is, do you?" I accuse, grinning.

"It's not like that!" he rushes to explain, abandoning his coffee. "Typically, they expect the rich and famous to trash the places we stay at, so they don't bother leaving the cleaning stuff around. Usually, they lock it away somewhere we can't even get to, but I can ask housekeeping..."

Whatever I might've said in response is interrupted when two doors open at the same time. The first is Slate, as he escapes the confines of what I can only assume is Prophet's room. Prophet follows close behind him with rigid shoulders that scream his fury, even if the man himself is silent.

The second is Dodger—fully clothed this time—with his hands in his pockets and damp hair hanging loose around his face.

Suddenly surrounded by the whole band, I bury my face in my hands.

This is not happening. They're all here, and that alone is making it hard for me to breathe. How do I even process this?

I can't. Not right now, and not under this much pressure.

"It's been nice," I begin, pushing to my feet. "But I've got to find myself a new hotel room now, apparently."

"You're staying." Slate actually puts himself in front of the door. "With us. Come on, *cariño*."

I stroll right up to him, press a single hand on his chest, and utter the word I don't think he's heard once in his life.

"No."

His jaw goes slack, and I would laugh at how stumped he looks if I weren't also on the verge of tears.

"You gonna tell us why?" he presses.

I shake my head, and a tiny, half-crazed laugh-hiccup escapes. "You need a why? You cancelled my hotel room, kidnapped me, blurted some stuff about soul mates, and—"

"So that wasn't as smooth as I'd hoped," he admits, unshaken. "*Lo siento*. But you haven't even considered—"

"Would you?" I demand. "Putting aside the blatant manipulation for one second, Prophet clearly doesn't want me here. Not to mention the groupies, the drugs..." I pause, grimacing as I realise how prudish I just sounded. "No judgement, live however you want, but that's not me. We wouldn't click, and that's just based on what I've seen in the last forty-eight hours. Plus, I *work* for you."

After tacking the last bit on, even though I know technically it's not true, I release him and grab my suitcase.

"I knew I should never have taken this job," I whisper, more to myself than them as I stride towards the elevator door and grab my phone.

Thanks to Slate's lack of consideration for personal space, my app has gotten close enough to detect the RFID tag of his door card. With a tap of the screen, I set my phone to match the frequency, and swipe it over the card reader.

The machine beeps and the elevator pings open. Thank god it wasn't a magnetic lock.

Later, I'll berate myself for being so obvious about my capabilities, but right now, I just need some air.

"F uck," Slate curses, as soon as she's gone. He whirls, running a hand over his braids as he paces the length of the room.

"Well, that's that," Dodger mutters.

That's one way to put it.

"That's *that*?" Slate retorts. "Dark—*our* Dark—just walked out on us, and that's all you can say?"

He turns to glare at me, and I shrug.

If he's hoping for an explosion of guilt, he won't get it. Nothing he does is going to make me think that dragging that adorable blonde bombshell into our lives is a good idea. He's trying to use her as a Band-Aid to fix the shit that's been tearing us apart. It was obvious from the start. Thank God that Darcy is smart enough not to fall for his shit.

Arlo is staring at the abandoned coffee cups on the table, caught in thought, blissfully unaware that he's the next object of Slate's ire.

"And *drugs*, Lo?" our bassist demands. "What the fuck? After all the work it took to get you off them?"

I'm actually with Slate on this one, but Arlo shakes his

head. "I flush every bag he gives me. I swear. I've been clean for years."

"Glasses off," Dodger demands.

Arlo sighs but doesn't protest, snatching the thin frames from his face and staring defiantly back at Dodge, letting the lack of yellowing and dilated pupils speak for itself. Then, for good measure, he shrugs up his sleeves, showcasing all the old puckered hash lines of old scars—and no new wounds. I've not seen any nose bleeds either.

If he's using again, the hallucinations haven't started back up.

At his lowest point, he picked his own skin so badly he looked like a polka dot canvas, convinced there were insects running around beneath the surface. One memorable time, we even caught him with a knife, trying to dig them out.

"I'm telling the truth." His resignation hangs in every word, because he's not expecting us to believe him, despite the evidence.

"So what did Darcy see?" Dodger demands, falling back onto the sofa with a groan.

"Probably Miguel slipping the shit into my pocket at the party." Arlo tugs his sleeves down, concealing his scars once more. "I'm sorry. I didn't mean to fuck up our friendship with her."

"Not your fault," I grunt.

It's not. It's more Slate I'm concerned with, but the bassist is currently too busy pacing to start a new plot to drag her into our life.

"It probably didn't help that you were practically making out with that groupie last night," Slate grumbles. "No woman wants it shoved in their face that their casual hookup is casually hooking up with others."

Typical him, focusing on everything Darcy said except the part where he was involved.

"I wasn't hooking up with her," Dodger protests, looking around like he expects any of us to be surprised about the fact he's been virtually fucking Darcy for years—news flash, he's not that subtle. "Besides, when Dark—Darcy—and I are together, I don't fuck anyone else. That woman was all over me, and I wasn't even there. You know how it is."

Dodger once confessed that a part of his mind just switches off when women start touching him—a throwback reaction from his past. But I'm willing to bet Darcy won't appreciate the excuse of *I'm sorry I played tonsil hockey with her, but I wasn't really mentally there for it, so it doesn't count.*

Arlo silences whatever Slate plans to say next by standing. "I'm going to find her."

"Find her?" Dodger looks at him like he's grown a second head. "We agreed: Darcy's staying out of our shit."

"Exactly," I mutter.

Everyone else we care about is tangled in this fucking mess with the cartel. Even if they weren't an issue, the band doesn't need another thing to fight over. I don't care if I have to make her hate me, I *will* keep Darcy out of it.

"Doesn't mean I want her thinking I'm just some useless junkie," Arlo retorts, grabbing his jacket. "Never mind that she already thinks I can't even clean up after myself. Shit."

He swipes his card, disappearing into the elevator before anyone can point out that none of us has a clue where Darcy has even gone.

I look back at Slate just in time to catch the barest hint of satisfaction in his gaze.

My hands curl into fists by my side, and I turn away, stalking back into my bedroom with a curse. Arlo may not know it, but I'm willing to bet that the softest member of the band has just made a move that Slate thinks will act in our favour.

My phone rings, and I soften instantly at the familiar tone.

"Wassup, sis?" I ask, without even looking at the caller ID.

"Your nephew would like to show you what he made in kindergarten today," Destiny answers, smiling. "Turn on video, stupid."

I sigh, grabbing a shirt and dragging it on before doing as she asks. My youngest sister peers back at me, balancing her toddler on her hip, while being careful of the baby bump that's just starting to show at her waist. My jaw aches, and I have to work hard to unclench it as the familiar bitterness that comes from seeing my siblings with their families resurfaces.

My two other sisters have settled down on the east coast, but Destiny and her husband Mikey chose to stay near our parents. She's also the nosiest of the lot, and barely a week goes past without her calling.

"Hey lil' bit," I smile into the camera.

"Uncle Ethan!" he cries, waving a piece of paper in the air. I catch a glimpse of glitter and maybe a bright pompom.

I want to grimace at his use of my first name, but I hold the expression back by sheer force of will. While the rest of the world uses my last name, my family stubbornly continues to call me Ethan.

"He can't see it like that," Destiny chides, helping Malik to hold his picture up.

"It's you!" he cries.

I chuckle. "So it is."

Malik's drawn a stick version of me with googly eyes and a pompom drum kit, being showered in glitter from somewhere above. Beside me, Dodger is screaming into a matching pompom microphone, and the others are there too, their names messily scrawled beneath them and their fuzzy pipe-cleaner guitars.

"Looking good," I praise.

Destiny presses a kiss to his chubby cheek and puts him

down. "Go find your dad," she says, shooing him away with a soft smile.

The moment Malik is out of sight, she frowns into the camera. "Mikey says there's a man lingering outside the playground at his kindergarten," she mutters. "I thought you got them to back off, Ethan?"

The bubbles of laughter die in my throat, falling like rocks to the pit of my stomach. "I did. I'll try again."

"You do that." She scowls at me. "Or I'll go down there myself."

"Destiny." I groan.

I don't doubt for a second that my fierce baby sister will, and that's the problem.

"Don't you 'Destiny' me," she retorts. "That's my boy they've threatened twice now."

I rub my eyes, nodding. "I know. I'll take care of it."

"Make sure you do," she growls.

Then, in true, temperamental baby sister style, she hangs up on me.

I look down at my phone, debating whether or not I should call Arlo.

No. He's wanted to meet Darcy for years. I'll give him one hour. Sixty minutes to assuage his curiosity before I drag him back to reality. I'm not sure if that's more cruel than putting a stop to it straight away, but it *does* need to stop.

Darcy deserves better than a noose around her neck.

Darcy
12

I keep a tight rein on my emotions as I go through the process of booking myself into the hotel, paying out the ass for a room that should've been taken care of—thanks, Slate—and making sure to use a fake name to prevent any more mystery cancellations. I chuck my suitcase in my room and head back down the stairs, resolving to buy myself an amazing breakfast to make up for my crappy morning.

Only for it all to fall apart as I walk straight into Arlo, waiting by the hotel doors.

"I'm not an addict," he begins, following me onto the sidewalk when I refuse to look at him. "I know what it looks like, but I swear to you, I kicked that habit."

"So Miguel just happens to give you packets of what? Baby powder?" I raise a brow. "Like I said, it's your life. I'm not judging how you spend it."

Arlo grabs my hand, pulling me to a stop. "He slipped me drugs, but I'm asking you to trust me. I didn't take them. I'm off that shit. I have been for years."

He's asking for my trust, all while carefully steering around the topic of what I saw. I raise a single brow, daring him to give me a good, solid reason to believe him.

"Come to breakfast with me," he begs. "Slate's trying to mess with things—that's just what he does—but we've never met in person before. I'd hate for you to walk away after years of friendship because we gave you a stupid first impression."

I look down at where our hands are joined, then up into his sunglasses, annoyed at how hard they make it to read him. My heart—which various terrible break ups have proved is *not* the best when it comes to common sense—gives a little pang. Shoving that stupid flutter aside, I try my best to think with my head.

One day, when I'm old and grey, will I regret not letting the gorgeous guitarist take me for breakfast?

Probably. Ugh.

"Fine," I reluctantly agree. "But just breakfast. And I'm not moving in with you."

He smiles, and it's a soft expression. "Never expected you to, Dark. Like I said, Slate pushes. That's just who he is."

Then, in a move so smooth he has to have practised it, he twirls me so his arm wraps around my shoulders without letting go of my hand. "There. Now, I happen to know a really good place that makes the best waffles I've ever tasted."

"Won't you be recognised?" I ask.

He shrugs. "Even if I am, most fans are harmless. They're happy to leave me alone after an autograph."

This close to him, the scent of his aftershave is slowly drowning out everything else. I'd hoped to get some distance from the guys to think, but right now, I'm struggling to remember why I was mad.

"So now that we're more than just internet buddies, do I get to know stuff about you?" Arlo asks. "Like about your family, or your life?"

"Does it go both ways?" I ask as we dodge the San Jose traffic.

He stiffens, then nods. "I... none of us have great pasts, just preparing you for that. I don't know if you know, but we met in juvie."

I do, because I've researched these four obsessively, but I'm not going to admit that. Besides, the reports I looked at told me nothing beyond the bare facts, and even those didn't add up sometimes.

"I have a lot of sisters," I hedge. "We were all adopted."

"Wow." Arlo stares down at me with a new kind of respect. "That must've been crazy."

"Our father is amazing," I add. "He's always made sure we have everything we need."

All true.

"And your birth parents, did you ever want to find them?" He pushes open the door to a cosy cafe, decorated in neutral tones, and leads me up to the counter where a small line of people is waiting to be served.

"They're dead, and I barely remember them," I admit. "They were part of a cult that believed in some messed up shit."

I leave out the fact that their cult leader set the church on fire with his entire congregation locked inside. I only escaped because I was small and sneaky. While Sunday School was being held in the basement, I crept out of the tiny window without anyone noticing to go and play in the park instead.

I remember vividly watching the proud, white-painted structure at the centre of the commune go up in a pillar of smoke. The destructive flames, and the way they resisted all the fire brigade's valiant efforts to tame it, fascinated me.

Later that same day, I ran away from the social worker who was going to take me to my first foster home. I waited until she stopped for gas, opened my door, and ran until I crashed straight into Man.

He prevented me from ending up trapped in the foster system, or worse...

"My adoptive father saved me," I finish. "What about your parents?"

He shrugs, but is saved from answering by the server asking for our order.

When we sit down in the far corner with our fruit and syrup-drenched waffles, he sighs.

"My parents were addicts," he admits. "They spent all our money on pot, speed, and coke. I got thrown into juvie for taking their stash and selling it on to my classmates so I had enough to feed my sister. My own parents sold me out—not because it was wrong, but because I was giving away their drugs."

How did he go from living like that, knowing the harm the drugs could cause, to taking them himself?

I bite my lip, staring hard into my coffee. "That's where you met the guys?"

Fondness eclipses his face for a second. "Yeah. The detention facility we were in had all these classes we were supposed to take, and music was one of the optional ones. Our band started out on crappy third-hand instruments in the basement of that hellhole."

We fall silent for a second, both of us focusing on our food.

"So, you really had no idea you were coming to work with us?" he asks. "That's a pretty incredible coincidence."

I shrug, not wanting to lie to him. "I saw a job and took it. It helped that your music is good."

He looks up, shocked. "You like our stuff?"

Snorting, I shake my head. "Why do you sound so surprised?"

"No reason." It's painfully obvious how badly he's trying to play it cool, but his hands have frozen mid-way through cutting his food, the waffle forgotten. "Just... most of the people who do don't wear pastel rainbow hoodies..."

"I must've left my studded choker at home," I deadpan, refusing to feel self-conscious about the softest, snuggliest item of clothing I own. "First Sully and now you. Honestly, the stereotyping is insane."

If I'd known wearing all black was such an important part of the job, maybe I would've blended better, and we wouldn't be in this position.

"What's your favourite song?" he presses, ignoring me. "Come on, you've got to tell me."

"What's yours?" I counter.

"That's like asking me to pick a favourite child."

I hum quietly, refusing to answer.

"I bet it's something from the old albums," he mutters. "'Snap'?"

I take a mouthful of syrupy waffle before answering. "A classic, but not my favourite."

"'Scuse me, man. Are you... You're not Arlo Estes? Right?"

Arlo turns an obliging smile in the direction of the kid who's approached him. "Hey."

A few seconds later, having had both his shirt signed and a photo taken, the kid returns to his own table, and I'm back at the mercy of Arlo's inscrutable gaze.

"'Fucking Fate'?" he guesses, naming one of the band's newer songs.

"Nope." I pop the 'p' sound at the end, enjoying this new game. "You won't guess."

"I just want to know which one of us wrote it," he says. "It's probably Prophet, but it might be one of mine."

He looks so hopeful that I resolve to never, ever tell him my favourite song, just in case I disappoint him.

"Don't you ever write any together?" I ask, changing the subject.

He shrugs. "Used to... at the beginning. Not so much in the last few years."

Another guy, this time in his late fifties, approaches our table. "Sorry, but I couldn't help overhearing..."

One photo and signed wallet later, Arlo pauses. "Hey, man, mind taking one of me and my girl?"

"*What*?" My head whips around.

But the older dude is already nodding happily. "No problem! My missus used to come to concerts with me all the time. Nothing bonds two souls like rock and roll!"

I grimace at the terrible joke, but Arlo takes it in his stride, handing over his phone to a stranger—who does that?!—and tugging me under his arm.

"Smile, Dark," he encourages.

I try my best, but my mind is already rushing through the hundreds of ways that fan could be funnelling Arlo's data away.

Just thirty seconds, and in his place, I could've connected his phone to my own device and installed a virtual backdoor.

"You shouldn't do that," I grumble, as soon as the photo is taken and Arlo's phone is back in his possession. "He could've done anything with your phone."

"If he ran off with it, I'd just buy a new one," Arlo shrugs.

Shaking my head, because he doesn't get it, I let him show me the photo. It's cute—and he's gorgeous, as I knew he would be—except I can see the tiny suspicious frown lines in my brow, and ugh, I didn't do the jawline trick, so I have a double chin...

Less self-sabotage, I remind myself gently. This picture is a memory, not a magazine cover. Judging myself by anything other than the happiness in our eyes is wrong. One day, it might be the only proof we even met at all.

Once this job is over, it's unlikely our paths will ever cross again. I'd like to have some mementos to remember this by...

even if I am feeling rather disillusioned with them all at the moment.

"Send it to me?" I request, handing his phone back.

He grins, and my phone *ribbits* a second later. "Now, back to your favourite song."

"Nope. You're not getting it out of me."

His pout is adorable. "But how can I add it to the set list tomorrow if I don't know it? At least tell me the album."

Rolling my eyes, I go to change the topic, but his phone rings before I can say anything.

Arlo frowns, raising it to his ear, then groans at the voice on the other side.

"Calm down, man. It's just breakfast," he says, though he's gotten quieter. "Look, Slate aside, this is our chance to—"

He cuts off, interrupted by the voice on the phone. It must be Prophet, or maybe even Dodger. Neither of them were happy to see me.

I stand, grabbing my bag. "It's okay," I promise. "I get it."

Arlo takes a breath and hangs up. "No, you really don't. I'm so excited to see you, and I wish—"

"Thanks for breakfast," I finish. "But I should be going. I want to explore the city before work tomorrow."

Arlo's face falls, and he nods. "It's been good to finally meet you," he says, and there's an open honesty in his expression that makes me believe him.

He doesn't try to stop me as I flee from the cafe and into the bright sunshine.

Upon my return to the hotel, I flop face-first onto my bed and let out a little scream.

This is not going how I envisioned. Meeting the guys for the first time, even having coffee with Arlo...

"This is why we swore off bad boys," I remind myself hollowly. "We have a plan, remember? Nice. Normal. Safe."

I spent my early twenties fucking around with the

dangerous ones. The toxic, sexy ones. The tragic hotties. The chemistry might have been there, but it wasn't healthy. I also got my heart stomped on one too many times, and none of those guys were ready or eager to move in and start a life together.

Hence the new plan.

I'm done with fixer uppers. A relationship shouldn't be a restoration project, and—

"Protesting wayyy too hard, Darce," I mutter.

Sighing, I prop myself up on my elbows and try to find the motivation to get on with my mission. At the very least, I need to get my laptop up and see if I can get into the hotel's records to find which room Gabrielle is in, and whether Miguel is staying here. Then I need a shower.

Head buzzing with the plan, I set up on the crappy desk and throw myself into the work.

Miguel isn't staying here—a shame—but Gabrielle is on my floor, and I'm betting her phone is attached to the free Wi-Fi. I hum as I work, grinning as I send a deauthentication signal. Her phone is knocked from the server, automatically mistakes my evil twin network for the hotel Wi-Fi, and locks on.

Gotcha.

I set my rootkit to download and head for the shower.

After the morning I've had, I can't be bothered to put my contacts back in, so I stick with my glasses and a pair of ripped skinny jeans with an oversized Starfleet Academy hoodie. My gun is holstered at my waist and reachable through a fake pocket.

Retail therapy, here I freaking come.

Darcy
13

I've managed to avoid them for a full day.

I hate shopping, especially alone, but it's kept me busy. After browsing almost every single alternative clothing store, I've managed to scrape together five new outfits to help me blend in. I'm not sure I like the idea of wearing so much black, but I can always take a leaf out of my sister, Royal's, book and return them all when this job is over.

If both Sully and Arlo commented on my look, then I'm sticking out.

Being noticed isn't the goal, so when I turn up at the arena the next day and get to work, I'm wearing ripped black skinny jeans and an oversized Hazardous hoodie. Free band merch is one of the perks of my job, and I'm already in love with the fleecy pile of heaven. The warmth is welcome given how they're blasting the AC in here.

My phone is on silent, and has been since last night, when Slate began his campaign.

It started with innocuous questions. Little prompts that I responded to cautiously. Before I knew it, the sneaky bastard had graduated to trying to figure out my room number.

It wasn't hard to figure out that he was trying to make his case again in person.

So I did what any self-respecting woman would. I sent him on a wild goose chase.

That won't work today. A new stage means a new safety talk, and this time they know who I am. So, like any mature, reasonable woman, I've decided to hide beneath the stage. The wires for the waterfall of sparks that kicks off the encore are loose, and I've had to crawl on my back like a crab to reach the connectors in the tight space.

"So you really managed to fuck with Slate yesterday."

His voice, so unexpected and close, makes me jump. My head comes up automatically, seeking him out without care for the solid metal bar above me. *Clunk*, my forehead connects, and I see stars for a second.

"Shit." I nurse my forehead as I glare at him through the nest of wires I'm tangled in.

"Whoa, jumpy much?" Dodger grimaces, offering me an apologetic smile and a hand up. "Need some help?"

I wiggle my way out from my hidey hole and take it warily.

Is this some kind of trap?

This close, the crushed velvet of Dodger's voice is over-whelming, messing with my senses. My body has been condi-tioned to expect pleasure when I hear him speak in that husky tone, and I bite the inside of my cheek as I silently beg myself to remain professional.

"I'm not used to men creeping up on me while I'm work-ing," I retort. "And Slate deserved a little payback."

He shrugs, as if he couldn't care less if his bassist was roaming the corridors of the hotel in search of room numbers which don't exist. "Probably."

"Where's the other three quarters of you?" I ask, looking around for them.

Aside from Gabrielle—who's ignoring us as she furiously

taps away at her phone a few feet away—and a couple of other techs messing with a misbehaving speaker above us, we're alone. The rest of the band isn't here yet, which means he's cornered me. Odd for a guy who slammed a door in my face when he found me in his hotel apartment.

"I left early," he shrugs. "I thought—" He pauses, running a hand through his shaggy hair. "I wanted to clear something up. You got the wrong impression, baby girl."

I raise a single brow, crossing my arms over my chest. "What wrong impression?"

He raises a dark brow, as if surprised I'm going to make him say it.

"Nothing happened between me and that groupie."

"Uh huh." I let my scepticism bleed through. "And why should I care if it did?"

Does he think I was born yesterday? Those girls were objectively gorgeous and were all over him like flies on honey. Dodger is attractive and sexy, and I certainly wouldn't be able to resist the advances of a bunch of hot men—wait. I *am* resisting the advances of a group of hot men.

Huh, go me.

Far from being put off by my words, he grins like I've given him a challenge. "I figured your big brain would be too smart to believe me without proof, so I brought a witness."

He reaches out to his left and drags Emma out from behind a crate. How long has she been there? The poor woman looks awkward as hell as she backs away.

"I do not want to be stuck in the middle of your girl drama," she begins, holding up her hands.

"Ems," he pleads. "Just tell her you saw all of us leave together."

The wardrobe mistress sighs, rolling her eyes, and for the first time I realise how young she really is. She can't be older than twenty, if that.

"They all left together," she echoes dutifully.

"Thanks, now go distract Slate, and remember, you heard *nothing*."

She lets out a groan. "Really, Dodger?"

He grins. "I'll let you ride in the Maserati if you can keep him and the others occupied until our safety talk."

Her eyes narrow. "Do I get to drive?"

"Maybe. Now, get going, brat."

Emma chuckles, shaking her head as she struts away. The easy familiarity between them might make me jealous, but I'm not reading any sexy vibes from either of them.

"I don't sleep with other women when our arrangement is in place," Dodger continues, folding his arms. "They touch me—fans do that—but it means nothing."

Next time, I'm going to find a better hiding spot. I did not sign up to explain that any other woman would consider groupies pawing him a breach of relationship exclusivity. It's not that she touched him. I'd expect a rock star to hand out hugs and hand shakes like candy. But having a girl straddling him, licking his bare chest? Yeah, that's where I draw the line.

"I told you, what you do with your groupies is your business."

"Then why did you bring it up when you were giving Slate all those reasons why you couldn't stay with us?"

Why indeed? Maybe because it stung like hell to see other women touch him—even if I'll never admit it. Of all the betrayals, his was the worst, and I don't even know why. I should've expected him to be fucking groupies every night. I certainly never specified he couldn't.

"I just don't want you thinking I'm not committed to what we're doing."

What we're doing? Is that the polite term for screwing each other's brains out across cyberspace?

"Our 'arrangement' is over," I reply evenly.

His eyes widen. "Baby girl—"

"I have no idea why you're so insistent on clearing the air about this when you haven't even so much as said 'hi, I'm so glad we could finally meet,'" I finish. "We've been phone-fuck-buddies for years, Dodge. But you still slammed the door in my face when I finally turned up. Make that make sense."

"I wasn't dressed!"

Okay. I take a deep breath and push my glasses up my nose. "Ordinarily, I'd consider that a valid excuse," I admit. "But you weren't showing any more skin than you were when that girl was licking your tattoos."

He waves my suggestion away. "They all do that. It means nothing."

I turn back to my wires, looking for the damn safety checklist, which must be abandoned somewhere in the chaos. "Fine, it means nothing. You can consider your point made."

A hand on my waist spins me around, and before I know it, he's pressed up against me, both hands on my ribcage as he presses me into the scaffold that holds the stage up.

I have a knife strapped to my forearm beneath my hoodie, but I don't draw it. Our eyes are locked in a silent battle of wills. The intimate connection quickly spills over, drawing other feelings out of the woodwork that I'd rather not share. Every single breath seems to push us closer together, and I become acutely aware of how little distance really separates us.

His lips inch towards mine, and for a second, I debate letting him kiss me. How many nights have I wondered what that mouth would feel like on mine? It would be so easy to give in and let him turn the anger scalding my veins into a different kind of heat.

I'm not that girl.

With a practised move, I duck and twist out of his hold.

"When I'm in a relationship, I don't kiss other people. I would never allow them to touch me like that. Call me crazy, but I don't think it's unreasonable to expect the same from my partner. I never demanded exclusivity before, but if you want to continue this—us—in person, then it's a hard line for me." My voice is rough, and I curse myself for the tremor at the end of it. "If you can't promise that, then I'm happier just being your friend. Besides"—I snort lightly—"you're all wrong for me, remember?"

I might as well have struck him. He takes a step back, then another, until I can no longer feel his breath on my face or smell the intoxicating scent of his aftershave. The crestfallen look on his face makes me rethink my words, and I bite my lower lip in indecision.

"Dodger..."

He shakes his head. "All right. I think you've made yourself perfectly clear."

Without waiting for me to apologise, he turns on his heel and disappears.

Feeling confused, and more than a little guilty, about the whole exchange, I glance around. The techs don't seem to have noticed our interlude, and Gabrielle has disappeared. I should return to work, but my focus isn't where it should be.

Am I overreacting? He said he didn't sleep with her, and being fawned over—while annoying—is part of his job. It won't go away. Ugh, I should hunt him down and talk about it like an adult... after I apologise for lashing out like that.

I end up on my phone, checking on the scripts I wrote to track Gabrielle's virtual life. Everything's running well. When I get back to my laptop, I can have a proper look around.

"Has anyone seen Darcy?" Sully booms from above me.

Shit. Safety check.

"Coming!"

I check the last wires in a rush, then climb up the steps to the stage. Arlo, Slate, and Prophet are all there, waiting beside Sully, Miguel, and a flustered-looking Gabrielle. I slow my steps, watching the way that she shrinks back from her boss.

"Where the fuck is he?" Miguel demands. "We don't have time for him to be off fucking around. I have an interview lined up and a photoshoot after soundcheck."

Gabrielle shrinks. "I don't know. He's not answering his phone."

"Send Jackson after him," Miguel demands. "He's head of security. He should be able to keep an eye on one temperamental singer."

"Yes, sir," Gabrielle says, tapping furiously at her screen.

"He'll be here," Sully says. "Calm down."

"We're on a tight schedule," Miguel retorts. "I wouldn't expect you to understand. Why are you here, anyway? Don't you have some motivational speeches to deliver or something, old man?"

Sully rolls his eyes and turns his back on the tour manager. "See you boys later. Listen to the girl this time. I don't want to have to dig out a fire extinguisher and deal with all that paperwork."

A man after my own heart.

"Start," Miguel snaps at me. "If he gets blown up, it's his own fucking fault. *Cabrón*!"

The manager strides off the stage, spouting a tornado of curses in Spanish and English, leaving Gabrielle to hurry along behind him with her phone glued to her ear.

"So," Slate begins, only to stop when I cut him off with a look, because I'm at my limit today after Dodger. "New outfit?" he finishes.

"I'm blending," I retort. "Now, the first song, we're starting with the flame—"

"You shouldn't blend," Arlo interrupts, and my head whips around to look at him. "You're perfect in your unicorn hoodies."

Do not glow. Do not glow.

Fuck, I think I'm glowing. Can I really be blamed, though? What woman doesn't want to hear she looks perfect in comfort wear? And my carefully curated collection of hot and cold weather hoodies certainly warrants compliments.

"*Flame throwers*," I continue, forcing myself to stay on track with a willpower I didn't know I possessed. "Which means that this whole area at the front of the stage is a risk zone."

My safety talk continues uninterrupted after that, and Dodger never turns up. He's still not there when the rest of the band traipses off the stage towards the interview that's been lined up for them. It isn't until the crowd is filling the stadium, the Rottenheim Twins have finished their set, and Yesterday's Cascade is halfway through theirs, that I finally catch sight of him with the others.

Miguel is with them, looking almost disturbingly calm after his earlier outburst, but I don't trust that for one second. I don't have a chance to move closer and listen in, because I'm called away again.

By the time I come up for air, almost an hour into their set, they're midway through the guitar solo that marks the midpoint of one of their newer songs. Arlo's fingers are a blur, every note pinpoint and precise.

Whatever else you can say about the band, they're professionals. The dedication it takes to learn to play an instrument like that while bouncing around the stage is incredible.

Dodger's head is banging along to the music, waiting for his cue. Then it comes, and he's there, stepping up beside Slate and crooning into the mic like it's a lover.

The beat picks up, Prophet's drumbeat carrying the melody higher and higher. Dodger's velvety voice—sure and steady with each screamed question—breaks on the final line, and he falls to his knees on the stage. The fans are eating it up, screaming as the bass takes over. Then Dodger rips his shirt off. A full-on battle ensues when he chucks the fabric into the crowd, but I don't even notice.

The moves his body makes are nothing short of sinful, almost more suited to a strip club than a metal concert, but it works. All of a sudden, I feel like an interloper, peering at the show from the side lines.

Watching them like this, lost in their element, sends a tiny twang ricocheting through my rib cage. Not for the first time, I wonder if sticking to my guns is the wisest idea.

For all their faults, they're my friends. I'm not one of those idiots who thinks sex messes up friendships: some of the best relationships I've seen evolved out of really close friendships.

Yet, are they even offering a relationship?

I don't even know where we stand. Dodger was happy to continue our casual arrangement, and maybe he'd have been okay with adding some boundaries if I'd just asked nicely. Slate was preaching "soul mates," but outside of his determination to have me, I'm unsure what he really wants. Arlo... I melt a little at the memory of our breakfast and how easy it felt to be in his presence, then just as quickly freeze over when I recall how Prophet ended it so prematurely.

At least the drummer hasn't left any room for confusion about his feelings on the subject.

Darcy
14

It's just past three in the morning by the time I get back to the hotel. I'm bone tired, so I don't even notice my phone ringing the first time. I wouldn't have noticed the second either, if not for the weird looks I'm getting from the other techs who walked back with me.

"You going to answer that?" Ricky—the guitar tech—asks as we file into the lift.

"Shit," I grab for my phone, swiping to answer before I've even processed who's calling.

"Morning, *cariño*."

My shoulders slump. "It's too early for this," I protest as the elevator dings onto my floor and I step out, waving farewell to my fellow roadies. "Let me sleep."

Thank god my room isn't far.

His dark chuckle echoes across the line. "You'd sleep better in one of the presidential suite beds. I swear the thread count on these sheets is—"

"Slate, I'm not having this argument," I retort, slamming my key card over the lock. "It simply wouldn't—"

My words cut off, and I blink at the utter devastation in front of me.

"Darcy?" Slate's voice echoes from the phone in my hand.

Shit. Shit. Shit.

I scramble for my suitcase, trying to ignore the acrid stench coming from my bed as I search. It's been chucked across the room—into the mirror, if the spiderweb cracks are anything to go by—and has landed upside down on the desk.

Still locked.

I breathe a sigh of relief.

My laptop and a few of my clothes are in there. I may be messy, but on missions, I'm always careful to keep my equipment locked away. Someone has obviously taken a knife to the hard outer shell, but I paid a good deal of money to make sure my luggage is impenetrable, and it's paid off.

All of my tech and most of my clothes will be fine.

My new purchases, however...

I hadn't gotten around to taking all of my new clothes out of their bags yet, and now they're scattered all across the room.

Along with blood.

Lots of it.

Probably animal, I rationalise, taking in the slashed curtains, soiled bedding, and broken furniture with dawning horror now that I'm sure my equipment is safe.

These are textbook intimidation tactics, but I haven't been here long enough to warrant this kind of reaction. No one knows about my links to the band.

I wander into the bathroom, grimacing as I realise there's more blood in here. In fact, someone has gone to the trouble of filling the bath with it. That's not the only damage. The sink is shattered, and chunks of porcelain have flown everywhere, tiles are cracked, the towels have been ripped up and tied into a noose which hangs from the shower head.

And on the glass shower screen, a single word has been painted in blood.

"Behave?" I read aloud, confused.

None of this makes any sense, and that's what makes it so terrifying.

"Darcy?!" Slate yells, and it takes me a second to realise that his voice is now in the room with me, and not echoing from the phone in my hand. "Where are you—?"

How did he find me? I whirl just in time to catch his entrance into my bathroom. I watch as his eyes find me, then slide past to read the word on the glass. His expression morphs from one of sheer panic to dark fury in the space of a second.

No confusion, I realise. He knows who did this, and maybe even why. The message means something to him, which means whoever trashed my room did it to get to the band, not me.

"Why would anyone do this?" I ask.

My innocence is fake, as is the wobble in my voice, but he doesn't know that.

I'm shaken, but not as badly as a normal person would be. I booked this room in a fake name, deliberately hiding my identity, which means they used the hotel's cameras to figure me out. That means bribing the hotel security, which takes money.

This was a warning from the Rosales Cartel.

Without answering, Slate snags my wrist and pulls me away from the screen and the message on the glass.

"This is my key card," he says. "It will give you access to our suite. Get in the elevator and stay on the phone until the doors close. I'll get security on this."

Really? Is his stupid plan to get me to stay with them all he can think of right now? My anger—ready and easier to deal with than the flicker of anxiety in my belly—flares to life.

"This isn't some stunt to make me move in—"

"This has nothing to do with that," he snaps. "Jesus,

cariño, if you think so little of me—" He groans and runs a hand over his face. "None of us would *ever* do something to hurt you. I'm sending you up to the others because I want you safe while we figure this out."

Awww, that's kind of sweet.

"Go. Please." It looks like it physically pains him to say the last word, and that's the only reason I do as he says.

I snag my case and laptop before I leave, because there's no way I'm giving security the chance to go through my stuff, and tuck my phone between my shoulder and my ear.

"Still on the line?" Slate checks, as I step into the corridor.

"Yes. Slate... is this normal?"

His breath hisses out, fuzzing down the phone. "Get in the elevator. I'll explain everything when I get up there."

That's not a denial.

The doors ping open, and I step in, pressing Slate's card to the reader. "I'm in."

"Good. I'll text Arlo to make sure that Prophet doesn't get to you first." He pauses. "*Lo siento, rubia*. You didn't deserve this."

He hangs up, leaving me alone in the mirrored box with only my suitcase. My glasses are askew, and I busy myself with cleaning them.

Slate didn't look surprised by what he found in my room, which means that this has happened before. That means *this* is the blackmail Miguel holds over them.

He's threatening the people who get close to them, and somehow he's figured out that includes me.

Behave.

Such an ambiguous message, but clearly aimed at one person. Dodger stormed off today and missed the interview and the photoshoot. The cartel chose me because I was the last person he was seen with. I thought we were alone, but no one is ever really alone back stage at a concert. Miguel could even have their phones bugged. I would have in his position.

"Darcy?" Arlo is in front of me, taking my case from my hand with gentle fingers. "Hey, you've spaced."

I grimace. "Sorry. Did Slate—?"

"He explained." The guitarist takes my hand in his and pulls me out of the elevator. "Come on, you've had a shock. We can get you something to drink, and I won't drop the mug this time."

"What the—?"

"Not *now*, Prophet," Arlo growls. "Do me a favour and get Dodger to come back. He's the reason this happened. He can fucking well fix it."

"All my new stuff," I grumble. "How fucking dare they? I was committed to blending, damn it!"

Arlo hushes me, guiding me over to the sofa and gently tugging me down. Prophet doesn't do what he asks. Instead, the drummer hovers behind me like a dark cloud.

"She was targeted?" he guesses.

"Fucking assholes!" I snarl, making both of them jerk upright.

"I was expecting more tears." Arlo rubs the back of his neck. "But anger works too. We got you, Dark. You just... do whatever."

His phone rings, and he snaps it up, answering without looking at the screen.

"Yeah, we've got her. You need to come up?"

Slate's voice is so quiet it's inaudible, as Arlo moves away with a last warning look at Prophet.

"Make her some coffee or something," he mouths at the bigger man before he disappears.

I'm so, so tempted to just grab my laptop and dump a whole load of viruses onto Gabrielle's computer as payback, but that won't help matters. My head falls forward into my hands, and my glasses dig painfully into the bridge of my nose.

Shit, my contacts were in my bathroom.

I take a huge, heaving breath, then freeze as two large thumbs rub across the sides of my neck and down to my shoulders. Long fingers join in, rubbing the tension out with gentle sweeps.

"I was trying to keep you out of this," Prophet grouches. "You should've stayed far away from us, angel."

My head snaps up, and I pin him in place with a glare. "You're not going to make some bullshit excuse about being an asshole to protect me, are you? Because I'm not in the mood."

He shrugs, as if to say, *fine, I won't say it*, and continues rubbing along my shoulders until the elevator pings again.

Slate and Arlo stride into the room with their heads pressed together. Prophet drops his hands like he's been burned, and a glance back shows he's folded his arms over his impressive chest.

"What's going on?" he demands.

"Usual shit," Slate growls. "Where's Dodger? He should be here."

"He hasn't returned yet," Prophet mutters. "I messaged him. He said not to wait up."

"Ring him," Slate orders. "We have to sort this out."

Arlo is already on his phone. "He won't answer."

My gut sinks, reading around what they're not saying. After I rejected him, he searched out someone who wasn't so picky.

"How bad was it?" Prophet asks.

"Worse than Sully," Slate says, grimacing. "But not as bad as Ems. Darcy..."

He trails off, and the rest of them look at me, uncomfortable.

"Coffee," I suggest. "Then you can explain to me why none of you are surprised by any of this, and we can take things from there."

Arlo heads towards the machine, quickly punching in some combination of buttons until the mug is full of caffeinated goodness before handing it to me.

"Thanks," I murmur. "Now, explanations. That... Why would anyone do that?"

Arlo sits beside me, staring intently at me. "I don't want to pry, but did you and Dodger have a fight, or...?"

I blush, taking a deep swig of boiling hot coffee to hide my reaction. "We disagreed on a few things."

"Someone must have seen and put that together with him missing all the PR shit Miguel had lined up," Slate curses. "They decided to go after her to make a point."

Prophet's head falls back, and he groans.

"You're being punished for not turning up to photoshoots?" I ask. "By who?"

"It's a long story," Slate hedges. "But you should know, we're in deep with some bad people. I'm not bullshitting you, but I think it's safer for you to stay with us from now on."

"It's safer for her to get on a fucking plane and get out now," Prophet growls.

"That worked so well when we tried it the last time," Slate grumbles. "They'll just terrorise her, and she'll be too far away for us to do anything."

Prophet says something in answer, but I'm too busy thinking to listen.

It's cute that they're worried about my safety. I should, by rights, be pushing for more details about the threat, but I don't have the energy right now. My earlier anger is wearing off fast, and my tiredness is back. Right now, I have two options: book myself a new room, or take up their offer. I'm not sure I can do the former this early in the morning without drawing too much attention to myself.

That's the weakest excuse you've ever come up with, Darce.

"If I stay with you"—because I can't leave, not midway through a job—"then there have to be rules. And I want a trial period. You could all leave the seat up and snore like tractors for all I know."

They all shut up quickly at that, shooting me incredulous looks.

Getting closer to the band will probably put me on a collision path with Miguel, but he's brought that on himself. He was always going to die, but now he's going to do so painfully.

I turn to Slate. "The soul mate crap stops."

He presses his hands over his heart. "You wound me, *mi vida*."

"We're friends," I insist. "I can't pick one of you over the others—"

Arlo's eyes widen. "You wouldn't have to."

His words stop me dead, and I take a reflexive sip of my coffee. "Excuse you?"

"We have a contract," he explains. "One woman for all of us, or none of us gets serious with anyone. A committed, closed relationship between the five of us."

"It was to stop some groupie getting in and splitting the band up," Slate adds. "I know polyamory isn't for everyone, but there are so many benefits—"

I hold up my hand, still trying to digest the fact that they've planned this. "Most of my sisters are with multiple partners. I'm well aware of the benefits *if* it goes well. I'm looking for something more serious. You know I want to settle down. Can you honestly tell me you guys are ready for that?" I turn to Prophet. "You don't even like me."

He shakes his head. "I don't want you pulled into his games. He's trying to use you as a Band-Aid to patch up—"

"It's late," Slate interrupts. "We can debate how this would work in the long term after your 'trial period.'" He air-quotes the words. "Any more rules you'd like to enforce?"

"No touching my shit. No treating me differently to the other roadies when I'm working."

Prophet scoffs and folds his arms. "You think we'd let our woman ride economy?"

Don't swoon at the sexist comment. Do *not* swoon at the sexist comment. "No, because I already decided next time I'm upgrading my seat. I'm a creature of comfort."

I noticed some of the other roadies doing the same on our flight here—including Emma—so why shouldn't I?

"We won't touch your stuff," Slate agrees. "But if we're dating, I want to take you out to nice places. Buy you pretty shit."

"Well, isn't this cosy," Dodger snaps. "Nice to know I was missed."

As one, the four of us turn to face the elevator. Dodger is a mess. His nose is busted, dripping blood down to his mouth. He's tried to staunch the bleeding with his sleeve, and now the fabric is stained red.

"Tell me you didn't go out and start a fight," Arlo begins, but Dodger waves him off.

"No. This was Jackson making sure I learned my 'lesson' for skipping the interview."

"The first part of your lesson, anyway," Slate growls. "The other half was left in Darcy's room, which is why we're discussing her terms for moving in with us."

"On a trial basis," I interject.

Dodger collapses on the sofa and grabs a tissue from the box on the table, pinching his bleeding nose and tilting his head forward.

"Fuck." His brown eyes meet mine, glazed with pain. "I'm

sorry, Darcy. I wouldn't have run off if I'd known they'd come after you."

His surprisingly sincere apology takes the wind out of my sails.

"I understand," I mumble. "I'm sorry, too. What I said wasn't fair."

"You were just being honest," he grunts, waving it off. "Terms, huh? Let me guess, rule one is no sex?"

Chewing at my lip, I shake my head. "I would like to have a conversation about expectations and boundaries before that."

His eyes fly wide, protests flying to his lips. "I told you I didn't fuck that groupie!"

"Wait, hold up. Sex is on the table?" Slate's grin is widening, but we both ignore him.

I shake my head. "I'm not accusing you of having sex with her. I'm a red-blooded woman, of course I'm up for sex. I also get that people are going to want to hug you and touch you just because of who you are. I'm just not comfortable with the level of touching I saw in that room."

"We can't stop fans touching us," Arlo replies, despondently. "But there's no need to touch them back, either. If we're always wearing shirts, it's not such a big deal, right?"

I grimace at the casual way he accepts the inability to enforce consent regarding his own body, but I get it. People are excited to see them.

"I'm not going to insist you wear shirts everywhere," I promise. "I'm not even saying no hugs or cheek kisses or whatever. Just... no kissing other people on the mouth, or having them on your lap... or licking you."

"Done," Dodger says, without hesitation.

"I'm possessive," I warn, sighing in defeat. "And I get bored easily. This whole idea is only going to end in tears."

No one has even addressed my other concern—that I want something permanent and long lasting. Something real.

"You got bored because you were dating limp-dicked business clerks," Slate corrects. "Dating four rock stars? I *dare* you to get bored of us."

Waving away his cocky confidence with a yawn, I stand and put my empty coffee cup in the sink. "So, where am I sleeping?"

That freezes all four of them.

"Where do you want to sleep?" Arlo asks, carefully. "There are four rooms. Two of us could bunk..."

"Oh no," Dodger snorts, a predatory glint entering his eyes. "She just said sex is on the table. Why the fuck would any of us share when we could have our own sexy Darcy to cuddle up with?"

He grabs the crystal fruit bowl and dumps the handful of fresh fruit out onto the low coffee table before righting it. Next, he digs into his pocket and fishes out a set of... car keys?

They hit the bottom of the bowl with a dull clunk, and he hands it over to Arlo.

"Darcy can bunk with whoever's keys she chooses."

"This is immature," Arlo mutters, but he's already patting his own pockets, searching for keys. "What if she wants to choose?"

"Do you have a preference?" Dodger asks me, brow raised.

He knows I don't. I shake my head, my tongue flicking out to moisten my lips. "No. This is good. There are no favourites this way."

Arlo deposits his own keys into the bowl as soon as I've given my approval, and a second later Slate drops his in as well.

I eye the basin warily, gnawing at my lip. I don't expect Prophet's to soar over my head and into the mix, so when they thunk against the crystal, I jump a little in response.

Whirling, I pin him in place with my gaze. What is his

game? Is he just trying to give me whiplash? To his credit, he doesn't flinch away from my stare.

Then he does the single most perplexing move available to the male half of the human race.

He shrugs.

What does that mean?

Slate catches my attention with a light cough. "Time to choose, *bebita*."

Dodger
15

The room is silent as she digs her hand into the bowl. My nose is throbbing, and my eyes keep fucking watering, which doesn't make it easy to see what she's up to.

I wonder if she knows that there are several hundred grand's worth of cars represented in that bowl. If she does, it doesn't show on her face as she lifts free...

Mine.

The breath whooshes from my lungs as I behold the keys to my GT Black Series dangling from between her thumb and forefinger.

God bless that car. Best investment I ever made.

Shit. Most anticipated night of my life, and my face feels like it's gone three rounds with a hammer. Fucking Miguel.

Darcy looks at Arlo first, watches him shake his head, then back to Slate.

"You lucky bastard," he mutters.

The closing of the door behind her is Prophet's only response.

"See you in the morning," Arlo mumbles, standing.

He pauses, like he's wondering whether he should wish

her a good night or offer her an out, but I already know that Darcy won't take it. She's curious. She wants to know if the chemistry we have on voice chat sparks just as fiercely in real life.

So do I.

She was so close to letting me kiss her underneath the stage. I know she was.

I shove out of my seat and offer her my hand. Being Darcy, she deliberately misunderstands me and places the key in my outstretched palm instead. Undeterred, I pocket it and stick my hand out again.

"Scared, baby girl?" I ask.

She should be.

"Only of the choking hazard," she retorts.

My grin pulls at my nose, but I refuse to wince. It's not broken, and it sure as hell isn't getting in the way of my first night with her.

Might ruin my plan for her to sit on my face, but we've got time, right?

My mind flashes back to what she said about a trial period, and I grimace. No. We might not have time.

If there's one thing Hazardous is good at, it's fucking up every good thing that happens in our lives. How long before Darcy realises what a mess we are and dumps our asses for some well-paid white-collar snob to raise her two-point-five kids and spend her days organising charity bake sales?

That's what she wants.

Not a bunch of metalheads caught in a deal with a cartel. Sure, we can offer her money and whatever scraps of our souls are worth giving, but it's not enough.

Hell, the life expectancy of a rock star is twenty-five years less than the average person.

She'd have to be mad to fall for Slate's plan and pick us.

All the more reason to make the most of it while it lasts, I convince myself, as Darcy finally reaches out and places her hand in mine.

Electricity arcs from the touch, and I clench my fist without meaning to. I ease up a second later, but she must have noticed.

She doesn't mention it, and I breathe out a sigh of relief, hauling her up and pulling her into my room. For once, I'm grateful I'm not a slob—I know girls hate that shit—as I push her towards the bed.

"Get comfy," I order, shutting the door behind me. "I'm going to shower, then I'll join you."

I'm not stupid enough to think the blood all over my face is a turn on, and I'm still sweaty and sticky from the stage earlier. I want her to remember this. The need to live up to every fantasy she ever had is a nervous pulse beneath my skin.

Normally, sex is just something I do. An itch to be satisfied, no different from eating or breathing or any other bodily function. If anything, fulfilling all the expectations was becoming a bit of a chore.

Not with her.

Being on the phone with Darcy as she moans her orgasm is a thousand times hotter than any other encounter in my life. Even though she wasn't physically there, I felt more than I did when I was a horny teen getting paid to fuck his way through an entire bachelorette party. I'm willing to bet reality is even better.

Rushing through the shower, I return, practically bouncing on my feet and—

Her snore fills the room before I can reach her.

I can't even be disappointed, because she's in my bed, hugging my duvet with one long leg twisted in the fabric. Her glasses are on my nightstand, and she's wearing the most adorable Pac Man pyjamas. Like this, she could be a true angel.

Those blonde locks are curling over my pillow, and her lashes cast sweeping shadows over her cheekbones.

Another deafening snore fills the room, and I grin.

Darcy snores like a train, and it's too fucking cute.

Batting down the erection that's plainly no longer needed, I grab my own pair of shorts and tug them over my hips before climbing in beside her. I'm spared the decision about whether or not to snuggle her when she practically claws her way across my torso.

Jesus. Is this girl made of literal ice? How is she so cold? I wince as her cold feet find my calves and start to leech the warmth from my bones, then grin. All she needs to do now is steal the covers, and Darcy will be the literal definition of a hostile sleeper.

I fall asleep with her breath huffing over my shoulder and a smile on my face, and I wake the exact same way. A glance at my phone reveals I haven't slept long—four hours at most—but that's not unusual for me. Her sleeping face is so unguarded, so trusting, and the intimate weight of her head on my arm is perfection. I physically can't bring myself to unwrap myself from her and leave the bed.

If I could wake like this every single morning for the rest of my life, I'd be a happy man.

The realisation stuns me for a moment.

Why can't I? Because of the contract? Because of her ridiculous notion that she'll be happier with John Doe, the accountant from the 'burbs?

She's our best friend. The past ten years have proven that Darcy just *fits* where no other woman has even come close. She's probably the only person alive with half a chance at bringing Prophet back into the fold.

The more I think about it, the more Slate's plan feels less like a ridiculous dream and more like a lifeline.

We can convince her. Buy her a nice house with a picket

fence and all the trimmings. I want to spoil the fuck out of her. We've spent ten years worshipping her from afar, and now I'm ready to do it from beside her. Or under her. Or over her... On the couch...

Briefly, I consider crawling down the bed and waking her with my mouth between her thighs, but she fell asleep before we could discuss her limits. I don't want to be that idiot who assumes his advances are welcome just because she slept in my bed.

So I creep out of my room and into the communal kitchen. I want to hear from Slate exactly what happened to Darcy's room last night. Music blasts from the gym, and I'm unsurprised that Prophet is already working out. Slate isn't a morning person, but I feel absolutely zero guilt in barging into his room and tipping a glass of cold water over his sleeping head.

"Asshole!" he splutters, jack knifing upright with a curse.

"What's the plan?" I demand. "Come on, I know you have one. I want in."

He wipes water from his eyes, a slow grin spreading across his face. "You changed your tune fast for someone who doesn't like to mix emotions with fucking."

"I haven't fucked her," I retort, shutting him up. "But this is Dark. She belongs with us. So tell me the plan, and then put your brain to solving the Miguel problem, because she's not getting put in the middle of that shit."

Slate sighs. "I told you. There is no easy 'out' when it comes to the cartel. We can protect Darcy the same way we protect everyone else. Good behaviour. Eventually, when we stop bringing in money..."

"Not going to happen."

He knows as well as I do that this life doesn't just let you leave quietly. There are always more ways for the people behind the scenes to wring money out of us. Comeback tours.

Anniversary Tours. Too-old-to-really-be-singing-but-fuck-it-we're-broke tours.

We don't even have to be as successful as we are for Miguel to make money out of us, especially since his main money maker in this whole thing is the drugs and the trafficking. My fucking microphones are kept in cases lined with bricks of blow. Our merch is tied up in so much money laundering it's actually painful to watch fans jumping up and down in it.

"Even if it doesn't, Sully's gathering evidence."

Sully's been documenting evidence for years. The problem isn't the lack of proof, it's the lack of people to give it to. For every good cop and upstanding judge, there are seven more in the cartel's pocket.

My heart sinks. "So the plan is to bring her into this with no way out?"

Slate swings his legs out of bed and stretches. "Look, man, I don't have all the answers. But I know, and you know, that Darcy is the only thing capable of bringing everyone back to how we used to be. We stand a better chance of getting out of this shit if all of us are on the same page, but right now, Arlo is practically a shut-in, and Prophet wants nothing more than to walk away and go back to stacking shelves in some backwater town. We need her."

I can't argue with him there.

"So what's the plan?"

He grins. "We play to our strengths. Arlo tugs on her heartstrings. You use those bedroom skills you're always bragging about to make her see sparks. Prophet pampers her, and I —" He shakes his head. "I'll come up with something."

"Woo her in Spanish?" I snort. "When are you going to tell her you don't even speak the language?"

"*Come mierda.*" There's no heat in his tone. "It's not my fault my mom didn't use it around me. Besides, I know the important words."

Both of us sober at the mention of his mom. Carmen Reyes is a sweet, quiet woman. She left everything she knew to marry Slate's dad, getting disowned by her family in the process. When he died, she had the severe misfortune of falling into a new relationship with an utter douchebag.

Slate hasn't spoken to her since he got out of juvie, but I know he has people keeping an eye on her.

At least the fact that she's not allowed anything to do with him means she's relatively safe from our bullshit. Small mercies.

"So what do we do when Darcy finds out?" I ask. "Because they already trashed her room. There's no way she won't ask questions when she wakes up."

"Trashed is too nice a word," Slate grumbles. "They smeared blood all around the room and pissed all over the bed."

My fists clench at my sides, and I resist the urge to pummel Miguel for the hundredth time.

"If she asks, we tell her there are some bad people who are targeting our staff to get to us, and our security is on it," Slate decides. "It's the truth, or close enough anyway."

Normally, manipulating the truth is my thing. I do it easily —too easily—but the idea of lying to Darcy sits wrong in my gut.

"Stop panicking." Slate reads my thoughts effortlessly. "And go back and make the most of what's left of your night. I still can't believe she picked you first."

I offer him a lazy grin. "You know I have the luck of the Devil."

"Whatever. Just means I have better odds when we land in Vancouver tonight."

"You sorting it so she's on our flight?"

Slate snorts. "You really think I'm going to have to?"

No. He won't. Prophet will. He can be as against Slate's plans as he wants, but the guy treats women like queens.

"Go." Slate waves a hand at his door. "And next time you decide to dump ice cold water on me, I'm going to return the favour."

Smirking, because he'd have to wake up early enough to manage it, I leave him to his plotting and head back to my own room via the coffee machine.

Darcy blinks open one eye as I enter, her gaze zooming straight to the mugs in my hand. I hold her coffee out like an offering. My own is black and unsweetened, but I know for a fact she takes hers loaded with cream and sugar.

"Morning," I chirp.

"Oh god." She visibly cringes, burying her head beneath the covers. "You're a morning person. I knew this wouldn't work out."

I snort, put her coffee and mine beside her glasses, and tug back the covers, bracing myself over her with my hands pressed into the mattress. "You can't give up on me over that." I pause. "Besides, I think I can convince you that mornings aren't so bad."

If she'll let me. For a second, the irrational fear of her rejection grips my heart and squeezes.

Her breath hitches, cheeks turning an adorable shade of pink. "Really?"

My voice lowers, and I duck my head until we're nose to nose. "Want to play, baby girl?"

Can she hear the vulnerability in the words?

This is all I have to offer her. If she won't accept it, then...

"What about your nose?"

"Not broken." I shrug off the injury, then pause.

Should I have covered the bruising? It's not pretty to look at.

Her hands trace up my forearms, trailing a buzz of electricity wherever she touches. I'm used to being touched. I've learned to switch off when it happens. I go through the motions of sex like a checklist. Lick there. Kiss here. Bite. Thrust.

Darcy isn't even doing anything overtly sexual, but I'm already more turned on than I have been in years. My dick is rock hard, tenting my shorts like a damned flag pole, trying to tempt her fingers to move past my wrists.

I know the minute she feels them, because she freezes.

My ink covers my scars pretty well, but it can't do shit about the messed up texture of my skin.

Distract. Divert. Deny.

I drop my lips to hers, claiming her mouth before she can say anything. The tension in my chest eases somewhat as she wastes no time in kissing me back. Her lips are so damn soft, and her tongue dances out to play with mine before she pulls back, eyes wide with alarm.

"Wait!" she cries against my mouth. "Morning breath! I haven't even showered!"

With a growl that I hope tells her exactly what I think of those excuses, I crawl on top of her and steal her mouth again, using my hips to press her into the bed.

"If you think," I begin, drawing back and grinding the evidence of my arousal against her. "That either of those things is a deterrent, then you severely underestimate how fucking desperately I want you."

She gasps, arching against me as her eyes fall closed. I take the opportunity to press a kiss to the tip of her nose.

"Say yes," I beg, shamelessly.

I think I'd willingly die just to get a taste of her.

My lips trace the line of her jaw, and I press another kiss to the soft skin of her throat, inhaling her naturally sweet scent. My tongue flicks out, and I breathe lightly over the wet patch until she shivers.

"Yes." The single word hisses out on a gasp.

"Good girl. You gonna behave for our first time?"

The grin she flashes me is all fake innocence. "I always behave."

That's a no, then. Good thing I love her sassiness.

Darcy
16

I'm breathless, and I don't even care. There's something drugging about the way Dodger kisses me. I can't think. I don't want to.

He cradles my face like I'm precious as his tongue strokes out to meet mine. His thumb strokes my jaw, tilting my face at just the right angle to thrust deeper. He's just as controlling in real life as he is normally, dominating every inch of the kiss until I have no choice but to relax and let him lead.

I grip his forearms, fingers brushing against the even ridges hidden beneath his tattoos a second time. In response, Dodger releases my face and grabs both of my hands, tugging them up until they're above my head.

"Keep them there," he growls, releasing me.

"But I want to play with you."

"Later." He grabs the hem of my top and pulls that up next, leaving it tangled around my upper body and exposing my breast. "Fuck. These tits are gorgeous."

He pauses, grinning as he cups them both in his hands. They overflow his palms. "Next time, I want to watch you suck on them, but this time, I'm not sharing."

Then, without waiting for a response, he dips his head and sucks one pink nipple into his mouth.

"Dodger!"

He groans against my breast, tongue flicking and swirling. Each movement teases the tiny bud tighter, and I mourn the sudden loss of his warmth until he sets his sights on my other breast, giving it the same treatment. My hands fist in his hair, determined to hold him in place this time.

Nipping my delicate skin as punishment, he draws back.

"Hands," he growls across my skin.

"Make me," I retort, then as an afterthought, I add, "Sir."

His grin cuts through my protest, and I can't help but feel I've been lured into a trap. "Gladly."

That quickly, his weight is gone, and he's on the other side of the room, searching through the pile of abandoned clothes on the floor.

When he returns with his belt, I swallow nervously.

"Worried, baby girl?" he asks, kneeling over me, his thighs wrapped around my abdomen. "You should be."

He makes a loop in the belt and quickly binds both my wrists together. It's a pathetic binding, really—Man taught me how to break out of much stronger bonds when I was seven— but that doesn't stop the shiver that runs across my skin as he attaches my wrists to the headboard.

"Not too tight?" he checks, testing the belt with a finger.

I shake my head. "No."

"Good. Now, where was I?"

His hands drop back to my breasts. This time, he pinches both nipples roughly between his thumbs and forefingers. I tug on my bonds, stretching towards him as the sting travels straight down my spine and my pussy gushes in answer.

He releases the right, only to spank it lightly. I cry out at the sudden sting before he sucks it away with his mouth.

"These are the most perfect tits," he swears, swirling his

tongue around the bud. "I swear I've dreamed of the day I'd get to do this." He sucks lightly, then releases my nipple to meet my eyes. "No dream of mine could ever live up to the reality of you."

My cynical inner voice tries to pipe up, reminding me that he could say that to all the girls. But the honesty in his expression can't be faked, and a little part of me melts in answer. The hurt that accompanied our initial meeting evaporates under his open admiration. The rasp of his stubble tickles my chest a second before he switches sides, breaking our stare to give my other breast the same rough, then soft, treatment.

I arch my hips, trying to hint at him that I want his touch lower, but he doesn't stop. His grip on my breasts turns from supportive to massaging, and I let out a tortured moan. I can't come like this, but my orgasm is still building, taunting me with what I could have if only he would show my pussy the same careful attention.

"If you don't fuck me in the next five seconds," I groan, "I'm breaking out of this and finishing myself off."

He barks out a laugh, stretching up to claim my mouth. "So impatient."

"You once promised to bury your head in my pussy and eat me out until I screamed," I point out. "Or was that all words?"

Dodger moves back, and his hands slip down, abandoning my breasts for the waistband of my sleep shorts. It only takes a small tug and the shorts slip down my legs, leaving me nude beneath. Starting at the inner curve of my ankle, he kisses his way up one of my legs, lingering at the crease of my knee as he slowly but surely makes his way to the junction of my thighs.

Those wide inked shoulders shimmy into place, and he wraps his arms around my legs, keeping me spread wide as he settles between them. My core aches as I take in the sight of the bruised, tattooed man who's eyeing my pussy like it holds the answer to world hunger.

"Soaked for me," he growls. "Just like I knew you would be."

He's not wrong, and the sound of his voice coming from between my legs doesn't help matters. My body knows this man, even if we've never been truly acquainted. I've been trained like Pavlov's dog to expect pleasure when I hear him speak.

"Do you need food?" he asks, taking me off guard.

"No?"

"Water?"

I frown. "I'm good."

"Just checking, because we're not leaving this bed for a long time."

We're... not?

I don't have a chance to answer because Dodger closes the gap between my soaked pussy and *feasts.*

"Fuck," I groan, my head falling back as my hips buck futilely against his grip.

I've been eaten out before, but Dodger is doing it like he'll die if he doesn't. His licks are desperate, fervent and consuming as he tastes me with single-minded abandon. Each brush of his tongue against my clit sends fireworks sparking through my soul, and when he dips lower, thrusting inside, the heat in my abdomen roars, demanding release.

"Please," I whimper. "Dodger, sir. I want to come."

He feigns nonchalance, but he can't hide the way his stare darkens at the address. "Should've thought about that before you sassed me." His words send warm breaths over my already sensitive nub and I clench as I catch sight of his glistening chin. "Now, lie back. I'm not done."

He dives back in, delivering a short suck to my clit that makes me jerk and cry out. The leather of his belt digs into my wrists, but I don't care. The only thing I can focus on is the liquid arousal lighting up my body. Every lap of his tongue is torturous bliss, because it makes my core clench on nothing, bringing the aching, empty feeling to the forefront of my mind.

The pressure is building, climbing higher and higher until my peak is in sight. Every cell in my body tenses, then cries out in concert.

My orgasm wrecks me, but Dodger doesn't let up until I've had two more. When he finally releases my thighs, there are hand prints on my hips where I've thrashed against his hold, and I'm panting.

"I want you," I say, before he can start again. "Now."

He grins, licks his lips, and then reaches over and opens the bedside drawer.

"Don't tell me hotels give you guys complimentary condoms."

He shrugs as he yanks down his shorts. "I'm not complaining."

Neither am I.

With the last shreds of fabric gone, there's nothing to hide him from my gaze. I tug against the belt, driven by the need to touch the lines of ink caressing his skin.

"I want my hands back," I protest.

He pretends to think about it for a second as he rolls the latex over his hard length. "If I untie you, are you going to bounce on my cock like a good girl?"

If I nod any harder, my head might fall off. "Yes, sir."

Dodger unbuckles the leather, rubbing my wrists gently before he twists us both until I'm settled over his hips.

Now free, I run my hands over his chest, tracing the lines of skulls and flowers as I brace myself. I reach down, pumping his cock once, then twice before fitting him to my entrance.

I can't help my groan at the stretch, and I lift back up before I can take him any deeper.

"Fuuuuck," he growls as I settle on him, taking him fully. "Darcy."

I can't move. I can't remember how long it's been since I felt this full. This good. I press a kiss to his lips while I wait for my body to get used to the invasion. Dodger's taste, mixed with my own, makes me squirm until I'm grinding against him.

His hands go to my hips, helping me. When just the tip remains inside, he slams me back down, and I moan as his cock slides right over the perfect spot. Without coaxing, I repeat the motion, lifting and dropping over and over as I chase the limits of our pleasure.

Beneath me, his face is lined with pleasure. His hands roam, shifting to cup my breasts, then down to slap lightly against my ass as I ride him with reckless abandon.

"So fucking beautiful," he murmurs. "Just like that. Keep going. Good girl. Damn, you're even better than I imagined, and I imagined a fucking lot."

The litany of praises continues to fall from his lips, his husky tones chasing me up and over the final edge until he finishes with a roar.

I collapse. His heartbeat thunders against his ribs below me as we both try to catch our breath. He rolls me over, pressing another soft kiss to my jaw before he heads to the bathroom to deal with the condom and wash up.

It's only after, when I'm snuggled against him, tracing the outlines of his hazardous tattoo, that everything sinks in.

Four orgasms. In one go. I didn't even have to use a vibrator or wait until he'd left the room to finish myself off.

How long has it been since that happened? Dread settles in my stomach as I fail to recall a single guy in the last few years of disappointing relationships.

I knew this would happen. I knew I'd get attached. I should've told Man to send someone else, and spared our friendship. There's only two ways this can end now: forever, or a broken heart.

My next breath is shaky, and Dodger freezes beneath me.

"What's wrong?"

I shake my head. "Nothing. Just... deep thoughts."

He presses a kiss to my forehead as my fingers leave his band tattoo and follow the chains from the blades of chaos over his shoulder and down his arm. The pad of my index finger finds another row of scars hidden beneath his ink, and I bend down to kiss them.

There are too many, and they're too even, for these to be the remnants of anything other than self harm. He lets me explore, but his muscles are tense as I follow their path down to the flames that circle his wrists.

I don't say anything, and he relaxes as it becomes clear I'm not going to start asking him about them.

"You know, your coffee is probably cold by now," he murmurs, stroking his fingers through my messy hair.

"Ugh." I don't have the energy to be upset about it.

I freeze. "Wait, what time is it? I'm supposed to be on a plane at five—"

"We're taking care of it," he interrupts. "You're flying on our jet."

Groaning, I let my head fall back onto the pillows. "I can pay for my own flights." Miguel will be personally reimbursing me for all my flights when I blast him into little pieces and wipe his accounts.

"Given that I know how much the agency pays you, I doubt it." Dodger scowls, then waves a hand at the door. "By all means, take it up with Prophet."

He might as well have told me to argue with a brick wall. I

can't even tell them all the reasons it makes more sense for me to fly with the rest of the crew.

How do you explain you need to integrate with your colleagues so that you don't draw attention to yourself because you're actually an assassin?

Part of me is also worried about what everyone else will think. I've only been around the band for three days and suddenly I've scored a seat on their jet. I'm about to go from invisible to gossip material, and that's not where any assassin wants to be.

I groan and shove away the sheets that have become tangled around our legs.

"Fine. I'll talk to Prophet."

Darcy
17

"**N**o."

"No?" I repeat, dumbly.

Prophet's arms are crossed over his chest and he towers over me with a single brow raised.

I had the perfect argument. I stated my case perfectly, and I'm ready to go. All I need is for him to get out of the way of the elevator. Why is he even awake now, anyway? Don't tell me he and Dodger are both morning people?

"No."

"I need to get on that plane," I insist. "All the other roadies are—"

"You're booked on our jet. We don't leave for another two hours."

"Why? You don't even want me around!"

His expression doesn't change, and he doesn't answer. Apparently, all of his communication points have been used for the day.

"The crew is going to think I'm sleeping my way to a better paycheck and benefits," I tell him bluntly. "I have to work with them, so I'm damn well going to travel with them."

"No."

We're back to one-word answers again. Great.

"Prophet, let me pass."

Gentle hands stroke my shoulders, and Dodger pulls me away from the door. "Come and have a hot cup of coffee. There's no reasoning with him when he gets like this."

"Dodger, I have to—"

"Even if you left now, you'd have to run to get through security on time. It's not worth it. Arlo is out grabbing us breakfast," he cajoles. "And I'm pretty sure he said he was getting orange muffins."

Oooh... Damn it, that does sound good. I can smell the coffee too.

"Don't think this is over," I tell the shirtless wall of muscle guarding the elevator. "You can't distract me with coffee every time."

I still don't understand his problem. He doesn't want me here, so why stop me getting on a plane?

"You're going to love our jet," Slate promises from his spot on the couch.

The bassist has been watching my standoff with Prophet for the last ten minutes, but he's wisely kept his mouth shut. Now he catches my hand and pulls me down to join him while Dodger hands me my coffee.

"And we can use the extra time to go out and replace the stuff you lost," Dodger adds. "We owe you that much."

"I can do that online with my own money," I insist. "Besides, Arlo said he didn't like my new clothes."

Slate brushes off my concern. "Let us pamper you, *mi reina*. Dodger makes far too much money for one person with his boring stocks as it is."

"Hey, that's nothing compared to what Prophet gets paid to write four-line-wonders for overpaid, whiny pop stars," Dodger says.

I press the heel of my palm into my forehead. "Stop it.

This money talk is making me uncomfortable. I'm more than capable of taking care of myself."

Although the news that Prophet is writing pop music in his spare time has me looking at him in a different light. Sure, I know a lot of artists can't write music—even Elvis didn't write most of his stuff—but I had no idea the drummer of a metal band would be the brain behind a lot of popular artists.

I take a sip of my coffee, thankful that Dodger made me a fresh cup.

"Fine. If I'm staying, then I'd like answers. Who trashed my room last night, and why?"

I doubt they're going to answer me honestly, but if I can get more information on how they're being blackmailed, then this won't be a total waste of time.

All three men share a look, but they're spared from answering as Arlo returns, almost running straight into Prophet's back as he steps out of the elevator.

"I brought breakfast!" he announces, stepping around the drummer to deposit a pastel-coloured box of heaven on the table. "Orange muffins!"

The guitarist opens the box and passes me a soft, fluffy piece of citrusy goodness with a flourish. "I remembered you said your sister made you some on your birthday last year. I'm not sure if they're as good..."

They probably have less of a chance of killing me, but I don't mention that. Hopefully, California's bakeries have fewer assassins working in their kitchen than the manor does.

Reluctantly relinquishing my coffee, I take a bite and groan. "Yes! Oh my God, they're almost as good as Karma's."

I quietly resolve to never, ever mention that to my sister. I value my life.

"When the tour is over, I'll cook for you," Slate promises, unexpectedly. "I'm pretty sure I can make you a pizza you love more than the abomination that is pepperoni and pineapple."

I roll my eyes, but don't comment. "I'm still waiting for an answer."

Arlo looks blank, but the others have no such excuse.

"I'm not dumb," I press, taking another bite. "People don't trash technicians' rooms and write bloody messages on their walls for no reason. I haven't pissed anyone off—that I'm aware of—and none of you seemed surprised by any of it."

"Would you accept a rain check?" Dodger hedges. "It's not an easy thing to explain."

"All you have to know is that we'll keep you safe," Slate says, brushing over the subject with too much calculated ease. "Stay with us, and you'll never have to worry about them again."

I frown, wondering if he honestly thinks such a bullshit line will work on me, but luckily for him, Arlo comes in with a sneak attack. He takes his sunglasses off, hitting me with a guileless baby blue stare as he twirls the frames around and around.

"We'll tell you everything, Dark. Just give us a chance to figure out how."

I bite the inside of my cheek, wondering how much of a show of token resistance I need to give. I'll let them get away with not explaining, because I already know that the cartel is responsible. While I'd like to understand how they got mixed up with a cartel, it's not necessary for my mission.

"And in the meantime," Slate continues, effortlessly shepherding the conversation. "Let us show you how good things could be between us."

I have to stifle a snort. He may as well have said: "Ignore the huge danger, Darcy, and while you're at it, fancy a turn on my pogo stick?"

"Slate." Prophet's tone is full of warning.

"You put your keys in the bowl," his band mate replies evenly.

I snort, because I know that doesn't mean anything. "Do any of you know a single living man who wouldn't put his hat in the ring if sex was on the table?"

Those mismatched eyes pierce me, flickering with emotion that I still just don't understand.

"If you can't tell me why I've been targeted, you can at least tell me how you expect a relationship to work," I continue.

"Easy," Slate says. "We pick a state, probably Texas, so we're close to Prophet's family, then we buy a big ass house. Then we give it a cute little white picket fence so it lives up to your expectations, and then set about filling it with all the stuff you want to be happy. Rugs and... candles and... girly shit."

I can't help it. I throw my head back and laugh. "Rugs? You think I want rugs?"

Slate shrugs. "You said you wanted to settle down. Settling down involves rugs and lampshades and ovens, and whatever other boring adult shit we have to pretend to get excited about. Like irons and cleaning stuff. My mom once spent three weeks cooing over a Dyson."

I can't breathe, I'm laughing so hard. "Slate, do you even know me? I don't cook, and I certainly don't vacuum. Wherever I live, I'm hiring a cleaning service. The only thing I care about is my rig and a damn good Wi-Fi connection."

He looks so taken aback that I chuckle again.

"If that stuff doesn't matter to you," Arlo begins, carefully. "Why are you so set on finding a nice guy to settle down with?"

I bite my lip, then shake my head. "Because I used to date bad guys, and all they ever did was stomp on my heart or disappoint me. Plus..."

Arlo's brows draw together in concern. "Plus?"

I take a deep break and look down into my coffee, wondering whether I should admit this.

"I've been doing a lot of soul searching in the last few years, trying to figure out what to do with my life. I want kids." I take a sip of coffee, using the scalding hot liquid to help me swallow the lump of vulnerability that's taken up residence in my throat. "I want my own family. I know it's a cliché, but I always have. Children deserve a good, stable household and parents who love them unconditionally. I'm getting older, and no one has said anything, but I just..."

I trail off, wondering how to put into words the intangible pressure that's just there.

By my age, my mother had already had me, and lost her life to the fire. My logical brain knows that the older I get, the harder it becomes to conceive. There are greater risks of complications. Even if I adopted, like Man did, I don't want to get so old I can't do things with my kids.

Assassins aren't supposed to want that life, but I do. Hell, I'm all in favour of being a strong, independent woman—and I'm not going to suddenly stop being one if I have a baby—but it's okay to want to be a mother too, damn it. I glance up, daring any one of them to laugh or criticise me.

Arlo clears his throat. "I think you'd be a fun mom, Dark."

The others don't say anything, and I bite my lip and steel my shoulders. This could be the end of the trial period. Not everyone wants kids. That's fine. But I'd rather not find out three years down the line that they're not interested. Especially with this arrangement. It takes a strong man to help raise another's kid, even if they are best friends.

"Once everything is sorted out, and we're not touring as much," Slate begins slowly. "It would be nice to have a family."

Something shadowed slips through his eyes, darkness

touching the edge of his words for a second. It's gone as quickly as it arrives.

"I don't have a dad," Dodger adds. "But if Prophet's there, I'm sure they'll turn out fine."

I turn to Prophet, waiting for his assessment, only to freeze at the raw, unhidden emotion in his eyes. A mixture of dark heat and pure want swirls in those mismatched depths, but his face itself is pinched, almost like he's in pain.

Without speaking, he turns on his heel and retreats into his room.

What does that even mean? Is he out?

Slate tugs me closer. "Prophet has always wanted a big family. He dotes on his nieces and nephews like they're his own. It's not you, or the idea of kids that he's upset with, *cariño*. It's us."

Not for the first time, I wonder what the hell is going on with the band. At times, they're so in tune, and others...

"We're sorting our shit out," Dodger promises, and my gut sinks. "Don't give up on us just yet, baby girl."

I can kill Miguel and his brothers, take out the cartel for good, but I'm not sure I can fix whatever bond has been broken between these men.

Arlo

18

"Vancouver, you've been an absolute blast!" Dodger yells, as almost twenty thousand fans bounce on their feet to the last echoes of Slate's bass. "Thank you so much for having us and have a safe journey home, all right?"

The lights go out, and I jog off stage, wiping the sweat from my forehead with one arm as I hand my guitar to Rick.

"Good show," Sully cheers, handing me a bottle of water. "You boys were great out there."

Someone hands Dodger a shirt, and he shrugs it over his bare chest, accepting Sully's praise with a fist bump, but I can't pay attention to them. I'm searching for Darcy, trying in vain to pick out her blonde ponytail as Sully shepherds us away towards the area they've set up for the VIPs.

Except, instead of a room full of more fans, he pulls us into a closet.

"Now, which one of you is going to tell me what's going on between you and our new pyro?" he demands. "Rumour has it her room was trashed, then she missed her flight and turned up on your jet just in time for setup? Are you fucking her? Because, boys, I understand the allure of a beautiful lady, but trust me, that there's a nightmare just waiting to happen."

I can't help but smirk. Sully can't really talk. He's a terminal bachelor, and some of the stories of his youth that fall out of him when he gets drunk are hilarious.

"It's not like that," Slate says.

"She's an old friend," I interject, before Slate can protest too hard and land us in worse trouble.

Sully is like a dad to us, and has been since Miguel first shoved us into the world of touring. The band trusts him without question, but unfortunately, he also has a dad's tendency to chew us out when we're doing something really stupid.

Something like pursuing a relationship with a perfect girl while under the thumb of a psychopath who has no compunctions about using anyone we care for against us.

"Oh, good. You cornered them." Emma slips into the room, shutting the door behind her. "I saw Gabrielle on her way to the VIP room, so we don't have long. Now. What's the deal with that girl?"

Our pseudo-dad *and* my baby sister heading the inquisition? I can't help my groan.

"Ems," I begin. "She's Dark Angel."

Maybe that will help her see why we can't back off.

Her eyes narrow. "That nerd girl you've been internet buddies with since I was a kid? No way. People you met online don't just suddenly show up in your life like that. That's too much of a coincidence." She pauses. "Has she asked you for anything? Money?"

My younger sibling is too suspicious for her own good, but I can't blame her. She's had too much first-hand experience of people who'd like to use her just because she's my sister. Our own parents, for one.

"She's practically allergic to our cash," Dodger grouches. "I'm trying to figure out how to get her a raise—"

"*That's* why we're getting a bonus this tour?" Emma whisper-screeches. "So you can sneak money to her?"

"She wasn't going to take it otherwise!" he retorts. "I tried to buy her lunch at the airport, and she sneaked away and paid for the whole table by herself when she went to the bathroom. Who does that when they're out eating with millionaires?"

Emma isn't fooled. "Someone who wants to worm their way in—"

Sully holds his hand up for silence. "It is a bit suspicious. Your oldest friend turns up after all these years—working for you, no less—and you're not even a bit curious as to how? Even if this *is* the mother of all coincidences, instead of protecting the girl by steering clear, you've decided to put her squarely in Miguel's crosshairs?"

"Exactly!" Prophet groans. "Talk some sense into these idiots. Please."

"Don't pretend you're not just as invested as the rest of us," Slate retorts.

Oh, please stop. I think, desperately. This fighting is endless, and discomfort creeps down my spine like goosebumps.

"You know what I'm invested in?" Prophet demands, and I take a step back as the tension between the two of them once again bursts into being. "Getting the fuck out of this band before this fucking deal we made kills someone. Do you know that they've sent fucking cronies to Malik's school *again*? Even kids aren't safe from these assholes."

Emma is watching me like a hawk, and I try my hardest not to shrink any further at the reminder that all of this is my fault.

I hate this. The arguing. The blame. The constant reminder that our once indestructible friendship is shattered into jagged little pieces, and only the fucking deal with the cartel is holding us together. The anger is a constant undercurrent whenever we're alone together, but it's been about a month since Prophet and Slate had a real blow up at one another.

The fragile hope which was humming in my blood turns sour as Dodger steps in, trying to keep the peace, as usual.

"We're all buzzed from the stage," he reasons. "We can talk about this later. Right now, we have to go and meet those fans, or Miguel will just arrange for something worse than a trashed hotel room."

That reminder shuts us up.

"I'm pretty sure they're planning some kind of deal to go down when we stop in El Paso," Sully says. "I'm keeping my ear to the ground, and I'll grab whatever evidence I can. We just have to find the right contacts to deal with this." He pauses. "Just hang on a little longer, boys. This can't go on forever. In the meantime, keep that girl safe. She seems nice enough, and if she's not involved, best keep it that way, yeah?"

He opens the closet door and ducks out before ushering the others out. I try to follow, but I'm not that lucky. Emma stops me with a hand on my jacket.

"Arlo."

I offer her a tired smile, somehow more worn out from that conversation than I was from hours of jumping around on stage. "Emma."

"I don't trust her."

I shrug, used to her protectiveness. "You don't even know her. At least give her a chance."

"Fine. But the second I find something, you agree to run fast in the other direction. Deal?"

I shake my head. "I don't make deals anymore. Dark was our friend before all of this—" I wave a hand at the stadium and my own, sweaty clothes. "She doesn't care about that stuff."

"She laughed at your art."

I snort. "Let me guess, the one with the kneeling orc?" Emma frowns, and I shake my head. "Inside joke."

My sister isn't placated. I can tell by the rigid set of her shoulders.

"She doesn't have Instagram. Or Facebook. Or even a TikTok."

Oh, the horror. I raise one brow. "Heaven forbid. She must be an alien. You know, not everyone wants to waste their life doomscrolling."

Personally, I leave all of the socials to our PR team. I deleted all my accounts when I first decided to give up coke as a way to remove the temptation. Ghosting everyone who was part of that scene helped a lot.

Perhaps I could've started new accounts again now that I'm clean, but I struggle enough dealing with what's in my own head without adding whatever some troll thinks about me to the mix.

Though, given Emma's phone addiction, I can see why she would think Darcy had committed some heinous crime.

"Tell her I want her to come shopping with me in Seattle."

I can't help but stare at her. "You want to take her shopping?"

Emma nods. "The gossip mill said her clothes were shredded. I'm your wardrobe mistress, after all. I can make sure she doesn't drag your style down."

A coil of dread unwinds in my stomach, and I have to fight hard to keep my grimace off my face. My sister appointed herself head of our wardrobe at sixteen years old. We let her, mainly because none of us likes shopping for ourselves, and she needed something to do in between online classes as we dragged her across the country on tour after tour. But is Darcy the type to enjoy having her clothes picked out and judged for her? I'm not even sure if she likes shopping.

"I'll tell her." I reach for the door handle, silently praying that Darcy forgives me for unleashing Hurricane Em into her life as I hurry after the rest of the band.

Darcy
19

I finish well after the rest of the band has been ushered from the arena, but when I leave the building an Uber is waiting to take me to the hotel. The receptionist doesn't even question why she's giving me a key to the floor where the band is staying, and before I know it, I'm in the darkened living area of yet another swanky suite.

Are they all asleep? Someone has left a lamp switched on by the couch, and my suitcase is leaning against it. I cross to my stuff on silent feet and unzip it quietly.

I'm tired, but this is a rare moment alone where I can finally get to work.

My laptop is out and fired up before I notice the list of messages on my phone.

[HzD]StoneRE1
I wanted to leave the bowl out, but the others might've sabotaged me *side eye emoji*

[HzD]D0dgeVip3r
Come find me I'm 1st door on the right

[HzD]StoneRE1
He got mixed up, take the 2nd on the left

[HzD]Fr0gg0
ngl I'm in the 1st left, but ur welcome if u
want. No pressure

[HzD]Proph3t
Very mature, Slate.

[HzD]StoneRE1
Fuck off P

[HzD]D0dgeVip3r
stop confusing her. 1st on right.

[HzD]Fr0gg0
Let Dark pick.

[HzD]StoneRE1
2nd on the left mi amor. You won't regret it
wink emoji

[HzD]Proph3t
Go to sleep. We have a plane to catch in the
morning.

I snort. I can't help it. In my mind's eye, I can
picture them lying in bed messaging the group, all hoping I'll
wander into bed with them while Prophet grumbles about
how they won't shut up.

Just for that, none of them get me. This couch is easily big
enough for little, old me, and it's softer than a cloud. Besides, I
have to work, and this is the first moment I've had to myself
for days.

Tugging on my pyjamas, because I work best in comfort, I

snuggle in with a blanket and pull my laptop towards me, only to freeze as I'm hit with a wave of nostalgia. This position reminds me of the dozens of evenings I've spent like this with my sister, Ivory, snoozing against me. The baby of our group has always suffered from night terrors, ever since she was a child. A lot of the time, she'd find me in the middle of a two a.m. gaming session, and I'd take a break from the screen to help her settle. As we grew older, she no longer needed milk and cookies, but would read beside me until she fell back to sleep.

Brushing away the pang of homesickness, I start by searching the network for the guy's phones.

"Oh, for God's sake," I groan.

They're *all* connected to the hotel Wi-Fi. Sighing, I quickly switch my phone's SSID to match the Wi-Fi and send deauthentication frames along the network to force their phones to disconnect. When the devices automatically try to reconnect, they mistake my phone for the Wi-Fi and voila, I'm in. Three clicks later and my sweet, innocent little tracking app has been downloaded onto all four of their phones.

I don't feel great about hacking my guys, but you never know when something like that will be useful. Hopefully, I won't ever have to activate the app.

That done, I return to the real threat here, Gabrielle. Firing up the rootkit on her phone with one hand, I quickly start skimming through her files. I've had an app recording her keystrokes for the last few days, and as I rifle through her stuff, I set another handy program to filter her typing history to search for likely passwords.

God, I can't help but admire someone whose virtual life is so neat. Everything has a folder, labelled and sorted alphabetically. All the files are dated. I almost feel bad that she made it so easy for me because it's so beautifully organised.

Each member of the band has their own file, and Gabrielle

has copies and backups of everything. Even the files kept by their juvie counsellors...

Ignoring that temptation—because some things should stay private—I click on a file titled "Surveillance" and start watching a random snippet of video footage.

I watch with dawning horror as Arlo enters a hotel room and starts stripping off his clothes without a care for the camera. From the vantage point, they must have hidden it on a shelf where it was unlikely to be noticed.

Not only are they blackmailing my guys, they have them under the kind of surveillance you'd use on criminals.

Gut sinking, I click on Dodger's name and find the most recent video. I watch with mounting horror as he brings a mug full of coffee to me, then braces himself over me to steal a kiss.

Nausea burns my throat, and I close the video, unwilling to see how much of our privacy they invaded. There are no words for the violation, and before I can think better of it, I check the file history.

No one has accessed it except for me. My breath leaves my lungs in a rush, and before I can think better of it, I delete and purge the file. Then I take an older video and rename it in its place, doing the same for all of her backups.

Hopefully, that should stop anyone getting suspicious for a while.

How the hell can anyone go along with filming others like that?

It only gets worse.

Their phones are bugged. They have hundreds of recordings of their calls, texts and even emails.

When I bumped into Gabrielle, I never thought she could be capable of something like this. How deeply is she involved? Is she a victim like my guys? Another doing her job to avoid Miguel's wrath? Her body language doesn't scream evil cartel assistant to me.

Whatever her reasons, she's in deep.

She wasn't mentioned in my briefing, but if I find evidence that she was a willing accomplice, I won't feel bad if she gets caught in the blast.

I close her files and switch over to her calendar. Gabrielle's obsessive organisation continues here as well. Every single part of the tour has been broken down and itemised.

Right down to the "family meeting" taking place after the concert in El Paso.

Bingo.

That's my chance.

It's the seventh stop on the tour. The band still has to play Seattle, Las Vegas, and Phoenix before we get there. Plenty of time for me to figure out a plan to get—

Footsteps sound. I slam the lid of my laptop closed, hastily shoving it back into my bag before I settle onto the cushions and do my best impression of sleep.

A door opens just as my head hits the cushioned arm of the chair. I take a deep in breath and let it out slowly, keeping my eyes as lightly shut as I dare. Before I can work up the courage to peek through my lashes, a warm pair of hands scoops me up from my spot on the sofa.

I'm cradled like a princess against a warm chest. I don't recognise the fresh, clean scent of his soap, so I don't think it's Dodger, and this kind of move is too subtle for Slate.

Which leaves Arlo. Sneaky Arlo. I didn't think the quiet guitarist had it in him to kidnap me.

I crack open one eye as I'm gently deposited on silken sheets and have to stop myself gasping in surprise.

Prophet tucks me in like I'm made of glass. The room is dark, but his silhouette is too broad to be anyone else. A finger traces my hair out of my face, tucking it behind my ear with such exquisite care that I melt a little.

"In another life," he whispers, so quietly I barely hear the words.

Then he leaves, shutting the door behind him. Leaving me alone in the massive bed with a case of whiplash.

"I don't understand that man," I murmur to the shadows.

Does he hate me and want me gone? Or does he want to tuck me into bed like a princess and take the couch?

I WAKE TO THE SCENT OF FRESH COFFEE AND THE quiet hum of conversation. It takes a second for me to work out where I am, and when I do, I can't help but sigh all over again.

I don't want to leave this warm, cosy slice of heaven, but I also don't want to miss out on coffee. Decisions, decisions.

As a compromise, I drag the covers with me into the living area, yawning as I go. The guys aren't in the kitchen, or on the sofa, where someone has left a neatly folded blanket and a pillow. It takes an embarrassingly long time for me to notice them at a table tucked away in the corner, and I blame my morning brain.

"She lives!" Dodger jokes, lifting a shiny silver cloche from a plate in front of the only remaining empty chair. "We ordered for you. The chef here is damned good."

Ignoring the breakfast wrap, I grab the huge mug of coffee someone has left out and inhale my first sip.

Perfection.

The wrap is the same, crammed full of my favourite foods, but without a mushroom or tomato in sight. I swear it's almost stalkerish how these guys know exactly how I drink my coffee and my least favourite foods, but I'm not going to complain.

"Hungry?" Slate asks, grinning at the enthusiasm with which I'm attacking my breakfast.

I groan. "Do you have any idea how much paperwork I had to do last night because someone tripped and stubbed their toe on my explosives cages?"

There's a special place in hell reserved for the inventor of injury forms. You'd think I shoved a rocket up Charlie's ass and set it off given the amount of paperwork that came with him tripping over the corner and faceplanting.

"Are you sure you like your job?" Dodger asks. "I'm sure there's something better paid…"

I shake my head. "I like blowing shit up." Understatement of the century. "Besides, I'm fine for money. Honestly."

I don't understand why he's so caught up about this. It's the third time he's brought it up, and it feels more awkward every time. I'm halfway to showing him my investment port-folio just to get him to drop the subject.

"When we land in Seattle, I think we should all go on a date," Slate announces, changing the subject.

"Ooh, yes!" I whoop, tiredness forgotten in the wake of my excitement. "I've always wanted to go to the Pacific Science Center! They have a tide pool and a butterfly house and—" I cut off, cheeks going red as I take in the band's expressions. "Sorry… we can do something else if you want."

I guess a nerdy day out probably isn't what they were thinking. Shit. I should've just said the movies or dinner or something… I guess it's not really the sort of place I'd expect rock stars to want to go. Well, really, I suppose it's a bit imma-ture for a thirty-something year old woman to want to go, but they know who I am. I've never pretended to be polished and sophisticated.

I'm a nerd, and I love butterflies, damn it.

"We can go," Slate replies, slowly.

Arlo looks more enthusiastic. "Should be fun. Do you think they'll have anemones?"

Prophet says nothing, but his eyes glint slightly—is that as close as I'll get to approval from him?

Dodger looks faintly amused by the whole idea. "More coffee?" he asks.

I offer him my cup in answer, and he sweeps it away to the kitchen with a soft parting kiss to the top of my head.

The rustle of paper draws my attention back to the table. Slate shoves four pieces of paper across the surface towards me.

"What are these?" I ask, confused.

"The other order of business," Slate answers. "Our latest health insurance checkups. None of us have been with anyone since the tour began. We're all clean."

I blink at him. *What is he getting at?*

"If you're comfortable, I'd prefer not to wear condoms," he finishes.

My brows shoot up. "Don't you want to know if I'm on birth control first?"

Slate just shrugs. "You're endgame for us. Whenever kids happen, they happen."

Something low in my belly flutters, and I have to swallow back the ball of emotion that jumps to my throat. My logical brain is working overtime to remind me that Slate's words are irresponsible, not cute.

"And your cavalier attitude wouldn't have anything to do with the fact that it's harder for the band to split up with a kid in the mix?" Prophet leans back, folding his arms behind his head in a relaxed pose that belies the rigid tension threaded through his muscles.

"We did agree to sort our shit out first," Arlo mutters but is ignored.

"You always have to push, don't you?" Prophet continues.

"She doesn't even know what she's getting into, but you'd lock her into hell with us anyway."

Internally, I grimace, because I know exactly what I'm getting into, but I also happen to have a one hundred percent success rate. I'm more invested in freeing these men than I have been in anything else; so despite Prophet's misgivings, Miguel won't be an issue for them much longer.

"I'm giving her the choice," Slate retorts, eerily calm. "Even if we all went our separate ways, we'd all still love the hell out of her baby."

"It doesn't matter," I interrupt. "I'm clean, and I've got the implant. There's…" I do the math in my head. "Still four months left on it. Long enough to finish this tour."

For the trial period to end.

None of them speak, and it takes me a second to realise that they're still waiting for my answer. Even Prophet is staring at me.

I check the paperwork, making certain for myself that their claims are true. One thing stands out to me.

"The date on Dodger's is more recent," I mumble.

"I figured you'd never believe I didn't fuck that groupie," Dodger mutters, placing my refilled mug in front of me and taking his seat . "So I got retested the next day."

"Bold."

"Just living in hope, baby girl. And it wasn't entirely unwarranted, now, was it?" He shoots me a cheeky wink, and I can't help but smile.

I sigh, but I can't lie, having experienced both before, I enjoy the spontaneity that comes without worrying over protection.

Pushing the pages back across the table, I keep my best poker face on as I consider it one final time. "I'm clean too." I got tested before the mission as a precaution because it wouldn't be the first time an ex screwed around before calling things off. "Yes."

Slate grins. "Thank fuck."

"If that's the case," Dodger murmurs, leaning in close. "Wear a skirt today, baby girl."

I look up at him. "I thought your turn was over?"

"The bowl is only for who you share a room with," Slate corrects. "Quickies don't count."

My brows creep up. "What counts as a quickie?"

Dodger runs his lips lightly up the column of my throat. "Anything under one hour and ten minutes."

"Specific."

Arlo snorts. "It's the flight time between Vancouver and Seattle. Don't you think you should ask her if she's okay with—"

Dodger pins him with a glare. "Darcy knows she can stop me whenever she wants to." He pauses, a wicked grin taking over his expression. "You should be thanking me; you're going to enjoy what I have planned. Bring your sketchbook."

Touring, I'm beginning to realise, is incredibly tiring. We're only on the fourth gig of fifteen, and yet, I feel like I've travelled the world as we board the private jet again. Sure, the luxury softens the blow, but it's the fifth flight in under a week.

I did as Dodger asked and wore my favourite shirt dress, following his commands, but not to the letter. Currently, it's flapping around my legs in the wind as I climb the steps onto the private jet. Thankfully, I had the foresight to overnight myself some new contacts before the concert yesterday, so at least I don't have to worry about the infuriating mix that is glasses, wind, and long hair.

It's small, for a private plane, but still comfortable. On one side of the aisle are two comfy armchairs, and on the other, a small conference table with two seats on each side. There's a more relaxed sofa and television area farther down the plane, but the band has chosen to ignore it.

Prophet has claimed the first armchair. His headphones are on, and he's tapping out a rhythm on the cover of a notebook with his pen. Slate is mirroring him in the second chair, playing on his phone, but he looks up as I pass him.

Dodger and Arlo have claimed the conference table. The former has his laptop out with spreadsheets open, while the latter is reclining in the seat opposite with a square sketchbook closed in front of him.

"Next to me, baby girl," Dodger calls. "Strap in for takeoff and give me your panties."

Here? In front of everyone?

I freeze, looking from him to the others. Prophet is ignoring us, but the rhythmic tapping of his pen skips a beat. Slate's eyes are dark, anticipatory, as he waits to see what I'll do, and Arlo is biting his lip.

Against my better judgement, I head for the seat Dodger is patting, my heartbeat picking up. I hesitate again before sitting, wondering if I should take my panties off now or later.

The flight attendant takes the decision out of my hands as she strolls in with a professional smile. My ass hits the cushion before I can think about it, and I reach blindly for the seat belt.

"Welcome back aboard. Can I get you anything to drink?"

"Soda," Prophet grunts.

"Two of those," Slate adds.

Arlo waves her away, and I'm so mortified that I do the same, but Dodger orders a coffee. The moment her back is turned, and she's headed back to the kitchen, he raises a brow expectantly.

My thumbs trace up the outside of my thighs, lifting the hem of my dress and hooking over the waistband of my panties. I actually debated not wearing any this morning, but chose to go without a bra instead.

"Dark, you know you don't need to—" Arlo begins, but I silence him with a look.

"I know. I... I'm game. I'll tell him if it's too much."

Dodger holds his hand out expectantly, and I rush to

comply. I have no idea when the attendant will come back, and I don't want to be caught.

The neon orange panties I pass him are one of my favourite pairs, covered in tiny fires with the words *warning, explosive* over the ass, and he smirks.

"Present for you, Lo," he says, wadding them up into a ball and throwing them across the aisle to his bandmate.

I gasp as the guitarist catches them and holds them against his nose, groaning, before tucking them safely into the pocket of his leather jacket.

Shit. I guess it is *always the quiet ones. Why was that so hot?*

The attendant appears with our drinks, silencing any comment I might've made.

"We're good for the rest of the flight," Dodger says, barely looking up from his laptop to acknowledge her. "Take the time off."

She nods, completely unfazed by his abruptness, then turns and leaves. The door snicks behind her, sealing me in with them.

"Still want to play, baby girl?" Dodger asks, voice dropping to the intimate tone that lets me know our dynamic has changed.

Inside the bedroom, he's in charge, and I love that. At first, I resisted. I'm an assassin, after all, more than capable of taking charge of any situation and completely unused to handing over the reins. It took me a while to trust him not to do anything to abuse that power, and to believe him when he said it would never be an issue outside of the bedroom. I also had to come to terms with the fact that I *enjoyed* submitting to him, which was probably the hardest part.

Over the years, our roles have solidified. I still find it fun to push his buttons, but I also love letting him take the burden of decision making from me, even if it's only for a little while. No thinking, just feeling.

"Yes, sir." Biting my lip, I shift slightly in my seat.

Without underwear, I'm painfully aware of how bare I am and the sensation of my thighs rubbing together as the plane taxis down the runway.

Dodger keeps me waiting until we're in the air, leaving me to stew over his actions as he calmly looks through graphs and...

"Are those stock reports?" I question, finally focusing on his screen.

He shrugs. "I like numbers. They make sense to me."

That's exactly the opposite of what I'd expect from someone so passionate. Cold, hard data seems more like it would be Prophet's thing.

The seat belt light goes out, and he undoes his own before looking at mine pointedly.

"Undo your belt, kneel on the seat, and take my dick out," he orders.

My hands scramble for the belt, and the clink it makes as it opens is like a gunshot in the quiet cabin. Kneeling on the seat takes some doing, and I quickly realise his game.

The second I bend over, everything will be on display for Slate and Prophet to see.

Taking a deep breath, I reach over and undo his belt, then his fly. His cock jumps eagerly in my hand as I pull it free. A pearl of clear liquid already formed at the top.

"You wanted to play," he reminds me. "So play."

He takes a sip of his coffee and puts it back down before reaching forward to type something.

I have to lean forward for balance, or at least, that's what I tell myself as I gently caress the velvet hardness of him. I pump once, using my thumb to swipe away the bead of pre-cum, and then bring it to my lips, experimentally.

"Fuck," Arlo whispers, and a light rustling makes me look over the table.

He's shifting through his sketchbook, charcoal in hand. His sunglasses have been abandoned on the table, leaving his frown of concentration visible. His blue eyes meet mine, and he winks before he looks back down.

"Eyes on me," Dodger growls, his free hand tangling in my hair and angling my head back towards him.

"That sounded awfully possessive for a man who clearly has some exhibitionist tendencies, sir," I tease.

"Do you really want to see what will happen if you sass me right now?"

The warning undercurrent in his voice is so, so tempting, but I also like surprising him. So, without warning, I duck my head, forgoing modesty to suck the dark head of his cock between my lips.

"*¡Mierda!*" Slate murmurs, and Prophet actually groans as the move treats both of them to the view of a lifetime.

Dodger says nothing, he just goes back to his spreadsheet.

So that's his game? Fine. We'll see how long he can ignore me. I wrap my tongue around the head of him, swirling like he's my favourite lollipop.

I duck down again, loosening my jaw to try to take more of his curved cock. The angle I'm kneeling at makes it awkward, and I can't go as deep as I'd like. I'm also keenly aware of the cool air against my pussy, and the way my breasts are pressing into the armrest between us as I lick and suck my way up and down his cock.

"Touch yourself," Slate moans. "Please, *chula*."

I come up for air and twist my head to look back at him. "Only if Prophet begs."

Is it bad that I really, really want him to beg? I don't get a chance to wait for his response, because Dodger's hand is there again, urging me back to his erection.

"I said, eyes on me," he scolds, before looking over my head. "Stop distracting her."

His fingers leave my hair and caress the line of my jaw before travelling down my throat to the buttons of my dress. In a few efficient flicks, the upper half is open, and my lack of bra is exposed. The angle makes my breasts spill out and I have to resist the urge to reach up and massage away the heaviness that's taken over them.

I draw back, tongue tracing the slit at the head and collecting more salty pre-cum, then adjust and try my best to get as much of him in my mouth as I can. The move has the added effect of making my skirt ride even higher—if that's possible.

"Please."

Prophet's single word freezes me.

I've never heard him say it aloud before. Perhaps if I had, I would've been more careful about making him beg in the past. That word, growled so darkly, is rich with a promise of punishment. Of retribution. I swallow instinctively, and Dodger, still buried in my throat, groans.

"Do it," the singer orders. "Fuck that greedy pussy with your fingers until they wish it was them fucking you."

His hands return to my hair, keeping it out of my face, supporting me this time instead of demanding. The help allows me to release his thigh with one hand and reach back between my legs.

God, I'm so wet already, and I moan as my fingers slide over my clit, rubbing the wetness over it as I bob up and down. I tease myself for several minutes, feeling desire coil inside my veins as I wind myself and the other two men higher and higher. Finally, when I can't take it anymore, I slide a single finger inside myself. My own silken warmth engulfs the digit before I pull it out and replace it with two more.

"Good girl," Dodger praises. "How does it feel, knowing all four of us want to replace those fingers with our cocks?"

I hum with him caught in the back of my throat, and his

fist clenches in my hair. The sting travels straight from my scalp down to where my fingers are slowly pumping into my weeping pussy, and my own walls clench hard around the two digits.

His words have triggered my imagination, and now all I can think about is someone coming up behind me, grabbing my hips, and filling me properly.

My next thrust makes me moan, and Dodger curses as the vibration goes straight to his dick.

"Up," he orders, hands going to my shoulders as he helps me rise.

"Dude, we were enjoying that view," Slate complains.

He turns me around, shoving the armrest up and out of the way as he pulls me down until I'm sitting on his lap. "Tough. This is my quickie."

I open my mouth to tell him that this most definitely does not qualify as a quickie, only to snap it closed as the head of his dick prods insistently at my opening. I reach down and adjust him, fitting him against me and letting gravity do the rest of the work.

God. Yes.

My head falls back and lands on his shoulder, my lips parting in a silent gasp as I sink down onto his cock. My shirt dress falls open, and Dodger wastes no time in undoing the final few buttons hiding my body, but I can't think about the view Arlo is getting. I'm too busy trying to adjust to the intensity of this angle.

"Shh, that's it," Dodger croons. "You just stay there."

Then, to my absolute astonishment, he goes back to work on his laptop. His arm wrapped around my waist keeps me from moving, and I suck in a breath as I grind down, but find no relief.

"Dodger," I complain, hand falling down to touch my clit.

"Ah ah ah," he chides, moving my hand away. "Sit there, keep me warm, and when I'm done, I'll get us both off."

What? He can't be serious? Every cell in my body cries out, begging for movement. For friction. For any kind of stimulation. My need is a pulse that ricochets out from my core with every heartbeat, and I squirm.

I can't thrust, not really, but every shift of his body inside mine causes tiny fireworks to flitter along my nerves. I've got to be making a puddle of wetness on his jeans, but he doesn't seem to care.

"Sir, I really, really want you to fuck me now," I whine.

"Stay still, baby girl," he tuts. "Can't you see Lo's trying to draw over there? Do you want to fuck up his masterpiece?"

True enough, Arlo is sketching away like a madman, flicking heated looks over the top of his book every few seconds. His fingers are dark with charcoal, and every so often his tongue darts out, getting trapped between his teeth as he concentrates.

"Stay put. When he's done, I'll fuck your wet cunt until you scream."

In answer, I reach up and cup one of my own breasts, playing with my nipple using my finger and thumb.

"Hurry up."

But neither Dodger nor Arlo seem in any rush. I half expect, given that Dodger's focus seems so consumed by his spreadsheets, that he'll go soft and slip out of me, but he never does. Even my attempts to spur him on, clenching my muscles around his girth and grinding my ass against him, do nothing to break his iron control.

Every now and again, the hand around my waist sneaks down, smearing my wetness across my clit. He stops whenever I get close enough that I can practically taste my own orgasm approaching. Leaving me squirming and moaning with need. Toying with me.

Edging me.

I've never had a boyfriend who could actually do it, and I'm honestly beginning to hate it.

"I swear to God," I pant, grinding down on him as he withdraws his hand for the sixth time. "If you don't fuck me soon, I'm going to rip your balls off."

His hand lifts from my clit to collar my throat, holding me still against his chest. "Want to say that again, baby girl?"

Slate chuckles. "If she's coherent enough to make threats, you're not doing the job right."

"Fuck you," Dodger groans, without heat. "You have no idea how fucking good she feels. Being inside her is a fucking spiritual experience. She's so damned wet. She's scorching my dick."

Not as unaffected as he appears. The thought makes me smile.

A throat clearing draws my focus back to Arlo. He's turned his sketchbook around on the table, and staring back at me is a two-page spread of my own body splayed over Dodger's. He's captured me with my eyes closed and my head limply resting against Dodger's shoulder. The style is instantly familiar, and my eyes snap up to look at him, mouth open with a gasp of surprise.

"*You* did those paintings in the gallery," I accuse, breath hitching as Dodger's thumb strokes the line of my jaw.

Arlo's shy, delighted grin lights up his face. "You caught me."

Dodger, evidently unimpressed with the distraction, shuts his laptop. Both of his hands move to my waist, and my breath catches as his shift causes his dick to jerk inside me.

"Lean forward," he says. "Bend over the table so Arlo can kiss you while I fuck this needy cunt."

He groans as his words make me clench hard on him,

increasing the perfect friction as he *finally* pulls out and slams me back down *hard*.

"Oh God," I cry, as stars wink behind my eyelids.

A hand fists in my hair, and when I open my eyes, Arlo is there, guiding my face closer to his. Capturing my cries with his own soft lips.

His other hand cups my breast, massaging the flesh until I'm under a lethal double assault.

"Yes!" I scream into his mouth as I come in a rush of sensation that leaves me boneless. All the frustration of Dodger's earlier teasing is unleashed in a tidal wave of pleasure.

But they're not done. Dodger continues pounding into me from beneath, and my orgasm rolls over, becoming a second, then a third. My body unleashes all the pent up orgasms of the last hour onto me at once. By the time he finally growls out my name and stills inside me, I've lost count of how many times I've come.

My flushed skin is pressed against the cool wood of the table, and I don't think I could move if I wanted to. Dodger tugs me back, arranging me over his lap until I'm wrapped in his arms.

I glance down at my body, taking in the black smears that Arlo's charcoal-covered fingers have left on my breasts and the dishevelled state of my clothing.

"I'm a mess," I complain, wondering idly what my chances of retrieving my underwear from Arlo are.

"Good." The satisfaction on Dodger's face is almost enough to have me coming again.

Fortunately, Arlo isn't such a barbarian. He leans forward, offering me a tissue.

"Thank you," I blush, watching him clean his own hands thoroughly. "Can I... can I have my panties back?"

He shakes his head. "I'll give them back when I'm done with them."

My cheeks burn, and I look away sharply. I can't decide what he means by "done with them," and the question haunts me as I struggle to return my clothes to some semblance of order.

"Oh, by the way," Arlo says, as the seat belt light bings back on. "Emma wants to take you shopping after we land. She heard you lost all your clothes."

She... does? Shit. I don't have panties on and one tissue is not enough to make me feel ready for an afternoon out with someone I barely know.

I shoot a pleading look up. "We can go to the hotel first, right?"

Dodger chuckles. "I think you should go out like this."

Playfully poking him in the ribs, I wiggle my way into my own seat, do up the belt and let him drag me towards him for a cuddle just as the plane starts to land.

Darcy
21

"**D**oes this look okay?" I ask the mirror. "No, wait. Sorry. You look gorgeous. Go out there and make a friend."

Positive self-talk for the win, right?

I look over my washed-out jeans and lightweight cropped pink hoodie. I bought it for the quote on the front that says "I'm not procrastinating, I'm doing side quests," but I love it for how soft the fabric is. I'm kind of nervous about going shopping with someone whose entire job revolves around clothes, but Emma didn't seem so bad when we've spoken before. Prickly, maybe, but some of my sisters are worse.

Plus, with the way the guys treat her, it's clear they're close. From what I've overheard, she's been with them since their very first tour, along with Sully. As head of wardrobe, I have a feeling she's going to be a formidable shopping companion.

I don't normally do shopping trips with anyone except my sister, Royal. She knows what I like and feels no guilt over dragging me out into the real world and pushing me into impulse-buying everything I look twice at.

Somehow, I doubt Emma is going to be as enthusiastic as

my sister, but I hope she'll still help me get over my indecisiveness.

The band is busy with a photoshoot, so there's no one to help me critique my outfit as I step out into the living area of the latest hotel and freeze as I come face to face with a young porter entering the suite.

"The band's stuff is already here," I begin, eyeing the backpack he's carrying. "So what the hell are you doing in their rooms?"

Instead of answering me, he turns and rushes for the open door. The security guard is conspicuously absent from the hallway beyond as he disappears down it.

Groaning, because after seeing Gabrielle's files I have a feeling I know *exactly* what that porter was up to, I head for the door myself.

At least that solves the question of how the cartel has so much footage. No doubt, that guy was getting paid a pretty penny for installing whatever equipment was in that bag while no one was supposed to be in the room. As Gabrielle controls the band's schedule and their agency provides security, they must know exactly when they can get away with installing the cameras.

This time, I've interrupted them. It might buy the band a night of freedom, or the asshole might just return when he sees me leave.

Not that it matters much. The first thing I did when I was sure I was alone was return to Gabrielle's folders and run a program that would corrupt all of the video footage while leaving the files in place. I set it to start with the older videos, and soon, all of them will be messed with beyond comprehension.

I still don't know her level of involvement with Miguel and his brothers, but perhaps that's something I can get out of Emma.

Taking extra care to lock the door behind me, I head out into the lobby and immediately pick out Emma's pink ombre hair waiting on a sofa by the revolving door. She's wearing a form-fitting white dress with a pink leather jacket and kickass boots.

Next to her, I look like a slob. Perhaps it was inevitable, given that she's the head of wardrobe, but I'm beginning to wonder if jeans were a bad idea.

"You ready?" she asks, standing as soon as she catches sight of me.

"As I'll ever be," I reply, trying for a smile that falls flat when she doesn't return it. "Where are we headed?"

"There's a mall just south of here," Emma suggests, already leading the way out of the hotel and onto the crowded street beyond. "Want to let me know why I got a text from Slate this morning telling me not to let you buy anything black?"

I grimace. "I'm *trying* to blend." For all the good it's doing me. "I don't want to be the only person wearing colourful stuff all the time. Plus, black is more practical for backstage."

Emma looks back at me and rolls her eyes. "Bullshit. You're never in view. All the gerbs are on timers. You can wear what you like, and no one would say anything."

"You don't think it stands out a bit much?" I protest.

"No more than fucking your way through the band by pretending to be their long-distance nerd friend."

Ouch. Blunt protectiveness slams into me with every word.

"I'm not pretending anything," I retort. "I've been friends with them for a long time, and the sex was not my idea."

Her blue eyes pierce me as she stops in the middle of the street. "Really? You expect me to believe that? What are you really after? A story to sell to the tabloids? Fame? Money?"

I fold my arms over my chest. "I take it this whole shopping trip is just a ruse so you can interrogate me?"

"My brother deserves to know exactly what your game is," Emma growls.

"Brother?" I blink at her. "Arlo. You're Arlo's sister." I don't know how I didn't see it.

I struggle to remember everything I've picked up about her over the years. I'm pretty sure she's ten years younger than him, an accidental baby. He took custody of her in her teens...

Emma's arms fold over her chest, and she shoots a challenging look my way. "So what?"

"So, if you're his sister, you should know who I am."

"I know who you *say* you are," she corrects, ignoring the people grumbling as they dodge around us. "Prove it."

She wants me to prove it? "Fine. Your brother's username is Froggo, after his childhood Frogger obsession. His favourite colour is green—because frogs. Seven years ago, on your sixteenth birthday, you moved in with him. I know because he spent your entire slumber party hiding in his room on Clans of Carnage with us, complaining there were too many girls in his house. The fire alarm went off, because you'd smuggled alcohol in, got drunk, decided to make smores on the stove, and burned them. He spent the rest of the night panicking about what he was supposed to do, since he legally became your guardian that morning and had no idea how to deal with underage drinking."

Emma's mouth has fallen open, and she's staring openly at me.

"I don't know how I never put Emma the kid together with Emma the costume designer," I mutter.

In my defence, it's a common enough name. But it's the sort of shit that should've been in the file, but then again, I skipped over a lot of the file because it was paperwork. I arrogantly convinced myself that I knew everything about them.

That was a mistake.

"So what if you *are* Dark Angel?" She finally sniffs. "Doesn't make it any less fishy that you've chosen to show up in their lives after all this time. I won't let anyone—old friend or not—use the band."

I run a hand through my hair. Her concern is touching, but inconvenient. I understand too well where she's coming from, but that doesn't mean I'm prepared to sit through her inquisition.

"I'm not using them. I'm here to do a damn job. I wasn't even going to tell them who I was until my damned phone outed me." Sighing, I start walking again. "Come on, if you're going to keep this up, I need coffee."

I push blindly into the nearest coffee place, getting a mocha to go. Emma eyes me warily, like she expects me to continue our argument at any second. When we make it back out of the shop without either of us starting up again, yet the frosty silence remains, I groan.

I know I don't owe her answers, but I selfishly want her to like me. It's not just because Arlo is her brother and I want her approval. The Emma I've heard stories about seemed like a good, if headstrong, kid. In a lot of ways, she reminds me of some of my youngest sisters—prickly, but ride or die for the people she loves.

"I don't blame you for being suspicious," I admit, defeated. "So let's get your concerns out of the way. Fame? I'm not interested. Tabloids? I have nothing to do with them. Money? I have enough to keep all five of us comfortable until the end of our natural lives."

She rolls her eyes, scoffing in disbelief. "No roadie is that well off."

"I'm a nerd," I correct. "When I bought my first bitcoin, it was worth less than a dollar. A virtual currency based on math? The very idea of it was too cool to pass up." Not to mention it's completely decentralised and anonymously distributed via the blockchain, making it perfect for discreet payments over the dark web, but I'm not going to tell her that part.

I am fed up with the band and those close to them thinking I'm a stupid blonde gold digger who can't work for her own money. I dug my own gold, damn it! Well, crypto-mined-slash-stole-from-bad-guys, but *whatever*.

Emma's sour expression has gone slack in disbelief. "Why work at all?"

I look her in the eye and give her the honest truth. "I really, really like blowing shit up. Now. Are we shopping, or can I go back to the hotel and order myself a pizza?"

Screw it, I could use the cheesy goodness right now. Maybe it will help chase away the icky feeling this conversation has left me with.

Emma's hand on my arm stops me before I can take my first step.

"I'm sorry." Her face is pinched, like the admission physically pains her. A tiny blush paints her cheekbones, giving away her embarrassment "I *might* have misjudged you, and I'm still happy to go to the mall with you if you want or hang out, or whatever." She pauses, shuffling on her feet. "*But* if you hurt my brother or the band, I'll crush you."

I pause, swallowing back my natural response and the ire from before.

"Netflix and Dominos?" I offer, cautiously.

She swallows, collecting herself, and raises a single brow. "What are we watching?"

That's how, several hours later, the band traipses into their hotel suite to find the two of us throwing popcorn at yet another rerun of *Say Yes To The Dress*.

"That mother-in-law is eeevil!" Emma crows at the screen. "That *thing* wasn't a dress. It was a pair of lacy curtains!"

"Randy will save her," I swear, earnestly. "Look, here he comes."

"Is it... safe?" Dodger whispers.

"I don't know," Arlo replies. "This could be a trick. There's no way they're both still alive."

Slate strolls up to the back of the couch, leans over to ruffle Emma's hair, then presses a kiss to my cheek. "Have a fun time shopping, *cariño*?"

"Don't let him fool you with all the swoony Spanish," Emma warns. "Most of his vocabulary is swear words."

"Don't you think it's past your bedtime, *hermanita*?" Slate asks and gets a handful of popcorn to the face for his troubles.

"To answer your question," I say, interrupting Emma before she can tell him what she thinks of his bedtime. "We didn't go shopping, and there's extra pizza in the boxes behind you, because Emma said they don't feed you at those PR stunts."

"Fuck, you're the best," Dodger says, heading straight for the food and passing slices out to the others. "I've been starving for hours."

"Of course I am. But that's my cue to go," Emma says. "I have no desire to see you all making sappy faces at one another." She stands, grabbing her jacket as she exchanges hugs with the band before heading to the door. "Laters."

She gives her brother a last, long squeeze, and mumbles something too low for the rest of us to hear, and then she's gone.

"So... you managed to survive Hurricane Em," Arlo begins, hopping into the space his sister left, slice of pizza in hand.

"Yeah, thanks for warning me that she was *that* Emma." I mock-punch him. "She's so protective of you."

"Sorry." He actually blushes. "It's not my fault that they put extra fierceness into baby siblings."

Prophet falls into the chair on the other side of the room, quietly picking pieces of pineapple off of his pizza. Philistine.

"Are you ready for another lucky dip?" Dodger asks, taking the seat on my other side. "Or did we wear you out on the plane?"

I hum in the back of my throat as my thighs clench at the memory. "It takes more than that to wear me out. Keys in the bowl."

Arlo scoops up the last handful of popcorn from the bowl Emma and I were sharing earlier, shoving them into his mouth as he drops his keys into the porcelain with the other. Prophet does the same, followed by Slate.

The guitarist picks the bowl up and hands it to me, at the same time that two hands wrap around my head from behind, covering my eyes.

"No peeking," Dodger whispers, the heat of him warming the back of my neck.

His breath tickles the shell of my ear, and I shiver as I feel for the rim of the bowl. My nerves flutter in my belly as my fingertips meet cold plastic and metal.

When I draw back and open my palm, the silence makes my heart flip.

Dodger's hands leave my eyes, and I look down at the fob shaped like a miniature car on my palm.

"Who drives a Tesla?" I ask, confused.

Behind me, Slate clears his throat. "Me."

Darcy
22

He scoops me from the sofa and into a princess lift before I can even process what he said. Squirming, because I'm not a lightweight by any stretch of the imagination, I go to protest, only to freeze when he throws me up in the air, spanks my ass lightly with one hand, and then catches me in one smooth movement.

Without giving me a chance to breathe, he turns and shoots a smug grin over his shoulder. "See you later, suckers!"

"Hey, what if I want a kiss goodnight?" Dodger complains.

"Should've thought about that before you teased us with that little show on the jet," Slate retorts, kicking open his door. "She's mine now."

Those ominous words are punctuated by the slamming of the door behind us, and I tumble unceremoniously onto the bed.

"The bulbasaur jammies are cute," he begins, stripping his tank top over his head and exposing a chest full of tats I just want to trace with my tongue. "But they've got to go."

"I think we should trade," I counter. "I'll take them off if you tell me what you're planning."

"Planning?" He offers me a cocky smile that reveals nothing. "Well, I'd hoped that we'd start with you showing me those beautiful tits, then move on to you sitting on my face until you come all over my mouth—"

I roll my eyes even as my thighs clench, loving his plan. "Slate. I mean it. What's going on with you and Prophet?"

He sighs, running a hand over his braids before turning to pace the room. "We have a difference of opinion," he finally admits. "Once we've resolved some... issues, Prophet wants to break up the band."

A stone comes to rest in my stomach. "Why?"

Slate shakes his head. "It messed up a lot of things for him. That family you mentioned? He's wanted one since we were in our mid-twenties, but thanks to how things are..." He trails off. "It doesn't matter. What matters is that the band is all the rest of us have. If he breaks it apart... we're fucked. You have no idea what life was like before. Prophet had a great family, but the rest of us weren't so lucky."

My heart breaks a little, but I reach out and snag his hand as he paces past, drawing myself up to my knees so I can hug him. My face is smooshed against his chest, his heartbeat racing beneath my cheek.

"If he leaves the band, it doesn't mean you have to split up. You could hire a new drummer—" I cut off as Slate groans.

"No. It does." He gives a little half-laugh. "I saw to that. Our band contract—the one we made as teens—states that if one of us wants out, the rest can't form another band or replace them. Hazardous doesn't exist unless it's all four of us." He gives a self depreciating shake of his head. "Another of my genius ideas."

I say nothing, just listening.

"Prophet's wrong, anyway," Slate continues. "The stubborn *pendejo* won't be happier if he leaves. He'll go back to some dead-end job that takes advantage of him until he dies.

He's only doing it to punish himself for getting his family involved. He loves the music more than any of us."

"Perhaps he needs the freedom to realise that for himself," I whisper into his chest. "Most of the time, clinging to people only drives them further away."

He sighs against me. "Does it look like I'm clinging, *cariño*?"

It looks like he's battling a bad deal with the cartel while dangling a Darcy-sized steak in front of his bandmates to try to convince them not to split up, but I don't say that out loud.

His hands come to rest on my head, fingers threading through my hair. "I just need to figure out how to remind him that this, right here, is everything he's ever wanted."

I have a feeling that might be harder than he thinks, but I say nothing, offering silent comfort through touch. His hands switch from stroking to tugging before I can say much more. His grip in my hair tightens, and he tilts my head back until I'm staring directly into those rich nearly black eyes.

"I believe I kept my part of the bargain," he murmurs, tracing the line of my lips with his gaze. "So... clothes off."

Then, before I have a chance to comply or ask more questions, he claims my mouth in a fierce kiss.

Trapped between his hands and his lips, I soften, then slowly melt. Slate may be a relentless bastard when it comes to getting what he wants, but there's a whole load of softer, unspoken emotions running between us. His kiss is an apology, a promise, and a declaration of intent all rolled into one seductive mesh of mouths.

It's the kiss of a man who craves me, yet openly plans to use me for his own purposes, and will never apologise out loud for either.

But here, now, in the quiet intimacy of his kiss, he pours his guilt, his need, and his resolve until I moan softly. When he pulls away, I blink for a second, lost in the onslaught of emotion, until he flops onto his back on the bed and grabs my thighs.

"I'm still dressed!" I protest.

He shrugs. "Tough. I gave you the chance to get naked."

I shake out of his grip, hooking my thumbs around the elastic waistband and flinging my shorts away. Slate grabs me again before they have a chance to hit the floor, and this time, he doesn't let me go until I'm hovering directly over his face.

My cheeks heat at the vulnerability of the position. Sure, I've been eaten out before, and sixty-nine is my favourite number, but I'm facing the wrong way to reciprocate, and even if I wasn't, he's fully clothed.

"Sit." Slate growls.

"Like this?" I lower myself slightly, until my pussy is centimetres from his face.

His sharp inhale makes my breath catch, and his answering growl vibrates against my core.

"Sit," he repeats.

I lower slightly more, only to squeak and jerk back when his palm smacks against my ass.

"Sit."

"If you die of suffocation…" I begin, dryly.

Slate loses his patience before I can finish. His arms wrap around my thighs, yanking my body down until my pussy is pressed against his face. His nose nudges my poor clit, and he growls as he fucking devours me. The vibration travels through him, directly to my core, and I can't help when my hips grind down, seeking more of their own accord.

My hands hang awkwardly in the air, fluttering towards his head as if to hold him to me, before I realise the futility of that action and change direction. My top lands in a heap somewhere and my palms caress the aching heaviness of my breasts. Slate groans against me, and my hands clench in answer, massaging my breasts until my mouth falls open on a gasp.

His tongue lashes my pussy, delving past my entrance in the search for more. He eats me out like I'm his favourite desert and he has to savour every last drop.

And when the inevitable happens, and he drives me over that invisible edge to an explosive orgasm, he. Just. Keeps. Going.

"Slate!" I shriek, trembling on top of him.

His hands clench on my ass as he says something, but I can't make it out. The words are too muffled. Still, the hum of them travels straight to my clit, sending me over a second time.

"Slate. I can't," I pant, when it looks like he means to keep going.

I'm too sensitive. Too overwrought.

For a second, I think he's listening to me. His grip on me loosens, and I manage to shift an inch away.

"You fucking can," he promises, breath washing over my tingling flesh.

Without further warning, he dives back in, his lips honing in on my poor, over sensitised clit.

"Slate!" The pleasure turns violent, blazing brilliantly across every nerve ending in a maelstrom that threatens to consume me.

My hands clench on my breasts, fingers trapping my nipples as his hands leave my ass only to come back down with a sharp *crack* that echoes around the room.

The sudden pain blends perfectly with the pleasure, soothing the ragged edges until I'm teetering on the edge of a third orgasm.

"Ah ah ah, you're coming on my cock this time. I want to feel your hot little pussy wrapped around me."

He lets go, and my boneless body tumbles to one side without him there to hold me up. Every single cell in my body cries out, straining for the orgasm that's slowly escaping my grasp while he pushes up and wastes precious seconds stripping. I landed on my front, but I twist my neck to watch over my shoulder as his jeans are discarded, followed by a pair of white boxers.

In seconds, he's completely naked, but he still hesitates at the edge of the bed. My eyes trace his tats, following the trails of lyrics across his ribs and lower to where his dick is bobbing eagerly.

"Hmm, decisions, decisions. You looked damn good riding Dodger's cock, but I've had a million fantasies of watching this ass jiggle as I fuck the living daylights out of you."

I stare at him, open-mouthed. The man has the audacity to leave me on the edge of an orgasm and then sit there debating sex positions while I'm spread open and needy just feet away.

"Just fuck me already!" I protest.

His bright grin is wicked. "Why didn't you just say so?"

Those large hands grab my ankles, yanking me to the edge of the bed before swapping his grip to my hips and pulling me up so my legs are folded beneath me. My arms fly forward, fisting the sheets as he lines himself up at my entrance and shoves home in one swift thrust.

I cry out, a warbling sound that still somehow fails to encapsulate the enormity of the sensations ripping through me as my body goes from empty to stretched to the limit.

"Fuck!" he groans, pulling back, only to slam back in just as roughly.

I told him to fuck me, and he does, jack hammering into my body as my nails claw into his sheets. The slick, wet sounds of our lovemaking fill the air. This position is primitive, but it also allows his cock to rub over sensitive spots I didn't know I had. My body quickly returns to the peak it was denied before, clenching and spasming around his shaft as he chases his own release. I'm so close, I just need that little something more to get me across the line.

Then, as if he's reading my thoughts, one hand leaves my hips and strokes down the crease of my ass. His thumb grazes the sensitive ring of muscle, massaging without pressing too deeply. The pressure, and the dark pleasure it evokes, are all I need.

I fall apart around him, sobbing out my pleasure into the softness of his mattress as his strokes lose their rhythm and his breathing turns harsh.

"Fuck. *Mi reina*. So damn good." He jerks out of me and comes with a groan, spraying my ass and lower back with the evidence of his release.

He rolls onto his back, panting and sweating. His eyes are glazed with pleasure, and it takes him a few minutes to recover.

"You look good wearing my cum," he murmurs, fingers tracing the stickiness into my skin as he recovers.

I stretch out across the covers with an exhausted sigh. "Can you get me a cloth or something?"

I'd go myself, but I don't want to find out if I can make it to the bathroom before gravity takes hold and I end up dripping a mess down my butt and onto the hotel's fancy carpet.

"Leave it." He drags me over his chest so my face is pressed against his pec as he continues to play in the mess we've made. "I get all caveman thinking about you wearing me on your skin."

I raise a brow. "You do *not* need to get any more caveman, mister. You freaking picked me up and carried me off to your cave already."

He barks out a laugh. "I'll give you that one, *rubia*. Let me have a few more minutes of neanderthalism before I clean you up."

There's enough smoulder in his dark gaze that I sigh and give in. "Fine. But don't think this will happen every time."

"Are you sure? Because there are at least three more places on your body I've fantasised about painting with my cum."

I count in my head... "Face, boobs and...?"

"Pussy," he smirks. "I want to watch it run down over your little clit..." He trails off, lost to the fantasy.

I don't know why that's so hot. Maybe it's because he's still drawing patterns in the cooling liquid across my ass with one finger, or perhaps it's just some long-dormant primal part of my psyche popping up to make itself known.

The spiral patterns he's tracing with his finger are actually pretty soothing. Without meaning to, I start mimicking the patterns across his skin, following the flowing lines of black script.

"Discipline equals freedom?" I ask, following three words down the side of his abs.

If it's a lyric, it's not one I recognise, and I thought I knew all the band's songs.

He shrugs. "Something I figured out pretty quick in juvie. As a teenager, I had a massive temper. I was just... *angry*, all the time. Sometimes for good reason, other times..." He pauses. "Other times it was just hormones, I guess. It's what landed me in that place with the others. But being a small kid with a big attitude doesn't get you far behind bars."

I keep quiet, biting my lip. Of all the guys, Slate's crime was arguably the worst. Aggravated assault with a weapon— although his step-dad was really trying to have him done for attempted murder. But since juvie records are sealed, there's no way that any normal person would know that.

"I don't know what the others have told you about our time there..." He trails off, as if hoping I'll interrupt, but I don't. "It was bad in a lot of ways. Dodger had it worse, but the boredom almost broke me. The walls are grey. Your bedding is grey. They serve you bland food. Apart from a few hours of classes, there's nothing to do for most of the day. Lights go out, and you can't do anything but sleep.

"Without creating a disciplined routine that gave me purpose and sticking to it, I would've gone mad. Having that structure, along with the two hours a day we were allocated in the music room, kept me sane." He pauses, fingers lifting from my skin as he glances down at his own abdomen. "After we got out, discipline kept me housed and off the streets until we managed to hit our big break. It got me through working two jobs while getting my online qualifications. The tat is a reminder that when I start to lose sight of myself, discipline will put me on the path back."

"You were inside for longer than the others," I murmur, leaving the statement intentionally open.

He stiffens, finger leaving my spine as he swiftly changes the subject. "Let me get you cleaned up."

Shifting out from underneath me, he heads for the bathroom. Despite the lingering exhaustion from round one, I can't help but watch his ass move as he goes. For all his faults, Slate Fletcher-Reyes has the ass of a god, and I could happily stare at it all day.

When he returns, warm towel in hand, he won't meet my eyes.

"You have the right to know this," he murmurs, beginning the task of cleaning me up with gentle strokes. "But it's not something I'm proud of. I went to juvie because I tried to kill my step-dad after I caught him beating *mi mamá*."

I freeze, sympathy gripping my heart and squeezing. "Slate, I—"

"My dad was killed in a hit and run when I was a baby. She married the bastard because he was a 'man of God.' He wasn't. He was just another slick, righteous *coño* passing as a preacher. The abuse must have been going on a while, but it wasn't until

I was fifteen that I came home from school and caught him smashing her head against the kitchen counter. I didn't think. I just reacted." His eyes finally meet mine. "If given half the chance, I wouldn't just stab him again, I'd finish the fucking job."

Death from multiple shrapnel wounds is infinitely more painful, but I don't say it aloud.

"I don't blame you," I whisper, instead.

"I got my mom to a shelter," he finishes. "Then I handed myself in. She still went back to him as soon as I was behind bars, though. The week before I was due to be released, I got a letter saying I wasn't to return home or contact my family."

"Assholes," I mutter, twisting and taking the towel from him—because I must be clean by now—before throwing it in the direction of the bathroom. With it out of the way, I tug him back into the bed, wrapping the covers around us both.

"It was brave, what you did."

After years of taking out the worst society has to offer, I know better than most that some people deserve to be removed from this world. Slate was just a kid, defending his mom against someone physically stronger and in a position of power. Someone who should've protected and cherished them.

I've half a mind to send their details on to Tabby. She considers taking out abusive assholes a hobby.

He scoffs. "It was stupid. I've gone over the situation a thousand times in my head. If I'd just had a handle on my anger, I could've videoed the whole thing and gotten enough evidence to put that dick away, or at least keep him out of our lives."

I press a kiss to his jaw. "You can't change the past, Slate."

"Nope, but I've learned a valuable lesson from it." His tone darkens, eyes glinting dangerously. "If you want to protect the people you care about, you have to be ruthless."

All my thoughts of sending Slate's step-father's details to Tabby flee in that second. I have a gut feeling that Slate is already well on the way to dealing with his step-father, and when he's finished, the man will wish he'd dealt with an accident at the hands of my sister instead.

Darcy
23

I fell asleep snuggling Slate, but when I wake, he's conspicuously absent. His side of the bed is cold, and there's a tiny folded note on his pillow. I trace the edges with one hand as I scramble for my glasses with the other. When I can finally focus my eyes enough to read, I snort at how messy his writing is. Such a mundane flaw for a rock star to have.

'Morning cariño,

I'm hoping I'll be back by the time you wake, but if not, thank you for last night. It was the best of my life. I can't wait for our group date today. Slate x'

Smiling, because the crazy man left me a love note, I shove my way free of the blankets and wrap myself in one of the plush hotel-supplied robes before heading towards the living area of the suite.

I make it three steps outside Slate's door before I stop dead.

There, on the floor, is Prophet, doing push-ups in the middle of the space. Not just normal push ups either. The show off is doing the fancy one-handed ones.

To make matters worse, he's not wearing a shirt. I can just

make out the dark lines of his band tat over his heart if I look hard enough. Damn. Why does the grumpy one have to be so... drool worthy?

Do not swoon. It's too early in the morning for attractive men, damn it!

He looks up, spots me, and then looks back down again. "Slate's at church," he grunts. "The others are still in bed."

The suggestion is clear: I should go and bother one of them.

Instead, I make my way over to the coffee machine and make myself a large mug of steaming heaven before returning to the sofa. Prophet freezes and shoots me an inscrutable look.

"Am I interrupting your workout?" I ask, raising a single brow.

"No."

There's a pause where he swaps hands, then shifts back to a regular plank position. His arms flex, and I take a swig of coffee to stop myself openly staring.

The two of us lapse into silence as he continues to work out, and I pick up my phone, swiping quickly through Gabrielle's inbox as I look for more information about the Rosales brothers' meeting.

Nothing. There are some vague mentions of "the usual spot" and "the villa," but nothing more definite. If that doesn't change, I'm going to have to download a tracking app to Gabrielle's phone and keep an eye on it throughout the night. Easier said than done when I'm responsible for not setting the guys on fire while they perform.

Regardless, I don't have much of a choice. As a backup, I set the tracker to install using the rootkit, before turning back to watch Prophet.

"You're not even struggling," I comment, as he does the thousandth push up.

It's unfair. He makes it look so easy, but all of my workouts end with me coated in sweat and my hair reduced to a pile of frizz.

"If you want to help, come and sit on my back," he retorts, swiping a hand across his face. "I could use the challenge."

Both of my brows must be in my hairline, but I tip-toe over to him anyway, still clutching my coffee. He drops to his knees, keeping his arms in position.

"Try not to move too much," he orders.

I fumble, almost spilling my coffee as I climb up onto him. God, his back is huge. Roomy, really. I settle, cross-legged, just below his shoulder blades, trying my hardest not to moon over his muscles. As soon as I'm in position, he shifts his legs back to where they were and starts to move.

Jesus, if these guys keep picking me up and lifting me like this, I might actually stop sucking in my belly pooch when I look in the mirror.

I take another sip of coffee, trying to distract myself from the way his body feels bunching and releasing beneath me. My pussy, apparently not satisfied even after last night, perks up, and I know I have to distract myself before the eager bitch does something embarrassing like leaving a damp patch on his back.

"So, Slate said you want to leave the band," I begin.

Prophet's pace doesn't slow. "And he sent you to talk me out of it? Typical."

"He didn't, actually." I pause, sipping my coffee. "But I wanted to hear your side of the story."

"There is no 'side' to this," Prophet retorts, pushing up from the ground and lowering. "Everything I've ever wanted has been shoved aside by this band." He lifts again. "The endless touring." Push. "The constant PR stunts." Push. "Even planning my fucking future." Push. "Because he's used his fucking law degree." Push. "To ensure we're bound together." Push. "For what remains of our incredibly short lives."

Setting aside the fact that Slate has a law degree and didn't even think to mention it, I take a deep breath and let it out thoughtfully.

Prophet's anger is barely contained in every word, but it's not directed at Slate. Not really.

He's angry at the cartel. And I'm willing to bet that underneath all that fury is actually a whole bunch of frustration and fear. He's the only member of the band with a large, close-knit family. That's a whole lot of targets for them to choose from.

"I can see how that's frustrating," I admit. "But do you love it? The music, I mean?"

He stops moving. "Kind of hard to justify loving a career that statistically gives you a shorter lifespan than the average Joe, comes with a two-to-seven times higher rate of suicide, and glorifies promiscuity and dying young."

I hum, taking care to keep my tone even as I answer, "I didn't ask about the job. I asked about the music."

No answer. Slowly, he resumes his workout, retreating behind his usual silence. I'm not surprised. I'm pretty sure that was the most I've ever heard Prophet speak in one go.

"What will you do when you leave?" I ask, switching the subject.

"I was working for an old army buddy of my dad's before the band took off. He was training me to run his gym. It was a good job."

I try to picture him running a gym, and I'm dismayed when I find it far too easy. Unlike the others, who've taken their metal personas to heart with their visible tattoos, leather, and piercings, Prophet could easily put on a polo shirt and walk out of this hotel as a normal guy.

Was that simply his preference, or something more deliberate? A subtler way of keeping his distance from the others?

This time it's my turn to stay silent. I'm caught between the belief that he should be able to choose his own destiny and the knowledge that watching him give up the stage for some job managing a gym would be like watching a lion willingly be declawed and defanged to fit in amongst the sheep.

Both Slate and Prophet have very convincing arguments, and I don't see a way for both of them to get what they want.

One of them has to bend.

"I wouldn't even *need* to work," Prophet mutters. "The band has earned enough money to retire several times over."

I've never heard someone sound so bitter about being loaded, and I take a reflexive sip of my coffee as he continues his workout below me.

"Off," he orders, after a few minutes.

I slip from his back, draining the last of my coffee and depositing the mug on a side table before turning back towards Slate's room. I should probably get dressed and ready for our date. Prophet catches me before I can take more than a step.

"I'm not finished."

Without any further explanation, he crouches down, slips an arm between my legs, and hauls me onto his back in a fireman's carry.

"Prophet!" I squeak, embarrassingly loudly.

Fortunately, he says nothing about the noise. "You said you'd help."

"Yes, with the push ups." My protests cut off as he starts executing perfect squats with me balanced across his shoulders.

"Man, you're making the rest of us look weak," Dodger complains, and I twist my neck to watch as he shuffles out of his room in nothing more than a pair of loose sweats. "Morning, baby girl."

"I didn't sign up for this," I grumble.

"Did Dark scream?" Arlo's head pokes out of his own room, brows creased with concern.

Prophet snorts. "She's fine. Go back to getting ready. We've got to leave when Slate gets back."

In response, the guitarist yawns and retreats back to his room.

Great. No help from him.

"Shouldn't I be getting ready too? I'm a girl. You know we take ages."

Prophet doesn't reply, but Dodger barks out a laugh. "You can't spend as long as Lo does on his hair. Em's got him using half a salon's worth of fancy conditioners and shit."

Emma knows her stuff, because Arlo's hair looks so soft that I really want to pet it.

"I still have to eat."

"I'll make you some toast," Dodger promises.

When the door to the suite opens, Dodger is feeding me my toast as Prophet uses me as a human barbell. I grin at Slate, waving from my current position suspended above the drummer's head.

"What on earth is going on here?" the bassist asks, incredulous.

He's the closest to polished I've ever seen him. If wearing a pressed white shirt with the sleeves turned up and the top button undone over a pair of jeans can count as polished. I suppose, for a rock star, it is.

"I'm being used as a weight," I deadpan. "I'm not sure whether I should be flattered or insulted, really."

"Flattered," Arlo answers. "Prophet is a total weakling. He couldn't do any of this stuff if you were the slightest bit heavy."

I grin at his blatant lie. Prophet, finally finished, lets me drop back onto my own two feet at last. I swipe the last of my buttery toast from Dodger and skip forward to hug Slate.

"Morning, *cariño*," he mumbles against my hair. "Ready to go see your tide pools and butterflies?"

"Yes." I can't help my grin as I dart away from the lot of them, heading for Slate's room and my clothes. "Let me just throw on some clothes."

The band may have its problems, but I'm determined that we're all going to have fun on this trip.

Prophet
24

Darcy is glowing. She flits between the plants of the butterfly house like a hummingbird, cooing over every single insect as if it's the most precious thing. Talking to them like they're old friends. She even reads every. Single. Sign.

Who does that?

Even Slate, the wordy genius among us, doesn't bother with much more than a passing glance to learn the names. Arlo ignores them entirely. He and Dodger are too busy staring at the blonde bombshell as she dances between exhibits.

She's such a science geek. I mean, I knew she was a nerd, but this is like seeing an entirely different side of her.

I'm well aware that I'm quickly becoming as entranced as the rest of them, but I'm also powerless to stop it. It doesn't help that every single time I do something to distance myself, I feel like shit afterwards.

I don't even know why I chucked my keys in that damn bowl—why I *keep* doing it. My common sense is screaming at me that Darcy—and everything she represents—is dangerous. She's the bait Slate has selected to trap me in the band for the rest of my life. If this relationship with her breaks down, it will ruin our friendship for all time.

I know this.

Yet somehow, I'm still hopeless when it comes to her.

Maybe it's because she's already under my defences. Ten years of hanging out, of hearing about her day, about her loser exes, her ups and downs, her arguments with her sisters. A decade of teasing and taunts.

I have a plan: get out of this band, save my family before they're killed because Arlo convinced me to sign that fucking deal, and get back on track to a normal life. I'm closer to forty than thirty, for fuck's sake. I should have my shit figured out by now.

Instead, I'm hitched to the Hazardous crazy train, like I've always been.

"Prophet, grab a picture, quick!" Dodger's voice cuts me out of my bitter thoughts, and I glance up to find a huge orange butterfly has made itself at home on top of Darcy's head.

She's trying her best not to move, but her eyes are almost crossed as she tries her best to catch sight of her hitchhiker.

"She must like my shampoo," Darcy whispers, awestruck.

My phone is in my hand before I can think better of it, snapping the shot. Not a moment too soon, because the insect flutters away in the next second.

Then she's there, in my space, tiny hands gripping my wrist as she turns my phone to examine the picture.

The corner of her lips turns down a fraction, but it's gone before I can point it out, replaced with awe. "Oh wow! That's huge!"

"The girl under it is pretty cute too," Arlo adds, peeking over her shoulder.

She waves him off with a tiny blush, then skips away. "Come on. The tide pools are this way!"

Before I follow, I send the photo to the group chat, grinning as the *ba dum tss* echoes from up ahead. When my phone dings a second later, I assume it's her, and check with a half-smile on my face.

No such luck.

> **Gabrielle**
> A last-minute photo op has come up. Get back to the hotel and bring the others with you. Dress for sailing.

"Come on, Prophet," Darcy calls from up ahead. "They have anenomenomes, anemo—you know! The colourful sea things with cute wavy hair!"

"Anemones," Dodger corrects, dryly.

The sound of a raspberry floats through the plants to me, and I glance down at my phone again. Gabrielle's message floats around on my lock screen accusingly, and every cautious part of me warns that, depending on Miguel's mood, ignoring her could see a repeat of what happened to Darcy's room. Especially if he learns that she was the reason we didn't follow orders.

Let him try, I think savagely. *We'll just buy her new clothes.*

All I want is one day to ourselves with our girlfriend. I mean, *friend* who happens to also be a girl and definitely not ours—mine. Fuck.

Tonight, we're on stage again, and after that, we've got early flights to Austin. We deserve a tiny break.

I turn off my phone and drop it into my pocket before jogging after the others, praying that I don't regret this.

I almost expect Gabrielle to try the others' phones, but if she does, they're just as guilty of ignoring her as I am. To be fair, it's easy to ignore your phone when Darcy is around, smiling so brightly as she gently dips her slender fingers into the tide pool and hums with happiness as the starfish tries to climb onto her hand.

"Should I add an aquarium to the list of requirements for that house you want?" Slate asks casually—too casually—as he leans against the side of the tank, watching her. "I'm sure we could have one of those cool glass walls with jellyfish in if you wanted."

Darcy rolls her eyes at him. "That's just ostentatious."

"Ouch." Dodger presses a hand against his heart in mock pain. "You realise we're rock stars, right? Ostentatious is part of the territory."

She laughs them off. "Well, I'm not, so I think I can live without that shit."

"But we'll need a proper gaming room," Slate continues, and I glare at him.

It's obvious what he's doing. Painting a picture of the future. Tempting me.

"Obviously," Darcy retorts. "But computers are far easier to keep alive than fish."

Arlo shrugs. "It says here they aren't fish. They're cnidaria."

Darcy chooses that moment to drop one of the biggest bombshells of my life. "Actually, there's technically no such thing, scientifically, as a fish." *What the...? No such thing as a fish?* "Regardless," she continues, without bothering to explain. "I don't fancy keeping something which can sting me as a pet."

Slate doesn't miss a beat. "I guess bees are out too, then?"

She shakes her head in disbelief. "I'm all for saving the bees, just as long as they stay far, far away from me."

"And me," I grouch, groaning internally as I realise Slate's plan has worked to draw me into the conversation. "You know I'm allergic."

Darcy blinks, then mumbles something like. "I thought

you were just allergic to smiling." Then her face brightens as she adds, "As long as my office is good, and we're close enough to a great pizza place, I don't care much about the rest of the house. It's more about the people who live in it, anyway." Her expression dims for a second. "Most of my sisters have moved out to be with their guys now, and I actually really miss having people around all the time. Not necessarily to talk to, but just the noise, you know? I like knowing that people are there."

I can relate. My two other sisters moved their young families out-of-state years ago in an attempt to shake the cartel. Even though Destiny stayed—too stubborn to give in when she was being threatened—I still miss Page and Shayla. Some small stupid part of my brain expects them to just be there whenever I return to our parents' house.

Darcy's lonely, I realise. Before I can so much as begin to fumble for the words to cheer her up, Arlo is there, dragging her into a sideways hug. "Well, you won't have to worry about being alone with four boyfriends."

"Yeah," Slate continues. "Most of the time, you'll probably just want to order us all out of the house so you can get some peace and quiet."

Her smile returns, and she shocks us all when she tilts her head back and kisses Arlo softly on his lips. "I suppose musicians can be quite noisy. I might have to get ear plugs."

If it was that much of an issue, I'd build us a studio in the yard.

I cut the thought off before I can fall into mentally planning the perfect space.

Because this is not happening. It's not the plan.

The plan is safety for my family, a normal fucking job, and a two person relationship where I don't have to worry about jealousy screwing things up.

Our guitarist is too stunned by her affection to reply, but

Slate swoops in. "If you're handing out kisses, *cariño*, I want one too."

Without pause, he pinches her chin between his forefinger and thumb and pulls her in for a kiss that fucking sizzles with chemistry.

I wish it wasn't so damn hot to watch. My hardon is pressing at the seam of my jeans like a heat-seeking missile focused solely on Darcy. I grimace and turn away, wishing I could adjust myself. Unfortunately, this place is packed, and that means I'm just going to suffer.

When we finally leave the centre, it's early afternoon, and time for the next part of our surprise. I know for a fact that Dodger booked lunch in the Space Needle, and a part of me can't wait to see Darcy's reaction to the revolving restaurant.

All my daydreams of her smiling face fade away as I catch sight of the familiar black escalade waiting for us on the curb outside.

Shit, where's Darcy?

My head swivels as I try to locate her before Miguel or his cronies can.

"*¡Mierda!*" Slate curses under his breath at the sight. "Darcy, go back inside. Now."

Fortunately, her position behind me means that my bulk is keeping her hidden. *Stay out of sight,* I silently pray. If they don't notice her, she's unlikely to get into trouble.

But being Darcy, she has to ask, "What? Why?"

"Baby girl, don't ask questions, please. Just trust us." Dodger is already steering her back towards the exit.

There's a suspicious glint in her eyes that I don't trust, but she allows herself to be sealed back to safety, just in time for the rear door of the escalade to swing open in invitation.

The message is clear: Get in.

Shit. Time to face the music.

Darcy
25

The second the band gets into the car, I fire up the tracking apps on their phones and watch as their dots coalesce on the map, before heading to the port. My phone *ribbits* a second before Arlo's dot buzzes violently —an alert connected to sudden movement of the gyrometer— before then his dot blinks out entirely.

Shit. Someone destroyed his phone.

At the top of my screen, his final message flashes up.

> **[HzD]Fr0gg0**
> Hey, sorry we had to jump out on our date like that. We're just doing some emergency PR stuff. Head back to our rooms and use Dodger's card to grab pizza. We'll see you in the arena.

Aww, that's kind of sweet that he was sorry for abandoning me, but at the same time, why was his phone destroyed? What the hell is going on? Stepping out into the crowd, I head towards the safety of the busy fountain opposite the science centre, sticking to the shade of the trees, along with the other tourists. A few more taps at my screen activate the mic in Slate's phone.

I press my speaker against my ear just in time to hear Prophet growl, *"That was unnecessary."*

Slate curses. *"You really want his face to look fucked up on stage tomorrow night?"*

"His puta *sister can hide it."* Miguel dismisses them. *"Your druggie friend needs to remember to look at me and not his fucking phone when I'm talking to him.*

"Gabrielle sent a message telling you to be ready for a photo-shoot hours ago, and instead I find you're all playing around in some stupid science park for kids! I have a hundred bricks to drop into the Puget Sound before midnight, and I can't do that without some spoilt rich pricks goofing around above deck to distract attention." He pauses. *"You're all behaving like you're not here to do a job. Don't forget, I fucking gave you that stage. I can rip it all away with a snap of my fingers if you fuck this up for me."*

"We get the point," Dodger says, tersely. *"We're here now. Let's just get it over with."*

"I don't think you do *get the point,"* Miguel argues. *"Because this is the second time you've decided to piss off and do your own thing on this tour. Third strike means blood,* cabrón, *and yours is too valuable."*

The car goes quiet, and I have to remind myself to keep moving.

"The girl was there," Gabrielle's voice is small, almost a squeak in the quiet. *"Our man saw her leave the building after we left. What would you like him to do?"*

Shit. I have a tail? Usually I'm sharper than this!

"She's just my latest fuck." Dodger's voice echoes from my phone, but I'm too busy rummaging in my bag to pay much attention. *"She's nothing."*

"Good job scaring her into our beds with your little trashing her room stunt," Slate says.

"If you want to get rid of her before she gets clingy, I'd appreciate it," Dodger finishes.

That's a lie. It's got to be, right? I shove the tiny, insecure voice that wants me to believe otherwise into the depths of my mind and focus on my tail.

Slipping my phone into my bag, I draw out the compact mirror, stop, and pretend to check my makeup. It takes a minute of filtering through people to find the one focused on me. When I find him, he's little more than a slim shadow lurking behind the ice cream stand on the other side of the fountain.

Keeping him in my sights, I take a path around the edge of the water, skipping between groups as I head for the busy pavilion. Once I'm inside, it's a simple matter of ducking into a staff-only area, pulling my sunhat and sunglasses out of my bag and ditching my jacket while I search for an exit.

I keep my steps purposeful and don't draw any attention.

There. Fire exit.

I shove through it and out into the courtyard beyond.

Good luck finding me now, asshole.

I order an Uber back to the hotel, ignoring my chatty driver in favour of keeping my attention on the guys. Once I'm in the suite, I switch to monitoring the situation from my laptop.

As payback for whatever Miguel did to Arlo, I carefully track the boat they're on until it stops in the bay and then report the location straight to the feds.

I don't have long before I have to leave for the arena, but as an extra fuck you to the cartel, I include a list of suspicious locations where Gabrielle's phone has been in the last day or so. Most of them are warehouses by the docks, and I'm willing to bet more than one of them contains narcotics.

I'm so distracted by my petty revenge that I'm late for setup, but Sully says nothing as I rush through my work and then speed through the safety talk. The boys are uncharacteristically silent and glum as they follow me silently across the stage, and it worries me, but when the lights go down and they take to the stage for real, you'd never know they were feeling off.

They're professionals who love their fans. They'd never give the crowd anything less than they deserve.

I try to speak to them as they come offstage, but they're whisked off to the VIP meet and greet before I can get close. Grumbling at how hard it is to get a hold of any of them, I send the group chat a message instead and switch my focus to packing up as fast as possible. As I work, I devise a plan to cheer them up when they return to the hotel.

When I make it back to our suite before them, I change quickly into my pyjamas, order pizza, and start up my laptop. When they get back, we can play MarioKart. I've got enough controllers, and no one can be mad after a few rounds of Rainbow Road.

Well, maybe Prophet can...

I don't know how long they'll be, but I make use of the time while I wait. Poor Gabrielle has no clue that her phone is my key to wiping every single fund from the Rosales brothers' ludicrously fat bank accounts. I won't do it yet, but I want to have everything in place for when I finally blow the assholes sky high.

She's had contact with all of them, phone numbers, email addresses; it's all there. Everything I need to quietly take over their digital lives. Sure, they have firewalls, security, all the usual stuff, but since I already have my access point, those things are meaningless.

She even has a list of all their properties, including a certain villa east of El Paso.

That's got to be the place where they're meeting. It fits with the tour plan and all the subtle references in their emails.

While my programs are running, I start checking out the stage for my mission. It's an old, privately owned villa in the hills. The lighting looks spotty, given the hundreds of unanswered maintenance requests, which means plenty of places to hide. The building is so old that the tiles are falling away from the roof, and the paint on the walls is peeling. The windows are grimy, and a quick check of the records shows it's registered under one of Roberto Rosales' aliases. It's also far enough from the city that I'll need to drive.

I send Man a quick email, letting him know I'll need a car delivered to the arena on that day, then settle into creating more back doors into the Rosales' network. I don't want to risk accidentally getting shut out on the day of a mission and going in blind.

It still takes hours. My eyes are dry and my back clicks as I finally step away from my laptop, but I'm still feeling pretty pleased with myself when the guys return. I stand up, ready to offer to reheat the pizza, but my words dry up as I take in Arlo's black eye and their solemn expressions. Taking a step forward, I try to hug him, only to be brushed off. My arms, unsure what to do now that I've been rejected, wrap around my middle, defensively.

The four of them are standing in a line, forming a solid unit of impenetrable muscle and tattoos as they loom over me. For the first time, how small they make me feel becomes an intimidating thing, rather than something to be smiled about.

"What's wrong?" I ask, hating the way my voice shakes. "What happened? Why are you looking at me like that?"

"*Cariño*—Darcy." Slate has to physically force himself to say my actual name. "We've been talking, and we think we were wrong about this." He gestures to the space between us. "It won't work. You're just... too much."

I bite my lip, gut sinking with dread at those two little words. *Too much*. Why is it never the other way around? Why can't the man ever just admit that he's not enough?

Somehow, the words coming from him feel a hundred times harsher than they ever were before. Perhaps because Slate *knows* how much that phrase irks me. How it's been used to hurt me in the past.

"Let me guess, it was fun while it lasted?" I can't help the bitterness coating the words as I take a step away.

"Exactly," Dodger says, cutting in. "We're not compatible, and today proved that."

Don't do this. "Let me get my stuff."

I know what they're doing, but it feels far too real. Because this time it isn't Tommy, or Dustin, or Eric saying those words, it's *my guys*. The ones I trust above all others. Thank God I've had practice keeping my head held high in the aftermath of a dozen other break ups. Otherwise, I might've caved to the desire to beg them to reconsider.

I'm all too familiar with the feeling of having my heart stomped on until all I have left is my dignity—and even that is hanging by a fragile thread right now. I have to fight hard to draw air into my frozen lungs, making my body move when all I really want to do is curl up into a ball around the bruised organ.

God, it's been a while since it hurt this much.

"You're not even going to fight us?" Arlo asks, astonished.

Grovelling never helped before, I think viciously, even as my shoulder raises in a nonchalant half-shrug.

"I figured it wouldn't work out. You guys are rock stars, after all. Why bother settling for commitment when you don't have to? It's fine." I pause. "I'm sure I'll have other options."

It's somehow uniquely satisfying to watch all four of them react to my words. I would say I feel sorry for being so callous, but then, I'm not the idiots who decided to dump me out of some stupid, misguided sense of nobility.

Now that I've had a second to think past the immediate pain, I have no doubt that's what this is. I should've expected it from the second Miguel threatened blood, but I let my emotions cloud my judgement. It's only natural that they're getting me out of the danger zone. I'd do the same in their place. It doesn't make it any less shitty, or fix the four-way rip in my heart, but I understand.

"I'm sure I'll find somebody," I continue, heading for Slate's room and shoving my laptop into my bag. "There are several billion other candidates, after all. If not, there's always plan B."

"Plan B?" Slate echoes, eyes narrowing.

I turn and roll my eyes at him, pretending like it isn't taking my all to keep a straight face, as I say. "Women don't need men to give them babies anymore, Slate. We have IVF and adoption for that. I think I'd do okay as a single mom."

That's a total lie. Being a single parent is tough as shit. It might have been one of the options on the table before I met these idiots, but it was never one I felt comfortable with. Given the demands of my job and the travel, it would've been unfair to my child.

I shove my chargers and dirty clothes into my case with trembling hands, zipping it up jerkily before heading for the door.

"For the record," I add, turning to face them one last time before I leave. Prophet is the only one with the guts to meet my gaze, and I memorise his mismatched eyes. "I'm glad we finally met in real life, even if it didn't work out. I'll keep out of your way from now on."

I shut the door behind me, ignoring the security guard posted outside as I start down the corridor.

A heavy thump, followed by the crash of broken glass,

follows me down to reception, but I don't look back. I don't even book a new room in the hotel. Instead, I walk the two blocks to a different one down the street in the dark, silently daring anyone to notice the burning tear tracks down my face.

Out of all the messy break ups in my life, this ranks amongst the worst. I think I always knew it would. That's why I resisted so much and insisted on my stupid "trial period."

In the end, it doesn't even matter. This would never have lasted beyond the end of the tour. Those four aren't ready for a long-term relationship, let alone children. There's too much unresolved shit between them for it to ever work out.

As soon as my stuff is unpacked, I pick up the phone and order a pizza. If I happen to sob on the phone... well, the dude on the other end of the line isn't getting paid enough to pretend to care.

S ully stands in the wreckage of our hotel room, open-mouthed.

There's pizza and glass everywhere, and I shift my weight from one foot to the other as I try to imagine what he's thinking right now. Dodger and Arlo are both gone, leaving me and Prophet to try to avoid the stare of our production manager.

Everyone thinks that Prophet is the one with a temper, but unfortunately Sully knows us well enough to know exactly whose fault this is.

"Well, I've seen some shitty behaviour from you boys in the past, but this..." He scrubs at his face with one hand. "What the hell happened? You're not fighting again?"

"Slate lost it," Prophet grunts, unnecessarily.

Like he's any better.

"How many hours did you spend in the gym this morning?" I retort.

I don't need him to remind me of how badly I lost control. I haven't had an outburst like this since—

I cut off the thought and go back to purposefully making myself feel every second of a deep breath, letting it out in a long, slow exhale. How many freaking classes did I take to get myself under control? How many therapy sessions? It's been years. I thought I'd mastered this.

This feels like a slap in the face. A failure.

"What happened?" Sully asks again, gentler this time.

Prophet just turns away, scrubbing his hand down his face. I guess it's up to me to explain, though it's the last thing I feel like doing.

"We broke up with Darcy."

Sully shakes his head. "All this over a girl?"

"Not just any girl," I retort. "*The* girl. Miguel threatened her, and we decided you were right. It's just not safe for us to have her."

Calling Darcy "a girl" is like calling the sun "just a star." Yeah, it's technically the same thing, but it massively under-states the impact she has on our lives.

The old man folds his arms and pinches the bridge of his nose. "You could've decided I was right before you started dating and saved yourself all this angst. She's already on his radar now."

"She's not." Prophet slumps on the sofa.

"We told him she was just Dodger's latest fuck toy." And I felt like dirt for playing along. "He made sure to keep whining about how clingy she was every time Miguel or his lackeys were in earshot."

Some of the shit he said made me want to deck him. Our girl's enthusiasm is a glowing thing that makes life seem fuller when we're around her. After a day spent loudly talking shit about her to throw Miguel off her scent, I was already wound tight. Coming back here to have her just walk out, without even fighting for us, was the match that lit the fuse.

The moment the words were out of my mouth, I knew I'd fucked up. I should never have let Prophet convince me that this was a good idea. My conviction started to wane the second

I saw the hurt in her eyes. Yes, Darcy's safety is everything, but every single atom in my body is telling me we made the wrong choice.

We should've just told her what she was really dealing with and let her decide. I know our past isn't exactly a glowing example of us at our best, but keeping this whole thing from her has just driven the five of us further apart.

"We have to get her back," I mutter under my breath. "Sully, we need a way out of this. Come on. There must be some evidence you've found that will be enough to get Miguel shut away."

I know we'll probably have to take a plea deal if Miguel is arrested. We'll probably have to serve more time inside because of it. For all that we're actively working against him, and we technically have nothing to do with his operations, we're accomplices because we earn money from the gigs.

I hate that dirty money, but we've done our best to do good with it. We've funded more philanthropic causes than any other band in history. Maybe Darcy will wait for us until we've served our sentence, but can we really ask that of her?

Do we have any choice, when the alternative is watching her move on with someone else?

Sully shakes his head. "We're not there yet, and we have to be careful with this. Just give me a few more days." He looks around, noting the open bedroom doors. "Where are the other two?"

I shrug. "They left."

I was in too much of a blind rage to notice them disappearing, but I'm not surprised that they did. Arlo hates conflict—always has—and Dodger doesn't deal well with stress because it triggers his insomnia, so he probably gave up and went for a walk.

"Left?! Boys, you have to be on a jet to Vegas in two hours."

"We're here," Dodger announces, striding through the open door.

His clothes are grubby and dishevelled, there are huge shadows under his eyes, and his hair is a mess.

Great. He definitely hasn't slept. I give him a pitying look that he throws off with a roll of his eyes.

"We have bigger problems. Arlo decided to get high." He drags the guitarist into the room and shoves him towards us.

"Stop pushing me everywhere," Arlo complains, his words falling over each other. "I'm fine. And I can get high if I want to. I'm a rock star, for fuck's sake. It's what we do."

The normal, quiet guitarist is gone. Dodger's holding his sunglasses, so we can all see Arlo's blown pupils and the way his eyes are darting from left to right. Great. Now we get to deal with his hyperactive alter-ego chatting shit for hours on end.

That's when the real hell begins. He'll deal with hours and hours of nerves and anxiety until he's ready to take another hit just to make it stop.

Fuck.

I look up at Prophet, silently asking for a truce. As much as he wants out, he still gives a fuck about Arlo, so I'm not surprised when he nods.

"Buddy system," Prophet grumbles with a sigh. "He goes nowhere alone, and *nowhere* near Miguel."

Step one, limit exposure and alone time. Our manager has always kept Arlo with a never-ending supply of blow, either directly, or via his "friends." When Arlo first tried to quit, things turned ugly, fast. It quickly became obvious that Miguel likes keeping all of us on a tight leash.

The slimy asshole caught on to our tactics and started slipping more and more drugs into Arlo's pockets, into the glove box of his car, every cabinet of his house. We even caught some taped to the underside of a hotel sink once.

So on top of quitting and dealing with the temptation of coke being literally everywhere he turned, Arlo had to keep up the charade of being an addict. At least he dropped his old friends ages ago. Now it's only Miguel we need to worry about.

"Agreed," Dodger mutters, falling back into the pattern with ease. "I've got the first hour."

"Hey, guys, it's no big deal. I've got this." Arlo grins, ignoring our worried looks. "I have the best idea for a song. I can already see the melody..."

¡Mierda!

There it is. The temptation. Euphoria. Every single cell of his body is up, alert, and awake. Confident in a way he never normally is.

It won't last.

Already, I can see the sweat beading at his hairline, and his hands tracing lines up and down his arms. When he was using regularly, he picked his skin to shit—coke bugs are no joke. Then there's the paranoia, the anger, the depression.

I sigh. At least he didn't overdose and end up in the ER this time. His life is in a much better place now than it was when he used to abuse the stuff. Perhaps that will help. After the rehab program, we learned a ton about supporting someone going sober, and we knew relapse was possible.

Hopefully, when he sees Emma's reaction and realises what he's done, he'll cooperate and go back to being clean. It won't make the withdrawals suck any less, but hopefully we can get him over this hill before Darcy notices.

When he comes down, he won't want her seeing this.

"I'll take second shift," I offer.

Sully sighs, pacing away from us. "You boys get your shit together and get on that plane. I'll get your evidence, but there's no point doing all this if you get yourselves killed."

———

ARLO STARTS TO COME DOWN MIDWAY THROUGH the flight to Vegas. It's easy to tell, but I think that might just be because I'm used to the signs. He stops talking so much and starts looking around more, checking for invisible threats. He's rubbing his arms, but hasn't started picking again yet.

I let Emma know what happened, and as predicted, she struggled with the news. Lo's baby sister is too tough to cry, but her breathing was shaky from the moment the news broke until I hung up the phone. She offered to help, but we all know how many memories this is dredging up for her. Ems spent her childhood dealing with junkies going through withdrawal, and Arlo's right not to want to put her through it again.

Instead, Dodger keeps close to our guitarist, fetching him water, forcing him to eat, and making sure the sketchbook is on hand as he switches rapidly between a familiar cycle of irritation, paranoia, and exhaustion.

At least he hasn't thrown up this time.

The second we land, we're thrust right into the thick of things. I take point during sound check and rehearsal, deflecting attention away from Arlo at all costs, but there's no fixing the fact that we have to see Darcy for the safety talk.

She's late, which isn't making the anticipation crawling beneath my skin any easier to bear. When she finally steps up on stage, she steals the breath from my lungs, and Arlo stiffens beside me.

"Shit," Prophet mutters, too quietly for her to hear.

She's not foregone her usual nerdy style, but her N7 dress is skin tight and clings to every curve of her body as she climbs the six steps up to the stage. I make a mental note to send a thank you note to whoever designed it, because the cut of the neckline shows off her gorgeous tits to full advantage. The hem is short enough that I want to get on my knees and beg her to lift the skirt just a few inches higher.

Add in the spiked collar around her throat, just begging me to replace it with my hand, and I'm a goner. She might as well walk all over me in her Doc Martens.

Then I meet her eyes behind the lenses of her glasses. The cool, indifferent stare she levels at the four of us over her clipboard freezes my ardour in my veins.

Yeah, her gaze seems to say, *you gave up all right to this*.

"The flamethrowers are going to announce you onto the stage, as normal," she begins, all business as she turns to point out the front of the stage.

Dios mio. Her ass in that dress is lethal.

"Fuck me." Dodger coughs to cover the curse.

To make matters worse, two minutes later, she drops her pencil and ends up bending over directly in front of us. Her heart-shaped ass is right *there*, and only two paces and her panties are between her pussy and my tongue. If I fell to my knees and tasted her, would she be tart with anger, or would she be just as sweet as before?

That's when I understand what this is.

Revenge.

We're the latest in a long line of disappointing jerks who've dumped her, and now she's trying to kill us.

We're going to be on stage with the mother of all erections, knowing she's down below, wearing that damned dress.

Prophet's eyes go heavenward in a prayer for deliverance, but I'm pretty sure the closest any of us could get to salvation is between Darcy's thighs, and we've locked ourselves out.

Not one of us manages to get any words out. We just follow her around like dumb sheep as she delivers the talk.

Then, when she disappears at the end, and we're left alone, her perfume lingers in the air.

"Remind me again why we're doing this?" Dodger

mutters under his breath as he passes me, his expression tortured.

"Some stupid, noble bullshit," I grunt. "I vote we go back to the plan."

Prophet's hand comes round behind me and cuffs me upside the head. "No."

I glance at Arlo, hoping for backup, only to find him spacing out.

"You okay?" I ask, softly.

"Yeah." One word, delivered softly, but by his sides, his hands are trembling. "Aching a bit."

No, he's not okay. "Come on. Let's get something to drink."

It's important to keep him hydrated; plus, I can hear Miguel heading towards us, and I don't want to risk him sneaking Arlo anything while the temptation to take more to stall the comedown is still strong.

Taking his arm, I guide him off stage on the hunt for a vending machine.

"Why haven't you all just given up on me?" he asks, breaking the silence.

I miss a step, stumbling before I manage to right myself. "Why the fuck would we do that?"

"I'm an addict. I got you all into this mess when you warned me not to get involved with Miguel. Now we're back to this again, all because I couldn't deal with my own shitty emotions."

"I'm a pushy bastard with a temper," I retort. "Dodger can't deal with stress to the point where he goes AWOL for hours at a time. Prophet is so stubborn that we could literally shove proof he was wrong in front of his nose and he wouldn't believe us."

His brows rise above the rims of his sunglasses. "Those are personality flaws, not a drug problem."

I'm pretty sure an addictive personality counts as a flaw too, but I don't want to get into an old argument. It won't stop how shitty he's feeling right now.

I shrug, uncomfortable. "When I got that letter telling me not to bother coming home, you remember what you did?"

Dodger and Arlo got out of juvie on the same day, two weeks before me. Dodger was in a shitty place, thanks in part to his mom dying while he was inside, so I wasn't going to bother him, but I told Arlo.

He shrugs. "That was a long time ago."

I jam the buttons on the machine, waiting impatiently for it to hand out our drinks. "You went out and found a bunk bed for your room in Dodger's house, so I had somewhere to sleep."

It was the most uncomfortable bed I've ever slept in, probably because he got it from a garage sale for cheap, but it meant the world to a kid who'd been unexpectedly made homeless.

Dodger never charged us rent, despite how useless we both were around the house. I was eating up money trying to put myself through online classes while working shit-paying janitor jobs. Arlo was desperately trying and failing to make a commission business turn a profit with his art while taking night shifts at a factory.

What little money we had left, we were scrimping together and spending on pedalboards, amps, and Gibsons just to score gigs at seedy bars in a vain effort to get noticed.

We both knew how Dodger was paying the bills, but he always made it clear that it was his choice.

"Yeah, well. You paid me back." Arlo runs his hands over his arms again, and I thrust a bottle of water at him.

"We look after each other," I finish. "That's why I'm not going to let Prophet break up this band. That's why when this is over, we're going to do whatever it takes to win her back."

"She'll have moved on," Arlo mopes. "She said it herself. She has options."

Taking a deep breath, I force back the fury at the idea of anyone laying hands on our girl and shake my head to clear the image of her with some faceless fuck.

"Darcy will take us back," I promise. "You heard Sully; we just have to make it to El Paso. That's our ticket to freedom. Then we can apologise to her. We'll pull out all the stops. Propose to her on the Eiffel Tower or something."

Arlo scoffs. "She'd hate that."

Eh, he's probably right. She's not really into clichés. Unfortunately, I think a proposal on the bridge of the UNSC Pillar of Autumn is out of the question. What really matters there is that Arlo never objected to proposing to her.

He's still in.

"We'll leave the romantic details to you and the makeup sex to Dodger," I retort. "The point is, this is all going to work out."

I hope.

Darcy
27

The next two days are awkward as hell. My heart might be broken into tattered pieces, but the rest of the world marches on, regardless. When I'm not working for the band, I hide in my room, diving into the cartel's servers and ignoring everyone. Hazardous plays in Phoenix and then finally moves on to El Paso, and the awkwardness between the five of us is tangible. Every member of the road crew is keenly aware that I'm no longer staying in their hotel room or flying on their jet—like it's any of their business.

The gossip mill is going wild, spitting all sorts of wild theories that range from the believable to the obscure. The best one had me dumping the band in favour of a relationship with Emma, even though she's not spoken to me once since.

Thankfully, Sully has been quick to snap the gossipers back to work. Once going so far as to offer me a sympathetic pat on the shoulder as he passed. I say a silent thanks for his interference as I pick my way across the backstage area just after setting off the final gerbs for the encore.

The brothers' meeting is scheduled for after the show. Too

close to the end of the concert for me to pack down with the rest of the crew and then go. So I have to sneak out.

Fortunately for me, backstage is chaos as everyone focuses on packing the trucks to drive to Austin overnight. I wore my darkest clothes in an effort to blend in, but I don't think it was necessary, given how little attention I'm paid.

Until I'm almost at the door. "Hey, Darcy?"

I turn, offering Nate, one of the lighting techs, a bland smile. "What's up?"

"Have you seen Sully?"

Sully? Usually, he's not hard to find. "No. Should I have?"

He groans and turns, head twisting from side to side as if he hopes Sully will pop out from a corner. "Don't worry. I'm sure he's here somewhere."

Thankfully, he's clearly too distracted by Sully's disappearance to ask where I'm going, and I breathe a sigh of relief as I slip out of a side door and head to the coordinates Man texted me two hours before the concert.

All of my stuff is neatly packed into the waiting Jeep, but I still check it all over before I change into the fireproof jacket and trousers that are essential in my line of work.

As a young teen, Man made me sit through hundreds of lessons on the importance of fire-safe clothing and how to tackle different types of fire. Running my fingers over the line of different extinguishers he's provided, I can't help but smile as a wave of nostalgia washes over me. I still remember our adopted father quizzing me daily for weeks until the difference between electrical, petrol, and paper fires was ingrained in my memory deeper than my own name.

Once I'm certain everything is ready, I silence the butterflies in my stomach and slip out onto the empty midnight roads. Anticipation thrums in my veins, eagerness making my fingers clench on the wheel as I weave my way through the city to the hills beyond.

I love my job. I love watching the moment everything falls into place and the entire horizon flashes with the beautiful glow of fire, and this feels even sweeter because this time it's personal.

Maybe I was destined to be a pyromaniac from the moment child-me watched that little white church burn to the ground with my parents and everyone else trapped inside. It certainly started me down the path.

My fascination with fire led to some... interesting developments when I became old enough to play with matches. Instead of confiscating everything flammable and sending me to therapy like any other parent, Man chose to help me use my obsession to take out my marks.

I've always been grateful for that.

My deep thoughts cut off as I turn the Jeep away from the main road and onto a dirt track. The desert offers very little in the way of cover, so I'll be forced to park further away than I'd like to avoid being noticed. Fortunately, Man provided the perfect car for a little off-roading, and I have no trouble going deeper into the arid hills.

Once I find a good spot to park, I crawl into the backseat to get set up.

My case clicks open, and I balance my laptop on the centre console as I click my little reconnaissance bot onto the underside of the delivery drone. I only need three drones for this mission. One to carry the bot, one to do a sweep of the area to prevent innocents from getting caught in the crossfire, and a third to deliver the payload that's going to ensure the Rosales brothers meet their end in a fiery inferno.

The camera feeds from all three drones pop up on my screens, and I check all of them before I open the window and throw the first out. I've got Drone 1 programmed to do a sweep of the hills and alert me to heat signatures—thank you, Tabby, for infrared cameras. The dry desert air rushes in, smelling faintly of earth with a slight herbal undertone I can't name as I start prepping the second.

Drone 2—the one with my little bot—takes to the air a few minutes later, once I've confirmed that the only activity by the villa is from the three SUVs parked outside. Unfortunately, they're idling, which means they're throwing off enough heat that it's impossible to tell how many goons are inside.

This drone flies straight towards the cars, approaching from a blind spot and slipping noiselessly to the ground just long enough to deposit the bot on the ground.

A few taps later, and my little hexapod buddy comes online, stretching out his limbs as his camera switches on. The drone dropped him perfectly behind one of the cars, and he's small enough that I can easily remotely manoeuvre him beneath the huge black vehicles and position him to spy on the meeting that doesn't appear to have started yet.

A chirp from my taskbar alerts me to another two vehicles climbing the small track up to the villa. Both large SUVs with blacked-out windows.

Someone's late, but is it Miguel, or his brothers?

I use the time it takes them to make it up the hill to adjust my bot until the camera can show me most of the driveway. I consider briefly turning on the night vision, but as soon as the two latecomers join them, they switch on their headlights. Together, all five cars form a rough circle of light that illuminates the dark space.

Their security gets out first, nodding silently to one another as they take positions facing away from the meeting. They're followed by Gabrielle and Miguel, who emerge from separate cars.

That seals it. If she's here, she dies with the rest.

The car above my bot rocks slightly as the other two Rosales brothers make their appearance at last.

Joaquin and Roberto are twenty years older than Miguel, and it shows. Not just in the grey streaks that linger by their temples, but in the way they carry themselves as they step into the light. Miguel has an anxious, jumpy energy to him that they lack.

Gabrielle dips her head slightly in a half-bow of acknowledgement, but she's ignored by everyone.

"You're late for your own meeting," Roberto begins, stepping in to slap his brother on the shoulder in greeting. *"Not the best start."*

Miguel just shrugs and releases his brother. *"Traffic."*

Traffic? In the desert? Ha.

Joaquin hasn't said anything, and he doesn't move forward to embrace his younger brother either. He looks to Roberto, then back at their cars.

"This traffic wouldn't have anything to do with the problems you've been having, would it?" Roberto asks, taking a cigarette from his jacket pocket and lighting up casually.

I tune out Miguel's careful reply and focus on setting up Drone 3. I'll have to get it higher than the others to avoid being seen. It's also more powerful, which makes it noisier, so I'll have to cut the power and let gravity drop it straight into their little meetup before I push the trigger.

Thankfully, most people never think to look up.

Carefully, I attach the payload to the underside of the drone, linking it to the detonator with a satisfying beep. The rotors whirr as they come online, but I don't send it out after the others just yet. I'll wait until everything else is in place.

As a backup, I start guiding my little bot between cars, carefully using his little robot arms to attach magnetic trackers beneath the wheel arches as a precaution. While explosions are fun, they're also a little unpredictable. I don't want anyone getting away without me noticing.

That done, I turn my attention back to the meeting, my thumb hovering over Drone 3's switch.

Only to stop dead as the door to Joaquin's car opens, and the band files out.

"Shit!" I curse, slapping my hand over my mouth before I remember there's no way they can hear me.

They're right in the middle of my hot zone, though none of them looks happy to be there.

To make things infinitely worse, Sully is pushed out of the car the elder brothers arrived in. He tumbles to the ground, already bruised, and all four of the guys wrestle with the security in an attempt to get to him.

Prophet almost manages it, ducking through his captor's hold in a calculated move that might've made Man proud.

But he's outnumbered, and he swiftly gets a kick to the ribs for his trouble.

"Your little project was halfway to busted, and you had no idea," Roberto remarks, drawing my attention to the furious expression on both his and Miguel's faces. *"While you were busy enjoying parties and making trades, your pet mules were using their loyal old dog to gather all the evidence they needed to have you strung up in another American prison."*

I watch as Miguel's expression goes from angry, to baffled, to downright furious.

"Sully had nothing to do with it," Slate growls. *"It was all us—fuck"*

He's cut off as the beefy man restraining him drives an elbow into his stomach, winding him.

"You were told to keep your mouths shut," he hisses.

"Let the boy speak," Roberto replies, taking a drag of his cigarette.

Slate's lips thin as he cradles his abdomen. *"He's just an old man. You've made your point. Let him go."*

Joaquin shakes his head, finally looking away from his

youngest brother. *"A rat is a rat, no matter its age. Betrayal will never be tolerated, not while I am head of this* familia.*"* He turns back to Miguel. *"You're still too young. Too rash. You want us to give you a seat at the table? Rid yourself of your delusions of immortality and learn to be more mindful of your enemies.* Abuelo *would be turning in his grave over how close you were to putting us all behind bars with your arrogance. You take too many risks,* mijo.*"*

He jerks his head at one of his goons, who grabs Sully by the scruff of his neck while two others open the boot of the car opposite. The older man is barely conscious as they start dousing him in petrol, and I'm grateful for it.

The band starts cursing and fighting up a storm, but they're forced to their knees, powerless to do anything but watch as tyres are forced over Sully's head to pin his arms to his sides. I've seen this before. I know what will happen if I don't intervene. I scramble for my drones, mind racing, as I try to figure out a way to stop this. My bot is forgotten, the feed still playing as Roberto strides up and slaps Sully around the cheeks until he comes around.

"You should never have gotten involved."

Sully's lips twitch up in a bloody half-smile. *"I'd do worse for my boys."*

The band is still there, still fighting and cursing while I try my hardest to think.

I can't use my explosives. Not without taking my guys out. The shit has hit the fan so fast I've got whiplash. What else have I got? Trackers? No use. The drones have speakers. If I couple those with some light and some smoke…

I disconnect the explosive in a rush, swapping it out for a smoke bomb. The white phosphorous payload should ensure no one can see more than a few feet in any direction. I need them disoriented if I'm going to get Sully out of this.

My carefully planned assassination has turned into a damn

rescue mission.

I practically throw Drone 3 from the car in my haste. We might not have the minute or so it's going to take to reach them. My eyes flick back to the feed from my little hexapod bot. Miguel is still on the receiving end of a lecture from Joaquin, but I can't see Sully.

Drone 1 solves the mystery of his whereabouts. They've hauled him to the top of the hill overlooking the light of the city. The heavy rubber tyres wrapped around his body stop him from struggling as Roberto takes a final drag of his cigarette, then flicks it at Sully's wobbling form.

No.

The gasoline they doused him with goes up in a whoosh of flame, and Sully screams as they kick him over the edge, sending him rolling down the rocky slope in a whirl of fire.

"Shit!"

Drone 3 bleeps its position, and I smash the enter key, triggering the release of its payload, which falls from the sky and right into the thick of things.

The cartel members scatter as smoke pours from between them. Guns are drawn. Shouts echo in the confusion as they all realise they're under attack and whirl to figure out where their enemy is hiding. Without pausing, I mash the bot's commands in next, followed by Drone 1.

Blue and red light beams cuts into the chaos. A siren squeals from Drone 1.

"Cops!" I don't know who yells it, but that's my cue.

Abandoning my laptop, I scramble for the driver's seat and slam the Jeep into gear, heading for the slope where they chucked Sully. I can trace his path thanks to the burning bushes, and when I finally reach him, he's stopped rolling all together.

"Come on, old man," I grumble under my breath, slamming on the brake. "You're too good to die at the hands of these scumbags."

Wrenching open my door, I rush to the trunk of the car. It's well equipped with all my usual safety stuff, and I say a silent prayer of thanks to Man as I grab a fire extinguisher. It feels like my legs are made of lead as I sprint towards the screaming fireball. The scent of burning rubber and smoke is heavy in the air, choking me as I pull the pin and aim the extinguisher at him.

White foam explodes out of the nozzle in a thick blanket. I swish it from side to side, but it still feels like it takes forever for the burning to fizzle out. When it does, it leaves behind a blackened and bleeding mess on the cracked desert ground.

He's no longer screaming.

That doesn't mean anything, I console myself. The smoke might have knocked him out.

I have to get him to a hospital.

My gut churns, and nausea burns at the back of my throat as I sprint back to the car, abandoning him just long enough to grab the fireproof gloves I keep on hand for emergencies. Even with those the heat makes freeing him from the already partially melted rubber a challenge. I do it anyway, stripping off my fire-retardant jacket to add more layers between me and the heat.

"Stay alive," I order, as I remove the final tire and he groans in pain. "You hear me, Sully? Stay alive!"

Hefting his burned and groaning body to the backseat of the car takes work. In the end, I roll him onto a fire blanket and use it to drag him over the desert floor and into the back seat.

The drive to the nearest hospital is long, too long, and his groans get quieter and quieter as we go.

"Stay alive for me, Sully," I demand, hitting the accelerator. "You're not going to die."

I have no idea what I'm going to say when we get to the hospital, but I'll think of something. If nothing else, I can call Man and ask for help, though it stings my pride to do so.

Shit. This was not how tonight was supposed to go.

Dodger

28

Miguel curses the four of us for the entire journey back to the city. We're all so numb we just sit there and take it. Gabrielle is shaking, pressing herself against the door in a vain attempt to escape the anger of the maniac in the car with us as he alternates between cursing her, us, and his security out in English and Spanish.

The SUV reeks of smoke, reminding us of the horror we just witnessed, and the driver is taking the longest route back to the hotel, trying to ensure we aren't followed.

All I can do is hope that the cops get them. I swear, if we're arrested, I won't even take a plea deal. I'll just testify with everything I've got to make sure these assholes stay in prison for the rest of their natural lives.

Sully. Fuck.

I can't believe they killed Sully. We've lost Sully.

The car rocks to a stop outside the same El Paso hotel we left hours ago, but we're not the same men. If hearts can bleed from grief, mine is haemorrhaging.

"Get the fuck out," Miguel orders. "No more fuck-ups, or I'll make what Roberto did to your beloved old man look like a party trick. You stupid shits have no *idea* what you just screwed up for me."

He doesn't have to tell us twice. Slate and Prophet throw open the doors, jumping out, and I lurch after them, dragging Arlo behind me. There's barely a chance for us to step away before Miguel's car speeds off, leaving us on the sidewalk.

"Fuck," Slate curses, but the word is broken. Hoarse.

I open my mouth to respond, then close it again. I'm not sure there are words for the hollowness in my chest.

Tomorrow, when we step off that plane in another damned city and perform like the circus animals we are, there will be no Sully cheering us on. No one to keep our spirits up before the performance, or tell it to us straight when things go to our heads.

The anchor that kept us all sane in this messy hell of an existence is gone.

Forever.

My skin is too tight. My thoughts are so fucking erratic I can't grab hold of them for more than a few seconds. A heavy emotional haze settles over me, obscuring the real world. For the first time since I was a teenager, I honestly consider whether pain would help me think clearly.

Only it didn't work back then, not really. I just focused on the physical hurt and let the emotional one rot inside me until my friends helped me find the strength to man up and face it.

Right now, I'm not alone. No matter how it feels. The rest of the band is hurting too.

"Get off the street," Prophet mutters, marching us forwards.

He's right. We're attracting attention. I'm sure it looks like the whole band has just been in a fight, and a camera flashes to my right before we can duck beyond the safety of the doors.

Fucking cameras. Can't we even lose Sully without our grief being plastered on the internet?

The four of us take the elevator up to our floor in silence, only to freeze when we step out into the suite. The light is on.

There, on the sofa before us, looking like a dishevelled angel, is Darcy. Dressed in black cargos and a matching tank top that don't match her usual colourful style, she has a ruthless air about her I've never noticed before. On the table before her is a bunch of wires and even a... clock?

"We need to talk," she says, uncrossing her arms and resting her elbows on her knees as she leans forward.

"*Rubia*," Slate murmurs, recovering quickest. "What the hell happened to you?"

She frowns, then glances down, eyes widening as she realises she's covered in soot and blood. That quickly, the hard, stoic mask she's wearing dissipates, replaced with the softer version of Darcy I'm used to.

My shoulders slump. Was this another part of the cartel's revenge? Sully wasn't enough? Guilt and anger battle inside me, finally winning over the hollowness.

"Oh. Shit." Her head falls back and she groans. "I'm fine. My clothes are fire-retardant, but getting Sully free was more difficult than I'd hoped."

All four of us stiffen at the mention of his name.

"Sit." She tilts her head towards the sofas. "I think it's time we're honest with each other."

Arlo does as she says without hesitating, taking the spot beside her. There's a slight pause, and then he gives in, dragging her onto his lap, where he holds her like she might disappear at any moment. Prophet is slightly slower, heading for the kitchen first and returning with a bowl of water, a cloth, and a first aid kit that he puts on the table.

"Let me clean you up," he grunts, kneeling on the floor beside them.

"You should hear what I have to say first," she counters, only to sigh in defeat when he doesn't budge. "Fine."

"We broke up with you," Slate says, reluctantly. "You shouldn't be here."

Darcy pins him with a glare. "Yes, that was a real dick move." She takes a deep breath, letting it out with a hiss as Prophet starts to mop at her soot-covered face with his cloth. "Anyway, first, you should know that Sully is in the hospital under a fake name. He's alive, but they've got him on a ventilator in the burns unit—Ouch! Arlo, stop squeezing me."

Our guitarist mumbles an apology, and his hands move to her hair instead, undoing her messy ponytail so his fingers can diligently tease out all of the knots.

I follow the movement until what she said finally processes. "How—?"

"You really think I just turned up working for you by coincidence?" She shakes her head and rolls her eyes. "I was sent here to kill the Rosales brothers. I'm an assassin, and if you boys hadn't been there tonight, this would all have been over by now."

Her words sink in slowly. Too slowly. By the time I've put it all together, Slate has slumped onto the armchair in disbelief and the water Prophet is using to clean her has turned a murky grey colour.

"Is this some kind of joke?" Slate mumbles, rubbing his temples.

Darcy's eyes narrow. "I got Sully out of there, didn't I? You don't think that was really the cops? No. That was all me. You're. Freaking. Welcome."

She takes a deep, shuddering breath, and for the first time, I notice how exhausted she looks. Then she jumps a foot in the air as Prophet starts on her neck.

"Stay still," he growls, answering her glare with one of his own.

Her eyes flash to his, and a moment of understanding passes between them.

"I have no idea when my next shot at them will be," she continues, glancing away. "Which means we should continue to stay away from one another. But it's become clear I need your cooperation if we're to avoid anyone else getting hurt." She waves her hand at the pile of wires. "Your phones are bugged. Your rooms are under surveillance. You have no idea how much footage they had before I corrupted the files, and now that Miguel has a closer eye on you, that's going to get worse. I can't keep corrupting videos without raising his suspicions."

My disbelief that Darcy—of all people—could be an assassin, flickers and fades with the pile of evidence on the table. This is either some really elaborate hoax or...

The truth.

I find the idea of Miguel spying on us easier to swallow than the idea of Darcy being an assassin. That fucker. Bugs in our phones? My hands curl into fists, thinking of all the times Darcy and I had phone sex. Was he listening in? Getting off? Wait... footage? I glance at her, trying to figure out how much footage there was.

If that asshole watched the two of us, I'll wring his damn neck.

"We were going to turn ourselves in," Arlo mutters. "Sully was supposed to be gathering evidence to put them away while we took a plea bargain."

Darcy's brows furrow as she takes in the news. "That's unnecessary. By the time I'm done, Miguel will have left the entire agency to you in a verified and witnessed will. He'll even have ended your contract without penalty. The money from his brothers—after I've taken my cut—will be split between good causes. You'll be free to continue your careers with a less toxic agency, or reform his."

"And you?" I ask, "What happens to you?"

Her nose tilts up. "You broke up with me. I don't see how it's any of your business."

She's right. I know she is. It remains the absolute worst decision I ever had to make.

"Baby girl," I begin, but she looks away sharply. "We did it to keep you out of this..."

"Anyway," she continues, ignoring my feeble excuse. "There are burner phones for all of you over there." She tilts her head in the direction of the other table, and I notice four boxes waiting. "The numbers are listed as Sully's emergency contacts... I didn't know if he had any family..."

Arlo shakes his head. "He never had kids. Said we gave him enough trouble."

We all knew that was a lie. Sully bounced around the foster system. Unlike so many others, his wasn't a negative experience, but after seeing what broken homes and absentee dads did to some of the kids, he never felt like settling down and having a family of his own. Eventually, life on the road and a bachelor lifestyle simply meant he adopted everyone he came across, us included.

"Well, they'll call you if anything changes. You could go and visit before your flight in the morning, but I'd recommend against it. You don't want to draw the cartel's attention to the fact that they didn't get their kill."

"What are his chances?" Slate asks, cutting straight to the point.

She sighs, fidgeting. "They've got him stable. He's not 'actively dying.' Recovery is going to be hell, but I think he *will* recover... to a degree. With burns, the risk of contractures is high, and that could limit his movement. Not to mention the effect of the smoke on his lungs, and—"

"Bet he'll be pissed if his moustache has been burned off," I mutter, almost laughing in relief at the random thought.

Prophet drops the cloth into the water for the final time, running it over the dirt on her lower arm, only for her to hiss.

"Stay still," he orders, putting the cloth down. "You've burned yourself."

Darcy barely spares it a glance. "Not the first time."

Prophet is already in the first aid kit, pulling out sterile wipes and gently cleaning the area before slathering it in ointment.

It's not a bad burn, but it's still painful to see it marring her skin.

The second he's done, she stands, pulling out of Arlo's hold. "I need a shower, so I'm leaving. I just came to tell you Sully was alive and to stay out of my way next time."

Slate catches her unburnt arm. "*Cariño*, we need to talk."

Darcy takes a deep, shuddering breath. "I knew what you were up to when you broke up with me." Her shoulders straighten, like she's preparing for battle. "You still hurt me, Slate. You knew exactly what breaking up with me like that would do to me, and you did it anyway."

"We were assholes," I admit, trying to deflect her attention. "But, baby girl, we were trying to protect you. We're always going to do that, even if you are a badass assassin."

She raises a brow. "I get that—and I feel the same way about you—but in the process, I lost my best friends. It was everything I feared would happen when we went down this path." She sighs and pins Slate with a look. "You didn't even try to hide the fact you were just trying to use me to fix your band. This whole thing"—she waves a hand between the five of us—"was built on a toxic foundation of lies from the very start."

Then, without waiting for any more of our bullshit excuses, she turns on her heel and strides from the room, leaving us in her wake.

None of us speaks for a while. I'm not really sure how you

follow up that whole conversation. Sully is alive—if barely—Darcy is an assassin, and if she succeeds, we'll be free men.

Arlo stands, and I move to follow automatically, only to freeze as he pins me in place with his glare. "I don't have coke in my room," he growls. "You already checked, remember? The best thing that ever happened to us just walked out of our lives for good, all because—" He cuts off, breath shuddering out in a rush. "Just... just leave me alone."

His door slams a second later.

Prophet takes a deep breath and lets it out slowly, then starts packing away the first aid kit.

He pauses in his doorway, looking back at Slate and me. "It was the right thing to do. She was too good for us."

Then his door is closed, and once again, it's me and Slate. I glance at my room, then dismiss it. On nights like this, I don't sleep. I lie in bed, getting more worked up. I grab my coat, ready to head out, but Slate steps in front of the elevator before I can go.

"Prophet's wrong," he says. "I should never have listened to him before. Look where it got us. We were on the right damned path until I started doubting myself."

I scrub my hand down my face. "We've ruined this."

Just like we ruin everything we touch. At least our band name is still fitting.

"So you're going to let it all fall apart rather than fixing it?" he demands. "You know we can't let her go, Dodge. She's it. The missing piece. Prophet's too stubborn or too noble to see it. Arlo is too lost right now to fight for her like he wants to. It's up to us." He pauses, then hammers the final nail in my coffin. "If she kills Miguel, and the band splits up, there's nothing left for either of us to go back to."

I swallow at the reminder. He's right. Prophet has his family. Arlo has Emma. Slate and I don't have anyone.

"She's right. We fucked up."

Slate shakes his head. "She's *it* for us, man. And she's wrong; the foundation wasn't lies, it was a solid decade of unshakeable friendship. That's not something we can replace, ever. That's something you fight for."

I grimace, unconvinced, but he doesn't budge.

"Do you love her?" he demands.

"What kind of question is that?"

"Do. You. Love. Her?"

I pace away from him, running my hand through my hair to get it out of my face. "You know the answer."

I've been in love with her since we first met. It's so wrong, but I silently prayed for her to break up with every one of those losers she was dating before, just so I could listen to her cries of pleasure through my headphones and pretend she was mine again.

Slate stops me before I can pace again, his hand on my shoulder. "So do I. Which means we need to apologise like our lives depend on it and fucking fight for her."

But what if we fight, and it all falls down, anyway? What if she never comes round, and the band falls apart, and everything we've worked so hard to save is left in ruins? And what can a bunch of delinquent musicians possibly have to offer an assassin?

I'm so conflicted as I meet his dark eyes, and he must sense that, because the harsh lines between his brows soften.

"Everything we want," he murmurs. "Is on the other side of fear."

Taking a deep breath, I blink and nod. "What's the plan?"

He swallows, looking away for a second. "She wanted honesty, right?" I nod. "Then we give her honesty. All of it. The whole sorry story."

Darcy
29

The flight to Austin is full of quiet grumbling. An email announcing Sully's sudden collapse and death from a heart attack was sent to the entire crew at five a.m. in the morning. No one believes it. The quiet discontentment makes me wonder how many of the roadies are aware of what's really happening between the band and the cartel.

I'm sure there are more than a few.

As I wheel my suitcase into yet another hotel, I resolve to keep my ear to the ground while I'm here. Without the band to keep me occupied, I might be able to get more information out of the other roadies.

First though, a nap. I swear Gabrielle is booking the crew flights at ridiculously early times just to mess with me. Once I'm through with that, I'll go back to hunting through her emails, searching for my next opportunity.

It won't be as easy next time. The cartel will be extra careful now that they know someone is on to their movements. With any luck, they'll think it's a rat, rather than an outsider with access to their network. Either way, my next attempt cannot fail.

I make it halfway to the bed before a knock on the door

freezes me. Silently, I check my gun is still in the holster beneath my arm, throw on a baggy hoodie with a fake pocket to disguise it, and look through the peephole.

"What do you want?" I ask, releasing my hold on my gun and cracking open the door.

Arlo and Emma are on my doorstop, though the latter is shuffling her feet, like she'd rather be anywhere else. The guitarist hesitates for a second, then pulls his sunglasses off.

"I came to apologise," he says. "What we did was wrong, especially after we promised we wouldn't be as bad as all the other shits you've dated."

Damn it. Stay strong, Darce. Resist the sad puppy eyes.

"I was hoping—" He swallows, glancing back at Emma, who gives him a small, encouraging smile before looking back at her shoes. "That you'd let me take you out to one of my favourite places in the city to make up for it."

I frown at him, trying to work out why this feels like a date even though we broke up. If it *is* a date, then why is his sister here?

"This time I guarantee Prophet won't interrupt," he adds.

I'm not sure if I'm considering it because Arlo had—arguably—the smallest part to play in the mess that happened in Seattle, or simply because he's always been so careful and considerate of my feelings before.

Glancing back at my room, and my unopened case, I chew my lip as I think over what this might cost me. I need to be looking for more opportunities to get this mission over and done with, not putting my heart on the line again with a band of guys who've already broken it once.

When I look back at Arlo, he's looking at his shoes, expression tight.

"Another time," he says, stepping back.

Oh, fuck it. "Let me get my stuff."

I don't let myself wait to see his expression as I turn and

double check my purse. It's too warm outside for a hoodie, and I hesitate, grimacing as I realise if I take it off, Arlo will see the gun beneath.

Well, he knows who I am. It can't be that shocking, right? Emma might, too, given how close the siblings are.

Sighing, I drag the hoodie over my head, ignoring the sharp inhale of breath from behind me as I check the safety out of habit before securing the weapon in a secret lining of my purse.

Wallet, purse, poison ring for emergencies... Wait. Where did I put my C-4?

"Dark... I don't think you need a gun..." Arlo mumbles. "It's just a park."

I raise an eyebrow. "We're in Texas. I'm hardly the only woman going round with a gun in my purse."

And there are far more deadly things in my purse. My phone, for one.

I double check the lock on my case, then give my outfit—a cute denim pinafore dress with a stripy top and sneakers—a once over in the mirror before I grab my key card and head for the door.

I try, and fail, to read Arlo through his sunglasses, but Emma keeps shooting concerned looks at my bag as we follow the slim corridor out to the main lobby and then onto the busy street.

"You haven't told her," I realise, but I don't elaborate. There are too many people here.

Emma's attention snaps to her brother, brows furrowing with concern, but she says nothing.

Arlo shrugs. "It wasn't my secret to tell. Besides, she's not here."

"She's right there." But I'm secretly glad he hasn't told anyone—even his only family member—about my mission.

He offers me a conspiratorial smile. "If we pretend she isn't, maybe she'll go away."

What's he playing at? Did he not invite her? Emma doesn't look insulted by his comment, just resigned and a little guilty. I'm about to ask what's going on when he diverts me into a coffee shop.

"This isn't our destination," he says. "But it's before ten, so I'm guessing you need coffee?"

Another little piece of me thaws as he orders for me, pressing the white chocolate mocha frappe into my hands before giving Emma a caramel one and herding us back out of the shop.

"What's going on?" I ask her, falling behind Arlo as he leads us across a street. Emma is busy checking her mascara in her tiny bejewelled compact, so she doesn't answer me for a second.

"I agreed to be a mute third wheel," she finally says, shooing me away with a sad half-smile. "He can explain himself, but he's not going anywhere alone."

Frowning, because her response has given me more questions than answers, I let the subject drop.

"So we're going to a park?" I ask Arlo, taking a sip of icy cold heaven as I walk a little faster to catch up with him.

"Kind of," he answers. "You'll see."

He turns a corner onto a tree-lined boulevard, looking far too at home in this city for it to be any coincidence. Before I can ask him about how he knows his way around so well, he takes my hand and tugs me past a tall concrete wall etched with words that declare we're entering a... sculpture garden?

Despite the busyness of the street we just left, the garden is tranquil and almost empty.

Arlo's pace automatically slows, and mine does as well. It's as if the park itself demands we slow and appreciate what's there.

I don't get modern art. I never really have. A lot of the time, I just feel like I'm missing the point. Maybe it's too subtle for someone as blunt as me, or maybe it's just not my thing. Still, I have to admit these sculptures add interest to what would otherwise be a regular park.

"Come on. My favourite spot is over here."

He tugs me across to a narrow staircase set into the wall and then up onto a glass and steel catwalk that seems to criss-cross over the garden. It's surprisingly spacious up here, and there are even thin benches spaced every so often to encourage visitors to linger.

The garden extends up here, along with the art. The trees are hung with more exhibits that change as you move around them. At some point, we lose Emma, but I catch sight of her again, sitting on a bench below, when Arlo pulls me to the rail and shows me the sculptures from above.

"She hates heights," he mutters, ignoring her stare. "I figured this would get us some privacy."

I look around, checking to make sure we really are alone. My eyes automatically scan for cameras, then people, before I feel happy enough to ask the question that's been bugging me since he turned up.

"Privacy for what?" I ask, confused. "Why is she following you? What's going on?"

Arlo sighs and collapses onto a bench. "She's following me because I did something stupid, and now I need a babysitter."

"Something stupid?" I take the seat beside him.

He takes his glasses off and tucks them into his pocket. "I relapsed." His words are so quiet I can barely hear them over the city traffic. "The night we decided to end things. I felt like shit, and when Miguel offered me some I just... I wanted to feel good again."

My heart sinks. "What does that mean?" I ask. "Are you using again now?"

I study his eyes intently, but his pupils aren't dilated, and he doesn't *seem* high.

He shakes his head. "It was a mistake. I'm not giving up all that I worked so hard for. I won't give Miguel the satisfaction. It's just... hard."

He says the last word so lamely, and I can't help but shimmy closer, offering silent comfort.

"It's my mess that got us into this in the first place," he mumbles. "The guys and Emma, they're too good to me, really." He takes a deep breath and turns away. "Anyway, I just... I brought you here because I wanted you to find out from me, rather than someone else."

He goes to stand, but I stop him with a gentle hand on his leather-covered arm. "How do I help?"

Arlo freezes, jaw clenching. "Please don't ask me that."

"Come on, we're friends. We've always been friends. I'm not going to leave you to face this on your own. If the others are helping, there must be something I can do."

Arlo

30

S he doesn't have a clue what she's doing to me.

Her earnest face doesn't hold a hint of guile. No matter what happened, what we did, Darcy would still help me if she could.

It makes me feel like dirt.

She wants an answer like "let me vent" or "buy me chocolate" or something *easy*.

It's not her fault she doesn't understand.

I learned years ago that to get over addiction, you have to have a life worth living beyond the high.

The words—the stupid, selfish, honest words—linger on the tip of my tongue.

Take us back.

Save the band from imploding.

Look at me like I look at you.

Love me as if I'm worthy of you.

I don't say them. I won't. Even though I planned this date hoping to undo all the hurt we did, I won't do it by guilting her into a relationship.

So I swallow the honesty back and settle for something more ambiguous. "I could use a hug?"

Darcy smiles and drags me close. I inhale the scent of her, trying to banish the phantom burnt plastic smell with the fresh fruity flavour of her shampoo.

I don't want her pity, so I release her far sooner than I'd like to.

God, I'm tired. It's been days since the initial comedown. It's not as bad as it was last time, but I only did one line before Dodger found me and dragged me home. Maybe that improves my chances.

Even now, the back of my throat is dry, and for a second I swear I can taste the awful gasoline taste of coke—even addicts will tell you it tastes like shit. The scent of it has been haunting me on and off since I woke up, and to distract myself, I glance back below to check on my sister.

Emma should be fucking mad at me; I deserve it. Instead, here she is, having my back again when she should be out there, living her life. She watched our parents fall to this demon, and now she's watching her brother fight the same one, even after I swore blind to her that I'd never touch the stuff again.

That time, I was in the hospital after an overdose.

I'm never going to let it get that bad again. It's bad enough I let myself fall this far.

"How did it happen?" Darcy asks, dragging me back to the present—damn it, I must've spaced again. "How did the four of you get mixed up with Miguel? My file wasn't clear."

I choke out a laugh. "He was in juvie with us. For a while, he was actually Slate's cellmate."

Back then, he was in for dealing, just like me. Unlike me, he was using as well. Slate knew and warned the rest of us to steer well away from him.

Who your rich daddy is isn't supposed to matter while you're inside, but it does. Don Rosales, the man who founded the Rosales Cartel, had enough money to grease the palms of everyone who came into contact with his bastard son. It also meant that when rival cartel members turned up, grudges sprang up quickly.

"There was a fight while we were inside," I continue. "And I accidentally saved his life." I lift the hem of my shirt, exposing the old, white scar just above my hip for a second before dropping the fabric. "Some asshole from a rival cartel had a shiv. I was in the wrong place at the wrong time. Anyway, I tripped and..." The rest was history.

I was suddenly under Miguel's protection. A member of the brotherhood, even though I never asked to be.

"When I got out of the infirmary, he offered me anything I wanted. Money. Drugs. Cars. Girls. A reward for saving his life. He even got my sentence reduced by two months."

Initially, I was hesitant. I knew, even then, that getting involved with his kind was more serious than the petty dealing I'd done before. Slate warned me, and back then, I listened. I wasn't yet desperate enough to accept.

"He kept pushing, even when we were released, and I kept turning him down..."

It got harder and harder each time. Emma was only six when we got out, but she'd suffered a full year without me there to look after her and make sure she was fed.

"Of course, my parents weren't going to let me back under their roof after I'd stolen their stash from them, so I took Dodger's offer and moved in with him. We were dirt poor, living in his mom's old house, which we couldn't even afford to heat properly. The building was falling apart, but we kept it clean, and I told myself I still wasn't going to take Miguel's money. Dodger was making just enough to cover the bills, and I was still hopeful that I could get some commissions."

We had enough to make sure Emma had clothes and food, though we had to be sneaky in getting it to her, given how hostile my parents were. When Slate joined us, we managed to scrape together enough for some shitty second hand instruments. Neither he nor I were making as much as Dodger could on a good night, but it was a contribution.

"It wasn't great, but I thought we were surviving okay. A year in, we even scored a lucky break and managed to buy ourselves gaming rigs with the extra money. Prophet's dad found him a beat up old van to drive our stuff to gigs. But then I walked in on Dodger one night."

I knew he was dancing at the club where his mother worked to pay the rent. He told us her old friend had gotten him a job there, but until then, I hadn't realised that he was doing more than just dancing.

I know Dodge won't care that I'm telling Darcy this. He's never hidden his past from anyone, and he's made it clear he doesn't regret it or find it shameful.

"He looked me dead in the eye, and there was *nothing* there, Dark. He was fucking this vapid, giggling old bitch, and he was just checked out. How could I sit by while one of my best friends whored himself out to buy us food to eat?"

I couldn't.

"And it wasn't just us. His money was going to Emma as well. Feeding my baby sister where I couldn't. For eight damned *years*, my friend was selling his body and soul to buy my sister's survival while I failed at producing art and playing guitar and called it progress."

I shake my head. The irony isn't lost on me that now I play in front of thousands and my work hangs in posh galleries, but my outlook on life is almost as bleak. Or it was, until Darcy arrived.

"Miguel knew we had talent. When I called him and said I wanted a loan, he asked what it was for. Originally, I'd just planned to bribe my way into an agency and get a deal. When he said he had another plan... I was desperate enough to roll with it."

"You signed the contract." The knowledge is there in her eyes.

I nod, the action more a jerk of my head than a true nod. "It was a year after we met online. I brought it back and convinced the whole band to sign it. I even hid who it was from. None of them would *ever* have touched it if they'd known. They trusted me, and I thought I was saving them."

Look where that got them. "For a while, it was good. Miguel was friendly. He put us up in a nice place, even helped me get custody of Emma. Of course, I know now that's because she was just more leverage he could use against me."

Darcy's face gives nothing away. "It clearly didn't last."

"We worked out why he was so eager to be involved. He wormed his way into every single aspect of our lives. A few months after our first album came out, he started taking me to parties where he knew there would be drugs. I guess he must've known it would be easiest to get me addicted. Dodger won't touch the shit; Prophet and Slate won't follow a crowd just to keep things peaceful."

Whereas all he had to do was surround me with the right people and pile on just enough pressure until I did a line to shut them up.

Then rinse and repeat until an addict was born.

The moment the band confronted him, things got nasty.

"When we discovered he was trafficking women amongst the other roadies, we refused to perform." I grimace. "They found Sully beaten in an alleyway to within an inch of his life the next day. Cartel enforcers started following Prophet's nieces and nephews to kindergarten when someone overheard him telling Slate he was going to quit. It got so bad that his two middle sisters moved their families to the east coast to get away. When I first went to rehab to try to get clean, some of their goons tried to rape Emma."

Luckily, my sister had years of living with our asshole

parents under her belt. After a few run-ins with unsavoury dealers looking for money, she started carrying pepper spray everywhere and took some basic free self-defence classes at school. The incident with Miguel's men still scared her to death.

It also made getting clean a thousand times harder, because I had to be sneaky about it.

There were days when the only thing which kept me going was the band, Emma, and Darcy's lighthearted teasing as we gamed together. There were even more days where playing with her online was the only thing that got me out of bed.

In so many ways, I owe this woman my sanity, and all I've managed to give her in return is a broken heart.

Darcy's hand has slowly risen to cover her mouth, but she lowers it when she notices.

Then, slipping off the bench, she crouches in front of me, putting her face directly in my line of sight.

"This wasn't your fault," she promises.

I let out a hollow chuckle. "Dark, this is *all* my fault. You can't even argue otherwise. My naiveté and good intentions got us into this mess, and my inability to stand up for myself sealed us in."

She pressed a finger against my lips. "You never meant for any of this to happen. Men like Miguel prey on people with kind hearts. They don't possess even a fraction of your goodness, and they use that." She pauses. "That's why there are people like me. To even the scales."

I offer her a sad smile and kiss her finger until she moves it. "It doesn't exactly make it better," I point out. "I caused this mess, and now our beautiful girlfriend has to come save us? Some men would be unmanned by that."

She raises a brow, asking a silent question.

"Fortunately, I'm not dumb enough to be one of them."

Darcy has always been every inch a warrior. Even when the

only thing I thought she was slaying was revenants and demonic spawn on the internet, I saw that about her.

Our girl is a contradiction. Nerdy, yet deadly.

It's hot as hell.

"I have never once failed to get my mark," she murmurs. "But this time, I'm going to make Miguel's death hurt. I promise you that."

Then, without warning, she slides her hand into my hair and pulls my face towards hers to capture my lips with her own.

Darcy

31

I don't know why I do it. Maybe it's because I've never seen him look so lost, or maybe it's the simple human urge to offer comfort to those who need it.

Fuck it. I'm not lying to myself anymore. It's because I love him. I always have. Trying to deny it is just not working.

I love the others, too—that's why what they did hurt so damn much—but none of them has really tried to make things right as Arlo has.

Right now, he's hurting, exhausted, and fighting a battle I can never really understand. But he still took the time to come and apologise to me, even though he didn't have to. Even though we broke up, and he owes me nothing.

At the mental reminder, I draw back, blushing.

I don't get far.

Arlo's hand snaps out, long fingers grabbing my chin and holding me still as he fuses our mouths together again. This time, our kiss is deeper. His tongue sweeps out to dance with mine, and I can't help melting into him. My eyes flutter closed, and my body tingles with awareness of him, demanding I get closer. Everything in me wants to kiss this man until our souls are so closely entwined that nothing on earth can tear us apart.

"What a surprise to find you two here," Dodger teases.

I jerk back, and this time Arlo lets me go. I barely have time to catch the twin trails of moisture bisecting his brutal cheekbones before they're wiped away and his glasses are back on. With all traces of his vulnerability erased, he turns to glare at Dodger and Slate.

The two of them are standing on the catwalk a few feet away, side by side and grinning from ear to ear.

"Did Ems tell you where I was?" Arlo demands. "What? Did you think I brought Darcy up here to get high with me?"

Dodger shakes his head. "Ems told us where you were because we asked her. We were coming to speak to you..."

"We wanted your input on our plan to get our girl back," Slate continues, offering me a wry smile. "And here you are, already on the case."

I stand, ready to stride away, but Arlo grabs my hand. "Stay," he pleads. "They might be idiots, but they mean well."

My walls, which are already halfway rebuilt after our intimate moment, tremble.

"*Cariño*," Slate murmurs, sensing the weakness. "We never wanted to hurt you."

Dodger meets my eyes. "I regret everything we did and said. Miguel threatened you, and I just about fucking died. I would've never forgiven myself if what happened to Sully happened to you."

"The way we went about it was stupid, but our hearts were in the right place," Slate finishes. "Can you give us another chance?"

Arlo slays me when I glance back at him and his lips form a near-silent, "Please."

It's one of those moments where it feels like time stands

still. The city is still moving around us, but the four of us don't move. I'm not sure we're even breathing.

"I'm not too much?" I mean for the words to come out a lot harsher, but they're an insecure whisper stolen by the wind.

"Never." Slate steps closer. "I shouldn't have said that. I just picked the words I thought would get you to leave us because I was convinced that was the only way to keep you safe."

"You could never be too much for us," Dodger promises. "We're made for you, baby girl. You fit us."

"I heard part of your conversation in the car with Miguel," I admit, looking away, guiltily. "I hacked your phones, so I figured our whole break up was about protecting me. I just didn't realise it would hurt so much."

"We'll make it up to you," Slate promises, with utter conviction in every word. "By our fiftieth wedding anniversary, you'll be laughing about this."

My brows rise. "Fiftieth, huh?"

He offers me a rakish grin. "Soul mates, *cariño*, remember?"

I shore up my walls, because that's not the only issue here. "And my job? You really don't have any issues with the fact that I kill people for money?"

They share a look, as if silently debating who will answer me.

"I mean, if you were slaying the innocent in cold blood, we probably would," Arlo finally admits. "But we know you. You'd never do that."

"My organisation only takes on the worst scum," I promise.

"Like Miguel," Slate growls.

I check that we're still alone before nodding. "He and his brothers, yes. The time before that, it was a senator who liked feeling up underage boys. And before that, it was a slimy English mogul who was running scams against the elderly and robbing them of their life's savings. We only go after the bad guys. Man—my adoptive father—makes sure of it."

"You're a badass," Dodger concludes. "And even if you were just an accountant or something, you'd still be our Darcy."

"If you're waiting for us to judge you for what you do, you've got the wrong band," Arlo finishes. "Between us, we've seen some of the worst shit the world has to offer. We know that the planet would be a better place if people like Miguel didn't inhabit it."

I swallow. "And what about Prophet?"

"I have a plan." Slate grins.

Arlo's head falls back, thunking against the barrier as a groan of exasperation falls from his lips. "Has there ever been a time where you didn't?"

I have to admit, Slate's plans are not filling me with confidence, given the low success rate so far.

"It's not bad this time," Dodger adds. "Tomorrow, Prophet is going to his parents, like he always does when we're in town. We're all invited because Mama P loves us. We'll just bring you along and introduce you as the band's girlfriend."

"That's a terrible idea," I retort, blinking at him in disbelief.

"Mama P will love you on sight," Arlo reassures me. "She's just that kind of person. Destiny, his youngest sister, is the same. His dad just wants his girls happy, so he won't say a word."

I'm unable to hide my scepticism. "And his mom loving me is somehow going to change his mind?"

"Just give it a chance," Slate pleads. "If this doesn't work, I'll let him walk away, no fuss."

Both of my brows rise in pure disbelief. Slate, give up on something? I don't believe it.

"Fine," I agree, because despite myself, I'm intrigued. "I'll come to dinner. But after this, no more pushing Prophet. I'm not going to force him to join us if he doesn't want to." That will just end miserably for all involved.

Arlo pulls me down onto his lap. "Now, can you two please stop interrupting my date? It's bad enough I have to have my baby sister shadowing me."

Dodger smirks. "How about I swap with Emma, and the three of us can go somewhere more exciting than a statue garden?"

"I wanted somewhere peaceful," Arlo grumbles.

"But you failed to show her your exhibition in the gallery down the road." Dodger raises a brow.

Arlo shrugs, and his cheeks flush pink. "I was working up the courage."

Damn it, there goes the last of my walls. I'm pretty sure Arlo, the softest, shyest of the band, is going to always be my kryptonite.

"Let's go and relieve Emma of babysitting duty," Slate suggests. "Then we can have a group date." He hesitates. "Unless... you don't want to."

It's visibly killing him to say the words. His brows are pinched, and his shoulders have dropped a fraction of an inch.

I take a deep breath and finally give in, letting the walls drop. "Yes, I'll go on a group date with you." I pause. "The trial period is over. I'm all in."

Slate whoops, snatching me from Arlo and lifting me into the air, twirling me around until I have to swat at his shoulder to get him to let me go.

"You're not going to regret this," he promises.

"Put her down," Dodger complains. "The rest of us want a turn."

Slate rolls his eyes but does as he asks, and Dodger wastes no time crushing me in an all-encompassing hug.

"I swear, baby girl," he whispers against my ear. "I'll never, ever let you go again. Even if it's dangerous."

"Good thing I've got enough firepower to protect all of us," I retort. "Now come on. I'm hungry, and you promised me a group date."

He releases me, and I instinctively reach back and grab Arlo's hand. He didn't come here expecting his apology to be ambushed by the other guys. He's taking it pretty well, but I don't want him to feel left out.

"There's a little cafe in the gallery," Slate says, leading the way and leaving Dodger free to take my other hand. "They do these amazing loaded bagels."

Just as he promised, the bagels were the best I'd ever eaten. The guys almost don't manage to tear me out of the tiny cafe, but in the end, the promise of seeing more of Arlo's art is too tempting to resist.

There's so much to see, and we wander around the brightly lit rooms slowly. The guys don't complain, even when I drag them this way and that, searching out all of the coolest pieces. My favourite is a room filled with amorphous sculptures which somehow manage to trap human sensuality in multicoloured glass.

Well, it's my favourite for all of five seconds, until we turn the corner.

"This is all you," I gasp, staring at the walls in awe.

Arlo's work is just as bold as before, a complete contradiction to the quiet man himself. The gallery has dedicated an entire room to his massive canvases, and I grin as I begin to recognise people from his life.

"Emma?" I guess, looking at a blown up painting of a teenager with a pixie cut glaring through the triangle of a clothes hanger.

"She was trying to force us into suits," Dodger comments. "Even at fifteen, she was bossing us around."

"You two almost caved that time," Slate grouches. "If not for Prophet, we would've been infamous as the preppy losers of the metal world."

I squint, pretending to imagine it. "Could've been cute."

Arlo shakes his head, shaking in quiet laughter. "I don't wear suits, Dark. Prophet might if his mom makes him, but the rest of us are allergic to that shit."

"I guess I'll just have to take Prophet with me whenever I want to feel fancy," I reply, grinning.

Dodger raises a brow, knowing I live for comfort wear. "Does that happen often?"

I snort. "Only when I need to seduce a mark to get close to them."

All three men freeze. Arlo looks away sharply, Slate's hands curl into fists, and Dodger pins me with a look I can't decipher.

"Is that something that happens often, baby girl?" he grates out.

Oh. *Oh.* They're jealous.

"Not anymore," I promise. "I'll find other ways now that we're together." The tension visibly fades from their shoulders. "It was never really my preferred method. Too close and personal. Some of my sisters go that route, but I find it safer to keep some distance between me and my marks."

Which is why my cameras and drones are so important. Visual confirmation of my targets prevents accidents. It helps that I always come prepared, and I've had years to master my technique.

El Paso was the biggest fuck up I've had in recent memory, and even that was arguably outside of my control.

I shake off my own self-criticism and move on to the next portrait.

"Wait, you painted your gaming rig?" It has adorable little frogs all over it in bright green.

Arlo murmurs something under his breath that sounds like "artist's block," and I laugh. Yeah, I'm sure that can make a person do all sorts of crazy things.

Fortunately, I don't have a creative bone in my body, so I'm at no risk of finding out.

"This is an old one," Slate whistles, drawing my attention away from the frogs and to a smaller canvas in the corner.

"Oh, it's you guys!" In the flesh rather than their avatars.

"Based on a photo of one of our first gigs after juvie." Dodger grins. "I remember that. I think I still have it somewhere."

Arlo's version is far better than a photograph. He's captured his band mates' souls in charcoal and paint. Everything from Prophet's dimpled, exuberant grin, to Dodger's sweat-slicked hair, and then Arlo himself, held in a headlock by one of Slate's tattooed arms.

"There was this one seedy bar that let us play for twenty minutes on a Friday night," Arlo explains. "We weren't even technically old enough to be in a bar, but we looked older than we were. The owner, Joe, gave us a month to start bringing in a crowd."

"Did you?" I ask, curious.

He shakes his head. "Nah. We were trying to play metal in a bar whose four regulars liked country and western. Of course we didn't."

"I still think that was down to his skunky beer," Slate grumbles. "But yeah, there was a reason we ended up signing that contract. Sometimes all the talent and hard work in the world just doesn't matter. At the end of the day, for most of the stars of this industry, it was all about who they knew, and we didn't know anybody."

And the only person they did know happened to be Miguel Rosales.

I move on to the next painting, only to find it's Emma again. "Why is she crying?"

Try as hard as I might, I can't picture Arlo's tough as nails sister weeping and hugging her knees as she is in the painting. Then again, I had my share of emotional meltdowns as a teenager. Looking back, I almost pity Man.

I can't help but be glad that no one decided to paint my first break up and put it up in a gallery for the world to see. Then again, these are old. Emma barely resembles this girl anymore, and Arlo's style is abstract enough that you might not put the two versions of her together. His musical career seems also to have remarkably little crossover with his artistic one.

Arlo scratches the back of his neck, clearly uncomfortable. "It was our parents."

When he doesn't elaborate, Dodger tilts his head as if to say "want me to take over?", and Arlo waves him on.

"Once Arlo had money, they tried to extort it out of him. Of course, by that point, the only thing he had to do with them was Emma, so they limited his contact with her until he gave them what they wanted. When Emma found out her brother was paying to see her on the weekends on top of the money he was sneaking her to make sure she had food, she didn't take it well."

Ouch. I can see how that would leave a scar. Arlo said his parents were addicts, so it's a safe bet they were using that money to get high.

"I ended up applying for custody, which I got when she was sixteen," Arlo adds, though I already knew that part. "Of course, then she had to deal with all the 'friends' who only wanted her for her money, and the ones who thought she could somehow introduce them to me and I'd make them into the next pop stars."

No wonder she's prickly. Looking through the lens of this new knowledge, so many of our previous interactions make sense. She didn't back off and relax around me until I'd proved that I had nothing to gain by using her or her brother, unlike practically everyone else she knew.

A wordless understanding passes between Arlo and me until I break our stare off to move onto the next painting.

Only to stop dead.

I know it's Dodger, but only because I recognise the way he holds himself, and because of the faint impression—more a shadow, really—of the crossed blades over his collarbones. Arlo left his face out of it, and it's not hard to realise why.

"Yeah, I look hot upside down," Dodger comments blithely.

As if a larger-than-lifesize painting of him, side on, hanging from a pole, nude, isn't hanging right in front of us.

Arlo rushes to defend himself. "It was a study of the human form. Shit, I forgot they had this."

"It was a study of my gorgeous ass," Dodger quips back. "Don't get shy now. You were the one snooping on my rehearsals, and it's not like I'm ashamed of it. My ass kept us fed for years." He leans in close to me, putting his mouth to my ear. "I still have that thong. Want a private show?"

Thong? How small is that thing? I can barely make out the line around his hips. Suddenly, all I can see in my mind is Dodger's muscled body, moving around a pole, arms flexing while I watch.

My arousal flushes across my skin, and I don't have to check to know I just soaked my panties.

"You like that idea," he whispers, moving in front of me.

His hands move from a respectable—if intimate—position at my waist and trace down my hips to cup the curves of my ass possessively. Against my stomach, the hardness of his erection is straining against his pants as if it's trying to break free and fuck me right here.

I glance up with wide eyes as his fingers play with the hem of my dress. Across the room, there are two elderly gallery patrons deep in discussion with each other about one of Arlo's other works. At any moment, they could turn around and see him nearly fondling me in public.

As if reading my thoughts, Slate shifts, putting his body between us and the rest of the room.

"I think Lo deserves a little something inspirational," Dodger murmurs. "There's a shortage of perfect asses in this world, and we wouldn't want him to lack for source material."

Slowly, giving me all the time in the world to object, he gathers the dress and lifts it. His fingers stroke against my skin, giving me goosebumps as he exposes my panty-clad ass to his friends.

Slate hisses out a breath, but Arlo is eerily silent. When I glance back, he's taken off his glasses and is staring transfixed at the way Dodger is holding me.

When my skirt lowers, I'm almost... disappointed.

That can't be right. We're in a public place, for goodness' sake! I do not want to take things any further. There could be cameras, and—

Except there aren't. The gallery is small, and I would've noticed a security system in the room when we entered. Even now, as I double check the corners of the room for them, I know I won't find any.

The couple from across the room is moving slowly closer, though.

So, taking a deep breath, I release Dodger and step into Arlo's arms.

Winding my fingers into his long, gold-kissed hair, I pull his ear down to my mouth and whisper.

"I love your art, but right now, I really need you to take me somewhere private and make love to me."

I thought my invitation was bold, but when Arlo turns his head and whispers in my ear. "What if I don't want to go somewhere private? What if I have something else in mind?"

My breath hitches, and I glance behind me to see Slate and Dodger share a knowing look.

"Depends," I mumble. "Do I still get fucked at the end of it?"

The slow, sexy grin Arlo offers me says yes.

Darcy

32

The three of them guide me around the gallery slowly, letting the anticipation build with every step we take. It starts off innocently enough, but teasing brushes of their hands across my ass quickly escalate to backing me into corners and kissing the living daylights out of me. By the time evening falls and we have to leave, my lips are kiss-swollen and my panties are soaked through. Arlo has his arm wrapped around my shoulders. His hand drops down to stroke the upper slopes of my breasts every so often.

If Dodger's thing is being in control, and Slate's is eating me out until I'm nothing more than a shaking wreck, I can't help but wonder if Arlo's is prolonged torture.

Given how quiet he is, I thought perhaps he would be into sweet, soft sex. The kind that winds you up and pushes you into orgasm gently, leaving you glowing for hours later. But after the plane, and now this, I'm beginning to wonder if it isn't something a little different.

A sharp pinch of my nipple through the fabric of my clothes draws a sharp gasp from me, and I blink, realising we've travelled farther than I thought while I was in my head. I have no idea where we are, but the three of them seem perfectly comfortable as they lead us along a street of rapidly filling bars and clubs and down a dirty alley.

They stop at a door which is painted with tribal designs and framed by bright red lanterns on either side. My brows furrow in confusion, and without pausing to explain, Slate hits the button on an unmarked intercom.

"Yes?" the mechanical speaker asks.

"Andraste," Dodger replies.

What kind of place requires a password?

"Welcome, sir." The intercom buzzes, and the door swings wide to reveal... darkness.

"Where are we?" I ask, confused.

"The Chantry," Arlo whispers against my ear. "It's my favourite secret place in the city. We helped Devon—one of Prophet's friends—open it last year."

The door swings shut behind us, and a mechanical click announces that we're locked in seconds before a new door opens to our left. A black uniformed server, bathed in a soft glow of candlelight, bows deeply as we catch sight of him. He's wearing a white mask that covers his entire face.

"Ms. Brown extends her apologies; she's out overseeing the expansion project in Denver. But your regular booth is ready for you, and she hopes you enjoy your visit."

Dodger nods, and that's apparently enough for the server. He turns and leads us down a flight of stairs and into a bar.

The decor is a strange fusion of industrial and gothic. The plain brick walls are broken up by pointed archways and lit by purple velvet-hung candelabras. There are no windows, and the lighting is low and warm, making the space seem cosy and intimate.

Our position beside the bar gives us a good view of the dining area beyond. There are several rows of velvet booths in the centre, occupied by beautiful people whose conversation rises above the orchestral rock music playing over hidden speakers. Around the edges of the restaurant are smaller, circular dining rooms, shrouded in the privacy of black lace curtains that half-hide their occupants from the rest of the world.

Though this place is undoubtedly posh, I'm not sure what to make of the atmosphere. Is it creepy? Is it cool? Is it both? I can't decide as our server leads us past the booths towards the far end of the room.

We finally stop at one of a line of private rooms along the back wall. Slate takes a spot on my left and Arlo on my right with Dodger slipping in on the guitarist's other side. Our server politely waits for us to slide into our seats before handing us our menus and disappearing with a soft bow.

From my position, I have a good view of the rest of the restaurant.

"I thought I'd seen everything," I murmur under my breath. "You have a regular table here? At a secret restaurant with a password?"

Dodger chuckles. "Surprised?"

I duck my head, fixing my gaze on the menu. It's one of those fancy ones where all the options are written in French and come with suggested wine pairings.

Good thing I speak multiple languages.

Slate's fingers capture my chin, forcing me to meet his eyes. "*Cariño*, we can leave if you don't like it. I promise you, though, the food is amazing."

I nod, because I trust them. "So... you bring all your dates here?"

Dodger chuckles. "No. In all honesty, we come here because the chef is Devon's wife, and she does the best chilli in the city. Plus, having a room like this means we're less likely to be interrupted by people wanting an autograph."

"That was Devon's idea," Slate finishes. "She's really into what she calls the industrial voodoo vibe."

"It's unique," I admit. "I've never seen anything like it."

Arlo's hand finds my thigh and squeezes. "What do you want to eat?"

He doesn't move his hand as we place our order, and once the server is gone, Dodger pulls our curtain closed, leaving us ensconced in our own tiny bubble of privacy.

As soon as the fabric is in place, Arlo's fingers slip higher up my skirt. All of his focus is concentrated on my lap at the point where my thighs meet, blocking further access.

"Let me in," he murmurs.

"We're in public," I hiss.

Only a piece of flimsy lace hides my shocked face from the rest of the restaurant, and the servers could return with our food at any time.

"I don't care," he says, eyes molten as he watches me. "Now shimmy that skirt up and part these pretty thighs. I think it's time we got Dodger back for how he teased me on the plane, don't you?"

I glance around, trying to judge how much would be visible through the curtain, but Arlo's fingers grip my chin, turning my head towards him.

"Don't think about them. This is about you and me. Trust me, Dark. I'd never let anyone see what belongs to us."

I see my own face, lips slightly parted, reflected back at me in his glasses.

"Take your glasses off," I challenge. "And maybe I'll consider it."

The corner of his lips twitches, but he does what I say, releasing my chin to remove them, then discarding them on the table with a flick of his wrist.

The fingers at my thighs stroke again, asking entry, and my pussy weeps, begging me to acquiesce.

Slowly, ever so slowly, I do as he wants, hitching my dress up and letting my thighs fall open.

Arlo's eyes smoulder as he watches. "You have no idea what you do to me, do you?"

I cup the outline of his cock over his tight jeans. "I have some inkling."

I can't help myself looking at the curtain again, but this time it's Slate who grabs my hair, turning my head towards him to claim my mouth in a desperate kiss.

"Let Lo play," Dodger says, scolding him. "It's his turn, after all."

Slate ignores him, continuing to steal my breath as Arlo's fingers tap-dance across the sensitive skin of my inner thighs. When he finally, blessedly, reaches my panties, he strokes over the cotton barrier with one finger.

I want to demand more. I want to curl up and hide.

My logical brain—never truly silent, even when I'm horny as hell—reminds me that the feeling of being watched is just the Spotlight Effect, but it doesn't make a difference.

It still feels like there are eyes on me as Arlo continues to leisurely stroke across the sensitive seam of my pussy.

"Soaked," he murmurs. "Don't you think you'd be more comfortable if you took these off?"

He hooks a finger beneath the edge of my panties as he says it, and a shiver runs up my spine as he releases it and the elastic snaps lightly back against my skin.

Swallowing my nerves, I nod, pulling back from Slate to hook my thumbs around the edges of the soft yellow fabric.

As soon as they're past my ass, I shimmy them down my legs, but before I can pick the panties up, Arlo's stolen them, tucking my underwear securely into his pocket.

It's official, he's a panty thief. That's the second pair I've lost, and I liked that set, damn it.

Giving him my best indignant look is hard when he and Slate are both pulling at my legs, stretching them wider beneath the table.

I freeze, caught like a rabbit in the headlights as the curtain parts and the masked servers start passing through our food. The pasta I'd been so excited to try slides across the table towards me, but I can barely summon the guts to smile and thank them because Arlo's left hand chooses that moment to find my clit and roll it gently between his fingers.

My thighs snap together, and my hands drop to my sides instead of reaching for the food like I planned. Dimly, I'm aware of Dodger waving away the offer of more drinks and the lace curtain falling back into place as the servers leave.

"How am I supposed to eat like this?" I ask, as Arlo's fingers—now trapped but still torturing me—continue to stroke with what limited motion he can get away with.

"Do you want me to stop?" Arlo asks, voice gone husky.

I shiver. "No." I can't think.

My thighs fall open, my body making the decision for me. My food—and our potential audience—is ignored in the face of the need he's steadily teasing to a crescendo.

"You're so perfect," he murmurs against my ear, leaning in. "Now, remember, don't make too much noise. You don't want anyone to know I'm getting you off under here, do you?"

Then, without pause, he ducks his slim frame down, slides beneath the table, and shimmies until his body is between my thighs.

Oh my god.

I've never in my life been eaten out at a restaurant before, but the warm breath washing over my pussy assures me that's exactly what he's about to do.

Dodger and Slate are grinning at me with knowing glances as Arlo starts pressing kisses along the creases at the top of my thighs. In this new position, his fingers have so much more freedom to play. His shoulders pin my legs obscenely wide, keeping me spread as his forefinger presses lightly against my entrance.

When he finally tongues my clit, I have to clamp a hand over my mouth to contain the moan that threatens to slip free. I scoot back, trying to get away before I embarrass myself, but there's nowhere to go. I'm trapped between the bench and his mouth as he slowly sinks a finger deep inside me and curls it up to rub against my G-spot.

"Eat up," Slate encourages, gesturing to my pasta. "It would be a shame to let it get cold."

I can't even summon the strength to glare at him. My face has gone slack with pleasure as my body hurtles closer and closer to orgasm with every flick of Arlo's tongue.

"How's yours, Lo?" Dodger asks.

Arlo leans back just long enough to answer. "Delicious."

I use the break to snatch up my fork, determined to at least act natural, but the moment he starts licking me again, it clatters noisily against the edge of my bowl.

"Better hurry up, Lo," Slate murmurs. "It appears our little *angelita* is not as good at multitasking as we thought."

"Play with her ass," Dodger says, as I pant, caught on the edge of rapture. "That always sends her over the edge."

Arlo freezes for a second, then grins against my sensitive flesh. "Oh, really?"

The finger in my pussy gives another curling thrust before slipping free, leaving me gasping and empty as it trails farther back to push insistently at my asshole.

"Lemme in, Dark," he says, between licks.

"We should plug her ass before we go to Prophet's tomorrow," Slate suggests as Arlo's finger slides past the sensitive ring until it's buried up to his first knuckle. "Tease the shit out of him."

Dodger's phone is out before I can shoot down the idea.

"Already ordering one. What colour would you like, baby girl? Pink, purple, or blue."

I can't answer him. If I open my mouth, I'm going to

whimper, or scream, and then everyone will *know* exactly what's going on.

"Pink." Slate decides for me as Arlo's finger sinks deeper at the same time he spears my pussy with his tongue.

I bite my lip, but Dodger slides in closer and frees it, claiming my mouth in a fierce kiss.

"You want to know a secret, baby girl?" he whispers. "Prophet is an ass man. Once he finally falls, he'll be begging you to let him fuck you back there."

"Don't let him," Slate murmurs, kissing my neck. "Torture him a bit first. He deserves it."

Arlo pulls his finger back, then pushes a second in beside it. The stretch and burn as he stretches me open makes me gasp, and Dodger uses the opportunity to twine our tongues together.

Slate's hand comes up to cup my breast through the fabric of my clothes, kneading the flesh until my thighs tense around Arlo's head.

Together, all three of them push me over the edge. My orgasm makes my hips buck wildly against his mouth, and my ass clenches on his fingers. I grind, thrash, and shake as pleasure courses through my body. The boys keep going, helping me ride the waves until I slump between the three of them, breathing hard.

"Gorgeous," Arlo praises, withdrawing his hand and sliding smoothly back up into his seat.

I reach for him, but he's already undoing his fly, freeing his cock from the confines of his leathers. The head is purple and angry, and when I wrap my hand around it, a pearl of pre-cum starts to bead at the tip.

"Up," Arlo growls, hands clasping my waist and lifting me until I'm straddling him.

I look up in shock, because even with the curtain, surely *someone* is bound to notice me riding him in the middle of a restaurant, but the look on his face tells me he's beyond caring as he lowers me down onto his cock.

"Arlo," I moan his name, and he captures it in his kiss.

"Move on me, Dark," he murmurs against my lips. "I'm yours. Take me."

One of his hands falls between us, his thumb angling to rub against my clit as I snap my hips back and forth over him. The wet sounds of us fucking fill the tiny space, and I claim his mouth again to muffle my quiet moans. With his thumb sending fireworks through my body with each thrust, it doesn't take long for me to tense.

I just can't seem to get—

Arlo's finger returns, penetrating my ass with ease, and I gasp at the sudden, dual invasion.

Every muscle from my toes to my fingertips locks and my spine stiffens as I come with a quiet gasp. My head falls into the crook of his neck, and he groans, my orgasm drawing his forth. His cock twitches inside me, and for a second, we just sit there, cradling one another. The other two retreat, giving us our space, and I sigh in contentment, burying myself into Arlo's chest. Then I start to panic as I realise we didn't think this through.

"What about the mess?" I hiss, trying to draw away.

His hands squeeze my ass, keeping me in place. "There are napkins."

My eyes are wide as I look down and catch sight of the objects in question. "They're fancy cotton ones," I hiss. "I'm not leaving one of those behind for someone to clean up."

His smirk undoes me. "Or you can walk to the bathroom with my cum dripping down your thighs. I know which one I'd prefer." My pussy clenches around him where he's still buried inside me, and he raises a single brow. "Something you want to confess, Dark?"

Where has the soft, quiet man from before gone? I have no

idea how to deal with this sexy imposter without getting flustered.

"Want me to order you to do it?" he whispers. "Then you can blame me for it when it turns you on."

I shake my head, because I may just have fucked his brains out in public, but I'm not sure I'm ready for that level of kinky stuff yet. Arlo just shrugs and hands me a napkin without forcing the issue.

"Dinner's still warm," Dodger informs us as I slip free of Arlo's grip and back to my seat.

"I'll be back for it later," Arlo mumbles, zipping his fly and squeezing past Slate as he heads for the bathroom.

Darcy
33

I eat my food in a daze, unable to help my burning cheeks as I dart glances at the rest of the restaurant. I wonder if anyone suspects what just happened in our booth. Would they say anything if they did?

The guys are acting as if nothing has happened, and when we're all finished, I try to sneak away to pay again, but Dodger practically jumps to get there first.

"Let me," I protest.

He pins me with a look so dark it's almost haunting. "Baby girl, I know you're independent, and I'm sure you could pay if you wanted, but... let me?"

Ordinarily I might've argued, but something in his tone convinces me not to.

I turn to Arlo and catch him sneaking the napkin I used to clean myself up into a pocket of his jacket. At least some poor server won't find it.

"Can I have my panties back?"

He shakes his head. "I think I earned them."

"Come on," Slate mutters. "Let's get back to the hotel."

We leave the way we came in, and I don't dare look back to

see if our activities left a wet patch. Oh well, it's leather, right? It's wipe-able.

Forcing down the sudden urge to hunt down some antibacterial wipes to clean a mess that may or may not—okay, it totally does—exist, I fall to the back of our group and let Dodger guide me out of the restaurant with his arm around my shoulders.

"Will you ever let me pay?" I ask, the lightness in my tone hiding my curiosity as we stride back down the street, now humming with clubgoers chatting happily amongst themselves.

Dodger's hangup seems to be money, and I can't help but wonder if it's related to what Arlo told me earlier.

"No."

"Do you mind if I ask why?"

He runs a hand through his hair and glances away. "You could, but I don't think you'd understand the answer."

"Maybe I won't," I admit. "But I can try."

He sighs. "You've never been poor, have you?"

I shake my head. Even before Man took me in, my parents were comfortable. Not rich, but nothing like what Arlo described them going through.

"Money's like a drug. Except it's not the money you're attached to. Not really... It's the security. Once you've lived at the bottom—the true bottom—not knowing where your next meal will come from or if you have a place to stay at night, then you get a taste of this"—he gestures around us—"you'll do anything to avoid going back to that life. *Anything*."

He scuffs his feet as he walks, not meeting my eyes. "I grew up watching my mom disappear into her room to fuck men for money every night. She spent her mornings carefully partitioning every single dollar into this folder full of plastic pockets, and each one was labelled." He looks me hard in the eye.

"Rent, food, electricity, school, emergencies. Most of what she earned went to feeding and clothing me. She rarely kept anything for herself."

I squeeze his hand. "She sounds like a good mom."

Dodger's shoulders slump. "I fucked it up for her. One day, one of her clients stayed over and left his wallet on the table. I was a teenager who'd just been told we couldn't afford for me to go on a school trip. It just seemed so unfair. How come this guy could literally buy my mom's body for a full night, but we couldn't manage a bus fare to the city? So I took it."

I blink. "You went into juvie for fraud." I know that much from his file.

"Yeah. It started a long, slippery slope," he admits. "I paid for that trip. Then I got into a habit of going through wallets and writing down card details—or just taking them. I bought myself a new pair of jeans and a backpack. Upgraded our internet package and got a calculator for math class. Little things. Things no one would notice on their bill."

"But you got caught."

He scoffs. "Yeah. I got stupid. Started buying bigger and bigger shit. Cocky asshole that I was, I figured no one had noticed so far. Why should they notice if I sent my mom on a cruise for Mother's Day? Why would they notice a car?"

"You bought a car?" My eyebrows rise into my hairline.

He shrugs. "Neither of those things outed me. It was a cocktail, actually. I booked myself a holiday to Europe, and they blocked the card when I tried to use it at a bar in Italy—I didn't think to see if it would work abroad. Anyway, the card company called the rightful owner about the suspicious transaction. The Italian police showed up, arrested me, and flew me back home to stand trial."

He stops, jaw clenching as he wrestles with his demons in

the middle of the crowded street. "I landed in juvie, and my mom was still trying to get work, except it was harder because word got out about what I'd done, and a lot of her men thought she'd been behind it all. So, not only was I in prison, I'd accidentally stripped her of most of her income with my stupid stunt. When she got ill, she didn't have the money for medicine. She didn't even get a proper funeral, and I wasn't allowed out to watch them stick her in the ground."

Oh, shit.

"Dodger, I'm so sorry." I pull him close, wrapping him in a hug. "You couldn't have known, though. You were just a kid."

"If I hadn't done it, she might've lived." His voice is dull now. "I went into juvie with a mom and came out as an orphan. I have to live with that. At the start, it was harder. The grief was... raw, I guess. I didn't know how to deal with my emotions when they got too much, and... well, you've seen my scars."

I have, and my heart breaks all over again for them. I hug him tighter, burying my head in his chest as I try to convey through touch just how much I wish I could've spared him all of that.

"Money could've saved her life." He pulls away, and I catch a glimpse of the anguish in his expression before he shuts down. "That's why I won't let you, or anyone else I care for, pay for shit. I know, logically, that you probably could, but what if one day, that hundred dollar food bill is the difference between you being able to pay rent and you being homeless?"

"No one can predict that," I reply. "All we can do is trust that we have people around us who will take care of us when we're struggling and return the favour if they need it."

"You guys okay?" Slate calls, tactlessly, from where he and Arlo have stopped ahead.

"Fine," Dodger calls, clearing his throat. "I was just asking Darcy if she thought Arlo would let me piggyback on his night."

"It might be Prophet's night," I retort, as we catch up, and the four of us start walking again. "What happened to the bowl?"

Slate rolls his eyes. "Prophet is too busy being noble to sleep with you. Plus, he can't have any idea you're coming tomorrow, which means it's Arlo's turn. He can sleep in your room to make sure you don't have to deal with any cameras or shit."

We all grimace at the reminder. "I've set all the footage on that drive to corrupt after a few hours," I mutter as we catch up to the two of them. "But yes, I'm game for a sleepover."

"A three-way sleepover?" Dodger presses.

"You're not stealing my night," Arlo warns.

"Oh, come on." Dodger pulls his best puppy eyes, effortlessly hiding the pain from before. "We all know you love being watched. I even promise not to snore."

Arlo's eyes narrow. "I don't believe you."

"I promise not to snore as much as Darcy does," he amends, dodging my playful elbow to the ribs.

"I do not snore," I protest, glowering at him as he shares a *look* with Slate that says I'm lying.

"You don't," Slate says. "Of course you don't. You're our perfect lady. You don't even fart. You just sprinkle unicorn dust, and—"

I mime shoving my fingers down my throat and retching. "Too much. I get that you should be grovelling, but stop spouting bullshit to get on my good side."

He just laughs.

"How about a cuddle pile?" I suggest when we reach the door to my room.

"We can't afford for them to notice we're all missing," Slate points out. "Arlo can stay with you tonight. With any luck, Miguel will think he's out at a party. Tomorrow morning, we'll come and get you ready for Prophet."

I blush at the reminder of what Dodger ordered earlier. "I've never worn one for a long time before," I admit. "Not around other people."

Slate grins. "Had you ever had sex in a restaurant before tonight?"

I shake my head.

"Did you enjoy it?" Arlo asks, and I feel his gaze boring into my head.

I bite my lip and grin. "Yeah."

"Then trust us," Slate finishes. "And if you hate it—and given how Lo's finger in your ass set you off, I don't think you will—then we'll take it out, and no one has to know."

"But if you love it like I think you will," Dodger finishes, crowding me against the door. "The rest of us are going to have hard-ons imagining you squirming all day long."

"What a shame." I slide my key card into my door and twist the handle. "I'm sure you can take care of each other."

Slate barks out a laugh. "Nah, I don't want my dick anywhere near their pasty asses."

Dodger presses a kiss to my lips. "Sweet dreams, baby girl. See you in the morning."

I kiss him back, then Slate, and watch the two of them disappear down the corridor wistfully until Arlo shuts the door.

"I call little spoon," he says, starting to strip off his jacket, only to stop halfway. "Turn off the light?"

I'm halfway to the bathroom, but I stop and cock my head at him. "You can't tell me you're shy now."

His eyes dart down. "No... it's just... my arms aren't pretty."

Frowning, because every inch of him is gorgeous, I shrug and keep walking. "Whatever you want, but I don't care."

When I return, he's already in bed, with only the lamp on the table to illuminate him. I tiptoe around him, pausing as he chokes out a laugh.

"Does that say *Stabby before 9 a.m.*?"

I shrug, glancing down at the cute knife-wielding koala on my chest. "It was a present from Naomi. She likes stabbing her marks."

He shakes his head and turns to face me as I climb beneath the covers. "I can't believe you grew up in a house full of assassins."

"You're looking at the original," I reply, smiling. "But yeah, it was fun. I loved having so many sisters. It's part of why I've always wanted a big family." I pause. "Now, you wanted to be little spoon?"

He flashes me a wicked grin and turns around so fast it almost gives me whiplash. "Snuggle me hard, Dark. Otherwise, I might fall out of bed."

I snort and wrap my arm around him, sneaking my upper leg between both of his and burying my nose in his back, breathing in his leather scent.

Then I fight the urge to stiffen as his arm emerges from the covers to switch off the lamp and I catch sight of the scars.

That's why he wanted the light out.

As much as it's killing me, I don't pry. I keep my breathing even, slip my glasses off, and slide them onto the nightstand. His skin brushes against mine beneath the sheets, and I feel the subtle raised bumps along his forearms.

My mind is racing, trying to figure it out. They aren't in neat and even lines like Dodger's. Arlo's scars are random and jagged.

He sighs beneath me. "You saw."

"You don't owe me an explanation." It's clear he's uncomfortable about them. "The fact that you've suffered doesn't change how I feel about you."

He turns, pressing a kiss to my forehead and embracing me until I'm pressed against his chest.

"On her sober days, my mom used to say God put a little more of Himself into artists," Arlo says. "That's why we feel the weight of the world so deeply. It must be true, because I've never met an artist who hasn't struggled with their mental health, but it makes me wonder; is God the same way?"

I bite back my automatic urge to shut him down. After what happened with my parents, I can *never* put my trust in any religion. But if Arlo needs that faith to help him navigate life, then I'm not about to argue. Especially when he's vulnerable.

In my experience, there's no great plan to this messy business called living, but that doesn't mean I see no value in hope and morality. I've seen how people cling to religion when everything else has fallen apart, and sometimes their faith is powerful enough to get them through.

"When I was using heavily," he says finally, when it's clear I won't answer his question. "I got these tactile hallucinations —they called it formication—where it felt like bugs were crawling under my skin. It was some freaky shit. I tried to dig them out, and in the process, I fucked up my arms."

"It must have been terrifying," I agree, quietly.

Arlo leans down and kisses me hesitantly. "There were days when I was working on getting clean when I didn't want to get out of bed. Do you know what made me?"

I snuggle closer. "What?"

"You. I lived for our game time. The others won't tell you, but when things were really bad, playing Runes with you was the only time that Prophet and Slate were civil to one another. You made it feel like I had my friends back."

This time, I move to kiss him.

He doesn't let me, stopping me with a finger to my lips. "I love you, Darcy. I've loved you since we first heard you sassing us over voice chat, and I'll love you until I die."

My heart gives a soft thump, then melts. "I love you too."

Prophet
34

The doorbell rings, and my hands—currently wrapped in Mama's bright pink rubber gloves—freeze in the hot water of the sink.

"Can you get that, baby?" she asks, from the other side of the kitchen. "I'm busy with the salad."

She's using the tone. The one that means trouble.

Silently wondering what she's up to, I shake off the water and plod through the house to the front door. Knowing Mama, I'm sure half the neighbourhood is waiting on the doorstep—at least that would explain why there's four times as much food as we normally have. She likes to do shit like this, pulling in people I knew from childhood because she thinks my lifestyle leaves me ungrounded.

But when I swing open the door, it's not neighbours, but the band on the front step.

"Nice gloves." Dodger snickers, raising his phone to snap a picture.

Shit. I rip the pink monstrosities off my hands with a scowl that promises death should he not delete that immediately.

"Oh, good. You're here," Mama says, sneaking up behind

me before I can slam the door in their faces. "Did you bring her like I told you to?"

Slate is grinning, which I realise far too late, because when he steps aside, Darcy is there. Her cheeks are flushed pink, and she's staring at her shoes like my mom's rainbow doormat is the most interesting thing she's seen all week.

"Here she is, Mama P," Dodger says, giving my mom his most innocent smile.

"Oh, sugar, you never told me how gorgeous she was!"

Then, in a scene plucked straight from my nightmares, Mama reaches out and catches Darcy's wrist, pulling her into the house.

"I'm Penelope," she begins. "But you can call me Mama P, like everyone else. Y'know, when Slate rang me up and told me my boy was hiding a secret girlfriend, and asked if I wanted to meet you, I couldn't believe they'd all actually found someone to suit all four of them—"

Darcy, caught up in the whirlwind that is my mother, is speechless as she's dragged into the house and towards the kitchen.

I glare at the remaining trio on my parents' doorstep. Even Arlo is here, fidgeting at the back.

I'm being backed into a corner, and I don't like it one bit.

"You. Called. My. *Mom*?" I hiss at Slate. "Low. Fucking. Blow." I can't even yell like I want to.

The second Mama hears even a hint of fighting, the two of us will be stuck together for the entire afternoon. On one memorable occasion, she made Slate and me share everything —cutlery and chairs included—and hug one another every ten minutes until we got along.

My mom is terrifying.

Slate shrugs. "All's fair in love and war, my brother."

"Arlo, Malik wants to show you his train set," Mama calls, and the guitarist gleefully slips past me, saved by my nephew.

"Ethan, you better go and summon your dad from his shed. Oh, and Dodger and Slate, can you help Mikey with the patio chairs?"

"*Sí, jefa*," Slate calls back, and I glare at him.

"Stop smooth talking me, boy," she calls back. "I already made your favourite mac and cheese."

Slate's grin turns soft, and I relax just a fraction. Guilt quickly rises, taking the place of my rage, at the reminder that Mama isn't just mine—not really. She unofficially adopted my band mates years ago, happily filling in for their own absent moms.

For all their quirks, I lucked out with my family, but the guys weren't so blessed.

Sighing, I let the two of them into my parent's craftsman style bungalow and follow them through the kitchen towards the back door. My mom is chatting away at Darcy in the other room, and my fists clench.

Why is she here? No. I don't need to ask that. She's here because Slate did something to make her change her mind.

Something that put her back on a messy collision course with our band.

The back door creaks under my hand, and I make a note to wire Destiny some more money to get it sorted. My parents won't take my money, but my sister's husband, Mikey, gets away with fixing the little things for them.

Dad's shed is tucked away at the very end of the garden. The glint of light in the window tells me he's smoking—again—and I'm proved right when I open the door and get a lungful of that familiar tobacco smell.

Every time I come in here, I lose the tension in my shoulders. No matter what happens, Dad's shed with its tool-lined walls and the lone star flag hung from the rafters will never change.

"If Mama catches you doing that, she's going to be pissed," I tell him, smirking.

He rolls his eyes and turns away from the mirror that's hidden inside his old military helmet. When he angles it just right, it serves as his early warning system should Mama come up the garden path.

The cig still hangs from his lips as he looks me up and down. "Dinner done?"

"She's ready for you to light the barbeque," I confirm. "The band is here too."

"Good." He shuffles over to his workbench and starts putting away his tools. "They bring that girlfriend your mom was excited about?"

So, he was in on it too? Why am I not surprised?

My dad may be quiet and reserved, but he's just as nosy as Mama. If not more so. No doubt, even my other sisters—who live in a different fucking time zone—have probably heard about this by now.

"Yeah."

"Good."

I thought my parents would be against the whole idea of us sharing a girl, even though they've known about our intentions for years. It's different to actually see it in practice. Apparently, they really meant it when they gave us their blessing all those years ago.

Dad and I lapse into easy silence as he finishes his smoke, then I follow just behind him as he limps down the garden path towards the patio.

"Going well," he grunts as we pass Dodger, Slate, and Mikey.

They do seem to finally be having more luck now that there's three of them to tackle the monstrous wooden patio set. They've even managed to haul the huge wedge-shaped table out of the garage.

Dad heads straight for the grill, unfolding all the pipes and dutifully donning the bright blue apron Destiny got him last year, which proclaims him king of the grills.

With my job done, I grab Dodger by the collar—I know for a fact if I talk to Slate right now, I'll lose my shit—and drag him to my childhood bedroom, praying to God with every step that Darcy is keeping my mother and sister occupied.

"Gonna let me go any time soon?" Dodger asks, as I carefully shut the door and shove him into the back of it.

"Why is she here?" I hiss, finally releasing his shirt. "I thought we agreed it was for the best that she stayed far away from us."

Dodger glares at me. "Things have changed."

"Why? Because she's somehow an assassin now?" I scoff, pacing away and running a hand over my short hair. "How many assassins do you think the cartel deals with on a monthly basis? Miguel is still alive!" I release a deep, angry huff of air. "Darcy's mission is going to get her killed."

Dodger frowns. "If you think that, you don't know her at all. How many people have you ever met with her brains? She saved Sully, and Miguel never even knew she was there."

I turn, intending to give him a piece of my mind, only stop short, and force myself back to the window.

He doesn't understand. Even after what happened to Sully, he doesn't seem to see the risks clearly. Or perhaps he sees them, and he simply has more hope than I do that Darcy can pull us through unscathed.

"I know she's smart," I snarl. "But all the brains in the world aren't enough. The cartel is ruthless—"

"You know, I'm pretty ruthless myself," Darcy interrupts, and I turn to find the door open and her framed within it. "Your mom sent me to find you. She says she wants you there for the baby photos."

Kill. Me.

As if on cue, I hear Destiny cackle.

"Mama, please don't!" I fly past both of them, trying to get to that damned photo album before Slate—

Too late.

He's perched on my mom's hideous, old, floral couch, looking in horrified amusement as my mom brandishes a photo of me as a toddler, wearing nothing more than a saucepan helmet.

"Mama," I groan.

"Sit down, baby. Darcy, you have to see this one. Destiny and Page used to dress him up for their tea parties when their daddy was doing an overseas tour and they needed another princess. Here Ethan is as Snow White."

Code red.

"Mama, I've got to show Darcy something," I say, grabbing her wrist. "In my room."

At least I can limit her exposure. I'm pretty sure my mom has shown the band that photo before, but what little remains of my dignity won't survive Darcy seeing it.

"Real men wear dresses," she objects as I use my bulk to keep her from looking around me and into the living room.

"Not saying they don't," I grunt, walking forward and forcing her to back up. "But you will never see that photo."

Or the next one in the pile, which, if memory serves, is of me playing an upside down recorder while covered in my mom's makeup and wearing her wig.

I manage to usher Darcy back into my room and close the door behind me with a lot less fuss than I anticipated. As soon as we're safe, I drop her hand.

Now we're in the very position I've tried my best to avoid. Alone. Together. With a bed.

I point at the mattress in silence, but I can't say I'm really surprised when she disobeys and heads for my old desk.

Crap, this place is a mess. Mama never touches anything in

here, insisting it's my space, even though I'm well past the age where I'd consider moving back in. The desk alone is covered in an old Yamaha keyboard with a missing C sharp key and hundreds of books, flyers, and magazines.

It's a dumping ground.

"Aww," Darcy says, plucking a piece of paper out of the mess. "It's you guys!"

Somehow, her seeing the flyer for one of our first gigs is more embarrassing than my mom's baby photo album. "Put that down."

I don't ever want to see the band's name written in WordArt again. For all the evil Miguel is responsible for, at least our branding is a hundred times more professional now.

She relinquishes it, only to pluck out another photo of us all as teenagers, fresh out of juvie. Shit.

Wrapping my hands around her waist, I pull her to me. My traitorous dick hardens the second her plush ass bumps against my groin, and I suppress a groan.

Her harsh inhale freezes me in place.

"Did I hurt you?" Damn, I need to be more careful. She's so much smaller than me, and I never, ever want to cause her pain.

Her cheeks are beet red, and she won't meet my gaze. I release her like I've been burned.

"Angel, I need to know if you're okay. Did I pinch you or something?"

"No," she squeaks, turning redder by the second. "I... erm. It's nothing."

I pin her with a look. "We're not leaving here until you—"

Darcy finally meets my eyes. "You didn't hurt me. Dodger plugged my ass before we came, and you jostled it when you..." Her fleeting courage abandons her, and she hides her face in her hands. "God, why does this stuff happen to me?"

If I was semi-hard before, just from having her body against mine, I'm painfully hard now.

Damn those conniving—they *knew*.

This is Slate's most devious plan yet. Bring her here, introduce her to my mother—the one other woman in the world whose opinion matters to me—then, as the death blow, spring her plugged ass at me.

"Let me see." The words rip from my mouth before I can take them back.

Darcy stops fidgeting with her hair, her hands dropping to the hem of her skirt as if she's honestly considering it.

Then come the six little words that spell my doom.

"Aren't you going to ask nicely?"

When she meets my eyes this time, the spark in her own eyes tells me she knows exactly what those words do to me.

"Wanna say that again?" I ask, wondering how far she's willing to sass me.

She opens her mouth, but I don't give her a chance to follow through.

A second later, she's bent over the bed, her blonde locks wrapped around my fist as I flip the pleats of her skirt out of my way and expose...

"Holy mother of—" I cut myself off with a groan. "I'm going to kill them."

She's wearing a garter belt. A garter belt and a tiny black thong that does nothing to disguise the pink gem winking from between her cheeks. She's so wet, she's glistening. I trace my shaking finger through the silken folds of her cunt before I can help myself.

"Prophet," she moans, her ass rising back, begging me for more.

I flick the plug in reprimand, and she gasps again.

"Stay still," I warn. "Or I'll spank your ass."

I might do it, anyway, just to watch it turn a pretty shade of pink beneath my palm. She deserves it for being a brat.

My control is hanging by a thread. All the good reasons I should stay away, protect her, are being slowly ripped from me with every twinkle of that gem. God, her ass is twitching around it, making it dance with each clench. Taunting me with thoughts of how she would strangle my cock if I fucked her back there.

Darcy was already my walking fantasy come to life; an angel incarnate. Now this image will haunt me every time I close my eyes.

"This is embarrassing," she complains.

My hand comes down without warning, spanking her just hard enough to sting, but not hard enough to truly hurt. "I'm looking."

If this is the only time I get to see this, I want it tattooed on my brain.

"If you're not going to fuck me, let me go," she retorts.

"Beg," I retort, and the possessive monster within me purrs at the idea.

"In your dreams." God, I love her fire. All riled up and sassy and *mine.*

The thought—so out of place—snaps me out of the haze, and I release her, throwing myself across the room.

"We are *not* doing this," I say, more for myself than her.

Darcy—to her credit—turns so she's sitting on the bed and stares me down. "There's more to this than you protecting me from the cartel, isn't there?"

Too fucking perceptive. "The cartel is a huge issue. If they don't hurt you, they'll hurt someone I care about."

"Sound logic," she replies. "But when they're dead, what then? Will you consider it?"

It's hard to believe that she's capable of the feat, but I won't say that. I trust her after all these years, even though she was keeping her profession a secret. Then again, we never exactly told her we were rock stars, either.

I could blow her off—give her some lame excuse—but I don't think she'll buy it.

"I don't share well."

I shake my head as I remember how eagerly I signed the band contract. I was full of the optimism and disregard for the future that was my hallmark in my teenage years, but I've had ages to think over what it would be like.

"We'll try to make this work, and my jealousy will kick in."

It was the reason I went to juvie, after all. I found out my girl was sleeping with half the football team behind my back. Then, while they were off chasing a ball around a field like a bunch of dogs, I snuck into their changing rooms, stole their keys, and carefully drove each of their fancy cars into the nearest river.

A small hopeful part of me tries to argue that that was literally almost twenty years ago, and that things are different this time, but I brush it off.

"There's too much room for misunderstandings and hurt feelings," I continue. "I'm not sure I could take it if I felt like you preferred one of us over the others." It would destroy what remains of the friendships I once had.

She doesn't immediately rebuke me or try to soothe me with easy promises. Instead, she gives my point a few seconds of careful consideration.

"You can't know unless you try," she finally says. "You've seen me with Dodger on the plane. Were you jealous then?"

God, no. I was more turned on than I'd ever been in my life. But that was one time. A long-term relationship would be different.

She must read my answer in my expression. "We're adults. If it stops working, we can communicate."

"And if we can't?" I challenge. "This could ruin our friendship."

Darcy pins me with a knowing look. "Haven't you been doing a good enough job of that by yourself?" She pauses. "You're pushing us away because you're scared. I get it." Damn, I wish she'd stop pinning me with those big green eyes. "The guys and I are committed to this, with or without you. I guess you just have to decide if the jealousy you might feel as part of our relationship is worse than the resentment you'd suffer watching us together from the outside. "

Then, as if she hasn't just cut my knees out from under me, she flounces off the bed and heads for the door.

When it slams behind her, the gust of wind knocks the photo she was looking at from its precarious position on the corner of my desk. It swirls in the air, then lands at my feet, and I bend to pick it up.

My younger self stares out, mismatched eyes judging me silently as he stands guard over the rest of the band, laughing and joking together.

I miss those days more than anything. We may have been dirt poor then, but we had each other's backs. Without Miguel, could we go back to that?

I'm not so sure. We spend so much of our time fighting that I'm not sure that killing Miguel and his brothers is enough to undo the damage.

Damage I caused.

The realisation creeps up on me slowly, but with the impetus of a baseball bat. I slump onto my own bed, rubbing my temples with my free hand as I stare at the picture.

You'd like to think that trials will make your friendships stronger, but that wasn't true in our case. Resentment and fear made me lash out. I don't even blame them anymore for the situation we're stuck in. Not really. But in the process of fighting to leave the band to try to keep my family safe, I've created a huge divide between us.

Hell, pushing Darcy away probably played a huge part in Arlo's relapse.

If Miguel dies, then I was an asshole for nothing.

For the first time, I try to picture life without the cartel. I'd have more free time without the constant touring. I could keep writing songs for money, work at the gym to pass the time. If the guys moved in with Darcy, maybe I could visit and—

The air leaves my lungs in a rush.

If the guys lived with Darcy, I'd have to watch them loving her, filling her with the babies she wants, raising children with her eyes and their mischievous grins. Any chance I had with her would be gone, and it would all be my own doing. And she's right. Whatever jealousy I might've avoided by staying clear of the relationship would come back a hundredfold just watching them enjoying the happiness they deserve.

The question is, am I too late to change that?

This latest plan of Slate's reeks of a Hail Mary. A last effort to bring me into the fold before they give up on me.

"Uncle Ethan?" Malik asks, peering around my door.

"Hey lil' bit," I call, putting the picture down. "What's up?"

He stumbles into my room, looking around at my old stuff with wide, curious kid eyes. "Nana said to come get you for dinner," he says, looking at me once again. "But we can hide here if you don't want her to know you're crying."

Shit. I reach up and swipe the back of my hand against my eyes, grimacing when I realise that yes, there's moisture there.

Malik uses both arms to claw his way up onto my bed, shimmying until he's beside me, and wraps me in a huge hug.

"You need to eat, lil' bit," I say. "You've still got a lot of growing to do. You can't skip meals."

"Okay," he says, not arguing. "Do you wanna talk about it? Did your girlfriend make you cry? Girls do that sometimes when they like you. My teacher told me that when Talisha told me off for not sharing my bouncy ball at recess."

His words run into each other so quickly that it takes me a second to put it all together.

Is some girl picking on him?

"I'm not sure that's always the case."

"It's okay," Malik continues. "When I shared my ball, Talisha let me play in the sandpit with her, and then we made this castle, and she said she was sorry for being mean, and then I said it was okay and she could always play with my ball."

I could live a thousand years and still not understand kindergarten politics, but fortunately, Malik is satisfied with a nod.

"Darcy didn't make me cry," I admit. "I was just... sad thinking about the future."

"Because your band is angry?" he asks. "I heard Nana and Mom talking about it. It made them sad too."

It did? I tried to keep the drama away from them, but I should've known Mama would pick up on that stuff. The woman has a supernatural level of perceptiveness when it comes to her family.

"If you 'pologise, they'll be happy again," he concludes, with a certainty that only comes naturally to five-year-olds.

"I'll try," I promise, slowly. "But things aren't always that simple."

Darcy
35

We tumble into the band's hotel suite a little after midnight. Arlo and Dodger have to almost hold me upright, thanks to the strength of Mama P's homemade cocktails. I'm a giggling mess, but the best part is, I don't even care.

My guys are here, I just survived an entire barbecue with a plug in my ass without anyone—aside from Prophet— noticing a thing, and I even got to thrash them all at family trivia night.

I am a trivia goddess, after all.

"Come on, you lightweight," Dodger murmurs. "Let's get you to bed."

He's got a gleam in his eyes, the same one that he wore when he carefully worked this silly plug into my butt, and a sharp stab of arousal punctures the happy fuzz.

"I'm not drunk," I promise, doing my best not to smile. "Just a little tipsy."

"I think she'd prefer my bed," Slate says, trying to weave between me and Dodger to steal me away.

Arlo elbows him in the gut. "What about me? I want to snuggle Drunk Darcy."

"You had her last night," Dodger retorts. "If we're taking turns—"

"If we're taking turns, it's my night."

Prophet's voice freezes the four of us in place, and a devious grin paints Slate's face.

The bassist turns slowly, schooling his expression as he extends a hand towards me in invitation. "As you wish."

I look up at the drummer in confusion.

Deep in the back of my mind, I remember that we just had this conversation. He wasn't willing to try a few hours ago. So why is he pushing for this?

My pussy, remembering how it felt to be under his scrutiny earlier, clenches in hope.

Prophet's face gives away nothing as he holds out a hand to me. "Come, angel."

My brain helpfully supplies another scenario when he might say those words in a far huskier tone.

Oh yeah, here comes Drunk Darcy's most elusive mode— horny as fuck. I slip my hand into his grip easily, sighing as he effortlessly arranges me so I'm pressed against his side.

Then he has to go and ruin everything. "Don't worry. I'm not taking advantage of you while you're drunk. But I think someone ought to take that plug out of you before you fall asleep." He pauses, looking over my head at the rest of the band. "In the morning, we have some things to talk about."

The four of them exchange nods, and Prophet dismisses them all by turning us and heading for his room.

The second the door closes, he releases me.

"First, I need you to tell me how to get rid of the cameras," he mutters.

I grin and fish out my phone. This means I'm getting laid, right? He just doesn't want anyone watching.

A few taps and the app I designed to detect radio frequencies pops up. I walk around the room, frowning as I trip on the uneven floor. Luckily, Prophet is there to catch me each time.

"In the alarm clock," I say, when I'm sure that I've checked everywhere. "That's it."

Prophet nods and rips his shirt over his head in one smooth move, chucking the fabric in the direction of the bedside table. It lands perfectly, obscuring any view of us, and leaving me free to explore his abs.

"You're so yummy," I say, then blink as I realise I said that out loud. "Oops."

His eyes smoulder as he looks at me, and his nostrils flare.

"Angel, I need you to bend over the bed for me. You're not sleeping with that plug in."

Grinning, because I know a sexy excuse when I hear one, I bend over and helpfully flip my skirt up.

"Sweet fucking Christ." Prophet sounds tortured.

"You can fuck my ass if you want," I say, trying to wiggle my butt enticingly, but I end up overbalancing. "Slate and Dodger said you would, and I'm game to try."

The plug felt hot going in, and I'm suddenly desperate for more.

"Darcy..." I turn and look over my shoulder to find him scrubbing a hand over his face. "You're not sober, and I'm not comfortable touching you until you are, let alone introducing you to—"

"I've done butt stuff before," I cut in. "It was awful, but I'm willing to do it again if you like it. Second time's the charm, right?"

I have a feeling *anything* Prophet does to my ass will be better than that awful, unprepared attempt years ago. He just oozes confidence.

"Doesn't matter," he retorts, hand stroking softly over my ass before his fingers come to rest on the plug. "Relax for me."

I clench harder, my earlier horniness quickly giving way to indescribable sadness. "No."

"No? Angel, you can't sleep with it in. It's bad for you." His hand has frozen, spreading me open but not going further. "If you don't want me to take it out, you can do it."

My eyes sting, and my breath starts to hitch. "But, you're leaving. If I can't convince you to stay, I'll never get to be your human dumbbell again, or make you beg, or... or—" I choke on the last word.

God, this is embarrassing, but I just can't seem to stop.

Prophet growls something under his breath. "Relax."

This time, his order is so sharp and shocking that I do as he says. Despite how angry he sounds, he's gentle as he tugs the plug free and sets it on the bed before picking me up and carrying me into the en-suite.

After a day with it in, the lack of a toy filling me up is hard to adjust to. My ass clenches on nothing as he sets me on the counter beside the sink, then turns and starts running the bath, tipping in a liberal helping of bubble bath.

When he's finally happy with the water, he turns back to me and thrusts both hands into my hair to angle my head so my face is tilted back, forcing my puffy eyes to meet his.

"Listen to me, angel. You do *not* have to sleep with me—anal, or otherwise—to get me to stay with you or the band. I did some soul searching. I listened to what you said. I'm going to fix things with the guys whether or not you decide to take me back."

"You are?" I hiccup.

"You're drunk." He shakes his head when I go to protest. "Drunk enough that I'm not happy you're in a place to consent to any of the things I want to do to you. If, in the morning, after we've talked and you've had your coffee, you still want me to fuck that sweet little ass of yours, it would be my honour. After that, I'm gonna hunt down the impatient piece of shit who made your first time hurt and pummel the shit out of him."

Then he drops his head and takes my lips in a sweet kiss.

I moan, tasting the salt of my own messy tears mixed with the flavour of him. His hands leave my hair and start stripping my clothes, but instead of touching me like I desperately want him to, he carefully picks my naked self up and deposits me in the water, surrounded by sweet smelling bubbles.

"Relax," he instructs.

"You're just gonna watch me?" I ask.

He shakes his head and picks up a bottle of shampoo. "No. I'm going to help."

Obediently, I slip back until my hair is submerged, then come back up.

"Fancy doing it naked?" Drunk me is an eternal optimist.

"My pants stay on." His hands are heavenly against my scalp. "Now stop tempting me."

His frustrating patience lasts all the way through my bath, then continues as he reminds me to take out my contacts, then carefully tucks me into his bed.

I would complain, but he slips in beside me and drags me in for a hug that kills any protest. His arms are huge, and one of them slides beneath my head, forming a comfortable pillow. The other wraps around me, hand closing possessively over my breast. The warmth of him sinks into my very bones, heating me from the outside in.

I can't help sliding my feet up against his calves, and he hisses out a breath.

"How are you so cold?" he mumbles, but I can only yawn in answer.

Darcy
36

When I wake, there's a hand sliding lazily up and down my back through the tee I wore to bed. Despite my pounding head, I grin, turning to press a good morning kiss to whoever put me to bed last night, only to freeze as I take in dark skin and a blurry, mismatched gaze.

"Prophet." His name is less than a whisper on my lips.

That quickly, I remember everything which happened last night, and my cheeks burn as I recall the way I begged him to fuck me, then cried when he refused.

"Advil is on your left," he murmurs. "With your coffee and your glasses."

I shimmy up the bed and grab all three, using the heavenly drink to wash down the drugs in one swig as I cram the frames onto my face. He doesn't interrupt, even when I cradle the mug and stare owlishly at him over the brim.

"Did you mean it?"

He props his head up on one hand and nods. "Yeah. I meant it." There's a long, vulnerable pause. "I'm sorry, angel. Pushing you away—and convincing the others to do the same —was one of the worst decisions of my entire life. I hated that it made you miserable, and I promise, if you'll still have me, I'll never let anything like that happen again."

I open my mouth to speak, but he's on a roll.

"You put your heart right out there, and I trampled all over it in the name of protecting you. Slate may have riled me up, but I could've handled it better."

Another long pause.

"Do you think... Do you think they'll forgive me?"

Will you *forgive me?* The words hang unsaid between us.

I take a deep breath and consider it as I sip more of my coffee.

"I knew what you were doing the whole time," I begin. "And so did the others. We all knew your heart was in the right place. It wasn't like you were blowing hot and cold for no reason."

If I know the others, Slate has already forgotten it. All he's wanted all along is for the band to stay together. Dodger and Arlo are harder to read, but they were both in on Slate's plan, so that's a good sign.

"They'll bring it up at every opportunity, just to tease you," I continue, thoughtfully. "But that's just what they do." The trash talking between the five of us when we're online together sometimes is unreal. "Of course, I know how you can guarantee my forgiveness."

Prophet gives me a look that's half hopeful, half distrustful. "How?"

I grin. "It involves one little word, some lube, and a whole lot of stretching."

His eyes heat as what I'm saying clicks.

"As much as I desperately want you bent over, begging me to fuck your ass again," he says, deliberately misunderstanding who would be begging whom. "I want to wait until I've talked to the others. Plus, we only have two hours until you need to be at the arena, and I'm going to want longer when I finally get my hands on your body."

"We could have a quickie now and talk to them later?"

He chuckles, and I swoon slightly. Prophet doesn't smile often. When he does, he's dazzling. "The anticipation will make it better."

Pouting, I gulp the last of my drink and shove out from the covers. "I don't believe you."

He leans over and lightly spanks my rear as I head towards the bathroom. "After the show, this ass is mine."

"I prefer to think of it as your cock is mine," I retort, shamelessly hiking my tee to flash him before shutting the door between us.

When I walk out into the hotel, wearing my favourite SG-1 hoodie and my most comfortable leggings, they're all so engrossed in their discussion they don't notice me at first.

"So after you've had her once, we're all even," Dodger says, looking at Prophet. "Who's game for a group orgy?"

"Me!" I scream at the top of my lungs, making all four of them jump. "Wait. No. I mean, only if everyone is cool with that, because I imagine DP has a lot of potential for accidental sword touching, and—"

Slate whoops, hops over the back of the sofa between us, and hooks me around my waist. His mouth descends on mine, drinking me in like he's been dying of thirst.

"Mmmm," I moan, as he draws back. "What was that for?"

"For bringing our brother back to us." His breath whispers over my lips, the words quiet enough that the others can't hear. "You're a miracle, *angelita*."

"Stop fantasising about our dicks touching and come have some breakfast," Arlo says, heading towards the small kitchenette. "There's mostly cereal—" My grimace as he turns around with the box of cornflakes stops him short. "No cereal?"

"Cereal often has less nutritional value than the cardboard box it comes in, and cornflakes were invented to stop people masturbating," I begin, donning a false air of haughtiness. "A lot of them contain more sugar than a doughnut, and doughnuts taste better, so…"

My hatred of puritanical breakfast runs deep, and I trail off when I realise I might've unintentionally put a little too much vitriol into my response.

"I'll just… put this back." Arlo edges away from me with a grin.

"Was that you saying you want doughnuts for breakfast, baby girl?" Dodger asks, grabbing his phone.

"Of course. But it's all true. You can look it up."

Slate shrugs. "Don't need to. I believe you."

Dodger rings someone, putting in an order for our doughnuts, then drops his phone to the couch.

"Have you got everything you need?"

I nod. "Yep."

Once I finish setting up, I can dive back into Gabrielle's files without her noticing and find a new date when the Rosales brothers will be together in one place.

Hopefully, I'll get another chance before the tour finishes.

I don't say any of this aloud. The guys' rooms are still bugged, and I took a big risk removing the cameras the last time. So instead, I say nothing and allow myself to simply enjoy the feeling of being around the band when they're not at each other's throats.

I'm still smiling and covered in powdered sugar as I wander into the arena, only to find the place in chaos.

Without Sully, things are slowly but surely falling apart. Gabrielle is trying to keep order, but she's the tour manager's assistant, not the production manager. She's also naturally quiet, so her words are mostly ignored by the bunch of louder, taller men around her.

"Hey," I snap at the group of them. "Back off and listen to her so we can get shit done before the band gets here."

Gabrielle shoots me a grateful look, then proceeds to quickly and efficiently outline Sully's plan, altered slightly to account for the quirks of the new venue. The more she talks, the more the bristling settles as it becomes clear she's got this.

By the time the group disperses, they're nodding amongst themselves and ready to work.

"Thanks," Gabrielle says. "Ugh, I thought they'd never shut up."

"You'd have got them to listen eventually," I reply, shrugging off her thanks.

I didn't do it for her. I did it because I didn't want the guys to turn up to a venue in chaos. They give their all on that stage for the sake of their fans. The least the rest of us can do is the same.

"Yeah." She sighs like she doesn't believe me, then actively flinches as Miguel's voice snaps across backstage like a whip.

"This place is a fucking mess. Where is Gabrielle?"

"Coming!" she squeaks, heading in his direction without even pausing to say goodbye to me.

Shit. Well, there goes the interim production manager. Surely Miguel can't expect her to do Sully's job and her own? The team needs someone in charge more than he needs her to hang on his every word.

I have my own stuff to get done, but if he doesn't send her back in the next half an hour, then someone else is going to have to step up.

Half an hour passes, and things are beginning to get chaotic again. Luckily, I'm ahead of schedule, so no one cares when I head down the corridor in the direction Gabrielle went.

Most of the crew is rushing the other way, bashing into me in their haste, and it doesn't take long for me to realise why.

Miguel is yelling so loudly I can hear his Spanish cursing from the other end of the corridor. Unfortunately, the hall is so clear that my lingering outside will be noticeable, so as I pass the door, I slip a tiny bot from my back pocket and drop it on the ground.

It's another hexapod, just smaller than my palm, with a camera, mic, and Wi-Fi connection. Bare bones, really, but it will do.

Ducking into the next cupboard I see, I snap my phone out and take control, directing my baby bot through the door and into the shadows of the corner. The room is clearly a disused office, but Miguel and Gabrielle have set up shop on one of the desks. She's clutching her laptop with white knuckles as he paces in front of the window. Her cell is on speakerphone on the desk.

"Your recklessness almost cost us our lives." Roberto's voice echoes softly from the slim device. I shift the bot closer, only to freeze as I realise the two of them aren't alone.

There are three security guys lined up against the wall. I didn't see them before, but fortunately, they're too distracted by Miguel to notice my bot.

Slowly, I edge my bot underneath a desk, trying to get a clear view of the youngest Rosales without giving myself away.

"You think I fucking planned this? It all went to shit because you brought them to a family—"

"No, mijo," the tinny voice snaps—Joaquin this time. *"It went to shit because one of us has a Belladonna in our midst. The only reason all three of us are alive right now is because those bitches don't do collateral damage.*

"The old man's remains weren't in the desert, which means he might still be alive. If we had been alone, that damned assassin would have wiped us out." He takes a deep breath and

lets it out slowly, before continuing in a more rational tone. *"Which is why Roberto and I will be organising things in Houston tomorrow."*

"I can organise—"

"No. You cannot." Roberto snaps. *"This has escalated. You have proved time and time again you are not ready for this responsibility. Gabrielle has been doing everything for you, and you haven't—"*

With a roar of fury, Miguel whirls, drawing a gun from his pocket. He fires once, then twice, then again, all with deadly accuracy.

I watch with my hand clamped over my mouth as Gabrielle's brains are splattered all over the dusty floor. The gun is fitted with a suppressor, but it's still loud enough that I can hear it without the mic from half a corridor away.

"I am more capable than some puta pendeja*,"* Miguel growls. *"I'll show all of you!"*

Then, without waiting for his brothers to respond, he shoots the phone as well.

Shit.

Miguel has lost it. It takes my fingernails digging into my cheek for me to realise that my hand is still over my face.

Gabrielle is dead, and if my guys aren't careful, they could easily be next.

I stumble out of the closet, on my way to warn them, just as a voice erupts from my phone.

"What the hell is this piece of—?"

Fuck! My bot!

A glance at the screen shows me that it's been picked up by one of Miguel's security guys. Without pause, I tap in the self-destruct sequence, enjoying the yell of shock from the room as I flee.

"The Belladonna must be in the building!" Miguel yells. "Find her!"

Shit. Shit. *Shit*.

I slow down to a fast walk as I reach backstage and dive towards the explosives cage, switching my phone to silent as I frantically shove myself into looking like I've been here all along. Glasses. Where are my glasses?

They're looking for a gorgeous woman. I need to nerd up and make myself invisible. Thankfully, my SG-1 hoodie is super baggy and hides my curves. With my sneakers and comfort-wear, I don't exactly look like a femme fatale assassin.

I should've known that someone with the cartel's connections would find out about my mission after that failed attempt. I've been too busy caught up in the band's drama to keep my ear to the ground.

"This is a security drill!" Jackson, Miguel's head of security, announces as I shove the frames onto my nose. "Everyone stay where you are and prepare to show your road crew lanyard."

The grumbles of protest cut off quickly, and I turn around to find that Miguel's goons are canvassing backstage with their guns drawn. Jackson's hand is badly burned, and I suppress a grin. At least baby bot didn't die without taking a chunk out of him in the process.

"Oh my goodness," I fake coo in my ditsiest voice as he approaches me, hand outstretched for my lanyard. "Are you okay? Do you need me to get you something to put on your hand? I think there's a first aid box in the kitchen—"

"Stay quiet," he snarls, glancing at my pass. "I'm fine."

I don't push it, keeping my expression full of fake concern until he turns and leaves.

Only when they've all left, moving on to other areas of the venue, do I allow myself to breathe a sigh of relief. The atmosphere loosens as the guns disappear, and people start murmuring amongst themselves, trying to figure out what the hell is going on.

Miguel doesn't yet suspect one of the roadies is responsible. Good. But my time is running out. Roberto mentioned Houston, and I'm pretty sure that's going to be my last chance. It's also our next stop on the tour.

When Miguel himself steps into the backstage area, several of the roadies head straight for him, already voicing complaints and concerns.

"*¡Cállense!*" he snaps. "I don't have time for your shit. Sort the fucking show out, and do it quickly. That's what I pay you for."

Without waiting for a response, he storms from the building, leaving the rest of the roadies flabbergasted.

Damn it! This is a complication I didn't need.

Darcy
37

T he next morning, I arrive at the new hotel in Houston, bone weary and more than a little grumpy. Without Sully to organise everything, or even Gabrielle, the crew only finished packing down in Austin at four a.m.. We were barely done in time to catch our plane.

Last night was awful, but seeing Dodger waiting for me in the lobby makes a little of the stress melt away. He takes my case from me and guides the two of us into the elevator. The second we're alone, I bury my face in his neck and take a deep lungful of his freshly showered scent.

"I know you're tired, baby girl," he murmurs against my hair. "But we need you to find those cameras before we go to sleep, okay? Emma's staying on our couch, and we don't feel comfortable having Miguel watching her."

I nod quietly against his hoodie, yawning. It won't take long, and I no longer care if someone alerts Miguel to the missing footage.

This is the last city he'll ever see.

The doors ping open, and I freeze at the sobbing coming from the room ahead.

This latest hotel suite is larger than the others, and the

guys have scored the penthouse, with views of the urban skyline beyond. Arlo is in the kitchen, rummaging in the refrigerator for something while Slate comforts Emma on the sofa. Prophet stands behind the two of them like a silent, protective gargoyle, not saying anything.

Emma does her best to dry her face as she notices me, but her crying has ruined her makeup, making the bruise decorating her face painfully obvious.

Who hit her? Anger eclipses my tiredness, and I carefully extract myself from Dodger's arms, digging my phone out of my purse and flicking open the app. I know, from habit, the most likely places to look for bugs—curtains, fans, mirrors, picture frames—but the app will ensure I don't miss anything.

"What is she doing?" Emma asks, as I climb on the table and start straining for the ceiling fan.

"Ompf," I grunt as Prophet strides over, lifting me onto his shoulder so I can reach easier.

One down.

"She's getting rid of all the cameras," Arlo explains quietly. "Miguel has our rooms bugged, and I don't want you sleeping in here if he's watching you."

Emma nods shakily. "Okay." She pauses. "This has something to do with her gun, right?"

I hold my hand up in the universal signal for *wait* and direct Prophet across the room. Only when I'm sure that every single room in the suite is clear do I tap his shoulder to set me down.

"Right," I begin, dragging my case over to the table and unzipping it. "Full disclosure: I'm an assassin, and I've been hired to kill the Rosales brothers." I plonk my laptop down and flick the screen open before returning to my bag. "All three of them will be dead by this time tomorrow." I grab a new baby bot and plug it into the laptop to begin a software update. "And after that, you will be free to live your life however you please."

Emma doesn't even look surprised. In fact, she recovers a little of her lost composure at the news. "Good. I was wondering when you'd turn up."

The band, who were steeling themselves for her reaction, are completely stunned by her nonchalant acceptance of my answer. I'm not.

"I figured it was you who got into contact with Man." She's so fiercely protective of her brother, that it had to be her.

"You hired an *assassin*?" Arlo's voice has dropped an octave in disapproval as he hands her the ice pack. Sighing, she presses it to her face.

Dodger, however, slaps her on the back. "Ems, you are the best."

It's clear, from Arlo's conflicted expression, that he doesn't agree.

"Hey, don't give me that look," Emma says. "It wasn't just my idea. Sully and I did it together when it became painfully obvious you needed a woman to come and sort out this mess. My decision meant you finally got to bone your nerdy virtual girlfriend, *and* she saved Sully."

The four men exchange exasperated looks, and I chuckle. "She's got you there."

"How the fuck can you afford an assassin?" Dodger chokes. "I thought you weren't touching your trust fund."

"I'm not," Emma insists. "Because it's not my money." Arlo sighs in exasperation, and she pokes her tongue out at him. "The Belladonnas took your case on for free."

The four men look at me, silently asking if that's even possible.

I shrug. "Man takes on more pro bono cases than you'd expect. Especially when it comes to scum like Miguel." And cases that Man knows are important to us. "Sometimes he'll assign one of us a mark that he knows we have a vendetta against." Like my sister, Ivory, who was assigned to end her childhood abuser. "Or he'll give us a case that allows us to protect those we care about."

Man will never confirm it, but I'm certain he gave Raven the marks which were most likely to coincide with the infamous Loxley Crew's whereabouts, because he *knew* about her connection to their leader, Otto. I have no idea how he located them, let alone uncovered their identities—I spent months hacking various government and criminal databases yet uncovered nothing about the thieves—but he *must* have.

I don't believe in coincidences.

Which is why I believe he took Emma's case. Man knew about my connection to Hazardous and gave me their file knowing I would never let one of the others touch it. He cares, though he'd never admit it.

"Did Miguel do that?" I ask, waving at Emma's bruised face to distract myself from my sappy thoughts.

She swallows, and nods. "He hit me when I tried to stop him taking my assistant." She pauses, breath hitching. "He was just dragging her out, but I managed to distract him long enough for her to run."

"Your assistant?" I ask, confused.

Slate crumples slightly in his seat. "His brothers traffic girls by giving them jobs in the crew as a cover," he admits, squeezing his eyes shut as he scrubs a hand down his face. "They usually end up in wardrobe, because Miguel thinks they won't draw too much attention there, and it fits with the lie they tell the girls—that they're coming to work. Then when he finds a buyer, they're taken and handed over."

"Marianne was picked up on the European leg of the tour," Emma whispers, dabbing the ice pack against her cheekbone. "In London. She was sweet, if a little awkward. I think she managed to get away..."

"I'm sure she did," I mumble, though I don't have too much hope, given how tight security was.

"You know Gabrielle was almost free of them, right?" Emma adds, still in shock. "She just had another year of work before her agreement with the cartel was up. They were paying for her little brother's medical bills. I caught her crying about it during her first week."

That makes a disturbing amount of sense, but I say nothing. In the hills above El Paso, I weighed her life and decided she was acceptable collateral damage because of her association. Guilt prickles across my shoulders until I have to physically shrug the sensation off. In the end, I didn't kill her. That blame lies at Miguel's feet, along with the destruction of so many other lives. At least her death was quick.

"Miguel won't have a chance to take any more girls," I finally say. "I'll make sure of it."

I drop my gaze to my laptop and quickly access the brothers' shared calendar.

"It looks like he's got a meeting set up with his brothers after the concert ends," I mutter. "Then they're heading for a yacht out on the bay."

I like boats. Boats are nice and easy to blow up with all that fuel on board, and they have the benefit of being far away from any innocent bystanders. Then there are helpful currents that will carry away bodies before they can become evidence.

Yup. That's my best bet. Blow up the boat.

I hum as I work, drawing up schematics. I'll need eyes on the meeting, and a backup plan in case their schedule changes, and—

A pair of hands land on my shoulders, massaging the tension from them. "It's late," Prophet grumbles in that deep voice of his. "I know you want to get started, but you have the whole of tomorrow to do this, and Emma needs to get some rest."

Oh. I forgot she was sleeping on the couch. "Sorry." I blush. "I got into the zone. I'll just..."

Before I can say anything else, he lifts me from the sofa and throws me over his shoulder.

"Night, guys," I call, craning my neck to look at them.

"Sweet dreams, *cariño*," Slate calls back.

"Night, Dark." Arlo chuckles at Prophet's antics.

"Hey, remember she's mine tomorrow night," Dodger calls. "And you've had two nights in a row. Don't think we aren't counting."

Prophet reaches back with his free hand and flips them all the bird. "We agreed."

They... did? What precisely did they agree to? Before I can ask, he's shouldering his way through his door and closing it behind us.

"You have two choices," he begins, tossing me onto the bed where I bounce on the mattress. "Option one, I massage the tension out of you, and you go to sleep relaxed and ready for me to fuck you in the morning."

I hum, pushing my way up onto my elbows. "And option two?"

"You still get the massage," he concedes. "But at some point, I'm going to bury myself in your dripping cunt and fuck you until we both can't walk tomorrow."

My grin creeps slowly across my face as I struggle to put on an unaffected air. "Decisions, decisions."

He quirks a single brow at me, eyes gleaming. "Do you want me to choose for you?"

No way. If I've learned anything about him, he has the self-control needed to go for option one.

"Option two," I squeak.

If his expression was heated before, it turns molten. "Clothes off."

"You first," I challenge, grinning as I cross one leg over the other in what I hope is a sexy move.

Far from being intimidated, Prophet puts his hands over his head, grips the neck of his shirt and tugs it over his head in one smooth move.

My lips part without my conscious permission, and my tongue darts out to moisten them.

"That's all you get for now," he rasps, leaning forward to pluck at the hem of my shirt. "Off. All of it."

My hands start following his orders without thinking. My hoodie comes off first, taking my shirt with it until all that separates his hungry gaze from my breasts is the patterned fabric of my bright green bra.

"Are those...?" he rasps.

"You don't like?" A bolt of self consciousness rocks through me.

He stares at the pattern of green helmets with yellow visors, and when he speaks, his voice has dropped an octave. "Angel, I'm doing my best to share with the others, but having another man's helmet plastered all over your pretty tits..."

"Master Chief is fictional!"

"I. Don't. Care." He reaches forward, and with one finger, deftly unhooks the front fastening. "Burn it."

Grinning, because his jealousy is kinda hot, I do the most inflammatory thing possible.

Shrugging off the bra, I shove down my leggings and turn over, exposing the back of my cheeky panties. The navy fabric is printed with the words *Property of Garrus Vakarian.*

Prophet's dark chuckle reassures me that I just went from "fucked" to "super fucked."

Mission accomplished, I grin into the pillow. The fabric swallows my gasp as he hooks one finger under the hem and traces it inward from my hip to the junction of my thighs.

"We're going to expand our merch line," he grumbles. "It's

our band's name on your ass, or nothing. In fact, maybe you could get our symbol tattooed right here." His finger twirls against the sensitive area of my inner thigh.

"No needles," I hiss. "No way."

"I'd kiss it better," he promises, hooking his finger under the waistband and dragging my final piece of clothing off.

I don't need to look to know he's tossed my favourite panties straight into the bin. I make a silent promise to rescue them later.

He climbs onto the bed, straddling my upper thighs without putting any of his weight on me. I can still feel the heat of his cock branding me as his hands find my shoulders and begin to knead.

"Ohh," I moan, sinking into the mattress as his wonderful fingers somehow find every single knot of tension and disperse it. "You're really good at this."

A grunt. It appears Prophet used up his ability to talk by threatening my underwear, but I can't bring myself to care as he slides those capable, calloused hands over my neck and down my right arm.

When he moves to my left, he pauses at the tiny grain of rice beneath my skin. His thumb strokes over the implant thoughtfully, and his head dips to kiss my nape.

"When he's dead, this comes out," he whispers against my ear. "And I'm going to fuck so much of my cum into you..."

He trails off, but my cheeks heat because I know what he means.

Once Miguel is dead, he's going to make sure we get the family we both want. I nod into the pillow, and he rewards me with a second kiss to my spine before he withdraws.

His hands finish caressing my arms and move down my back, fingertips grazing the sides of my breasts but never going further. He spends longer than he needs to on my ass, caressing until I'm actually trembling and moaning into the pillow. His thumbs spread my cheeks, rubbing against my back entrance with careful strokes that make my pussy gush against the sheets.

I'm beginning to think this massage was just a way for him to torture me. I need something. Penetration. Friction. Anything.

"Prophet," I moan.

"Not yet, angel. I still have to do your front."

He's going to kill me.

"I want you to—" I cut off with a groan of frustration as his hands move down to my thighs.

No amount of begging will speed him up as he carefully rubs my feet then rolls me over and starts again from the bottom of my calves. My heart is pounding, and my skin flushed by the time he reaches my belly, but my hands come down on autopilot as he shifts his caresses to my abdomen.

"Can we just skip that part?" I ask, trying to shimmy his hands up to my breasts.

"Nope." He lowers his head, pressing a kiss to my navel. "I'm in love with every single fucking inch of you. Let me show you how much."

His thumbs rub up either side of the slight pooch, and he presses another kiss to my navel as I fall back, eyes burning.

"I love you too." My breath whispers out as he finally stops and trails his lips up my sternum to claim my lips.

His hands cup both of my breasts, testing the weight of them in his palms before lightly strumming the rapidly hardening buds of my nipples. He alternates between softly rubbing and kneading my breast with his whole hand until I gasp and buck against him.

He shifts until his hips come to rest between my thighs, and he uses our position to keep me pinned as his mouth explores every inch of mine. I nip at his full lower lip, impatient, but he draws back.

"Patience," he chides, sliding down until his stubble grazes my throat.

"No," I retort, digging my heels into his ass and grinding my lower body up. The rough denim of his jeans *finally* grants my clit a fraction of sensation I crave. "No patience. Fuck now."

He chuckles against me. "No."

I have a moment to pout about how unfair it is that he can make a single word sound so final, before his hands shift, abandoning my breasts. One arm braces himself over me while the other grabs his own waistband and shoves his pants down.

That's when I see it.

A single word tattooed along the left side of his Adonis belt, just below where the waistband of his pants would sit.

Please.

The cursive is flowing and gorgeous, and the artist has added tiny black wings on either side. It's the only ink he has other than the band tattoo over his heart.

Mouth falling open, I go to say something as he braces himself over me, but the length of his cock brushes right over my clit at the same time. Whatever I might've said is lost to the groan as he slides the hard length up and down, coating it in the wetness that's been building since this whole thing started.

He's too gentle, so I do what anyone else would in my situation, flipping us over until I'm on top so I can grind against him like I so desperately need to.

My upper hand doesn't last long.

With a snort and a move that should be illegal, Prophet escapes my hold and ends up behind me with his hands on my hips and his cock sliding against my ass.

"Keep trying to top me, and I'll fuck this ass before you're ready."

"I'm ready now."

His hand leaves my hip to lightly spank my butt. "Not yet, but you will be."

Then he leans over to where his own suitcase is open and pulls out something. Before I even manage to process what I've seen, he's rubbing the cool silicone of a butt plug between my folds.

"Where did you—?" I cut off on a gasp as he slides the plug slowly into my pussy.

My inner walls clench, and I almost come now that I *finally* have something filling me.

"Get it nice and wet," he murmurs. "Yes, angel, you're taking it so well."

The toy is larger than the one he took out yesterday, and he works it slowly in and out of me, making sure I coat every single inch of it before he withdraws it and rests the tip against my ass.

"Breathe out." His voice is husky, and obeying him is a compulsion I don't want to ignore.

The plug goes in easily at first, the first two inches slipping in with no resistance. The third is a struggle, but Prophet notices when I stiffen, and his free hand strokes over my back. "Keep breathing, angel. You're almost there."

He pulls the plug back and then pushes it in farther, giving me tiny thrusts that tease me into accepting another torturous inch.

"It burns," I whimper, hands fisting the sheets.

He freezes. "Do you want me to stop?" I shake my head so rapidly that he laughs. "Good. Keep going."

When the thickest part of the plug finally pops through my sphincter, I let out a shaky breath. The fullness is incredible, and I can't seem to stop shifting, relishing the feeling of my inner muscles tensing and releasing around the toy.

"Grab onto the headboard," Prophet murmurs. "Don't let go."

As soon as I do what he says, he lines his cock up with my entrance.

Holy shit. I guessed he was big, but with the plug in my butt, his girth becomes terrifying. The head of him eases forward, and I cry out into the mattress.

"It's okay," he whispers against my back. "You can take me. Your body was made for me, angel. Relax. I'm going slow."

He pushes forward a little more, then pulls back, only to slide in again, just as far. Thrust by thrust, he works himself inside me, rubbing against the plug through the thin barrier of skin which separates them.

Then his hips finally, blessedly, meet my ass.

"I'm in, angel. You've taken all of me so well." His body lowers, covering mine, and his next words brush against my ear. "Hold on."

With that warning, he draws back and plunges back in.

My breath leaves my lungs in a soundless gasp, my knees tremble, and my back arches at the sudden invasion, pushing my breasts out. That's just the beginning. His sweat-slicked body fucks into mine in hard, slow strokes that stretch me to my limit.

Each time his hips meet my ass, the plug jostles, reminding me of its presence.

"One day," Prophet grunts, reading my mind. "That won't be a plug. It'll be me in your ass while one of the others takes this scorching cunt. We'll fuck you until you pass out, and then we'll wake you up and we'll go again until you're full of our baby."

The mushroomed head of his dick brushes against my G-spot, and I cry out at the combination of the sensation and his filthy words. I want to scream. I want to beg. I want to collapse in a writhing mess beneath him.

I can't. Because Prophet is holding me up by my hips,

keeping me in place as he wrecks me. My lips are spilling word-less mumbling praises, but I can't hear any of them over the harsh animal grunts of his breath as he chases our pleasure.

"Come for me," he pants. "Come on, angel. Show me what it feels like when you break apart on my dick."

I can't deny him anything.

My body trembles, and my toes curl as heat explodes out in a rush. Every muscle in my body clenches.

"Fuck. Darcy." He chokes out my name a second before his dick jerks, triggering a second, smaller orgasm.

He rolls the two of us until I'm splayed out with my back to his chest. The motion jostles the plug and makes me moan.

"So perfect," he croons in my ear, pressing a kiss to my throat. "I don't know how I ever thought I could live without you, but I swear, I'm going to make it up to you every day for the rest of our lives."

He may have taken me roughly, but he's gentle when it comes to cleaning our mess up. I fall asleep, warm and pampered, with him wrapped around me like my own muscled blanket.

Darcy
38

It's time.

I sneak down into the rooms beneath the arena, carrying a backpack crammed with everything I need. I smuggled most of the explosives into the cage yesterday, so the only things I'm carrying are my drones, bots, a few grenades, and my emergency C-4. My phone—my greatest weapon—is in my hand, and I swipe my thumb absently over the screen as I think through the talk I had with the band and Emma this morning.

Needless to say, none of my guys were impressed with the idea of leaving me alone, or me putting more trackers on their phones. Eventually—after a lot of arguing—Emma and I managed to convince them it would be safer for me if I didn't have to worry about the boys getting in the way.

I have to be free to spy on the Rosales brothers' meetings without worrying that they'll turn up on the boat unexpectedly, like they did at the villa. I also need to be able to warn them of a change of plans, which is why I've also rigged an alert that will connect to the radio frequency of their in-ear monitors while they're on stage if there's an emergency.

Miguel is losing it. That makes him unpredictable. Having several contingency plans in place is just common sense.

First though, I need to see what's going on in the brothers' meeting, which started just a few minutes ago. And I have to do it without neglecting my job as a pyro. My phone buzzes, and I quickly swipe to see the live feed from the stage, check where the band is standing, then set off a waterfall of sparks, before returning to my current task, planting my own cameras.

Unfortunately, Miguel's goons are everywhere in the warren of tunnels beneath the arena. The increased security is likely due to his brothers' presence, and they're probably on the look out for more bots.

Fortunately, I have the arena's schematics on my phone. I can sneak my bots through the vent connecting an unused room to the one where the meeting is taking place. I just have to get there first.

I turn a corner and come face to face with none other than the head of security himself: Jackson.

Shit.

"Oh, thank goodness." I grin, trying to make the expression as genuine as possible, despite the dread eating me up from the inside. "I was trying to find you. I have a lot of experience with burns, and I just wanted to make sure—"

"For the last time, I'm fine," he snarls, shoulder-checking me as he strides past. "Don't you have some actual work to do?"

I count to three, pretending to be frozen with shock at his rudeness, when in reality I just really want to turn and put a bullet through his eyes. The second his footsteps are gone, I roll my eyes and continue walking.

He's so lucky he's not my target. I won't be sad if he ends up on the boat when it goes up in flames.

The room I want should be right... here!

Checking both ends of the corridors to make sure that no

one is watching, I twist the handle and slip inside, closing the door behind me. At one point, this was clearly some kind of function room, but currently it's empty. The chairs and tables have been stacked up against one wall, leaving the vent visible and easy to access.

Prying the cover away from the wall takes a while, and I have to stop twice to set off more pyros upstairs. When I'm done, it's a simple matter of guiding my little bot through a straight vent, using the little laser Tabby gave it to shear through the bolts on the other side, and then...

Voila. I'm in.

This time, I'm not getting caught. I sneak my way through the room, hiding in shadows as I try to get a good angle on what's going on. I hit the jackpot when I find a table covered in a dust cloth that hangs low to the floor, camouflaging my bot while allowing enough room for my camera to see underneath.

The three brothers are sitting at a table in the centre of the room, swigging lazily at beer bottles as they chatter away in Spanish. So close. My fingers itch to send a bigger bot with a payload that could wipe them all out, but it's too risky. An explosion down here could bring the entire arena down on our heads, killing dozens of the concert goers above us.

"What you've said, mijo, *aligns with our information."* Roberto sounds carefully calm, in the way people often do when they're about to break bad news. *"The Belladonna they've sent after us is focusing on you. She's taken out your surveillance, interfered with the old man, and now you say she's spying on you? All of this... well, it's why we've decided to shut down this arm of the business."*

Miguel's bottle slips from his fingers. *"Shut it down? But I'm so close to scaling it up. It's been the perfect cover for years, and I'm so close to luring in new talent—"*

"There will be other chances to prove yourself," Roberto

promises. *"For now, we need to bunker down and cover our tracks here. The band will need to be silenced. Overdose the addict. His death will give the others an excuse to quit touring. They'll stay quiet, or we'll follow through on our threats to their families."*

My heart ices over. They want to kill off my guys to cover their tracks? Fuck that.

Part of me wonders if I shouldn't give them the easy fiery death I had planned. Perhaps I should take a page out of Ivory's book and play with them a bit first.

"This was supposed to be my *arm of the business,"* Miguel retorts. *"You can't just snap your fingers and shut it all down. I'm making money, aren't I?"*

Roberto gives him a patient look. *"You are making* peanuts, mijo. *What product you manage to shift in a year is nothing in the grand scheme of things, and the cost of all this pageantry isn't cheap."*

Miguel is quiet. Too quiet.

While his brothers are cool and collected, I'd have expected some kind of outburst from him by now.

Evidently Joaquin thinks the same, because he leans over to pat his younger sibling on the shoulder.

"Do not take this to heart," he says, gruffly. *"This is the Belladonna's fault, not yours. Once we are back home, we can create a plan to take her out, and maybe then you can get more experience managing our operations at the docks."*

"We can talk about that later," Roberto mutters, putting down his own beer. *"Once we're safely aboard our yacht and far away from the assassin."*

Miguel stiffens, then relaxes, shoving his way out of his seat. *"You're right,"* he admits. *"Come. Let's speak on the yacht. As you said, there's no time to waste."*

His older brothers relax, and Joaquin nods, heading for the door.

I need to move fast. They're heading for the boat way too early. Hefting my rucksack over my shoulder, I—

BANG.

BANG BANG.

My hands fumble with my phone in my haste to figure out what just happened.

BANG.

"ASSASSIN!"

It takes me a second to realise that that final gunshot, and the accusatory voice that accompanied it, aren't coming from my phone. Ignoring the pinch in my shoulder, I turn and come face to face with Jackson, pistol raised and pointed at me as he talks into his radio with the other.

"It's the bitch the band was fucking. I need cleanup."

Shit.

He made one fatal mistake: not finishing me off straight away.

Drawing my own gun, I fire on instinct, taking him out in one neat shot to the forehead. I don't waste time watching him slump to the ground or admiring the blood splatter. He's just a pawn, and I'm here for the brothers.

Only, it appears I'm too late to take out the two older Rosales. On my phone, Miguel is standing over their corpses, golden glock in his hand. Roberto is face down on the floor and unmoving, but Joaquin has managed to catch himself on a chair. With one hand, he reaches for his youngest sibling in a silent plea, but a final shot finishes the eldest Rosales brother off before he can say anything.

Shit.

I swipe across my screen, firing a tracer bug from the bot before Miguel can vanish. The tiny dart hits the back of his collar, and affixes itself. Before I can do anything else, more security—drawn my way by Jackson's shout—rush through the door.

More gunshots. Shit. My plan is falling apart. I take out my attackers and take cover beside the door. With one hand, I blindly swipe across the surface of my phone, activating the warning beacon.

My guys have to get out of here.

I glance down at my shoulder, and the dark stain growing rapidly across the sunshine yellow of my hoodie.

Damn. This was one of my favourites.

As it is, the writing, which once said *Not a hot mess, just a spicy disaster* is getting hard to read. Shoulder isn't too bad. He likely only missed major arteries by sheer luck because I was fumbling with my phone. It's my left arm, which means I can still shoot. I've got until I lose fifteen percent of my blood volume before I become impaired. Forty percent until death.

Shit, I have to staunch the bleeding, then I have to move.

Squeeeal. Dodger's name flashes up on my phone, and I tap open the message before I can stop myself.

[HzD]D0dgeVip3r
What's happening? Talk to us.

> **D4rk4ngel**
> Get everyone out.

This complication means I'm not going to make it to that yacht in time. Which means Miguel has to die here.

Ripping my hoodie off hurts like a bitch. The second it's out of the way, I press my hand to my wound *hard*. With the other, I rummage in my rucksack, grimacing as pain shoots down my arm. I have basic first aid stuff, but not much, so I pack the wound as best I can and wrap it with a bandage. It's not perfect, and it won't last, but it's what I've got.

While I work, I set my phone to show footage of the band on stage. Dodger has stopped the show, and I watch as he directs the fans to leave as quickly as possible.

Good. If they block the exits, the chaos will make it harder for Miguel to get away.

Bandage done, I strap as many weapons to my body as I can and gingerly edge my way out into the corridor. Miguel should be just around the corner.

Another hail of gunfire stops me, and I duck back into the room, returning fire blindly.

"Kill her!" Miguel cries. *He's right there.* "She murdered my brothers!"

I fire again, cursing my shoulder as it burns. Fuck. I don't have time for this.

Grabbing a grenade from my belt, I chuck it down the corridor. I get a brief moment of satisfaction from the cries of shocked men who didn't expect me to bring explosives to a gunfight before it detonates with a deafening boom that shakes the walls.

The second the immediate danger is over, I sprint away. Another hail of gunfire follows me, but their aim is off, thanks to the smoke.

I need to regroup. I have the tracer on Miguel, but I work best with a plan, and right now, all of my ideas have fallen through. This isn't the place for a showdown with a crazed drug lord. I don't have my fireproof clothes, I'm injured, and I have no exit strategy.

But I have no choice.

I swipe between apps, bringing up Miguel's location... Looks like he's headed for...

Wardrobe?

Dodger
39

S he's not answering her phone.

Slate and Arlo are still on stage, directing what's left of the crowd away from the building using their mics. After the blast which rocked the arena from below, the audience didn't need much convincing of the bomb scare we made up. Even the road crew is emptying out, and security... is fucking absent.

Probably because they were all hired by Miguel, which means they're busy hunting for Darcy.

"I think they're all gone," Prophet announces, bouncing his drumsticks against his thigh, restlessly.

"Time to go after our girl," Slate growls, and I couldn't agree more.

We might not be qualified to help her, but I'll be damned if I'm going to flee outside with everyone else and leave her to face Miguel and his cronies alone. Especially when it's clear something has gone very wrong.

"Stay exactly where you are!"

All four of us freeze as Miguel's voice cuts through the empty arena. I spin in place, trying to figure out where he is, but all I can see is his security bursting onto the stage, guns pointed at us.

"*¡Hijos de puta!*" Miguel curses. "You hired an assassin, didn't you?"

Finally, he steps out from behind the black curtain, shoving Ems forward with a gaudy golden gun pressed to her temple. She stumbles, falling into Prophet's drums before she can right herself. When she looks up, I can already see a fresh bruise forming against her cheek and a fiery spark of fury trapped behind her eyes.

Shit. I grab Arlo's arm, stopping him when he would've stormed forwards.

"Do you even know what you've cost me?" our manager demands. "This entire operation has gone down the drain. A decade of work, destroyed, just as I was about to expand."

"I'm going to cut off your dick with my pinking shears," Emma growls. "You think—"

"Shut up." He jabs the golden muzzle of the glock against her skull harder. "Did you think I wouldn't find out? Did you pay her extra to fuck you?"

"I need you to get him on the edge of the danger zone." Darcy's voice echoes sharply through my in-ear monitor, and I have to fight hard not to react. *"I can set off the gerb beneath him, which will stun him long enough for you to grab Emma and run."*

The trouble with the earpiece is that I have no way to communicate back to her.

"Keep him talking," she advises, audibly out of breath. *"Don't set him off. He just shot both of his brothers."*

I share a glance with Slate, and I see the wheels turning in his eyes. So she's speaking to all of us. Then the impact of what she just said sinks in.

Shit. If Miguel just took out the two heads of the cartel—

his own half-brothers—Emma is in serious danger. He won't think twice about shooting her.

"Look, man," Arlo mutters, stepping forward with his hands up. "We have no clue what you're talking about."

Wrong thing to say. "You think I'm stupid? I *made* you. All of you. All this—?" He gestures wildly at the stage. "Thousands of people worshipping you. All you had to do was keep your heads down and your fucking mouths shut."

"Miguel," Slate tries again, and I notice he's actually taking a few steps back.

Trusting him, I follow his lead, retreating and dragging Arlo with me.

His grin—already crazed—turns positively cruel at the perceived weakness.

"We had nothing to do with hiring any assassins," Slate reiterates. "That's the truth. Let Emma go. We can still salvage all of this. The rest of the tour will—"

"There *is* no more tour," Miguel snaps. "You four are a liability. You think, after you broke my trust, I'm going to just let you carry on and wait for another knife in the back?"

He takes a step forward, forcing Ems to walk around the drums, but it's not far enough. I can see the black tip of the gerb two feet in front of him.

We can't back up any farther, or we'll run out of stage.

"Come on," Darcy mutters in my ear, and I wonder if she knows she's still connected to me.

Her voice is thin, and the words end on a pained groan. My heart hammers at the inside of my ribcage in answer.

Is she safe? She wants us to grab Emma and get out, but what about her?

I glance back at Prophet, but the stoic drummer is staring intently at the stage, like he's trying to see if Darcy is hidden beneath us and calculating a way to get to her.

"You don't have to do this." Arlo backs up another step. "Just give me my sister, and we can pass this all off as an accident. I'm sure your men have the assassin handled. She's just one girl."

"What would you know, *cabrón*?" Miguel retorts, shoving Emma forward again. "All you've ever cared about is your next fucking hit. You're just another dumb addict."

"He's not," Emma growls. "He's a hundred times the—"

Miguel brings the glock down hard at Emma's temple, and I take a step forward before I can stop myself.

"Shut up, you stupid bitch."

Emma tumbles forward, cradling her skull, and Miguel follows after her. I'm so concerned for her that I don't even notice that the move has put the two of them squarely over the top of the gerb until Darcy mutters in my ear.

"Finally. Get ready to grab her and run."

The slight whoosh of ignition is all the warning we get before every single gerb on the stage lights up at once.

Miguel rears back as he gets a face full of flames, and his goons panic as the stage starts to rapidly fill with fire and dry ice.

A drone drops from the ceiling, dropping a small canister to our left, followed by another, and another before it disappears back into the rafters. The resulting whine, followed by a loud flash and an ear-splitting bang, sends what remains of Miguel's forces cursing and yelling. There are six in all, and they explode one by one, sending cartel members ducking and diving to try to avoid the effects.

We're far enough away that we're not blinded, and we have our earpieces to thank for not being deafened, but security has no such protection.

Unlike me, Slate isn't frozen in place in awe at Darcy's handiwork. He rushes forward, snatching Emma up and carrying her back to our group as Arlo frantically tries to extinguish the flames crawling up her skirt.

"This way," Prophet shouts, already jumping down into the arena where a path has opened up.

Arlo gives up on battling the fire and rips the skirt from Emma's body as Slate carries her past the two of us. I hesitate as Miguel staggers up, pressing his hand to the charred mess that is his face. The pain has distracted him, and he's dropped his gun.

Without pause, I stride up to him, kick the gun away and put all my strength into a second kick to his face.

"Rot in hell," I spit at him, before turning.

"Dodger, get your pretty ass out of my hot zone!" Darcy yells in my ear.

"You better be waiting for me outside, baby girl," I mutter back—knowing she can't hear me as I flee into the thick white smoke after the others.

I barely make it to the emergency exit before the huge boom rocks the building. The lights flicker, the walls tremble. If I didn't know better, I'd think it was an earthquake.

Shit. "DARCY!" I yell, turning, only for an arm around my abdomen to pull me back.

I turn, half expecting it to be Prophet, but the rest of the band is in the same position as I am. The police are here, and they're currently trying to get us clear of the trembling building.

The officer holding me—a kid with wide fearful eyes—looks completely out of his depth as he tries to talk sense at me. "Sir, the building is unstable! You have to get clear."

"My girlfriend's inside!" I yell back, still struggling.

Another boom, louder and more terrifying than the first.

"Get him out of there!"

Things start to blur as multiple hands reach out and yank me clear. I can't take my eyes off the door, even as I'm pulled out into the carpark. Darcy. We've got to find Darcy.

"Someone's got to go in there," Prophet argues from behind me. "There are still people inside."

"Sir, right now, we need to—"

But whatever the officer is going to say is cut off as, with a cloud of smoke and a deafening thunderclap of noise, the arena explodes.

The blast is so powerful that all of us are blown off our feet. Heat singes my skin and every hair on my body stands on end as adrenaline courses through my nervous system.

The rush of air that passes over my head is so powerful that it sets off car alarms and shatters windows. Someone grabs my collar and yanks me away, but I keep struggling.

Darcy.

No.

She's still in there.

"Darcy!" I scream, throat burning as I cough through the smoke.

But my yell is just one of many, caught up amidst the cries of hundreds of shocked fans.

"If anyone's still inside, they're *dead*!" the officer yells in my ear, desperation leaking into his tone. "Come on! You don't know if it's going to blow again!"

Like my body has been waiting for that one final word, all the fight leaves me. His grip on my torso changes from restraining to supportive as I collapse.

He's right.

There's no way anyone survived that. Amidst the thick dust, the crumbling arena is slowly becoming visible. The area where backstage was... is completely gone.

She's gone.

In my chest, my heart crumples as the pain becomes too much and it shuts down protectively. I'm so numb that I barely feel the officer drag me farther away.

Darcy
40

S hit. Shit. Shit.

I double check the wires on the explosives cage a final time. It's a rough, last-minute improv job, but the C-4 should trigger enough of the other combustibles to destroy the building.

My bandage is soaked through, and my blood is now painting me, making my hands slippery as I swipe bloody marks across my phone screen. My breathing is coming in choppy pants that don't seem to fill my lungs, but thankfully, my drone's video feed shows me that Dodger is finally leaving like I told him to. As much as I loved seeing Miguel get a kick in the teeth—literally—I need the band at a safe distance.

The chill creeping across my limbs is a bad sign.

Damn it. I'm better than this.

My thumbs are a blur over my phone screen as I start the final hack, wishing I'd automated the entire process. Every single Rosales-owned computer will soon be showing my *Game Over* screensaver, and their wealth is already being funnelled into my shell accounts.

All that's left to do is press the detonator.

I glance at the exit doors on my left, stumbling towards them. My coordination is failing as the blood loss starts to slow me down, but I don't have time to worry about the wound. Already, I can hear the cartel starting to recover from what I've done. On my screen, Miguel starts to stir, one of his men stumbles closer and starts dragging him away as my drones continue to drop smaller frag grenades around them.

My thumb slides over the button as I pass through the first door. The countdown pops up straight away.

Ten.

I make it to the corridor.

Nine.

I trip, but grab hold of a steel edged black equipment case, using it to right myself as I head for the glowing green fire exit signs. The building is shaking, which isn't helping. By the time I look back down at my phone, three more seconds have passed.

Dread pools in my stomach, and I open the group chat and send a single message.

D4rk4ngel
heart emoji

Four.

Damn it. I can do this. I press the power button eight times rapidly, activating my emergency beacon.

Just two doors to go until I'm out. A spurt of adrenaline pushes me forward a few more steps.

Two.

One.

The blast lifts me, propelling me forwards. My head smacks into something hard, and the world goes white.

Slate
41

I'm not sure any of us have spoken in the last three days.

We ended up at Prophet's house, crowded into the spare room. Mama P keeps prodding us to eat, but even Prophet, who's usually anal about mealtimes and sleep schedules, doesn't manage to keep much down.

The police took our statements, but we told them nothing beyond that we'd been informed there was a bomb threat and evacuated the audience. Then we had to tell the feds the same thing. They already knew that Miguel was working with the cartel, but we faked ignorance, and they took us at our word.

Now the press is reporting that it was an attack by a rival cartel. Our reputation has been saved, ironically, by our fierce record of philanthropic donations to youth drug rehabilitation centres.

None of our crew, or our fans, died in the blast. There were a few injuries, and Emma has a few minor burns, but that's it. Miguel, his brothers, and his men were the only documented casualties.

Because Darcy D'Angelo has been wiped from the face of the earth.

Darcy saved us all, took out the cartel, then ceased to exist.

There's no record of her body. Her contract of employment is gone. Even her stuff disappeared from our hotel room, leaving no proof she was ever there.

We're free men, but it doesn't feel like freedom without her here. It feels like hell. Her last message taunts me every time I open my phone.

"Ethan, baby?" Mama P calls from the hall. "There's someone here for you."

I do love Prophet's mom, but she's had just about every friend and neighbour over in the last three days to try to cheer us up. Fuck, she had her pastor here praying over us yesterday.

Prophet doesn't even bother moving his gaze from the TV, even though I'm pretty sure he's not paying attention. "I'm not in the mood."

When the door opens anyway, I'm the only one who even bothers looking up.

I don't recognise the man who enters the living room, but I recognise the way he moves. Like a soldier. All martial confidence and smooth grooming.

Prophet's dad has marine buddies who walk the same way.

"You're Man," I realise, my voice cracking. "She told us about you."

I'm a coward. Can't even say her name.

The others finally look up, drawn out of their fog by the mention of her.

Man doesn't speak, just extends a hand and cocks two fingers in our direction before turning on his heel and walking out of the door.

Arlo is off his feet in a second, striding straight after him without hesitation.

I share a look with Prophet and Dodger, hardly daring to let myself believe this is real. Prophet's jaw works, and he swallows before standing.

"We have to know," he mumbles. "Even if it's just a... a body."

His voice breaks on the last word, and he hurries out after Arlo, wiping his hand down his face as he goes.

"He's right." Dodger stands and offers me a hand, which I take with a deep, fortifying breath.

It turns out Darcy's adopted father brought a Bentley. We pile in, letting the stony-faced driver shut the door after us before getting in and starting the engine. None of us talk, and Man doesn't either. Soon the silence is deafening.

I'm full to the brim with the unasked questions.

Why is he here? What does he want? Does he know who Darcy is to us? Does he know what happened to her?

The hollowness in my chest aches with the final question. Though I'm not as eager as Arlo to grab hold of hope—I've been disappointed too often—I can't help but wonder...

Why would he be here if she was dead?

Are we going to her funeral?

It takes hours. I follow our route on my phone, trying to figure out where we're headed. When we reach the outskirts of Houston, I swallow the lump of emotion in my throat. I didn't want to come back here. I don't think I can stomach seeing the city that took her from us.

The driver finally pulls up outside a mid-rise classical revival style building, then gets out and opens a door for us.

Man leads us up the steps, presses his thumb against a concealed scanner, and enters without knocking.

Inside is calm, but sterile... It's not a typical clinical setting, so I don't make the connection until a male receptionist in scrubs greets us.

This is a hospital. A very well-funded one.

My heartbeat picks up speed, but I crush it.

Hospitals have morgues too.

"Mr. Belladonna, nice to see you again. Are these the friends you mentioned?"

Man nods once.

"Well, they're still in the same rooms as last time. Go on up. Please, feel free to stay as long as you like. Visiting hours don't apply to our black card members."

Man nods, then beckons us to follow him again. We take two flights of stairs, passing doctors and nurses in scrubs, as well as their well-dressed clientele.

I suppose it makes sense assassins wouldn't use a regular hospital, but this is just weird.

When he opens the door to a private room, my breath whooshes out of me as I see the person in the bed is male.

"Well, boys, those disappointed faces are darn righ' insultin'," Sully drawls raspily. "I'm fine, so get outta here. I'd rather be staring at the pretty nurses than your ugly mugs."

That draws a half-hearted chuckle from me. The old Texan looks rough. He's plastered in some strange plastic wrap that seems to be spread over the burns covering a good portion of his body. It's only been ten days since the events at the villa, but whatever they're doing to him must have helped, because he looks a hell of a lot better than I thought he would.

"Glad you're alive, old man," Dodger croaks.

He snorts. "The one you're looking for is in the next room. Go on. But I expect flowers and chocolates next time you visit. And one of you better smuggle me a pack of puros too, but hide it from the docs. They don' like me lighting up."

"Sneaking in contraband already, Mr. Sullivan?" a nurse asks, brushing past us and into the room.

"Never, Lara," he swears, the picture of innocence.

"Mmm hmm," she says, crossing over to him.

"He's in good hands," Dodger mutters, pulling me back out of the room before we can watch any more of the old man's terrible flirting.

Man is waiting by a second door, and my breath falters, hands curling into fists. I can't take this anymore. Either her body is in there, or she's alive, and not knowing is killing me.

I go to shove past him, but his hand on my chest stops me.

"If you don't love her, don't walk through that door." His voice is quiet, but surprisingly cultured.

What kind of—? I remove his hand and push open the door.

Only to come face to face with the most machines I've ever seen attached to one person in my life.

Holy shit.

Buried under wires, and tubes, and casts and bandages, our girl's angelic blonde hair peeks out.

"Dark," Arlo whispers, shoving past my frozen ass and approaching the bed. Somehow, he manages to dodge the tubes and IV lines and make his way to her side. He can't take her hand without dislodging her cannula, so he settles for stroking a thumb reverently along her hairline.

Dodger is the next one to break free of his paralysis. He takes her other side, and his face is actually wet as he rests both hands on her bed's side rails and just stares at her. Prophet shoves me forward, and the two of us end up at the end of her bed. I can't even touch her toes; they're wrapped tight in bandages. What little skin I can see is black and blue.

"Mr. Belladonna?" A cool female voice with the slightest hint of an accent asks. "I'm here if you'd like an update on your daughter's condition?"

I turn to find a short but curvy doctor in scrubs waiting quietly with Man by the door.

He nods, then introduces her. "This is Doctor Ebrahim. One of the world's leading reconstructive surgeons specialising in crush wounds. Doctor, these are my daughter's partners."

She nods. "Darcy is very lucky to have so many devoted men in her life."

"Will she recover?" Dodger asks, voice breaking.

Doctor Ebrahim's smile is small, and her brown eyes twinkle with sympathy. "With time. She's suffered a gunshot wound to the shoulder, which fractured her scapula and nicked a major blood vessel. Then there are several crush wounds, including the main ones to her lower legs. Luckily, since the anterior and interior tibial nerves were intact in both cases, we believe we'll be able to salvage both limbs without shortening or amputation."

Shortening? They do that? Wait... amputation?!

The back of my throat burns, and my fists clench by my sides.

"We expect her to come 'round in a few days, but we're keeping her in a coma until the swelling on her brain heals. We're predicting six months until she regains full ambulatory motion, though it could be longer if she requires more surgeries."

My mind short circuits.

Six months of healing.

Oh, cariño. Why would you bring that building down if you were still in it?

Even as I silently ask the question, I dismiss it. I know why.

Our girl is fiercely protective of those she loves. If Miguel and his goons were chasing after us, she would've done whatever she had to to keep us safe. Even raze an entire arena to the ground.

Now she's fighting a completely different battle.

My eyes land on her phone, lying silent on the bedside cabinet. The glass screen is cracked, and the chassis has warped under the stress of whatever fell on top of her.

My thoughts are racing, and it takes a conscious effort to bring myself back to the present. Ironically, I find myself reaching for the breathing exercises I learned years ago to control my temper.

What I need right now is control over something. I can't fix Darcy's broken bones. I can't lower the swelling in her brain or wipe away the bruises covering her.

What I can do is figure out our next steps. She's going to need a place to recover, and we can't exactly offer her Mama P's sofa.

Our apartment in Florida is out too. As is our holiday place in Hawaii. She's going to need to be close to her specialists, and stairs are out of the question.

"How long until she's discharged?" I ask, interrupting the list of injuries that Doctor Ebrahim is still listing off.

The doctor's hand comes up to fiddle slightly with the fringing of her headscarf as she thinks. "A month, perhaps longer. It's hard to tell until we see how she responds to the treatments."

So we'll need accommodation as close as possible to this place until she's discharged. With Miguel gone, there's nothing to stop us from cancelling the tour. In fact, I'm sure most people will be expecting it. What kind of band would go on touring after their concert was literally blown up?

"Dodger, you'll need to announce the cancellation of the rest of the tour," I begin, though I don't envy him the task of dealing with whoever is left at Miguel's sham agency. "Prophet, find us a place nearby to stay until she's ready to leave. Arlo, sort out getting some of her stuff here so when she comes around, she doesn't go stir crazy."

Darcy will hate being confined to that bed, but we can make it bearable with her favourite streaming services and a gaming laptop. Hell, we'll bring LAN parties back if it keeps her happy.

"What are you going to do?" Prophet asks.

I roll my eyes. "Find us a dream home to fill with all the babies she wants when she recovers." Because she just put herself through the wringer for us, and I intend to make sure she knows how grateful I am every single day for the rest of our natural lives.

I turn, glancing back at the bed for a second, before walking straight into Man.

He raises a single brow, and for some reason, I understand the question he won't ask.

"She's ours." And we're hers. It's not so much a claiming as an acknowledgement of inevitability.

In this world, some souls are destined for one another, and she's it for us. It doesn't matter if she never walks again. Until the day we die, and beyond.

"We'll take care of her."

Man nods, straightens his suit, and leaves the room.

I'm going to take that as his blessing.

Darcy
42

There's something in my throat, and I don't like it, but when I try to pull it away, my arms don't respond.

"Darcy."

Who's that? Why are they familiar?

Fear creeps through me as I realise I can't move. My eyes won't open. My hands won't move. I can feel fingers tracing lightly over my own, but I can't grab them.

What the hell happened to me?

"Her heart rate is spiking."

"Go get the nurse."

"Hey, Dark. Don't panic, beautiful. We're here. We're all here."

Far from being comforting, I just fight harder. *Who's we?* The voice seems familiar, but I can't place it. Am I being drugged?

Before I can fight anymore, the blackness takes me again.

SOMEONE IS SINGING. CROONING. OH. I KNOW THIS song. Half a melody erupts from my throat before I can stop myself from trying to hum along to the tune.

The singing stops.

"Hey, sleepyhead? You there?"

I blink, but my eyes are full of sleep. No—wait.

"Where are my glasses?" I try to ask, except my tongue feels glued to my mouth, so what comes out is actually "Whermeglusses?"

There's an audible fumbling, and a second later, the familiar weight of the frames slides into place, bringing the room sharply into focus.

The first person I see is Dodger, and I smile in confusion. "Hey, aren't you supposed to be on stage somewhere?"

"We're retired, baby girl," he murmurs, and his eyes start to glisten slightly. "Streaming only from now on."

Oh. A jolt of alarm hits me. "But I liked watching you hump the floor."

"Jesus, how many drugs is she on?" Slate asks, and I twist my head to search for him, but it doesn't work very well. Someone's got my neck stuck.

Dodger half-chokes on his laugh. "I'll hump the floor for you any time, sweetheart."

Oh good. Somehow, that reassures me enough to let me fall back to sleep.

"MISS BELLADONNA, IT'S NOT HOSPITAL POLICY TO allow weapons—"

"Our father already approved it with management." *Is that... Harlow? No, it can't be.*

I set down my tablet as the door opens. It's a rare afternoon where all four of my guys have had to leave me alone. I wasn't expecting any visitors, and the last people I expect my poor flustered nurse to admit are two of my sisters.

"Are those for me?" I ask, grinning, as Tabby hefts the gift basket laden with guns across the threshold.

She doesn't answer, passing me a loaded Glock before she heads for the window and begins checking the locks. Classic Tabby-Cat. Behind her, Harlow is carrying another—less dangerous—hamper full of cupcakes, pastries, and other baked goods. I eye them with suspicion as I check the safety on the Glock before shoving it beneath my pillow.

"Karma sent these," she says, plopping her burden down on the table by my bed.

"And Raven had no part in it?" I check, eyeing the mouth-watering array with a healthy dose of suspicion.

A week ago, Raven sent a bottle of pillow mist that had been liberally laced with one of her potions. Instead of helping me sleep, as I'd assumed it would, it sent me into fits of laughter. The guys hadn't understood what was wrong until Prophet fell victim as well, and by that point, it was too late. Dodger sprayed Slate, who accidentally caught Arlo when he tried to return fire, and minutes later, the entire room was awash with gut-busting giggles. It took hours to wear off, and my nurse was less than impressed.

I'm going to get her back for that... when I can walk again.

"No, she's too busy basking in the glow of winning your 'prank war,'" Tabby says, off-handedly, as she begins screwing something to the window frame. "She hid a camera in the packaging, so you're going to have to delete the video when you get out of here."

Taking a pack of antiseptic wipes from her bag, Harlow vigorously cleans the plastic visitor's chair before she takes her seat, flicking her hair out of her face. She's more tanned than when I last saw her, thanks to all the travels her guys have taken her on.

"You look good." Both of them do, actually.

Although Tabby lacks Harlow's tan, there's a relaxed look about her that isn't normally there. Both of them are dressed casually, but I know they're armed.

"I'd say the same, but..." Harlow trails off, and I snort.

"Hey, at least my face is healing." A lot of the superficial bruises there are fading, but I have a long way to go until I can get out of this damned bed. Hopefully, I won't need any more surgeries on my legs now, but it all depends on what the doctors decide.

"Okay, I've replaced the locks on the window," Tabby announces, heading back to her basket. "I've got a scanner I can put on the door. You've got three boxes of ammo there. I've also got throwing knives, frag grenades, a drone with a mini machine gun mounted onto the base..."

I smirk, because her plan to defend me while I recover is the closest to a declaration of love I'll ever get from her, then grab the first baked item—a gooey triple chocolate brownie—from Karma's basket and bite into it with a moan. Tabby continues reading out her list of weapons as Harlow settles back in her seat, biting into one of Karma's cupcakes. The two of us share a look that's equal parts amusement and exasperation.

My sisters are the best, and I can't wait to see what the guys make of my "get well soon" gifts.

"WOW, THAT SUN IS BRIGHT." I WINCE, COVERING MY eyes with a yellow-and-green bruise-covered hand as Prophet expertly manoeuvres my wheelchair out of the hospital doors.

It's taken two months, but I'm finally breaking out of

here. I still have at least four more months of rehab, but I fully intend to enjoy being outside for what little remains of the summer.

"Ems should be meeting us at the car with coffee," Arlo says.

He's almost bouncing on his feet beside me with excitement and has been since the hospital finally signed me off to leave. Slate and Dodger are already at our mystery destination, which leaves Arlo and Prophet as my escorts.

"Here we are," Prophet grunts, pulling my chair to a stop alongside a beast of a car.

"You own a G-Wagen?" I can't keep the disbelief from my voice. "Really?"

It suits him. Large and bulky and practical. If it were anyone else driving, I'd have said the car was making up for a tiny dick.

"If you're looking for the flashy pretty boy cars, Dodger has you covered," he says. "I wanted something that would survive a zombie apocalypse or a car chase with a drug lord."

"Oddly specific," I mutter, as he puts the brake on my chair and then bends to scoop me out of the chair before depositing me in the passenger seat. "Wow, this is... How high am I right now?"

They chuckle, but no one answers. Seriously.

"I'm here!" Emma calls, crossing the road with her hands full of takeaway cups.

For the last few months, she's been amazing. Not only has she set up her own design boutique in the city, but she's also sat with me on the few occasions when the guys couldn't be there. Together, we've finished all nineteen seasons of *Say Yes to the Dress*, and most of *The Bachelor*.

The moment she reaches me, she passes my cup through the window, and I sigh in relief at the first blisteringly hot sip.

The one cup of filter coffee the hospital provided for

breakfast was nowhere near enough for me. If it wasn't tepid, it was borderline tasteless.

Okay, I'm a coffee snob, but there are worse crimes.

"Is there pizza where we're going?" I ask, enthusiastically.

That's the other thing I've missed. Apparently, it isn't on the hospital menu.

"As much as you can eat," Prophet says.

I'm so busy enjoying my first real coffee in weeks that I don't notice everyone else has clambered into Prophet's ludicrously large car until he starts the engine and cruises out onto the streets of Houston.

"Is it far?" I ask, as he takes the main road out of the city.

"A couple of hours," Arlo replies.

"Get some rest," Emma encourages, and I groan.

"I've *been* resting."

All I seem to do nowadays is get tired way too quickly. I fall asleep at weird times, and while I know that's just my body trying to heal, it still sucks.

"You'll need your strength for the exercises the doctor prescribed," Prophet reminds me.

I sigh and let my head thunk back against the rest. "I hate exercises."

Just because they're good for me and I do them doesn't mean I have to like them. The gruelling routine that Doctor Ebrahim and her team of personal torturers—ahem, trainers —has created for me to regain use of my legs is just evil.

At least when I worked out before, sparring and jogging kept my brain engaged. Not like this endless repetition that I've been doing recently.

The only benefit is the Prophet has appointed himself my workout buddy, so at least there's eye candy to watch while I suffer.

I don't mean to, but I drift off again to fantasies of him

doing push ups with me on his back. When I wake, we're pulling up to a huge colonial style manor with dark green shutters and a five door garage.

It's almost as big as the Belladonna Mansion, and I raise my brows.

"Who lives here?"

Arlo chokes out a half laugh, and I catch Emma rolling her eyes in the rear-view mirror.

Slate steps out of the double doors, closely followed by Dodger and even... Sully?

It takes an embarrassingly long time for my brain to join the dots.

"You guys bought a house?"

Prophet grunts in affirmation.

"If it's not what you like, we can buy a different one," Arlo rushes. "We chose this one because there's a ground floor suite that we can turn into a home gym when your legs are healed enough for stairs, but there were others..."

I scoff as my door opens. "I highly doubt there's an abundance of mansions with five door garages just waiting for us to pick one out."

"If there aren't, we'll build one." Slate's easy confidence oozes out of him as he lifts me out of my seat and carries me through the front doors.

The way he looks at me, even with my rolled up sweats and bulky brace-covered legs, makes me grin.

"I'm not cleared for any kind of strenuous activity for at least the next few weeks," I remind him, as he tries and fails to keep his eyes from wandering along the v neck of my tee as he carries me into the kitchen.

"Counting down the days, *mi amor*," he murmurs, kissing the top of my head. "See that island there? I have daydreams about bending you over it."

"Pizza first," I insist. "Prophet promised you had some."

"You heard her," Emma says. "Pizza first, gross lovey dovey shit later."

Darcy
43

My arm throbs like a bitch, but I keep that information to myself as I watch our home come into view. January this year has been colder than ever, and an icy layer of sleet obscures the windshield as Prophet pulls up outside.

For the first time in six months, I can open the car door and step out by myself, without a cane or crutches. Walking unaided is the biggest gift, and while my legs will still twinge from time to time, today was my last follow up appointment with the torture-therapists.

"So…" I begin, rushing up to the porch. "I vote that we start in the kitchen."

"Start?" Prophet asks, unlocking the door.

"Then we'll move on to the den." I shoot a grin over my shoulder as I waltz in. "But I'm partial to doggy on the stairs, so we'll have to stop on the way."

Prophet's eyes twinkle as he finally catches on. His hands encircle my waist, and he pulls me back against his chest, leaning down to press his lips to the spot just below my ear.

"You sure you're ready for this, angel?"

The careful concern in his tone has me melting.

The one and only time we tried anything sexual since my injury, my orgasm caused my still-healing calf muscles to cramp. Hard. It was an incident that none of us will forget in a hurry, even if it didn't have any long-lasting consequences. After I screamed the house down, all four of my guys decided to pull the plug on sex until I got the all clear.

It's been a *long* six months. Made longer by the fact that I joined them for workouts in the gym every morning.

In short, I'm hornier than I ever remember being, and I am beyond ready to have the gang bang they keep taunting me with.

Plus, I have a surprise for them.

"I'm beyond ready." I pry his hands free and dance out of his hold. "Let's go find the others."

I don't have to go far. The others are gathered in the den, poring over... sheet music? It's my favourite room in our home, purely because it's essentially a cinema room with giant bean bags in place of chairs. Right now, the three of them are lounging around as Arlo strums on his guitar, and Slate adds a bass line into the mix.

"Prophet, get over here," Dodger commands, tucking his pen behind his ear as soon as he spots us. "We've got a good melody going, but what do you think we should do with —Darcy?"

I grin as my top falls to the floor, leaving me in just my bra. As much as I love the way they've gradually fallen back into writing music together again, I have something more important to talk to them about.

Grabbing my left arm, I twist to proudly display my tiny, throbbing wound.

It's nothing compared to the bullet scar on my shoulder—which has since been covered with my own tiny Hazardous band tattoo—but it still hurts like a bitch. I guess being shot and crushed did nothing to improve my pain tolerance.

"Is that...?" Arlo trails off.

I grin at the startled look in his eyes that's quickly turning to a stormy heat. The moment the tour was cancelled, his trademark glasses came off, and he hasn't worn them since. He has no need to pretend to hide a coke addiction now that Miguel is gone, and with the cartel out of the picture, he's been able to talk to a professional, who's helping him deal with any hiccups along the way. He's still not at the stage where he's comfortable wearing short sleeves, but nothing makes me happier than being able to read every single emotion as they play across his face.

"My birth control ran out a few months ago," I admit. "But I got it taken out today."

Butterflies take up residence in my stomach. We've talked a lot more about children since we moved in together, and we're all on board. We've discussed which of the rooms would be a nursery, how we'd manage the school run, what we'd do if our kids were bullied for having more than one dad, and just about every single hypothetical scenario we could imagine.

But this is still a big step.

Sure, I have no idea how long it will take my fertility to settle down to normal now that the implant is out, but the chance is still there that if we do this now, there could be a baby joining us in nine months.

Prophet is the first one to actually act. The other three are still processing. He has me pressed up against the wall in under a second, his mouth fused with mine as his erection scalds me through the fabric of our sweats.

My breasts heave, brushing against the fabric of his top as he devours me like I'm the very air he needs to keep breathing.

"If you're not sure..." he mumbles, in between kisses. "Fuck. Please be sure."

In answer, I nip at his lower lip. "I've never been more certain of anything."

"Wait, wait, wait..." Slate struggles to disentangle himself from his guitar strap as he climbs to his feet. "Prophet, we had a *plan*, remember?"

The drummer breaks the kiss long enough to give him a death stare. Some silent communication travels between the band, and I pout in frustration as I'm gently lowered to the ground.

"This better be a good plan," I grumble. "Do you have any idea how horny I am right now?"

Dodger chuckles. "I think we can relate."

"It's a good plan," Arlo interrupts, grabbing my hand and tugging me out of the den. "You'll like it."

He doesn't release me until we're standing facing the kitchen island, and the cheerful square box on top of it. Steam is rising from the cardboard, and I can smell the pizza within.

"Food?" I ask, confused. "I... I think we can reheat it later?"

I never thought I'd pass up pizza, but...

"Open it," Dodger encourages, and I turn to find they're all behind me, herding me against the sideboard.

My brows furrow, but I do as they say, turning back and flicking open the—

"Oh my God." The words tumble out as my brain short circuits.

There, on top of the stuffed crust goodness, chunks of pineapple and pepperoni have been artistically placed to spell out two little words.

"Marry us?"

I whirl, catching myself against the side as I realise they're on their knees in a semi-circle, fingers brushing as they offer a glistening tangle of metal to me. Each guy is technically holding a different gold band, but those bands are connected together in such a way that they can't be separated.

"I am... so confused right now," I admit. "What...? How does this...? Do I wear them on different fingers?"

Instead of a traditional circle, each thin band is a wiggly shape that doesn't make sense. Each one is embedded with a tiny ruby, and there's a larger diamond in amongst them as well.

"We got you a challenge," Arlo says. "It's a puzzle ring. There are four rings, and they fit together to make one."

My smile slowly spreads, crinkling my cheeks as I catch on. "One for each of you."

God, they're proposing to me and I'm only wearing my bra and sweatpants.

"Still waiting on your answer, *cariño*," Slate reminds me, and my mouth pops open as I realise he actually looks a little nervous.

Like my answer was ever really in doubt. "Yes. Of course."

"Great, now, solve it so we can go back to fucking you senseless," Dodger growls.

I take the metal from them, playing with the loops. "Did it come with instructions?"

They all look at Arlo, who shrugs. "No?"

Thirty minutes later, after Slate gave in and Googled the solution, my new ring sits proudly on my finger. The pizza has been abandoned in the kitchen, and the five of us retreated back to the den. The four bands sit snugly together, and the weird wiggles that confused me before have settled into an intricate Celtic knot, with the four rubies surrounding the diamond in the centre.

"It's beautiful," I whisper, stroking over each of the lines.

"It will look better when you're naked," Dodger says, stroking my hair away from my neck to press a kiss to the skin there.

I've somehow ended up sitting in his lap, my ass bracketed

by his thighs as the others lounge around us on their own beanbags.

"I agree," I murmur, turning my head so I can kiss him. "But don't you think there are a few things to sort first? We should pick a date, and then there's the matter of whose last name to pick..."

I'm teasing, of course, but the way their faces go slack with disbelief is entirely worth it.

"The date is Dodger's birthday," Slate says, reaching behind me to undo my bra snaps. "Because it's closest, and he'll want to unwrap you. As for your last name, I think that's obvious."

"It is?" I gasp as he tugs the fabric away and stares hungrily at my exposed breasts.

"You get the last name of the reigning Rainbow Road champion."

"So yours, then?" Darcy Fletcher-Reyes... It doesn't sound too bad, but I don't particularly like the idea of choosing one over the others, even if it's just their last name.

"Well, you can't exactly have Prophet's. That would just be confusing." Slate's words earn him a cuff upside the head from the drummer.

"She can have my name if she wants it."

Dodger's hands rest on my bare waist. "I vote we have a tournament to figure it out. All of us put forward one game, and then we play each of them until a winner is decided."

"No way. You're gonna pick some obscure beat 'em up with weird button commands," Arlo complains.

Dodger quirks a brow. "And you're not going to make us play some vintage arcade shit?"

"Or we head back to CoD and see who manages to get a 360 noscope first try," Arlo says, leaning back on his beanbag to grab one of the many sketchbooks he's abandoned all over the house. The second it's in his hands, he starts to flip through it in search of a clean page.

Slate visibly cringes. "I could've gone my entire life without hearing that phrase ever again."

Arlo looks up from the book just long enough to shoot him an offended look. "Hey! It was our *thing*."

Prophet drops his head into his hand. "That was when we were *teenagers*, Lo."

"You guys are so lame, and my last name is *not* being decided by that," I protest, shoving my sweatpants down along with my panties in my haste to end the discussion. "I vote I leave my name exactly as it is. Or I just become Mrs. Hazardous."

"We can table the discussion for now," Dodger murmurs, his hands coming up to cup my breasts. "But for the record, I think Darcy Cartwright is—"

"I'm not taking the last name of a man who won't even tell me his legal *first* name," I retort, only to drop my head back on a moan as he sucks on my throat before licking the spot.

"I barely even remember my legal first name," he replies, breath whispering over the damp patch his tongue has made on my neck, making me shiver. "I've been Dodger ever since I was a kid. Just like Prophet is Prophet."

My thoughts are turning fuzzy, but that might be because he's circling my nipples with his thumbs, teasing them into hard points as the others watch.

"Besides," he continues, pinching both buds hard until I moan. "I love the way it sounds when you scream it as you come all over my cock."

His voice, combined with his filthy words, makes goose-bumps flare across my skin. He knows exactly what he's doing to me, because he releases my poor tormented nipples a second later, then takes my hand in his and brings it to my breast.

"Show me how you suck your own tits," he murmurs. "You know I've always wanted to watch."

Arlo's head snaps up. "She can do that?"

In answer, I raise one breast to my mouth and let my tongue swirl out around the dark pink skin of my areola.

The stick of charcoal he's holding snaps, but he barely pauses to discard the top half before his hand starts gliding furiously across the paper.

"Keep going," Dodger murmurs in my ear. "You want to give him plenty of inspiration, don't you?"

His hands slide down my rib cage to rest on my upper thighs. With the gentlest of pressure, he spreads my legs apart, exposing my pussy to the hungry gazes of the rest of the band.

"Who wants the first taste?" Dodger asks.

Slate moves forward eagerly, and to my surprise, Prophet lets him. For all his worry about jealousy, or perhaps because of it, he's probably the best at sharing out of the group.

"I'm going to grab a few things," the drummer mutters, mysteriously. "Don't get too carried away without me."

Slate's on me before I can ask what Prophet is up to. The bassist lies flat on the floor and kisses his way up the scars on my calves. The evidence of my ordeal is healing, but my skin remains pink and shiny in places. He takes his time laving each mark tenderly, kissing the sensitive skin beneath my knees, then stroking a path up my thighs as Dodger holds me open for his friend's use. Slate's first lick against my pussy makes an audible wet sound as his tongue swipes a path across my entrance and up to my clit.

"Darcy's getting distracted," Arlo complains.

"Keep playing with those tits," Dodger growls against my ear. "You wouldn't deprive Lo of his masterpiece, would you?"

I hadn't even realised I'd stopped, but my mouth eagerly returns to the task as Slate continues eating me out.

God, he's good at this. My hand clenches hard against the

softness of my other breast, knuckles turning white as he lashes my clit with sure strokes. Dodger notices and releases one thigh to pry my fingers away.

He raises my hand to his mouth and lightly sucks on the tips of my fingers. The sensation travels straight down to my clit, making me clench, hard.

Why is that so hot? Fingers are not supposed to be an erogenous zone.

It's so hard to focus on my breasts while Slate's eating me out like he's forgotten the need to breathe, but I do my best. Then, when he adds a finger and starts slowly working his way inside me, I lose the will to try. My head falls back against Dodger's chest, and he chuckles as I tremble against him.

"Does it feel good, baby girl?"

"Yes," I moan. "Too good."

Slate slips a second digit into me, and the room begins to fill with the noise of him lewdly finger fucking me. He curls them inside my pussy until he finds the spot that makes me jerk like a livewire. It's been too long, so I'm not surprised when my orgasm barrels into me out of nowhere. My breath whooshes out of me, and pleasure arcs up my spine.

Slate doesn't stop. No. He just wraps his arms tighter around my thighs and doubles down on my hypersensitive flesh. Dodger takes both of my breasts in his hands and pinches my nipples again as I hit a second peak in moments, drawing out my release until I'm squirming and gasping for breath. Another orgasm is on the horizon, and my muscles tense as I strain to reach it.

"Not yet," the singer whispers against my ear. "Prophet's brought you some toys to play with, and then we're going to take turns filling up your pretty cunt."

"And her ass," Prophet adds.

"You sure you know how making a baby works?" Slate asks, chin glistening as he pulls away, allowing Dodger to rearrange me so I'm straddling him. "Or have you forgotten in your old age?"

There's a slap, which I assume is Prophet cuffing Slate upside the head, before the drummer takes his place behind me. His hands slide over my ass, spreading my cheeks while his thumbs press inward at the back ring of muscle. He plays there for a few seconds, stretching me, reminding me how good it feels, before he pulls away.

"I'm going to plug this ass, angel. Then Dodger's going to fuck your pretty pussy while you suck Arlo off. Then, when you're nice and stretched and open for us, Slate and I are going to fuck you at the same time."

Does he expect me to object? "Please."

A cold dollop of lube lands just above my asshole, and Prophet lets it drip down slowly before he starts to work it inside me with his finger.

"This plug is bigger than before," he warns.

"You can take it, can't you, baby girl?" Dodger croons, his hand slipping between us to fondle my clit as Prophet awakens a whole different set of nerve endings with his careful stretching.

"Yes, sir," I mumble against his chest, my words ending on a gasp as he catches my clit between two fingers and pinches.

I'm on the verge of coming again when Prophet draws back, replacing his finger with the cool, firm press of silicone.

"Breathe out," he coaxes.

"Taking it so well," Dodger says, pressing kisses to my face. "God, I wish I could see your ass stretching around it."

"You can have her ass when we reach round two," Prophet promises.

"Round two?" I squeak, trying to distract myself from the burn as the plug slips deeper.

Prophet leans in closer and presses a kiss to my shoulder. "You didn't think you would just take off your top, dangle the possibility of a family in front of me, and get away with only being fucked once, did you?"

The rest of them laugh, privy to some joke I don't understand.

"You're not leaving this room until you're so fucked full of cum that it drips out of you," Slate says.

"Probably not even then," Dodger adds.

"You realise it will take some time for my hormones to even out?" I ask, groaning as the flared end of the plug *finally* comes to rest against my sphincter. "It might take months…"

Or longer still. My heart pangs as the statistics flash through my mind again.

"We've got nothing but time," Arlo reassures me as Dodger undoes his zipper and frees his erection. "I'm going to love drawing you when you're all round with our baby, Dark."

Dodger angles our bodies, then presses his cock inside slowly. The fit is a hundred times tighter with the plug in my ass.

"Oh God." My breath hitches as he pulls back just a little, then works his way forward again.

Then Arlo is there, holding his erection out in offering, the head bobbing just inches from my face.

I lick him, then draw him as deep into my throat as I can, savouring the distraction from the battle for space going on below.

"Shit, Dark," he hisses, as I bring one hand up to fondle his balls. "You're so good at this."

Playing with him allows me to relax enough for Dodger to bottom out in my pussy. He stills as soon as he's in, and I work hard to control my breathing. The fullness is incredible, but I also have the irrational fear that if he moves, I'm going to split in half.

"You feel like heaven," he mutters. "You're drenched, baby girl."

I pull away from Arlo's cock. "It's too much," I whimper.

"You want to stop?" he asks against my lips. "Or do you just need a second to get used to it?"

I bite at my lip and wiggle experimentally against him. "Go slow."

"Okay."

His hands fall to my hips and start guiding me up and down over him, helping me to ride him at my own easy pace while I return my focus to sucking Arlo as deep as I can. Hands stroke gently across my body, their callouses a deliciously rough contrast to the softness of their touch. Eliciting moans and desperate whines from my throat as their fingertips skate over my skin.

My mind can't seem to decide whether to focus on the cock in my mouth, the stretch taking over my pussy and ass, or the soothing strokes across my spine. Together, they're almost too much, stoking the embers of my previous orgasm rapidly back into flame.

Dodger lets me control the pace, so when I start to speed up, chasing the promised high of my own pleasure, his hands are there, lifting and lowering me to the new rhythm. Our flesh slaps together, the acoustic noise echoing over the harsh sound of our breathing as we draw nearer and nearer to the edge.

Then someone—probably Prophet—grabs hold of the plug and starts fucking me with it in tandem.

Arlo's cock falls from my mouth, and I cry out as pleasure spikes, then cascades.

"Fuck," Dodger shouts, slamming hard into me one last time before his cock jerks.

I'm still coming down from the high when Arlo lifts me off Dodger, pushes me down into the beanbag, and stuffs his cock into my still-quivering cunt. It only takes three thrusts before he's spilling inside me as well.

He draws out with a groan, then flops onto the bag beside me, tracing my hair out of my face as he leans up to press a kiss to my lips.

"Are you okay?" Prophet asks me. "Legs fine?"

I do a quick inventory, then reach my arms out to him. "I'm fine. I want more, though."

Dodger groans. "Insatiable."

"Good thing there are four of us," Slate adds, taking my hands before Prophet can and lifting me up into his arms. "Hold on tight, *bebita*."

With one hand beneath my still-plugged ass to hold me in place, he uses the other to angle his dick towards my pussy, sliding in easily. As soon as he's buried as deep as he can go, he rearranges us so that his arms are hooked beneath my knees, with my feet digging into his ass and my arms wrapped around his neck for support.

He grins over my shoulder at Prophet. "Were you planning to join us?"

I follow his gaze, and frown as I realise the drummer is rolling on a condom, but I don't have a chance to ask why as he finishes and comes up behind me. I let my head fall back onto his shoulder and glory in being surrounded by two men who love me absolutely.

Then he tugs the plug free, discarding it to the floor without caring where it ends up.

My spine stiffens, but he's already there, lubing up his cock and pressing it against my asshole. "Don't tense, angel. Just breathe and focus on how good Slate feels in your pussy."

Tilting my head back, I claim Slate's mouth in a desperate kiss as Prophet's cock replaces the plug. God, he's so much bigger than the toy, and I nip at Slate's lips as gravity forces my body to yield to the dual invasion.

"My God," I choke out as he finally bottoms out.

"Your ass is mine, angel," he groans against my ear. "Now hold on to Slate's shoulders."

I do as he asks, my nails digging into Slate's muscles as the two of them draw out and then start alternating their thrusts. Moving with the kind of synchronicity that I've only ever seen them display on stage. They play my body like I'm their instrument, thrusting at just the right angle so that Slate rubs over my G-spot while his pelvis grinds against my clit.

It's wet, messy, raw fucking, and I love it. The sounds that escape my mouth are nothing short of animalistic as I stretch to accommodate the two of them.

"I'm not gonna last..." Slate grunts. "Come for us, *reina*. Come all over our cocks."

Prophet shifts, moving one hand around between my body and his bandmate's to find my slippery clit and trap it between two of his fingers. Then he leans down, rubbing his stubble along my throat as his lips caress my ear.

"Please."

I detonate, clinging to Slate as my toes curl, and my thoughts become a blur. The bassist freezes, buried deep inside me, then he groans and buries his head in my hair. Pressing a kiss to my temple, he withdraws and staggers back, still watching with hooded eyes.

Prophet carries me over to the beanbag, his cock never leaving my ass as he arranges me on my hands and knees and then starts thrusting in earnest.

A second before he's about to come, the reason for the condom becomes clear as he pulls out and rips the latex off before shoving his dick into my pussy. He fucks into me once, then twice, before groaning as his own orgasm hits.

"Stay there," he murmurs, drawing back and pressing my shoulders down into the bag when I would've flipped over.

Prophet's fingers scoop up the cum which has escaped and spreads it up to my pussy, before forcing it back inside. While he works, the others move to surround us, claiming my mouth with tender kisses.

"Fuck, that's hot," Dodger mutters under his breath.

"Weird as hell, though," Arlo adds, then rolls his eyes at the death glares the others shoot him. "What?! We spent the last thirty years of our lives trying *not* to get girls pregnant. This is literally a one-eighty."

I giggle, because I understand exactly what he means. "You'll get used to it," I promise, as Prophet finally gives up and allows Slate to pull me into his lap. "After all, we have plenty of time to practise." I pause, grimacing when my tummy rumbles. "So, when do I get to eat that pizza?"

Four snorts answer me, and I snuggle deeper into Slate, kissing the band tattoo over his heart while Dodger shuffles away to go and fix us some food.

Yes, it's been a long road to get here, but I'm finally exactly where I always dreamed of being.

"For the record," Slate whispers in my ear. "I really like Mrs. Hazardous."

NINE YEARS LATER...

"Mom?" Freya's voice echoes down the hall, and I quickly finish typing the final line of command code before shutting the lid of my laptop.

The TV screen mounted on the wall of my office displays the live cam footage of my target's office in Dubai erupting in flames, but I manage to switch it off before my beautiful daughter pokes her head through my door. Her mismatched eyes—a carbon copy of Prophet's—blink innocently at me, despite both of us knowing she's not supposed to come in here when I'm working.

"What's wrong?" I ask, confused. "You were supposed to be getting ready for your slumber party with Daddy S."

"He got distracted by Sophie." Freya sighs in the over dramatic way she does. "Can you help me find my lombax pyjamas? Pleaseeeeee?"

I huff under my breath in amusement. As much as my eldest would like everyone to believe she's been neglected ever since Sophie was born, she's got all four of her fathers—and a few of her aunts—wrapped securely around her eight-year-old fingers.

"Freya." Slate groans, pushing open the door. "*Princesa*, you know your mom's working."

"It's okay," I murmur. "I've mostly finished."

I tap my phone on, then swipe the bot I made into action. It can clear out the mark's bank accounts and start the process of funnelling the funds into our accounts.

Not that we need the money. The band's record label is thriving, and I'd never have to work a day in my life if I didn't love it so much.

Hazardous's music, now unhindered by Miguel's bullshit, has only grown better. Though they haven't toured again since our showdown with the Rosales cartel, their renewed willingness to collaborate with one another has led to the creation of five new albums, all of which proved an instant hit with their fans. Add in the hit new music streaming app I created for them, we could retire tomorrow if we wanted to.

But I don't.

Apparently, even dropping a building on my legs wasn't enough to cure me of my fascination with explosions. Thankfully, Man still sends the odd case my way, and advances in robotics in the last few years mean I can deal with them remotely. Seeing things go *boom* on a screen isn't anywhere near as satisfying, but my guys aren't too fond of me going out into the field after the Houston incident.

"Come on." I stand, locking my phone before holding my hand out to our daughter. "Let's go find those jammies."

Instead of taking it, she launches herself at Slate and climbs his body like a koala.

"Oof," he grunts, but doesn't complain as she attaches herself to his chest like a barnacle.

"Sophie's got Arlo playing fairy princess again," Slate

informs me. "I turned my back on Freya for five seconds to be a dragon, and when I turned back, she was gone."

Sure enough, when we enter the den, Arlo is hunched up on a child's stool, wearing a too-small pair of fairy wings and patiently letting our youngest put braids in his hair while Dodger smirks and takes photos. One of the girls' white dress-up wigs has been smooshed over the guitarist's head, and Sophie's play makeup is smeared badly around his lips. She's even attempted to give him a badass scar over his left eye, and my mouth physically hurts from the repressed laughter bubbling in my throat.

"Smile, Princess Arlo," Dodger croons.

"Princess *Geralt*," Sophie corrects, her precocious little voice half-raised in song. "Honestly, Daddy D, you're not very good at playing fairy princesses if you can't even remember his name."

"You'll have to get him his own wings," Arlo encourages, raising one pierced brow in a silent promise of retribution that goes right over our daughter's head. "Then he'll understand what it really means to be one."

Sophie purses her lips in serious thought but abandons her game the moment she spots me.

With a loud exuberant cry, she runs up to me, dragging Arlo with her. "Mommy! Look, I made Daddy into a fairy princess!"

"So you did." It's so hard to keep my grin from turning into a full-blown laugh as I meet Arlo's eyes. My cheeks ache with the effort. "He's a beautiful princess."

Freya wiggles until Slate has to put her down, and for a second, I just take in the sight of my two daughters. Both have dark hair, but that's where the similarities end. Sophie is a girly girl who lives for her favourite purple princess gown, while Freya is a tomboy who'd rather be climbing trees or playing astronauts.

My two girls are oil and water, but I wouldn't have them any other way.

Arlo winks at me, and I pull my poor, tortured husband in for a kiss. He tastes of cherry lip gloss and coffee, and I savour him for a second before I start to pull away.

"Ewww. No kissing!" Freya groans.

"Is it her bedtime yet?" he mumbles against my lips.

"Are you ready, Freya?" Prophet calls. "We've got to be at Auntie—" His words trail off as he pushes through the other door and comes face to face with Arlo in full fairy princess regalia.

"Don't say a word," Arlo mutters.

"It's okay, I videoed his entire glow up," Dodger says. "We're saving this."

"When your daughter wants to play fairy princess, you play fairy princess," Arlo grates out. "Now. Freya, your pyjamas are already in your bag, and Auntie Ems is ready for—"

"I want to go to Auntie Ems's house!" Sophie blurts. "I can show her my makeup skills! I'm gonna be just like her!"

"You can go soon," I promise. "But Freya has a slumber party with Amy today."

The two cousins were born three months apart and have been inseparable since then. Amy may have been an "accident," but Emma is an amazing mom, and it's been nice to have them living so close.

Unfortunately, Freya is at that stage where having a younger sibling cramping your style is embarrassing at best and downright annoying at worst.

Sophie pouts, but she's quickly distracted when Dodger pulls a familiar cream DVD case down from the shelf.

"While she's gone, we thought you'd want to watch this with your mom."

"*Princess Bride*!" Sophie squeals, nearly deafening me,

before turning to Arlo. "Daddy, you're not wearing the right outfit!"

Arlo's shoulders sag slightly in relief. He's much happier to dress up as Westley than Princess Geralt. Unfortunately for him, his long, blonde-streaked hair makes him Sophie's favourite doll—after me.

"Ready?" Prophet asks Freya, who's released Slate in favour of double checking that her favourite lombax pyjamas are in the bag as Arlo promised.

"Yep!" she chirps, bouncing up to press a quick kiss to my cheek before running to grab Prophet's hand. "See you later, Mom!"

"Bye, sweetie," I call.

But she's already gone.

"Drive safe," I murmur, pulling Prophet to me for a kiss before he follows after her daughter.

"Always," he promises. "When I get back, want to practise making baby number three?"

I shoot him a coy smile. While we're not actively trying for a third, we've talked about it a bit. I wouldn't be upset if it happened, but my girls are more than enough for me right now.

"What about the new expansion for Runes of Chaos?" I ask. "It just dropped this morning. I thought we were going to check it out..."

Besides, the band is considering doing a relaxed tour, with less explosions and no cartel connections in the next year. It will be a good chance for our girls to travel, and I know that, as much as they might protest otherwise, they do miss being on stage. They're even trying to convince Sully to come out of retirement for it—and I'm pretty sure they're going to succeed.

"Screw the game," Prophet mutters. "I'd rather stare at you than a screen."

"Get going," I say, ignoring the way my heart flutters happily at his words. "Freya is excited to see Amy again."

He sneaks another kiss before he goes. "Love you, angel."

"Love you too," I mumble against him, but I meet the eyes of all four of them as I say it.

It's such a cliché, but I really do fall more in love with them every single day. My nerdy rock stars turned out to be everything I ever dreamed they could be and more, and I can't wait to see what the future brings us.

THE END

DRESSED TO KILL

Welcome to the dangerous and enticing world of the Belladonnas - where the women may be beautiful, but they're more deadly than anyone could ever imagine.

Assassins. Women for hire.

Is there really a difference?

These women dress for success... and that success is usually found while standing over the bodies of their targets.

Ten USA Today and International bestselling authors bring you a dark and decadent world full of spies, con men, assassins, and deadly secrets.

Will these deadly flowers be able to find love?

Harlow by Katie May and R.A. Smyth
Selena by May Dawson
Ivory by Kira Roman
Royal by Ann Denton
Raven by Kris Butler
Naomi by Alisha Williams
Karma by Amber Nicole
Darcy by Marie Mistry
Tabitha by Stacey Brutger

Acknowledgments

While I've got your attention, I'd like to thank you for reading. This was my first foray into contemporary romance, and I had so much fun writing Darcy's story, so thanks for taking a chance on her (and me)! If you'd like to be extra awesome, please consider leaving a review. They help authors like me enormously, and I always enjoy seeing what people think.

I'd also like to thank Katie May for asking me to be part of this world, and all the other authors involved. I've never done anything like this before, and you were all so lovely to work with! Readers, you should check out the other books in the world, honestly, they're all soo good!

There's always a team effort behind the scenes to put out any book, and I would be remiss not to give them all the credit they rightfully deserve. My Betas are my rock, and for this one they had their work cut out for them. Love all of you, and your eagle eyes.

Thanks also to the amazing Lisa, for the laughs and your hard work checking all of the Spanish in this book. It was so lovely to meet you, and Slate probably would've sounded like a moron if not for you and the 'Tex-Mex council.'

El, without whom my English ass would've been lost writing a story set in the USA. Thank you for answering my early morning questions about what people in Texas eat for breakfast.

Katie, my editor, who still hasn't gotten fed up with me after all this time. You're a champion and I love you.

I also have to thank those who talked with me about their

experiences of coke addiction and recovery. I sincerely appreciate the courage it took to share something so personal knowing it would be used and put on display like this.

And my poor, suffering, brother who put up with endless questions about the music industry and cars. Love you, idiot.

Snow, Candice, Stacey, Colette and the other authors who help me keep going in the sprint room when I'm convinced all of my words are shit. Thank you so much, and I hope you know you guys are all doing awesome.

Finally, to the chaotic mess that is my family. Stay crazy.

BOOKS BY MARIE MISTRY

About the Author

Marie Mistry lives in rainy Britain but spends most of her time escaping into imaginary worlds, whether that is in books or video games. She writes paranormal romance but has written books in other genres in the past. She has a mild obsession with happily ever after and true love which she blames on a childhood full of Disney goodness. She loves interacting with fans in her reader group, and feel free to stalk her on any of her social media or via her newsletter.

Printed in Great Britain
by Amazon